More praise for *Acid Bath* . . .

"Finely crafted . . . The book is literally hard to put down . . . excellent."

—*El Paso Herald-Post*

"Nancy Herndon's characters, descriptions, and situations are both intellectual and laugh-out-loud funny . . . extremely potent and great reading."

—*Mostly Murder*

"Elena Jarvis is tough but appealing, and Herndon's tongue is firmly in her cheek."

—*El Paso Times*

**And don't miss the
second Elena Jarvis Mystery,
Widows' Watch!**

D1173606

MORE MYSTERIES FROM THE
BERKLEY PUBLISHING GROUP . . .

CAT CALIBAN MYSTERIES: She was married for thirty-eight years. Raised three kids. Compared to that, tracking down killers is easy . . .

by D. B. Borton

ONE FOR THE MONEY

THREE IS A CROWD

FIVE ALARM FIRE

TWO POINTS FOR MURDER

FOUR ELEMENTS OF MURDER

KATE JASPER MYSTERIES: Even in sunny California, there are cold-blooded killers . . . "This series is a teasure!" —Carolyn G. Hart

by Jaqueline Girdner

ADJUSTED TO DEATH

THE LAST RESORT

TEA-TOTALLY DEAD

MOST LIKELY TO DIE

MURDER MOST MELLOW

FAT-FREE AND FATAL

A STIFF CRITIQUE

FREDDIE O'NEAL, P.I., MYSTERIES: You can bet that this appealing Reno private investigator will get her man . . . "A winner." —Linda Grant

by Catherine Dain

LAY IT ON THE LINE

WALK A CROOKED MILE

BET AGAINST THE HOUSE

SING A SONG OF DEATH

LAMENT FOR A DEAD COWBOY

THE LUCK OF THE DRAW

CHINA BAYLES MYSTERIES: She left the big city to run an herb shop in Pecan Springs, Texas. But murder can happen anywhere . . . "A wonderful character!" —*Mostly Murder*

by Susan Wittig Albert

THYME OF DEATH

HANGMAN'S ROOT

WITCHES' BANE

ROSEMARY REMEMBERED

BONNIE INDERMILL MYSTERIES: Temp work can be murder, but solving crime is a full-time job . . . "One of detective fiction's most appealing protagonists!" —*Publishers Weekly*

by Carole Berry

THE DEATH OF A DIFFICULT WOMAN

THE DEATH OF A DANCING FOOL

GOOD NIGHT, SWEET PRINCE

THE YEAR OF THE MONKEY

ELENA JARVIS MYSTERIES: There are some pretty bizarre crimes deep in the heart of Texas—and a pretty gutsy police detective who rounds up the unusual suspects . . .

by Nancy Herndon

ACID BATH

LETHAL STATUES

WIDOWS' WATCH

LETHAL
STATUES

Nancy Herndon

BERKLEY PRIME CRIME, NEW YORK

LETHAL STATUES

A Berkley Prime Crime Book / published by arrangement with the author

PRINTING HISTORY
Berkley Prime Crime edition / July 1996

The Putnam Berkley World Wide Web site address is http://www.berkley.com

ISBN: 0-425-15384-3

Berkley Prime Crime Books are published by The Berkley Publishing Group, 200 Madison Avenue, New York, NY 10016.
The name BERKLEY PRIME CRIME and the BERKLEY PRIME CRIME design are trademarks belonging to Berkley Publishing Corporation.

PRINTED IN THE UNITED STATES OF AMERICA

10 9 8 7 6 5 4 3 2 1

For the Eastside Herndons
Don and Nell

Acknowledgments

Many thanks to the members of my critique group, Elizabeth Fackler, Terry Irvin, Jean Miculka, and especially Joan Coleman; to Marion Coleman for information on deer hunting in the Davis Mountain area; to Bruce Dodson of the Kmart Auto Center for automotive information; to UTEP Assistant Basketball Coach Gilbert Miranda for weight-lifting information; to my son Bill for information about Trojan Horses and other such mysteries in the computer world; to my husband, Bill, for choosing, installing, and explaining my computer equipment as well as being a great cook, companion, and purveyor of unusual facts; to my editor at Berkley, Laura Anne Gilman; and, as always, to members of the criminal justice system, especially Narcotics officers, in El Paso, Texas.

N.R.H.

1

Darkness and silence shrouded the university library. The first floor held only one pool of light—in the atrium, where soft amber floods bathed a statue. Copies of that statue existed in every size and material, from a larger-than-life bronze on the quadrangle to plaster miniatures in the university bookstore. The original in the library was life-sized, five and a half feet of pure white marble. It depicted a young woman, slender and boyish, hands raised joyously, left leg bent up at the knee as she danced, one lock of her short hair flying. Caught forever in her carefree joy, her clothing so flimsy that she seemed nude, the *Charleston Dancer* radiated her own music, for there was no sound other than that which echoed in the mind of a viewer pausing to appreciate her lithe, slender grace. She had been chosen by the founder as the spirit of the university he had endowed and to which he had left his estate.

Another amber light shone on the second floor, this one glowing from a computer screen. It illuminated the face of a young woman who was as alive as the dancer was inanimate, who was as dark as the statue was white. Under her fingers the computer keys compressed silently, letters and numbers flowing across the screen. This girl was beautiful as well, if at the moment less joyous, less carefree than the statue on the floor below.

As she worked in a three-sided computer cubicle, her concentration was absolute, her attention fixed on the hand-

1

written notes that hung from a clip arm attached to the side of
the monitor. Hurrying to finish, she was less wary than usual.
Yet, even if she had been more alert to danger, she might not
have heard the stealthy footsteps coming down the aisle
between the stacks and the computer row.

A man's voice behind her said, "I've been looking for
you."

Wrenched from concentration to panic, she swiveled her
chair. Her heart raced; her hands trembled as she looked up.
Shock gave way to action; she grasped the metal arm that
held her papers, hardly feeling the sharp edge that cut into her
fingers. One certainty filled her mind: she could not afford to
be caught. Ripping the clip arm from the computer, she
launched herself out of the chair, turning, swinging back-
handed, and struck him on the side of the head.

The blow opened a gash under his hair that staggered him
and enabled her to dash past and head for the stairway that
curved gracefully to the atrium. Risking a fall, she raced
down, one slender hand on the rail. Curses and the sound of
his steps followed her. Because she had been a runner and a
hurdler in high school, and still ran for the joy of it, she hoped
to escape. If she could get out of the side door, she could
disappear among the palm trees, or dive into the dense
flowering shrubbery that grew in defiance of stony desert soil
and dwindling water supplies.

With a soaring leap she flew over a sofa, but her trailing
foot touched the middle cushion on the way down. She
stumbled, then caught herself; she had lost precious seconds,
but *he* would have to skirt the obstacles while she was
heading for open ground. Now even with the statue, giving it
hardly a glance, she lengthened her stride.

The man saw the girl's leap with amazement. She ran like
an antelope, swift and smooth, but he dared not shoot her
down as he would have shot an animal in the brush. He
pounded around the sofa toward the statue, knowing that in
seconds she would widen the distance between them.

Because he had so great a stake in catching her, he acted
instinctively. Placing one hand on the slender ankle of the
statue, another at the shapely knee, he gave the figure a

powerful shove. The dancer teetered on her perch, then plummeted forward. For a moment he thought he had failed, because the runner had cut away from him to the right. However, one marble hand caught the back of the fleeing girl's head and knocked her to the floor.

They went down side by side, the marble arm appearing to embrace its victim. The pursuer stopped short of the two fallen women and stared at the results of his impulsive act. At least he'd halted her escape. He knelt, then frowned, for the amber light picked up red in the black of the girl's hair; her blood dripped from the white marble fingers of the statue. He sat on his haunches studying her, then reached out to search for a pulse on the girl's long, slender neck. Nothing.

He tried again. No life fluttered beneath his fingers. He'd screwed up. She was dead, which at the least meant a setback to his plans, and at the worst, big trouble. The wink of gold beside her head caught his eye. Instantly he saw the possibilities, and lifted the thin chain away from her neck so he could slip it and the gold coin on it over her head. If anyone knew she wore it, her death might be taken as having occurred during a robbery.

Rising quickly, he headed toward the stairway. On the second floor, in her cubicle, he shuffled together the papers that had scattered on the floor. One, speckled with a few drops of blood, still hung from the clip arm with which she had hit him. He tore it free and stuffed all the papers into her backpack. Let them wonder what had happened. Why she was in the library. How the statue came to fall on her.

When he studied the metal clip arm, he saw blood at both ends. Puzzled, he wiped it clean with his handkerchief. He knew he couldn't eliminate the blood traces completely— police methods would turn them up—but if he turned off the computer and reattached the clip arm to the side, returning everything to normal in the cubicle, no one would think to inspect it. And when he turned off the computer, her work would be lost. Perfect. No one would associate her with this particular place or with him.

He glanced around quickly, searching for other evidence of his presence or hers. None. Covering his finger with a clean place on his handkerchief, he threw the power switch. The screen went dark. Then he left as silently as he had come, satisfied that nothing obvious, nothing that wasn't microscopic, remained of his presence but the dead girl and the broken statue. It was as if he'd never been here.

2
..

The beeper went off just as Los Santos Crimes-Against-Persons Detective Elena Jarvis picked out the dining room rug she was going to give herself for Christmas. The store owner, a curly-haired woman named Nell with a quintessential Texas accent and an open-hearted Texas friendliness, turned from the rug pile to eye her daughter.

"It wasn't mine, Mom," said the young woman, displaying her silent cellular phone as evidence.

"It was my pager," said Elena, sighing. "If this one doesn't have any flowers in the middle, I'll take it. Can I use your phone?" These days Elena never seemed to manage a full day off. She wondered what it was this time. Someone shooting down Christmas shoppers at a mall?

Nell and her daughter heaved aside the rugs at the top of the pile to reveal an uncluttered scrollwork circle in the middle of Elena's choice. "Perfect," said Elena. Nell directed her to the office of the Brass Shop, a wholesale-retail operation hidden in an industrial area of the city. The store sold everything from fluted, frosted glass lamps to giant brass elephants, from oak furniture and area rugs to brass bookmarks decorated with enameled butterflies. It was a treasure trove of bargains that Elena's neighbor, Omar Ashkenazi, had told her about once she'd convinced him she couldn't afford a real oriental rug. As she left the carpet room, Nell's son-in-law joined the family in a complicated folding-back-

5

and-edging-out endeavor to release Elena's rug from the bottom of a four-foot pile.

It was just what she wanted, and the price was right. Because her living room looked so great now that her mother had woven gorgeous southwestern fabrics to cover the upholstered furniture, Elena had decided to do something about her dining room. Having found a rug, she might now refinish and reupholster the heavy Spanish table and chairs she had bought secondhand. Not that she had used the room since her divorce from Frank the Narc. During their marriage, weekly poker games had been played, beer spilled, and chips crumbled on the table.

She poked her head into a warehouse-sized office, piled everywhere with merchandise and ruled over by a huge man stretched out on a recliner. He was growling into the telephone at someone who had bounced a check. Elena started to back out, but he caught sight of her and waved her to a chair, continuing his irate conversation. Removing a pile of gauze skirts and a cat from the chair, Elena sat down and tucked loose strands of dark hair into her French braid.

The man, evidently Nell's husband, turned as noisy cackling started up in a wire-enclosed runway that led from the office to the yard. The cat stopped glowering at Elena and bolted for cover. Elena craned her neck. Geese! The man plunged his hand into a bag beside his recliner and threw goose munchies through a door in the wire mesh. The geese shut up. "Tomorrow, or I call the cops," said the owner to the bad-check writer and hung up. He looked toward Elena. "Who're you?"

"A cop," she replied. "But I'm shopping, not investigating. Unless you murder your deadbeat customer."

"Easier to sic the geese on him. They're better than cops and meaner than dogs." He brushed long, light hair out of his eyes.

"What kind of chair is that?" she asked, never having seen anything quite like it.

"A podiatrist's chair."

"Right." Did he have a doctor who made house—no, business—calls to work on his feet? "Your wife said I could use the phone."

"You buy anything?"

"A rug."

"She give you a discount?"

"She didn't say."

"Thirty percent," he decided, and slid a cordless telephone across the desk. "Leave your card. Then we'll know who to call if we find a corpse. Want to hear a good joke about a lady cop?"

"No thanks," said Elena, punching in the number of Manny Escobedo, her sergeant. The owner looked disappointed, but Elena heard enough policewoman jokes at work. "It's Jarvis. What's up?"

Manny explained.

"So what am I supposed to do? Arrest the statue?" After listening, she agreed to go on overtime for a solo visit to Herbert Hobart University, where a coed had been brained by a statue. Elena knew which statue: the *Charleston Dancer*. And now, apparently because of past cases she had investigated at the university, she had become the person the LSPD sent to investigate mayhem among the palm trees. She'd have to get her rug later. If she put it in the back of the pickup, the H.H.U. students might vandalize it. They were too rich to bother stealing it.

3
..

Tuesday, November 29, 9:10 A.M.

Chief Clabb of the University Police Force had put on
weight and developed a tic in his right eyelid since Elena last
saw him. "Everything's going wrong," he said, placing his
hand over a gap between two straining uniform buttons, as if
covering one gaping area would hide the others. "Look at the
statue. It's missing an arm. And a leg. The founder himself
bought it in Spain and had it shipped back shortly before his
death. It's part of our heritage here at the university."

They were standing in the atrium, pink marble under their
feet, lavender and pink art deco couches scattered across the
area among giant ferns in pots decorated with parades of stiff
Egyptian funerary figures. Behind the multicolored ribbons
produced by the H.H.U. police to use as crime-scene tapes,
curious onlookers gawked.

"Lots of famous statues are missing parts," said Elena
soothingly. She had sent several campus policemen and the
night guard who discovered the body to check for signs of a
struggle or illegal entry, anything amiss that might shed light
on this strange death. It got them out of her hair and kept them
from screwing up the crime scene, if it was a crime scene.
Other H.H.U. cops were keeping the crowd away until the
Identification and Records unit arrived to gather evidence and
the medical examiner, to take charge of the body. "The *Venus
de Milo*, for instance. She's missing both arms."

"She's not missing any legs," Chief Clabb pointed out.

8

"Now our statue looks like a cripple instead of a dancer." The lower portion of the dancer's leg had been broken in the fall.

"What about the girl?" asked Elena, staring down at the two figures in inanimate embrace, the marble arm across the corpse's back. "Student? Employee?"

"Student," said the chief mournfully. "Our first African-American."

Elena hadn't known there were any at Herbert Hobart, enclave of the rich, white, and not particularly inclined to academic pursuits. Why would a black girl come here? Not for H.H.U.'s academic prestige, not on an athletic scholarship. The school had an elaborate intramural program but no intercollegiate athletics.

"More bad publicity," said Clabb. "And after all the other terrible things that have happened."

Elena had been studying the body of the slender, handsome girl, who looked like Nefertiti without the headdress. She might have stepped off one of the fern pots. Dark skin. Close-cropped hair, now matted with blood where the statue had caught her. "What terrible things?" Elena asked. "Have there been racial incidents since she enrolled?"

"I meant the poet who was murdered last spring. You should remember that; you solved the case."

I also dated the murderer, thought Elena glumly. She had solved the acid bath case, nearly getting herself and her friend Sarah Tolland, chairman of Electrical Engineering, killed in the process. "Anything else?"

"That secretary accused of killing his father."

Elena had solved that one, too. Caught the serial killer, the last person anyone would have picked.

"And the pro-lifers," said Chief Clabb. "Surely you've read about them. We thought when the clinic-protection law passed, the fines and jail terms would scare them off, but they're still campaigning against our Health and Reproductive Services Center. Now we're getting threatening notes. They're going to burn us down. Blow us up. One note said, 'Death to the baby-killers.'"

"Oh?" Elena's attention sharpened. "Did this girl get a note? Is she connected with the clinic?"

"The doctor got a note. The president got a note. *I* got one.

Everything was so peaceful here the first few years. And before that, when I was head of security for President Sunnydale's evangelical ministry in California. We never had corpses in the sanctuary. Just tax problems."

Elena knew all about the university president. He'd gotten into trouble with the I.R.S., lost his tax exemption, and been forced to give up TV evangelism, California-style, to become president of Herbert Hobart University, a reward for having converted the founder before Hobart's tragic death. Herbert Hobart had died of electrocution while creating one of the video games that made him rich.

"And now this!" moaned Chief Clabb. "Another murder. What will all those rich parents say? Well, *her* parents probably aren't rich, but . . ."

Nobody seemed to care about the deceased. They were more interested in the statue, the parents, and the scandal. "We're not sure it's murder," Elena pointed out.

"Statues don't just fall over on students. And she wasn't supposed to *be* here in the middle of the night. Students don't have keys."

"We'll have to ask the guard about that," said Elena, trying to imagine a scenario in which the girl could have died accidentally. Nothing came to mind, although there was no question that the *Charleston Dancer* had hit the student. The marble hand of the detached arm had bloody fingers.

"I've sent for my best man to help you in your investigation," said Chief Clabb, his eyelid spasming wildly. "Assistant Chief Eleuterio Vasquez. A fine boy. My protégé, you might say."

Elena just bet the assistant chief loved being called "a fine boy." About as much as she liked being called "girl" or "babe" or "sweetheart" by her colleagues. She didn't argue with the chief about the assignment of a co-investigator. Her own partner at LSPD, Leo Weizell, was off to Cancun to celebrate the impregnation of his wife, the trip a gift from her family, who hadn't thought Concepcion and Leo were ever going to add to the accumulation of grandchildren, nieces, and nephews. And this Vasquez would have inside information about the university—she hoped.

Charlie Solis of I.D.&R. and Assistant Chief Eleuterio

"Tey" Vasquez arrived at the same time. While she was talking to Vasquez, Elena could hear Charlie muttering, "That's a hell of a big statue to dust for prints."

The assistant chief was a stocky, muscular man who made the lavender uniforms of the H.H.U. force look masculine instead of art deco. Maybe it was the added touches, the cowboy boots and the wraparound dark glasses he didn't remove. He interrupted an approving examination of Elena and assurances that the two of them would have no trouble clearing up this "little matter" to tell Charlie Solis, "You'll find hundreds of prints on that statue and every other *Charleston Dancer* on campus. People touch them for luck. I do myself."

Charlie scowled and ordered the I.D.&R. team into action. Elena muttered, "Oh great!"

"Maybe it fell over on its own," suggested Vasquez. "The students are always fooling around. They'd think it was funny to jerk the statue loose and leave it teetering."

"When a statue toppled and killed a citizen of ancient Rome," said a voice from behind the crime-scene tape, "the statue was tried, found guilty, and ground into rubble. Good morning, Detective Jarvis."

Elena nodded to a short man with a goatee, a beret, and a cigarette holder. She'd met him at a dinner party given by Sarah Tolland. Elena tried to imagine the D.A. bringing a case against a statue. "Nifty idea, Professor Rambeaux."

"What's her name?" Elena asked Tey Vasquez, gesturing toward the deceased.

"Didn't Chief Clabb identify her?" Vasquez glanced at his superior. "That's Analee Ribbon."

"OK. We'll want to find out all we can about her." Elena was impatient to begin, her interest in the dead girl building. Analee Ribbon shouldn't have been in Los Santos, where there were so few African-Americans; she shouldn't have died. Elena wanted to know not just what had happened, but why. "I'll need her records, the names of her family and friends. We have to find out what she was doing the last day of her life, why she was in the library in the middle of the night, what—"

"Her records will be at the registrar's office," Vasquez broke in.

Elena moved toward the medical examiner, Onofre Calderon, who was squatting beside the body, going through the back pockets of the girl's jeans. "Anything you can tell me?"

"Statue hit her on the head," said Calderon. "I figure maybe they had a fight. She's got cuts across the fingers of her right hand." He turned the hand for Elena's inspection. "Like maybe the statue had a knife, an' the victim grabbed it. Then—"

"You need a vacation, Onofre." Elena was used to the quirky humor of the medical examiner and his staff, but she didn't want Chief Clabb or any of the professors and students to hear.

"The statue didn't hop off, Calderon," said Charlie Solis. He had been examining deep scoring on the pedestal. "It's been shoved off the base."

"She died between two and three last night," said Onofre cheerfully. "More or less. Know more after the autopsy."

"It would take a real strong guy to knock that statue over," said Charlie. "You gotta wonder why. There must be easier ways to kill a girl than braining her with a statue. And what was she doing while the perp was pushing the statue over? Standing around? Running away?"

Elena wanted to know, too.

"You always catch the weird ones, Jarvis," said Calderon. Having bagged the hands, he signaled to two assistants with a body bag and a gurney.

Elena hated to see the young woman go into the bag; there was so much beauty, so much promise in that face, so much lithe power and grace in the sprawled body.

4
∙∙

"I figured out where I've met you before," said Tey
Vasquez as they drove to the registrar's office, Elena enjoying
the beautiful late fall morning. The sun was shining, the sky
above the mountain as blue as lupine, the temperature in the
sixties. "Do you remember me? We took a couple of criminology classes together at UT Los Santos."

Elena turned to study him. It was possible. She'd finished
her degree at UTLS after marrying Frank Jarvis and trans-
ferring from the University of New Mexico. But she often
found it difficult to recognize people wearing sunglasses, and
this guy never seemed to take his off. Vasquez? Vasquez?
They could have met in the casual way students do, said hello
before class or in the halls.

"You were married to a cop." He grinned at her, an engaging
smile displaying even white teeth. "If you hadn't been married,
I'd have hit on you for sure."

His hands were brown and blunt on the steering wheel as
he drove through crowds of students, blasting the horn to
scatter them in defiance of the pedestrian-right-of-way policy
that ruled on most campuses. There was a masculine cocki-
ness about him that both attracted her and set her teeth on
edge.

"Sorry. I don't remember," Elena replied, telling herself to
back off. She was a sucker for Hispanics. Her father, Sheriff
Ruben Portillo, and all her relatives on his side were Hispanic,

as was almost everyone she'd grown up with in Chimayo, New Mexico, not to mention seventy percent of the population of Los Santos. But she didn't need macho. She'd had that with Frank, and it hadn't worked out.

Frank thought he could play around and then smack her when she complained. Well, he couldn't; she'd dumped him on the spot. Anyway, Vasquez was her partner on this case. Romantic complications wouldn't help them solve the crime, so she shrugged. "It was a long time ago."

"Not that long. You still married?" He glanced at her ringless finger.

"Divorced. What can you tell me about Ms. Ribbon?"

"Ms.? You a feminist?"

"I'm a Crimes Against Persons detective. I'm interested in professional conduct and clearing homicide cases before all the clues dry up. What about you?" she asked pointedly.

"I can take a hint," he replied good-naturedly, "and I don't know shit about homicides—only what I read in the criminology texts, so you're in charge."

Elena relaxed. "What have you been doing since you graduated?" she asked, feeling more friendly.

"I didn't—graduate. Got a job offer. My mother was sick, looked like she might lose a leg to diabetes, so I quit school and went with the Robbins Security Company because they had good insurance and no clause about previous conditions. Couple of years later, when she had the diabetes under control, I moved from Robbins to H.H.U. Figured I had a bigger future here. In case you think Clabb has a college degree," he added defensively, "he doesn't."

"And you're his fair-haired boy—figuratively speaking," she said.

He looked pleased. "The chief say that?"

"More or less."

Vasquez nodded. "Sometimes he's an asshole, but he's going to do me some good before he retires."

Asshole? Elena glanced at Vasquez in surprise, then reminded herself that Clabb had the sort of paternal, condescending attitude that would probably tick Vasquez off. Although she had the same problem with her superior,

Lieutenant Beltran, she didn't go around calling him an asshole.

Vasquez swung into a parking space reserved for campus police, walked with Elena into the administration building, and did a little light flirting with the registrar's clerk as she pulled the files on the deceased and directed Elena and Vasquez to an empty desk. Vasquez took the leather-covered swivel chair, leaving Elena the straight-backed visitor's seat. He might have designated her "in charge," which she was, given the agreement Herbert Hobart had with the LSPD, yet he scanned each paper before handing it over. But since the papers came to her quickly enough, she didn't complain. No sense causing trouble if she didn't have to.

The take she was getting on the deceased was fascinating. The girl had been a junior with a 3.8 average. She had both an ROTC scholarship and an academic scholarship, and she was a computer science major.

"You gonna read the name of every course she ever took?" asked Vasquez, tipping back in his chair and crossing booted ankles.

"Maybe one of her classmates killed her," said Elena, continuing to study the girl's record.

"Maybe. But if they did, they got folks with the big bucks to get them off," said Vasquez. "Or haven't you noticed the criminal justice system works better for the rich?"

"I've noticed," Elena muttered, and read on. Here was something interesting. Analee Ribbon had been drawing pay as a computer researcher on a project run by Sarah Tolland. Elena knew what her next stop would be.

"Take a look at this family, will you?" Vasquez asked, handing her a sheaf of forms filled out when Ribbon applied for admission.

Elena read the material and saw nothing particularly surprising. In fact, Analee Ribbon seemed to have been better off than most American youngsters; she'd had a two-parent family that looked stable and prosperous. She listed her mother as Lavender Lee Ribbon, owner of a cafe named Lavender's Gumbo, and her father as Ray Lee Ribbon, jazz musician. There were three siblings, two male, one female; two had been to college. Analee had been the youngest.

Obviously the Ribbons could afford to educate their kids—maybe not at H.H.U., but then Analee had received a lot of money in scholarships and salary.

Elena went on to look at the deceased's high school record. High grades, lots of activities, lettered three years in track (440 and hurdles), 1390 SAT. A higher score than Elena's. So why had Analee chosen H.H.U.? Being black, female, and smart, she could have gotten into somewhere prestigious like—what? Smart Hispanic kids from Los Santos were getting into M.I.T. Why hadn't Analee gone someplace like that?

"You don't see it?" asked Vasquez impatiently. "Her father's a musician. Musicians are all dopers. Especially the black ones."

Great. She had a bigot helping her investigate the death of an African-American. Next he'd be saying the daughters of musicians are dopers.

"Hey, it's the truth," snapped Vasquez. "Read the newspapers."

Maybe. she couldn't afford to overlook possibilities because she was trying to be politically correct, any more than she could let his prejudices affect her investigation. "I want to interview Sarah Tolland," said Elena. "Ribbon worked for her."

"Only until September," Vasquez pointed out.

"Even so, it was a two-year-plus association. Dr. Tolland must have known her pretty well."

5
..

"Colin, hi," said Elena, giving Professor Stuart a hug when she encountered him in the outer office of the Electrical Engineering Department. "How's Lance?" she added, then wondered if it was proper to inquire after a gay man's partner as you would a fellow officer's wife.

"Ask your mother," Colin replied. "He's up in Santa Fe accepting an award for Southwestern poetry and planning to have dinner with her tonight."

"Terrific." She turned to Virginia Pargetter, the departmental secretary. "Can we see Sarah?" she asked pleasantly.

"She's busy," was the stiff reply. Mrs. Pargetter continued to dislike Elena for having arrested Sarah last spring during the acid bath case.

"Are you two here about Analee Ribbon?" Colin asked in an undertone.

Elena nodded.

"Damned shame. She was a great kid. Bright, a computer whiz, and her father, Ray Lee Ribbon, is as good a jazz trumpeter as I've ever heard. Never could figure out why the man stays in Houston. Doesn't do out-of-town performances, as far as I know." Stuart, a jazz buff, shook his head at the loss to music lovers. "I just learned about Analee," he continued. "Sarah's going to be upset."

Elena sighed. "Were you going to tell her?"

17

"I was, but I'll happily defer to you. Let Detective Jarvis in, Virginia," he advised the secretary, "unless you want to be the one to tell Sarah her favorite student's dead. I sure don't." Which he proved by leaving.

Virginia scowled at Elena and Tey Vasquez. "Since *you're* here, it must have been murder."

"We don't know yet how it happened," said Elena.

"Well, if you're thinking Dr. Tolland had anything to do with it—" Virginia began combatively.

"I don't think that," Elena snapped. Virginia Pargetter might be superefficient, but Elena considered Sarah's valued secretary an obstructive pain in the ass. "Can you tell us anything about Ribbon, Ms. Pargetter?"

"Mrs.," snapped Virginia, and buzzed her boss. "Detective Jarvis to see you, Dr. Tolland."

"I hope you don't have your eye on Stuart," Tey murmured to Elena. "He's gay."

"You're *kidding*," Elena replied. "We've dated." She experienced a childish pleasure when Vasquez backed off a step, as if she were contagious.

"Believe me," he said urgently. "Stuart is gay! Or at least AC-DC. I hope you didn't—" He stopped, looking embarrassed.

Elena almost laughed out loud as she walked into Sarah's office. Vasquez probably thought all gay men had AIDS, and so might she. Well, she *had* gone out with Colin—once. He'd decided he was gay the night of their date—an ego-buster if ever there was one.

"Sarah, I've got some bad news," said Elena, sitting down. As gently as she could, she went on to tell Sarah about the strange death of Analee Ribbon. "So anything you can tell us about her will help," Elena concluded.

Distraught, Sarah ran her fingers through gray-blond hair. "It had to be an accident," she said. "Analee was a wonderful girl. Bright. Funny. Charming. Everyone loved her."

"I guess you thought a lot of her yourself, Professor," Vasquez suggested. He had parked his butt on the edge of a walnut credenza and crossed his booted ankles, looking casually cool, like a motorcycle cop who fancied himself a biker for the good guys.

"She was my best student!" said Sarah, whose distress shadowed her eyes. "She'd never have chosen H.H.U. if it weren't for me."

"Then how come she dropped out of your research project?" Vasquez whipped the question into the midst of Sarah's agitation.

She stopped talking and stared at him. "When did Analee die?" she asked.

"Sarah, we don't think—" Elena began.

"Just tell me when she died," said Sarah, obviously remembering the last time she'd been accused of a murder, when the victim was thought to be her ex-husband.

"Between two and three this morning," said Vasquez, resettling his sunglasses but not removing them.

"I was with Dr. Zifkovitz of the—"

"Sarah, you don't have to—"

"All night, Dr. Tolland?" asked Vasquez, pencil poised over a small notebook.

"We went to dinner," said Sarah, "then back to his place. He's in the Art Department." Her cheeks were stained with angry color as Vasquez nodded and jotted notes with a smug grin. Elena could have killed him.

"Now, you asked me why Analee dropped out of my research project," Sarah said coldly. "She claimed the press of studies, and she *was* carrying a heavy class load, although her resignation surprised and disappointed me."

"How *much* did it disappoint you?" asked Vasquez.

Elena turned to him, fuming.

"She was taking two of my classes, Mr. Vasquez, and making A's in both. There was no rancor between us, if that's what you're implying. Analee seemed as disappointed to leave the project as I was to lose her."

Vasquez shrugged. "We have to ask. Have to cover every angle. Right, Detective?" He'd glanced at Elena and noticed, evidently for the first time, her reaction to his line of questioning.

Elena returned her gaze to her friend. "I'm so sorry, Sarah. We'll find out what happened."

Sarah nodded sadly. "I can't believe she had any enemies. Even Virginia liked her."

Elena's pager went off, and she asked to use Sarah's phone. After several minutes of conversation, she said to Vasquez, "They've found something at the library."

6
⠂⠂

"You never asked how she was getting in and out?" demanded Vasquez in a sarcastic drawl.

The guard stood his ground. "Analee was workin' for Dr. Tolland. She musta give her a key. Professors got their own; you know that." The guard stared resentfully at Vasquez while Elena gave the assistant chief a "cool it" look. She wanted the guard's cooperation. At the rate Vasquez was going, they wouldn't get anything else from Mr. Tully, although she had more questions.

"What was your impression of Ms. Ribbon, Mr. Tully?" she asked pleasantly, stepping between the sixtyish guard and Vasquez. Tey had insisted on coming with her, although she had suggested he head for the dorm and corral Analee's roommates. Now, having offended Sarah, he was screwing up this interrogation. "Did she ever say anything about enemies?"

"Enemies?" Hiram Tully hawked, then, looking embarrassed, swallowed when he realized there was no place to spit. "Ever'one liked Analee. Even them rich kids, an' she wasn't one of 'em. She was a regular gal. Real nice."

"Did she tell you lately that she was working for Professor Tolland?"

"Din' hafta. Tole me all about it last year. She didn't have her own computer back at the dorm like the rest. Likewise she was on scholarship, needin' to study and livin' with rich

21

blabbermouth roommates. She come over here at least three nights a week ever' year since she was a freshman. Real hard worker, that Analee."

"And you saw her last night?" Elena asked. "About what time?"

"Din' see her last night. Only saw her dead this mornin'," said the guard, who looked sincerely distressed. "She musta come in after I went up on Four to monitor them screens."

"When was that?"

"'Round two, like always."

Vasquez started to interrupt, but Elena gave him a "don't do it" look. "Did you see anyone on the screens?"

"Nope," said the guard, "an' I din' see that there nekked statue fall on her neither, but then the screens only look at stuff the security company thinks someone might steal, like office machines an' computers. Don' expect nobody to steal a nekked statue nor push it over on someone."

"And you didn't hear anything?"

"Not three floors away, shut up in that there surveillance room. Wish I had. I'd a been down here in a flash." He stared hard at Tey Vasquez, as if Vasquez might try to refute that claim.

"But I knew right off she'd been workin' here last night when I seen the gadget on the computer. It were hers; she always brung it in an' took it home. Reckon she come in late to use the computer an' got killed afore she finished up."

Elena nodded, studying the clip in its plastic evidence bag. "If she was using the clip, there must have been papers on it," she murmured thoughtfully. "I wonder where they are."

"Couldn't say," said the guard. "Cleaning crews wasn't workin' last night. Analee, she's been avoidin' the nights they come through waxin' an' buffin'. This year, anyways. Usta joke with 'em jus' like she done me, but this year she had more work to do. Said she needed quiet."

Was there really so much difference in the workload from the sophomore year to the junior? Or was there something troubling Analee, making it harder for her to concentrate? Had she been afraid and using the library as a hideout? One would have thought she'd feel safer in a dorm full of people

hen in an empty building. Elena needed to talk to roommates
and friends.

"You've been very helpful, Mr. Tully," she said, smiling at
the man, who looked tired and rumpled, his heavy gray
eyebrows standing out at unlikely angles, as if he'd rubbed
them. He'd been on duty since midnight. "You can go home
now." She turned to Charlie Solis, who was in the computer
cubicle, dusting for prints. "You getting anything, Charlie?"

"Partials on all the keys," he replied. "Only the power
switch was wiped."

"Maybe the killer turned it off after he got her with the
statue," suggested Elena.

"My guess is she got him first," said Charlie.

"Plenty of kids use those computers," said Vasquez. "I'd
think, what with prints overlaying one another—"

"We'll see," said Charlie.

"How do you mean she got him first?" Elena asked.

"Blood on the clip arm. It's been wiped, but it's there. I
sprayed because of the cuts on her hand. Blood where she
grasped it, blood on the other end where she hit him. Even got
a little off the floor tiles."

He had been talking as he worked. "That about does it," he
said to his assistant. "Let's get this stuff back to the lab." He
picked up the bagged clip and muttered, "Heavy. Must have
hurt when she hit him."

Vasquez chuckled, hand resting comfortably on his holster.
"You're going to insult Detective Jarvis here by assuming the
killer was a man."

"Not many women could push that statue off the pedestal,"
Solis muttered.

"Come on, Tey," said Elena. "Analee's roommates should
be waiting for us at the dorm. If they really are blabber-
mouths, the way the guard said, maybe they'll have a lot to
tell us."

7
..

"Cadet Major Melody Spike," said the petite redhead who
opened the door of the suite in which Analee Ribbon had
lived. Melody Spike wore a peculiar twenties-style uniform,
a shift with epaulettes and military buttons, mauve instead of
khaki, hem above the knees. As Elena's hand was being given
a no-nonsense shake, she couldn't resist asking to what military
organization the major belonged.

"United States Army Reserve Officers Training Corps"
was the answer.

ROTC? Did the army know that its uniform had been so
extensively modified? Elena had already been informed by
the housemother that Melody Spike was the daughter of Big
Hank Spike of Houston, a man so rich that the collapse of the
Texas oil and real estate markets hadn't driven him into
bankruptcy. Maybe he had bribed the secretary of the army to
overlook his daughter's fashion eccentricities. Maybe he *was*
the secretary of the army. Elena often felt like Dorothy in Oz
when she was at H.H.U.

"My roommate, M. M. Daguerre," said Major Spike,
gesturing to the woman just entering the room. "She's a
graduate student in psychology, although woefully unin-
formed on women's issues."

Maggie, the LSPD computer expert in Identification and
Records, shook Elena's hand as if they had never met, then
shook with Vasquez, who was gaping at her. At five-eleven,

Maggie topped him by an inch. She wore baggy jeans and a sweatshirt that said, "H.H.U., A Good Time and a Good Education." The motto encircled a drawing of the *Charleston Dancer*. However, even that shapeless outfit didn't disguise Maggie's chorus-girl legs and spectacular breasts, not to mention her shining black hair and exotic green eyes. Vasquez was stunned, as were three-quarters of the cops at headquarters. So what was she doing here? And why was she pretending she didn't know Elena, and making it clear with a hearty "Nice to meet you" that she expected Elena to do the same?

"Ms. Daguerre," Elena mumbled, finding it hard to pretend that Maggie was a stranger. To distract herself, she concentrated on the sitting room, particularly the sofa, the back of which swooped from a high curve at one end to a low curlicue at the other, and was covered with a print fabric featuring Egyptian females in headdresses high-kicking their way across the sofa cushions, pyramids in the background. Beside it a six-foot bronze snake, rising from its coil, balanced a white frosted-glass ball on its head. A lamp? Elena found it really creepy.

"I see you've noticed our art object," said Melody Spike. From the coffee table, she picked up a bronze cowboy on a bucking bronco, which Elena had *not* been looking at. "You'd think they could do better by us. Western statues were popular during the art deco period, but they don't belong on the Egyptian floor."

"I kinda like cowboys," said Maggie, dropping onto a love seat that matched the sofa.

Vasquez, again Mr. Cool, was leaning casually against a wall. He quickly adjusted the creases of his uniform trousers to better display his boots.

"You *would* like cowboys, Daguerre" said Melody. "A woman who doesn't like French haute cuisine and refuses to provide a cover for her bed or drapes for her windows can't be expected to have good taste in art objects." Melody turned to Elena and Vasquez. "Each floor here is furnished in a different style of art deco—Frank Lloyd Wright, Mayan revival, Egyptian—and each suite has an art object. Ours doesn't match our decor. Naturally, I've filed a complaint."

"Naturally," murmured Elena.

"Hey, you don't like the cowboy, I'll put him in my room," said Maggie.

"You, M. M., need your consciousness raised," said Melody. "You should join the ROTC. Women can't expect to take a place in the power structure until they form a substantial presence in the military." She turned back to Vasquez and Elena. "I suppose you're here about Analee. Sit down, and I'll tell you who killed her."

Raising an eyebrow, Elena took a seat beside Maggie. Vasquez moved closer, leaned his butt on a breakfast table that faced a small balcony, and crossed his ankles again for optimum boot display. Although Elena doubted that his fancy footwear had ever seen a horse, the boots made an interesting combination with the lavender H.H.U. police uniform.

"It was L.S.A.R.I.," Melody said, as if she had been a witness and was prepared to name the very person who had pushed over the statue.

"Bull," said Vasquez.

"Did Ms. Ribbon have something to do with the health center?" asked Elena.

"What's L.S.A.R.I.?" asked Maggie.

"Los Santoans Against Rampant Immorality," said Melody. "They have two wings. The Anti-Abortion Brigade and the Anti-Fornication Brigade, both determined to limit women's rights by any means, including murder, as we now know."

"Why would they have it in for Analee Ribbon?" asked Elena. She was willing to listen, although it seemed to her that if L.S.A.R.I. wanted to kill someone, they'd have chosen Greta Marx, the doctor at the Health and Reproductive Services Center, not some coed.

"She joined L.S.A.R.I. as an undercover agent for us," said Melody. "The Feminist Coalition. We use standard F.B.I. tactics—infiltrate the enemy and find out what they're planning. Then we circumvent them. For instance, when they decided to spray-paint 'Baby Killers' on the clinic walls, Analee warned us, and we warned the campus police—not that it did any good. Before the police retreated in disarray, L.S.A.R.I. managed to spray-paint them, too, and leave their silhouettes on the walls." She glared at Vasquez. "Where were you when your men made fools of themselves?"

Folding his arms, he replied, "Chief Clabb's men, don't you mean? I was off that night."

"Next time we get word of activity, I'll call out my ROTC unit," said Melody.

"You're not going to be getting any more inside information if your mole is dead," Vasquez remarked.

"Just my point," said Melody. "They killed her."

Mole? mused Elena. Melody came off as a nut, and Vasquez was egging her on.

"Who else would have a motive?" snapped Melody. "Analee was very popular."

"Who did she date?" asked Elena.

"L. Parker Montrose," said Melody. "He's white. Although I've suspected that Analee had black boyfriends at UT Los Santos. She was over there several nights a week. In fact, she was rarely home in the evening. She led a very active social life."

Elena wrote down the name of the boyfriend and elicited the information that he was an H.H.U. student, wealthy, well connected socially, and that his parents were furious because he was dating a black woman.

"Isn't that ridiculous?" exclaimed Melody. "It's not as if Analee wanted to marry him." Melody didn't know the names of any African-American boyfriends; she just suspected their existence. "After all, L. Parker and Analee only dated once a week—her idea—so she must have been getting it some-where."

"Getting what?" asked Maggie.

"Sex," said Melody. "She was a feminist."

"I thought feminists didn't like men," said Vasquez, grinning.

Elena could see that he was enjoying himself.

"If all the H.H.U. force is as dumb as you—" began Melody.

That put and end to Vasquez's good humor. He didn't like being called dumb. "Look, girl—" he interrupted.

"—and those three idiots who got themselves spray-painted, it's no wonder you had to call in the city police. And don't call me 'girl.' For your information, women have as much right to sexual satisfaction as men, and feminists demand it."

Elena cleared her throat and flipped the page of her notebook. Maggie was still sprawled beside her on the sofa, grinning at the show. "Ms. Daguerre, can you shed any light on who might have killed Analee Ribbon?"

"I spend all my time working and studying," said Maggie. "I don't have time for sex or girl talk."

"Or bedspreads or cultural appreciation," muttered Melody. "There's more to life than books, you know. At least, Analee had social concerns. *She* believed in a strong national defense and feminist action."

"Hey, the ROTC paid her, and so did the Feminist Coalition," said Maggie.

"We only paid her expenses on the L.S.A.R.I. assignment," snapped Melody.

Elena made note of that, asked to see Analee's room, and left the two women arguing. "Coming, Vasquez?" she called over her shoulder, then stopped short. The bedroom was decorated in green wool and lavender satin. It looked like a schizophrenic whorehouse. Was this where Analee Ribbon had lived?

"That's *my* room," called Melody Spike. "Hers is on the left."

Elena exhaled in relief. She'd have been surprised and disappointed if Analee Ribbon had been into green wool and lavender satin. For Melody Spike, the decor was no surprise. The major was the kind who gave feminism a bad name. Probably had never held a job in her life and had no idea what discrimination against women was about.

Analee's room was more sensible—no bedspread or throw pillows, no crystal perfume bottles scattered across a dressing table, no outfits color-coordinated to panties and bras lying on the floor. Elena wondered if Melody had a set of underwear whose silk and lace matched every outfit in her wardrobe. "Look at that," she murmured to Vasquez. "The sheets match the Egyptian-chorus-girl sofa and love seat."

"I didn't notice the sofa, not with that Daguerre girl sitting on it. She has a *great* body." He began to pull papers from

Analee's desk while Elena went through her dresser drawers. "Spike's kinda sexy too," Vasquez added.

Elena shook her head. She didn't see Assistant Chief Tey Vasquez and Cadet Major Melody Spike as a very likely couple.

8
..

Tuesday, November 29, 12:45 P.M.

Elena was hungry and annoyed. Vasquez had flipped care-
lessly through the papers and the engagement calendar in
Analee's desk, given the rest of the room a cursory look, then
said, "Let's get some lunch." When she insisted that they keep
searching, he shrugged and said, "Suit yourself, but there's
nothing here." He then left, making Elena feel that she was
the flunky and he, the boss. He hadn't even offered to bring
food back.

Gritting her teeth, she went carefully through everything
he'd glanced at. In an address book she found telephone
numbers with the University of Texas at Los Santos exchange. Maybe she'd located the boyfriends, lovers, whatever, that Melody Spike suspected. Jealousy was a good
motive for murder, especially a murder that seemed impulsive
rather than planned. Nobody *planned* to push a statue over on
the victim, did they? She jotted down the 747 exchanges and
went on to copy names that she hoped might be L.S.A.R.I.
people. Ora Mae Spotwood, for instance. That sounded like
an anti-abortion name.

On telephone bills she picked up a Houston area code.
Analee's family? Thank goodness Elena didn't have to call
them. A representative of the vice president for academic
affairs had pulled Elena aside at the crime scene to say that
Dr. Stanley would prefer to notify the family himself.

What were they like? she wondered. Lavender's Gumbo

30

and a jazz musician. Interesting parents. She found only one piece of correspondence: a postcard with a picture of the Astrodome on one side, on the other a Houston postmark and the message, "Send the money to me." It was signed "Bose." Who was Bose? Someone, Analee presumably, had written across the message with a blue Hi-Liter, "In your dreams." Elena turned up no more correspondence. The Ribbons evidently didn't keep in touch by mail—unless Analee had thrown the letters away.

And where were the girl's financial records, her checkbook? The desk contained nothing else except class work. Where was her purse, for that matter? The police had found no handbag or backpack with the body or in the computer cubicle. Surely the motive for the killing hadn't been robbery. You didn't push a statue over on someone to steal her purse. Had Analee gone to the library carrying nothing but her computer clip arm and her unauthorized key? Sarah Tolland denied having given Analee a key to the library. There should have been papers on the clip arm. None had been found. Had Analee been killed for the missing papers?

Elena looked under the bed, under the mattress. She checked the bottoms and backs of drawers, pockets of clothing hanging in the closets, under the edges of rugs, behind and under chair cushions, growing more puzzled because she found no financial records. Everyone these days, unless they were trying to live on welfare or Social Security, had a checking account, a credit card.

Finally she found what she was looking for in a hollowed-out Bible. A slim black lockbox. Unless Analee distrusted the maids—of which Herbert Hobart had more per student than any university in the country—this box contained something she didn't want anyone to see.

Elena broke the lock and found a checkbook and a savings account book. Analee had been a meticulous record keeper. ROTC and academic scholarship payments were neatly recorded in the register, reimbursements from the Feminist Union and—here was a surprise—biweekly payments from L.S.A.R.I. What had Analee been doing for the anti-abortionists? Was she a double agent? Had the feminists found out and killed her? Elena shook her head. She was getting as weird as Cadet Major Melody Spike.

The most curious entries, however, began after the only payment this fall from Sarah's research fund: a series of five-thousand-dollar deposits followed by large withdrawals, the checks made to cash. Where was Analee getting the money, and what was she doing with it? Twenty-five thousand dollars, unexplained, raised big questions. After putting Analee's financial records back in the box, Elena sat down on the window seat to think about the case. Before she got very far, Maggie Daguerre poked her head in.

"I got back from lunch as quick as I could," she said.

"I hope you brought me some."

"No, you don't." Maggie made a gagging sound. "You wouldn't believe the crap they serve us. Today I think we had duck liver in brain sauce. Jesus, what I wouldn't give for a Big Mac or, better yet, an order of *fajitas* and beans."

That sounded good to Elena. She was hungry. "So what're you doing here? They're saying at I.D.&R that you're on vacation, not that you've quit the force."

"I haven't quit, but I'm sure not on vacation." Maggie sprawled on Analee's bed. "I just couldn't say anything while the major was here. Jeez, can you imagine living with a rich, militaristic, sex-crazed feminist? It's no wonder Analee never stayed around. She'd have had to listen to Melody having sex with everyone and his brother. Which *I* have to put up with—and me turning into a nun since I got to this town full of midgets. The only man on campus taller than me is my chairman, and, as Melody so charmingly puts it, 'Erlingson doesn't fuck students.'"

Elena grinned. She'd heard a lot about Maggie's dating woes since they met on the acid bath case. It was ironic that such a beautiful woman couldn't get a date. As far as Elena knew, Maggie had gone out only with Sergeant Manny Escobedo, a really good guy but a lot shorter than she. "That still doesn't explain why you're a student here. And in psychology."

"I'm undercover." Maggie laughed derisively. "I'm thirty-two, and my captain comes into my office to say I'm going undercover as a twenty-two-year-old graduate student. At a place with no graduate program. In the middle of the semester. Christ, some cover! And when I get here, the chairman of Psychology signs me up for three courses, half credit because I arrived at midsemester with fake grades from UT Austin. Then he assigns me a research project, which he asks me about every week. I'm working my butt off! And getting fed all this fancy French garbage, and getting lectures from my damned roommate about my clothes and how I don't have a bedspread and no feminist consciousness and—"

"But Maggie, what are you *doing* here? For the department?"

"Oh. Well, some asshole is selling diplomas from H.H.U. at twenty grand a whack. How about that? The university won't give their first real degree until next spring, and they've already got alumni who seem to be dumber than their students. Have you met any of the students—besides Melody, I mean? What a bunch of twits."

"OK, but why are *you* assigned to this?" asked Elena. "Why not someone from Fraud and Forgery?"

"Because the Chamber of Commerce and the city council and the chief and even my captain are falling all over themselves to keep H.H.U. happy. Because H.H.U. puts so much money into the local economy. If I tell you about this, you'll keep it quiet, right?"

"Of course. Who'd believe me?" Elena started to laugh.

"It is pretty weird," Maggie admitted. "But it's a computer scam, and I'm into computer security, so I'm supposed to track down the scammer because they can't find him themselves." She sighed and sat up. "Seems like they discovered the fake transcripts in the computer last spring—some registrar's clerk found one. So Charlie Venner—you remember Charlie?" She glanced at Elena for confirmation. "The little lech who's head of the computer center? Charlie's supposed to find out who got into their system, which, of course, he can't manage because he's too busy trying to get it on with his female employees."

While Maggie was relating this tale with relish, Elena tried not to laugh.

"So they give up on Charlie and hire some professional talent, but by that time it's summer and the scam stops—

which makes them think it's a student, and they're hoping he won't come back."

A student? Elena thought of Analee Ribbon.

"No such luck. More transcripts this fall. Twice as many after October."

When Analee's big deposits started.

"They panic and call the LSPD, who sends 'em a computer scam expert from Fraud and Forgery. He's got forty other cases and not much interest. Harley Stanley's having a kitten. Says the LSPD's gotta send someone better, someone who can go undercover and doesn't look like a cop. My captain volunteers me; Fraud offers Beady Trent."

"Who's that?"

"New guy. So the V.P. looks at my resume, and he's ecstatic. Seems like the honchos promised the chairman of Psychology a graduate program and then never delivered, so he's threatening to leave. Which makes me the answer to Harley Stanley's prayers. I've got an undergraduate degree in psychology.

"My cover story—if you can believe this—" Maggie shook her head incredulously "—is that they bought me away from UT Austin with promises of tuition, room, board, money, and so forth to keep Erlingson, the Psych chair, happy—in the middle of the semester yet. While I'm solving their computer scam and playing grad student, they get a chance to find some real graduate students for him.

"I, of course, point out to my captain that I'm thirty-two years old. He says, great; they'll only need to change one number on my undergraduate transcripts to make me look twenty-two. So here I am."

"And—what's his name?—Erlingson went for it?"

"Well, he was pretty surprised to get a new student in the middle of the semester, but he muttered something about an administration that thinks money can buy anything, and then he started piling the work on me."

"So have you found out anything?" Elena was thinking again of the unexplained five-thousand-dollar entries in Analee's financial records. According to Sarah, Analee had been a computer whiz.

"Yeah. I've found out that going without sleep makes me crazy."

"No, I mean about the computer scam. Have you—"

"Sure. I've found all the fake transcripts and even fake letters of recommendation. That was easy. I just cross-referenced dorm registrations with transcripts. Up popped the fakes because the fakes never attended H.H.U. The university system had *no* security, but we already knew that—what with hot-zipper Charlie Venner being head of the computer center. But hell, even Charlie's beginning to look good to me, so you can tell how hard up I am." Maggie's mouth curled sardonically.

"Anyway, the man hadn't changed the passwords since the school opened, so I made him change them. Two or three times, because new transcripts came in after we made the changes. The first ones were entered from library terminals; now they come from everywhere. Whoever's putting them in can disguise the terminal he's using or else has keys to every office on campus."

And Analee apparently had an unauthorized key to the library.

"So I'm looking for a Trojan Horse."

"A what?" Elena pictured a big wooden horse, rolled into the library so a crook could slip out at night and enter fake transcripts in the computer. Some exhibit from the Classics Department? Maybe the Trojan Horse belonged to Professor Rambeaux, who'd made the remark at the crime scene about ancient Romans grinding up killer statues. Maybe *he* was the killer, returning to the scene of his crime. "Wouldn't a Trojan Horse be easy to spot? It'd have to be big enough to hold a person. What gave you that idea anyway? It's bizarre!"

"A Trojan Horse, dear, is computerese for a line of code put into the system so the hacker can sneak back in when you do something to keep him out. I'm working for read-only access in offices that don't need more. Of course, no one wants to give up anything even if they don't know what it means. Shit! I've been here a month."

"Do you have anything to eat?" Elena interrupted. "I'm starving."

"Analee kept granola bars," said Maggie. "They're in our

fridge. And Melody stocks all kinds of exotic stuff. Me, I don't keep anything. The meals are putting fat on me." She gestured angrily toward a body Elena wouldn't have minded owning.

"Help yourself," said Maggie generously. "Analee's dead, and Melody wouldn't notice anything missing. Her company helps themselves."

Elena scooted into the sitting room and gathered up a can of root beer, a granola bar, and a jar of marinated aritchoke hearts, which were pretty good but not very filling. While she ate and Maggie talked, Elena made notes occasionally, even though she really didn't understand a lot of what Maggie had to say about the diploma scam. "Did you ever think that Analee might be your perp?" she asked when Maggie had finished describing her sleuthing strategies.

"Analee? No way. She was a great kid. Told the best racist jokes I've ever heard. And she was smart. I mean *really* smart."

"And she knew a lot about computers," Elena pointed out. "Also, she has unexplained five-thousand-dollar deposits to and withdrawals from her account this fall."

"The computer scam started last year. It just took them forever to catch on, although you'd think, when they discovered in April that they'd been issuing degrees, they'd figure something was wrong."

"So maybe the original guy took on a partner. Maybe he had to, once you started making it hard."

"When did the payments start?"

"First of October."

Maggie shook her head. "I didn't get here until the end of October. Anyway, it couldn't be her. She was great." Maggie thought it over. "Still, you said five thousand? That's a quarter of a diploma."

"Keep her in mind," said Elena. "Maybe the partner got sick of sharing."

Melody Spike entered Analee's room without knocking. "What are you doing here, Daguerre? I thought you had a job at the computer center. If you have free time, you should be campaigning."

"Campaigning?" Elena cocked an eyebrow at Maggie.

"I got nominated for Christmas Queen," she muttered.

"You could have refused the nomination," said Elena, grinning.

"Not really," snapped Maggie. Turning on her roommate, she added, "I'm not campaigning. I consider it beneath my feminine dignity." And she flounced off.

"That's just the sort of person we feminists want elected," said Melody. "Someone who disdains beauty and beauty contests."

"But she's a knockout," said Elena. The idea of thirty-two-year-old Lieutenant Maggie Daguerre campaigning in a college beauty contest was a hoot.

"But completely indifferent to her looks," said Melody. "I caught her cutting her hair with her toenail scissors. Can you imagine? It's a wonder her reproduction Lalique mirror didn't crack at the indignity."

9
..

Tuesday, November 29, 2:15 P.M.

Maggie had left for the computer center and Melody for
an ROTC drill, both assuring Elena that she was welcome to
stay and use their phone. She did. First she tried the two
University of Texas at Los Santos numbers. No answers.
Then she called the UTLS operator and discovered that the
numbers were indeed dorm rooms and belonged to males.
Elena jotted down the names, Ahmed Mohammed and
Bulward Pankins.

The operator refused to speculate on whether the names
belonged to African-Americans. "We're an equal access
university with an open admissions policy," she said. "We
don't ask or answer questions like that." Elena felt as if she'd
just been labeled Bigot of the Year.

Muttering under her breath, she betook herself to Maggie's
bathroom to unbraid, comb out, and rebraid her hair, which
was straggling loose from its businesslike French braid. The
thick, black mass of it demanded a heavy-duty, double-
toothed comb, which she kept in a sling purse with her gun,
badge, and other necessities.

When she looked into Maggie's mirror, she felt as if she
were seeing a photo of her head in an aquarium. The mirror
was round and etched with delicate frosted fish and bubbles,
in the middle of which swam Elena's lightly tanned face, a
little Indian with high cheekbones, dark eyes, and sharply
etched black eyebrows; a little Spanish with the thin nose; a

little Anglo hippie with the long hair and generous mouth. She glanced down. And a *whole* lot unprofessional when you considered what she was wearing—narrow-hipped jeans, flat-heeled cuffed boots, and a sweater that was on the snug side. No wonder Vasquez had ogled her. But Vasquez seemed interested in every female he met—even Melody Spike. Did he genuinely like women, or was he just horny?

Elena left the bath—each suitemate had her own—and used Maggie's phone to track down L. Parker Montrose. He wasn't in his room, the number of which she got from the H.H.U. operator, so she called the registrar's office for his academic schedule. His course-in-progress was Commodities Market 310, Lab, in the auditorium of the business administration building. She had time before it let out at 4:30, so she called a friend at one of the newspapers and asked about L.S.A.R.I.

"They've picketed Planned Parenthood," said Paul Resendez. "They've harassed doctors who do abortions. Some of them even got arrested at H.H.U. after Congress passed the laws protecting clinics. But aside from spray-painting the health services building, for which they didn't actually get caught, they haven't done anything violent or destructive, although some of them seem to want to.

"Of course, some of them act like butter wouldn't melt in their mouths. Their secretary, Ora Mae Spotwood, for instance—she'd head of the Anti-Fornication Brigade. The chastity-nut branch." He laughed.

"Now, Father Bratslowski is another can of worms. He's the president. Of L.S.A.R.I. and everything else. *He* talks tough. And the vice president, Chester Briggs—according to my sources, he's been known to advocate violence. He just doesn't do it where he can be quoted." Elena jotted down the three names and tried to call them.

Father Bratslowski, who supported everything from water for the *colonias* to an open border for any Mexican citizen who wanted to emigrate to no abortion for any reason, was out of town at a retreat for migrant workers. Elena hadn't known migrant workers could afford retreats. In reply to questioning, the housekeeper at the rectory said that "Father" had left yesterday morning and would be back late tomorrow.

Unless she was lying, the priest hadn't killed Analee; he had an alibi.

Elena called Chester Briggs's house. She identified herself, and the woman who answered said, "My brother's not at home." Before Elena could ask when he'd return, the woman hung up. Elena wrote down his address and called Ora Mae Spotwood, who said she was about to leave for her quilting circle but would be glad to talk to Elena the next morning, provided Elena realized that Los Santoans Against Rampant Immorality was a law-abiding organization whose purpose was to foster chastity, wholesome living, and piety, and to save the lives of the innocent unborn. Elena said she'd come by at nine.

Then she tried the University of Texas at Los Santos numbers again, unsuccessfully, and decided she'd better head for L. Parker Montrose's class before he, too, eluded her. She took her time walking over and slipped into a seat at 4:15. The scene was fairly astonishing: students, mostly male, waving bits of paper and shouting at each other and at people on the podium, one obviously a professor, about grain and soybean futures and hog bellies. Hog bellies? A big board in front of the auditorium changed numbers with confusing speed, and if it weren't for outbreaks of laughter among the students, she'd have thought she really was in a commodities market.

Then a bell rang, and the students stampeded for the door. Elena jumped up and threw her arms across the exit, shouting, "I need to talk to L. Parker Montrose."

Nobody owned up to being L. Parker Montrose, which Elena considered suspicious until the professor assured her that L. Parker was out of town.

"Since when?" she asked.

"Since this morning," said a young man wearing shorts and a white cable-knit, V-necked sweater, and carrying a tennis racket. "Poor guy caught a 6:30 plane. I know; I drove him to the airport."

"Ah." Girlfriend dies in the middle of the night; boyfriend escapes on an early morning plane. Sort of an O.J. Simpson scenario. "Why couldn't he drive himself?" she asked, sure that all students at H.H.U., except maybe the late Analee, had their own cars. "Was he planning a long absence?"

"Hey, you don't leave a Ferrari in the airport parking lot, even for a couple of days," said the student, aghast.

"So you expect him back in a couple of days?"

"He's on a field trip for the Resort Evaluation class. Think he went to New Zealand." The student was tapping his racket impatiently against a pristine white tennis shoe.

Did New Zealand have an extradition treaty with the U.S.? Elena asked the professor a few questions about Montrose, but only by dint of flashing her badge and physically restraining him after the students disappeared. One of the three girls in the class lingered.

"I think he's the student who bought wheat futures and lost a bundle," said the professor. "And I think he has blond hair."

"And blue eyes," said the girl. "Are we going or not?"

"I have a date," he said to Elena, and walked off with the student.

Elena left, wondering how many professors dated students. Maybe Maggie would manage to snare a tall prof while she was undercover. Glancing at her watch, Elena headed for the lot where she had parked her truck. With luck she could get across town in time to pick up her rug. Nell had said the Brass Shop closed at five—even if there were ten thousand customers outside waving hundred dollar bills.

"Detective Jarvis?"

She looked up and spotted Michael Futrell, a good-looking criminology professor. Light brown hair, hazel eyes, warm smile, well built. She'd met him at a bicycle race in Chimayo. She was guarding a murder suspect; he was watching his twin brother take third place. He'd even called her for a date, but she couldn't go and he'd never called again. Dating in the nineties—if you could find someone interesting, he never called back. If he did, you wondered whether he had AIDS.

"I suppose you're here on the Analee Ribbon case."

"Did you know her?" Elena asked.

"No, but I know her boyfriend. He's taking a course with me."

"Really. What's he like?"

Michael glanced at his watch. *Shoot*, Elena thought. *He's in*

*a hurry—probably to get home and dress for a big date with
a student.* "Hey, I can make an appointment for tomorrow if
you don't—"

"Not at all," said Michael Futrell. "I just thought—if
you're not busy—and you're through for the day—maybe
we could—ah—go out for a drink—or dinner."

Elena looked down at her jeans. "I'm not—"

"I guess you've got other plans," he interrupted. "I shouldn't
have—well, an appointment tomorrow would be—"

"No," she said, happily postponing her rug until tomorrow.
"I'm just not dressed for—I mean this was my day off. It was
a come-as-you-are deal. Analee was dead; they wanted a detective on the scene."

"You look great to me," said Futrell. "How about beer and
pizza? I'll tell you everything I know about Montrose."

"OK," said Elena, wondering if beer, pizza, and questions
about a suspect could be considered a date.

"We'll have to walk," said Futrell, looking embarrassed.
"My car's in the shop."

"I've got my truck," said Elena. They went to a place
called Gourmet Pizza Academia. Elena was almost afraid to
look at the menu, but it listed pepperoni, so she ordered that
and a Bohemia from their all-import beer list. Michael
ordered sun-dried tomato and pesto pizza and a beer from
Ireland that looked like molasses. He then insisted that she try
the sun-dried tomatoes and pesto, which turned out to be so
tasty she let herself be talked into eating half of his in
exchange for half of hers.

So there, Sarah, she thought, directing a silent shot toward
her friend, Dr. Sarah Tolland. *I can appreciate foreign food,
too.* Sarah was always complaining about Elena's plebian
tastes when it came to foreign cuisine. "Tell me about L.
Parker Montrose," she urged Michael. "He's conveniently left
town, so I can't question him."

"Well, Montrose thinks he's a big man on campus because
he's dating a black woman, especially since his parents
disapprove. He never fails to mention that."

"How would he feel if he found out she had other
boyfriends?"

"I think he'd be furious if it came to his attention that Ms.

Ribbon wasn't—ah—exclusive in her affections and didn't properly appreciate the honor he's doing her."

"Furious enough to kill her?" Elena asked, pushing away the Chianti bottle with the candle, which had just dripped hot wax on her finger. Behind Michael's head a Roman arena decorated a poster labeled Verona. Along the wall on either side were other Italian travel posters—so spectacular they made you want to run out and jump on the first plane to Rome. Not that she could afford to.

"Well, I can postulate a situation," Michael was saying. He put down a half-eaten wedge of her pepperoni pizza and looked thoughtful. "He hears that she's dating someone else. He knows she's always at the library, so he goes over there—although how he'd get a key and why he'd want one is beyond my imagination. A less devoted student than Montrose is hard to find. I've always suspected he bought the term paper he turned in last year, but I couldn't prove it. Anyway, let's assume he has a key."

"Same problem with her," Elena admitted. She was picking tasty olives out of her salad and popping them in her mouth. They hadn't been pitted like your average canned supermarket variety, so getting the pits out of her mouth without looking tacky was a problem. "We don't know where she got her key."

"Well, we'll hypothesize that Montrose got in, confronted her, and turned nasty over her dating other men. Montrose is the kind who *thinks* he's broad-minded, but he's really an immature exhibitionist."

"Sounds awful."

"His only redeeming feature is a quirky sense of humor."

"She evidently had one too," said Elena, who had just discovered an anchovy under a lettuce leaf. She moved it to the ashtray. "Go on. What happens after he gets nasty?"

"Maybe he hit her. Any sign of that?"

"No. Except for the blow from the statue. Actually, we think she hit him. And drew blood."

"Ah. Even better. He insulted her, and she hit him. *Then* he'd be furious."

Elena nodded and picked up the story. "So he chases her down the stairs. And in a fit of temporary insanity, he pushed the statue over on her. Then he gets a high-priced lawyer, spends a few months in a plush mental institution, his expensive doctor declares him sane, and he's out." Elena scowled. "The assistant chief here was saying this morning that the system works a lot better for the well-heeled than for poor minorities."

Michael nodded gloomily. "The brilliant African-American girl dies; the wealthy white kid goes free. How about some *tiramisu* and espresso?"

"Will I like it?"

"You'll love it. It's like a coffee mousse on a crust with chocolate sprinkles on top. I promise you won't want to sneak it into the ashtray." He signaled to the waiter and ordered.

"Of course, maybe L.S.A.R.I. killed her."

Michael frowned. "How do they come into it?"

"Maybe they don't. I have an appointment with one of their officers tomorrow."

"Be careful," he warned. "They're dangerous people. Look what happened to those doctors in Florida."

"It's hard to believe someone named Ora Mae would shoot me," said Elena, grinning. The waiter put down a plate of something delicious looking, also probably very high in calories. Still, if she was going to risk her neck tomorrow interviewing people who put a higher value on life in the womb than out, she might as well have fun tonight. "How strong is that coffee?" she asked.

"You might want to put some sugar in it."

They spent two more hours drinking coffee and getting acquainted, talking about new forensic techniques the LSPD couldn't afford and other topics of mutual interest. When she dropped him off at his faculty apartment house, a boat-shaped building with portholes and other art deco touches, he leaned, laughing, across the gearshift and kissed her. Just a little brush, but it was nice, and maybe rather daring from a man who admitted that when she'd refused his first invitation several months back, he'd been afraid to call again. Tonight, he claimed, had been the result of impulse; he'd seen her, thought she looked great, and forgotten, initially, to worry about being refused.

Thought she looked great. What a nice thing to say. She

hoped he'd call again. If he didn't, maybe she'd call him. After all, it was the nineties. There were supposed to be liberated women and sensitive men out there. She considered herself liberated, and maybe he was sensitive. That would be a nice change from her ex.

Humming a mariachi tune, she drove home with a cold wind buffeting the pickup and the headlights of oncoming cars growing in the dark like alien spacecraft until they flashed in her eyes, then disappeared into the black distance. Elena liked to drive at night. It gave her a heady sense of isolation.

She thought about Analee, a lovely dark girl with the white marble arm of the statue lying across her, blood dripping from its fingers. It wasn't a scene she'd ever forget. And she was damned well going to find out who had killed Analee Ribbon. Elena knew she couldn't control what the courts did afterward; Vasquez was right about the way the system worked, but she'd find the killer.

10

"All *right*!" said Elena, spinning around in her gray tweed chair at Crimes Against Persons. She'd asked for a rush on the typing of blood traces on the clip arm, and the information was on her desk when she arrived: O negative on the end where Analee had cut her hand, A positive on the other end, where they thought Analee had hit the killer. The autopsy hadn't been done yet, so Elena didn't have a blood type on Analee, but. . . .

She thought back to her first case involving H.H.U. and an interview with Dr. Greta Marx, a crusader for birth control and abortion at the Health and Reproductive Services Center. The memory of their conversation convinced Elena to call the doctor instead of showing up in person, which might expose her to another embarrassing lecture on responsible sex. Nor did she have time for a personal visit. Ora Mae Spotwood, the chastity lady, expected her at nine o'clock.

The doctor, as it turned out, had known and liked Analee. "When my blood pressure went up to one fifty," said the doctor, "—that was after L.S.A.R.I. spray-painted the clinic— Analee suggested that I have Buildings and Grounds take off the 'Baby Killer' graffiti and leave the silhouettes of the campus police who got in the way of the vandals." Dr. Marx laughed. "It worked out beautifully. The president saw the silhouettes from his limousine the next day and stopped to compliment me on my

46

new art deco decorations. Poor man hasn't a clue. Whereas Analee was brilliant—and amusing."

Elena wouldn't have guessed that Dr. Greta Marx had a sense of humor.

"If I knew who murdered her—"

"You could help me find the killer."

"How?" asked the doctor.

"Well, it could have been the spray painters."

"Wouldn't surprise me."

"But it might have been a boyfriend, in which case I need her bloody type and his."

"From me? You're asking me to release privileged information?"

Elena sighed. "Do you realize how long it takes to get information from the coroner and the state lab? She's dead, and L. Parker Montrose—"

"Obnoxious little snot."

"So I've heard."

"Don't know what the young women see in him."

"He's already skipped town. If he killed Analee, he could get out of the country before I can stop him. And the L.S.A.R.I. people. The longer they stay free, if they're responsible, the more time they have to think up alibis and round up members to lie for them. DNA matches take forever, but quick blood-typing would give us a head start. I don't even have Analee's yet."

"If I give you information, it's unofficial," said Dr. Marx. "You can't say where it came from, or you'll get me in trouble with the patriarchal bastards in the county medical society."

"I'll just use it to zero in on her killer."

"She was a fine young woman," said the doctor. "Very conscientious about matters of birth control and disease prevention. I hope you yourself are—"

"I am!" said Elena. "I'm very careful." She knew better than to say she wasn't having sex. Greta Marx would never believe that; she thought everyone was having sex—irresponsibly.

"Hold on," muttered the doctor. A minute later she returned to the phone. "Analee was O negative. Montrose is A positive."

"Bingo!" exclaimed Elena. Montrose had just become her prime suspect.

"So go out and find the little psychopath."

"Montrose is a psychopath?"

"You consider pushing a statue over on someone sane behavior?" the doctor demanded.

"No," Elena agreed. She called the university to see if they had a number for L. Parker Montrose's parents and a field-trip destination in New Zealand. Surprisingly, she got both, but New Zealand turned out to be New England; Montrose was checking out bed-and-breakfast lodges that were part of a ski-touring package in Vermont. First, she called his parents' home in Westport, Connecticut, and was told that Master Parker was "away at university." *Master Parker*? She grinned and put through a call to Vermont. Montrose had registered at a lodge, but he wasn't in. The field trip seemed to be for real; the clerk had actually seen him.

A glance at her watch sent Elena hurrying to check out a car for the visit to Ora Mae Spotwood, quilter and chastity advocate. The woman lived in the Upper Valley, in a two-story brick house with white columns. Plantation in the desert, Elena thought dryly. Why didn't people just use thick adobe and blend in with the landscape, as well as save on their heating and cooling bills?

This place was new—the yard had not yet been taken over by the shrubbery made possible by a Rio Grande water allotment. It looked bare compared with older neighborhoods in the area. Two fairly large trees were obviously struggling through a recent transplantation. They were set in raised, brick-enclosed circles with thick rosemary plantings mounded on top, spilling over the brickwork, and covered by pale blue flowers with a freeze-dried look.

Because of the quilting, Elena had expected someone grandmotherly. Ora Mae Spotwood, however, had maintained a Southern female perkiness into middle age along with her big hair and an accent straight out of East Texas. The quilting turned out to be a class she taught, not some cozy coterie of older ladies getting together to sew and swap their grand-mothers' patterns.

Elena, when invited, sat down on a firm-cushioned, conservatively striped sofa and accepted a cup of decaffeinated coffee. "I'm here about the death of Analee Ribbon," she began.

Mrs. Spotwood gasped. "Analee's dead?"

Elena nodded. "Killed early yesterday morning in the university library." The woman seemed to be in shock. "It was in the paper," said Elena. "On the front page."

"I've canceled my subscriptions," said Mrs. Spotwood. "I refuse to support the liberal media elite who are destroying Christian values and American family life."

"Oh." Unable to suppress her curiosity, Elena asked, "What about TV?"

"It's part of the same conspiracy. Sex and violence—that's all they air. Have you ever heard anyone advocate chastity on TV?"

"Well, I—"

"Of course, you haven't. I belong to TOTT."

"I'm—ah—not familiar with—"

"Turn off the Tube. We have fifty thousand members among Southern Christians."

"Well, about Analee—"

"She's really dead?" Mrs. Spotwood dabbed at her eyes with a handkerchief. "I can't believe it. What happened?"

"Some one pushed a statue over on her."

"One of those disgusting *naked* statues?"

"Well, actually they just *look* naked, but yes, that's what—"

"I knew we shouldn't have let her volunteer. Now they've killed her."

"Who, Mrs. Spotwood?" asked Elena. Everyone had a theory on this case. Some of the theorists had to be trying to take the light of speculation off themselves.

"Those feminists. Those fornicators and baby-killers. They must have found out that she was working for us."

"What was she doing?" Elena asked, remembering the payments from L.S.A.R.I. recorded in Analee's records. "Evidently you were paying her."

"Oh, not paying her," Mrs. Spotwood protested. "Analee wouldn't have asked for anything. We offered because she needed the money, poor girl. Neegrah families can't afford places like H.H.U., although why her parents would let her attend such a school—the immorality there! You wouldn't believe it!" Mrs. Spotwood poked an errant flower back into an otherwise neat arrangement.

"But her parents probably didn't realize," she added. "Obviously they're good people. I could tell that because they raised such a fine daughter. Analee was absolutely loyal to the cause. She joined us because she knew that fornication is ruining Nigrah family life. She told me that herself the first time we met. And, of course, she understood that abortion is a genocidal plot. Analee's such a good Christian. Her sister's a minister."

"Is she?" murmured Elena, finding this flood of information interesting if somewhat confusing. "So what were you paying her to do?"

"Not paying her, Detective. Helping her out. Her mission was entirely voluntary."

"What mission?" asked Elena patiently.

"The gathering of information. Not that she had a chance to report anything. They must have caught her and killed the poor child before she could."

"What kind of information?" asked Elena. She knew what Melody Spike had wanted Analee to find out from L.S.A.R.I., but she couldn't imagine what Analee could have found out for Ora Mae, even if Analee ever planned to be a double agent, which sounded bizarre.

"Why, anything that would help us put a stop to the sexual immorality that flourishes on that campus and to the abortions performed by that evil Marx woman. I consider it very significant—her name. She's probably descended directly from the father of the Communist menace."

Elena hadn't heard it called "the Communist menace" in a while, except by a murdered neighbor who had thought *glasnost* was a Communist plot. Maybe Mrs. Spotwood suspected the same thing. Before Elena could question the lady further, the doorbell rang and Ora Mae went to answer. Elena heard a man's voice saying, "I've brought the flyers by. You'll have to—"

"Oh, Chester, the most terrible thing has happened." Mrs. Spotwood ushered in a stocky, bald man wearing a windbreaker over a plaid shirt. "This is Detective Jarvis. Detective Jarvis, Chester Briggs, our vice president."

Elena remembered the name from her talk with Paul Resendez at the newspaper—who'd be fascinated to hear that he belonged to the liberal media elite. Chester gave her a suspicious look and didn't offer to shake hands, although she had risen to do so.

"What news?" he asked.

"Someone has killed Analee."

Ora Mae looked as if she might weep. Either she was a talented actress, or she had really liked the victim.

"Saw it in the papers," said Briggs. "If I were you, Detective, I'd find out where Dr. Greta Marx was when it happened." He had turned an intense gaze on Elena. "A woman who kills babies wouldn't think twice about killing a black girl."

"Dr. Marx would need a motive," said Elena mildly.

"What are you? One of those females who thinks it's all right to get pregnant and then commit murder to take care of your mistake?"

"Chester!" admonished Mrs. Spotwood. "Detective Jarvis is a policewoman."

"The last I heard, abortion wasn't against the laws of man, just the laws of God."

"I'm very interested in hearing why you think Dr. Marx would have killed Ms. Ribbon," Elena persevered.

"Because the black girl was supposed to find out the names of students who'd had abortions at that clinic."

"Did she?" asked Elena.

"Maybe she did; maybe she didn't." Briggs put a bundle of flyers down on Mrs. Spotwood's coffee table. "I gotta get back to work. You'll have these out by tomorrow, Ora Mae?"

"The Children's Brigade will take care of it after school," said Mrs. Spotwood.

"It's been suggested that someone from L.S.A.R.I. may have killed Analee," said Elena.

"None of us did," said Briggs, and left before Elena could ask where *he* was the night of the murder.

Mrs. Spotwood said, "We are *not* a violent organization, Detective. We cherish *all* life." She sounded huffy and didn't reseat herself, thereby signaling that she expected Elena to leave. "I hope you'll keep me informed about your investigation. I was very fond of Analee. We all were."

Elena wondered whether Chester Briggs was. He hadn't called the victim anything but "the black girl." "I hope you'll understand that I have to ask everyone who knew her this, Mrs. Spotwood. Where were you yesterday morning between, say, one and three?"

Ora Mae Spotwood blinked in astonishment. "Why, I was sleeping beside my husband, as I have every night for the last thirty years."

"I see. I wonder where Mr. Briggs was."

"Sleeping in his sister's house, I assume. Chester is not one for after-dark carousing. He devotes himself to his business, his widowed sister, and the cause. A fine man. I wish I could find him a wife. It's a shame he has no hair. Even the most moral-minded of us appreciate a good head of hair." Ora Mae patted her own teased, lacquered, tinted curls.

On that note, Elena took her leave before she embarrassed herself by giggling. These people weren't funny; in fact, some of them were dangerous.

11

As she drove toward the university, Elena's gaze rose to the Thunderbird, the great red sweep of its wings dominating the west side of the mountains. She imagined it coasting on the wind, waiting to drop down on the developers who hoped to usurp its slopes. It was huge—a rust-red bird of prey stained by iron oxide into the golden brown morning folds of the Franklin Mountains.

It affected Elena as it must have affected the Apaches who had sheltered there, waiting to swoop down like avenging demons on earlier intruders—the trundling wooden carts of the Spaniards on their way toward Santa Fe and, later, stage-coaches and army detachments and whoever in the nineteenth century braved the Jornada del Muerto up the river from the pass.

She hoped that the Thunderbird would never be scraped away or covered over by the machines of men who were more interested in making money than in preserving the legacy of the past. Surely, if they disturbed that figure from Indian mythology, its destruction would bring a curse on the city.

Smiling at her own superstition, Elena turned the car in at the gate of the university, circled the quadrangle, and pulled into the lot of the pink police building. Tey Vasquez stood on the steps, coming on to a freckled coed with curly beige hair who evidently felt the appeal of a uniform and a pair of sexy sunglasses. When Elena approached, he said, "Catch you later," to the girl and then, "Where have *you* been?" to Elena.

"Interviewing Mrs. Spotwood. You didn't want to come. Remember?"

Vasquez shrugged. "The Ribbon family's arrived. They've checked in at the Guest House, so we'd better get over there, find out if the girl had criminal connections in Houston."

While they walked over, Elena brought him up to date on her discoveries about Analee's finances and the blood types.

"Five thousand dollars, huh? What do you bet it's drug money?"

"Or part of the diploma scam," said Elena. "I assume you know about that."

"Yeah, but I doubt it. *She* wouldn't have the contacts to run it. You think there are a lot of blacks who have twenty grand to buy a fake diploma?"

"Beats me." They entered the Guest House through a great curved arch framed by mosaic tiles. In the lobby the Ribbons were easily located as the only group of tall, grief-stricken African-Americans. A young woman, evidently the sister, was haranguing President Sunnydale on the subject of a university memorial service for Analee.

"*Ah'm* conductin' the service," she said in a voice that echoed through the lobby and caused other guests to turn and stare. "You people got her killed—"

"I assure you, Miss Ribbon—" began President Sunnydale.

"*Reverend* Ribbon," she corrected him. "Ah'm the founder of the Church of the Omniracial Mother."

"I think I've heard of it," said President Sunnydale, eyes brightening. "Monterey, California?"

"Houston, Texas," she snapped. "An' *Ah'll* deliver the eulogy over mah sister's body."

"Of course, Reverend Ribbon." President Sunnydale beamed at her. "We must get together for a chat. We evangelists—"

Dr. Harley Stanley, the vice president for academic affairs, cleared his throat. "The investigating detectives are here, sir. They wish to speak to the family."

The older woman, who looked a good deal like Analee, although taller and lighter-skinned, turned a bitter glance on Elena and Vasquez. "You caught him yet?"

"No, ma'am," said Elena, "but we will." She murmured briefly to Dr. Stanley, then led Lavender Lee Ribbon into the manager's office, which had been vacated for their convenience. Elena sat on a sofa beside Analee's mother. Vasquez took the chair behind the desk.

"You have my sympathies, ma'am," said Elena. "Your daughter seems to have been a remarkable young woman."

"Mah most promisin' child," said Lavender Lee Ribbon, dark eyes shining with unshed tears. "Named after her grandmother, hopin' she'd follow in the Lee family line of great cooks. Turned out Analee didn't have a talent for food, but she did know the value of a dollar, just like her mama an' grandmama. She'd a made somethin' of herself." The tears overflowed.

"Her professors certainly thought so," Elena agreed. "I talked to Dr. Tolland yesterday; she said Analee was a brilliant programmer."

"Whatever that means," muttered Lavender. "If mah Analee hadn't been so lovin' of computers, she'd never a come here, an' she'd be alive today. But I s'pose you don't wanna hear about that."

"Anything you can tell us, Mrs. Ribbon, will help. The more we know about her, the better our chance of finding the killer."

"For instance," said Vasquez, "is there any criminal activity among the family or her friends back in Houston?"

Elena cleared her throat. "Mr. Vasquez is the assistant chief of police here on campus." What she didn't need was a racial/ethnic standoff. "The chief assigned him specially to this case because the university is—well—horrified over Analee's death. I'm a detective from the Los Santos force."

Lavender Lee Ribbon didn't seem particularly impressed with their credentials. She glared at Vasquez and said, "Well, now, Mister Assistant Chief, Ah'm proud of everyone in mah family. We own our own house. Mah aunt left it to me. That's why we moved from New Orleans in the first place. You own *your* own house?"

Vasquez evidently didn't, because his mouth turned sulky. Elena mumbled that she did, not sure to whom the question had been directed.

"Glad to hear it," said Mrs. Ribbon. "Ah always feel more comfortable with home owners. An' Ah own mah own business—Lavender's Gumbo. Best gumbo anywhere—includin' New Orleans. Ah'm the gumbo queen of Houston, an' mah husband, Ray Lee, is the best jazz trumpet an' blues singer anywhere. But he's not a man to go runnin' off on outa-town gigs an' forgettin' his family. He's a real fine husband an' daddy."

Mrs. Ribbon had a rich voice and a Southern accent like sweet syrup. Elena found pleasure in listening to her.

"As for mah children, Mister Assistant Chief, three outa four turned out good, an' that's better than most folks can say these days. Thelonius Lee, now that boy's big on dreams an' short on brains, so he run afoul a the law, but he's out on parole, an' Ah never let him outa mah sight. He's gonna take a turn down the path a virtue whether he wants to or not."

She nodded emphatically, and Elena believed her.

"Now you wanna know about mah Analee, Mister Assistant Chief? Look at her grades, look at all the fine things she's done in her young life, look at *her*. She was a beautiful girl, smart an' ambitious. Some white man musta killed her. Jealousy. Didn't like a black woman goin' places." With that, Lavender Lee Ribbon, anger tightening her mouth, rose and stalked out.

"How do we get more information about the one on parole?" asked Vasquez. "Didn't I tell you there'd be criminal connections?"

Elena rose and punched the I.D.& R. number on the phone. "If you hadn't insulted her, we've have found out more," she said. Once she had made her request for information on Thelonius Lee Ribbon and left her telephone number with I.D.&R., they called in Ray Lee Ribbon. If the others were tall, and they were—Analee had been not only the youngest but also the shortest in that family—Ray Lee towered. Six-eight, at least, Elena estimated, as she invited him to sit beside her. She felt like a midget, but not at all intimidated. Analee's father had kind eyes, now very sad, in a dark face. The victim had inherited her color from him; her features, from her mother.

"You got any idea who killed her?" he asked, sounding like a man in the middle of a nightmare.

"That's what we're trying to find out," Elena said gently. "Anything you can tell us will help."

"You think Ah know?" His eyes were clouded with grief. "All mah life Ah never cared about anything but mah wife, mah children, an' mah music. Ah was *there* for mah children. Even Thelonius Lee, mah youngest boy. He plays a fine sax. Jus' he got dreams too big for what a musician makes. But he's learnin'. His mama an' me, we're takin' him in hand. Analee, now, she never gave us a minute's worry. No reason for anyone to kill mah Analee."

"Maybe when she wrote or called, she mentioned something that might give us a clue," said Elena. "Boyfriends, girlfriends, enemies." He kept shaking his head. "Did she ever mention anyone who was unkind to her?"

He shook his head again. "Analee was good about callin'. Like Ah said, she wasn't one to worry us, me an' Lavender, but she always talked about her grades an' such. Made us real proud. You think some boyfriend killed her? In a white university, she wouldn't be havin' boyfriends."

So they hadn't known about L. Parker Montrose. Mr. Ribbon didn't seem like the kind of man who would take murderous offense over a white boyfriend; nonetheless, Elena wasn't going to mention Montrose. The telephone rang, and Vasquez took the call. He'd been antsy through the interview, swiveling his chair, tapping his foot, ignoring the father. "For you," he said to Elena, holding the phone out when the person at the other end obviously refused to give him information.

"Better get back to mah wife," said Ray Lee Ribbon. He rose with slow deliberation and headed toward the door. When Elena started to protest, Vasquez frowned, nodding toward the phone urgently. She took the hint and let Ray Lee go.

Because of the news I.D.&R. gave her, she would have called in the younger brother next, but Langston Lee Ribbon presented himself on his father's heels. He was dressed entirely in black—mourning? she wondered—and took a seat on the sofa. Still thinking about the younger brother's record and its implications for the case, scrabbling for a first question, she said, "Tell us something about yourself, Mr. Ribbon." She knew that he was twenty-seven, but nothing else.

He turned to stare at her, a handsome man, tall and slender with a face that was—what? Sensitive. As if the wrong word would tip him into depression. "Ah'm a student," he said in answer to her question. "An' a writer."

"Student where?" asked Vasquez, turning his dark glasses toward Langston Lee Ribbon.

"Well, actually, Ah'm a postdoctoral fellow."

Elena blinked. That meant he had a doctor's degree.

"In creative writin'. At the University of Houston. Got mah B.A., M.A., an' Ph.D. there. Suppose Ah could go teach somewhere, but Ah like Houston. Like mah mama's cookin'. Ah was a student with Donald Barthelme. Reckon you've heard a him."

"No," Elena admitted. Vasquez was antsy again.

"He's famous," said the brother reproachfully. "Dead, too. Ah'm in mournin'." He nodded, looking down gloomily at his black clothes. "He was a postmodernist."

"Ah," said Elena encouragingly. She had no idea what that meant.

"Cancer killed him. Ah quit smokin' right after the funeral. Stopped writin' short stories. He wrote short stories. Before he died. For *The New Yorker*."

"Impressive," murmured Elena. She guessed it was best to let him keep talking. Maybe he'd hit on something relevant to his sister's death, which he hadn't mentioned.

"Ah was named after Langston Hughes. Guess you don't know who he was, either."

Elena didn't.

"He was black. An' a poet. Now Ah'm writin' poetry. Mostly elegiac." He took a notebook from his pocket. "Writin' one for mah sister's service. Analee." He stared at his poem, wrote a line, then asked, "What killed her?"

"A statue," said Vasquez.

"Makes a good metaphor," said Langston Lee Ribbon, "the dead killin' the livin'."

"What can you tell us about your sister?" asked Elena when he seemed to have run out of conversation.

He considered the matter. "She was beautiful. Funny." He thought some more. "Liked money. Never read a poem, 'cept mine, 'less she had to take a test."

"Where were you when she died?" asked Vasquez.

"Houston," said Langston, as if anyone would know that. "In my carrel. That's where Ah always am, 'less Ah'm home. Did the statue just fall over or what?"

"We think it was pushed," Elena answered. "Would you have any idea who might have done such a thing to her?"

"A messenger of evil," said Langston, and wrote another line in his notebook.

"We need to talk to the other brother," Vasquez said to Elena, as though Langston weren't in the room.

Langston rose and tucked his notebook into his pocket. "Ah'll get him."

"What did Identification and Records say?" asked Vasquez.

"The younger one got busted for dealing coke when he was eighteen," Elena murmured. "Got out on parole last summer. He's one of the guys freed when the state prisons were so overcrowded. The board was looking for anyone who hadn't committed murder with an axe or an Uzi."

"He'll be mixed up in it somehow," said Vasquez.

"Maybe."

The younger brother came in, looking nervous. For an ex-drug dealer, he was the most conservatively outfitted young man Elena had ever seen—close, ordinary haircut (no dreadlocks, no shaving up the side); well-pressed, pleated slacks; loafers with tassels; a button-down-collar sport shirt in a low-key green plaid. "Thelonius Lee Ribbon?" she asked, just to be sure.

"Bose, OK?" He sat down beside her but on the far edge of the cushion, which took some doing; he was tall and husky, not slender like his brother. "Mah daddy name me Thelonius after Thelonius Monk—you know? The piano man? But Ah cain't play no piano." He glanced at Vasquez. "Cool shades, man." Vasquez scowled.

"Bose?" Elena connected it immediately with the postcard in Analee's desk. "Send the money to me," it said. "In your dreams," Analee had written across the card.

"Is that short for Bozo?" asked Vasquez—meanly, as if the young man's compliment had been an insult.

Ribbon glowered at H.H.U.'s assistant chief. "Be for the speakers. Bose speakers. Best there is. If Ah hadn't wanted me some so bad, likely Ah'd a never got in trouble."

His criminal career, evidently short-lived and disastrous, had been inspired by a desire for stereo equipment? Well, why not? Elena had read about kids who got killed for their sneakers. "Why were you writing Analee to 'send the money to you'?" she asked.

Bose looked taken aback. "Jus' a li'l joke," he mumbled. "Like she told Mama she be doin' real good an' didn't need no help, so Ah say send me some—you know?"

"Or maybe you're back in the drug trade," suggested Vasquez, "and she was dealing for you. Maybe she got killed in a deal gone bad."

"You think Analee dealin'? She so mad Ah was, she never visit me in prison. Mama mad, but she come visit. Anyway, Ah'm clean. Ah'm on parole—you know? Workin' for mah mama. At Lavender's Gumbo. That's her place, her restaurant—you know? Ah ever git off parole an' kin go in clubs again, Ah'm gonna play gigs with mah daddy."

"Your sister died Tuesday morning between two and three," said Vasquez. "Where were you?"

"Sleepin'. In mah mama's house. An' she do bed check."

Elena marveled at his English. Everyone else in the family spoke standard English with a Southern accent; Bose spoke a street patois. Had he sounded like that before he went to prison?

"She worse'n mah parole officer. Never take her eye off me."

"But a mother's a perfect alibi. She'd lie for you, wouldn't she?" said Vasquez. "Your parole officer wouldn't."

"Don' let mah mama hear you say she lie," Bose retorted. "Ah don' know nothin' 'bout what happened to mah sister. Ah wasn't here."

That was all he'd say. Elena wondered whether guilt or fear of the police made him uncooperative. Of necessity, they moved on to the sister, Reverend Zora Lee Ribbon.

"Who were *you* named after?" asked Vasquez sarcastically.

She fixed him with an eye as commanding as her mother's. In fact, Elena imagined Zora looked just about the way Lavender would have looked at twenty-nine. Zora was the eldest of the children, tall with an earth-mother figure. The founder of the Church of the Omniracial Mother, whatever that was.

"Mah mother named me after Zora Neale Hurston. Not likely you know who she was."

"Who was she?" asked Elena, interested and hoping to get the sister talking, to lessen the hostility Vasquez projected.

Zora turned to Elena. "Got a few races in you," she commented. "No black, but in mah church we take women of all colors. Zora Neale Hurston—African-American writer an' anthropologist. Do you good to read her work, Detective."

Elena nodded. "I'll look it up. We hope you can—"

"Zora Neale chose to study her people an' to write about them. Ah chose to lead mine."

"Great," said Vasquez. "About your sister—"

"A sinner," said Zora. "More interested in money an' material success than in the true soul power of the woman."

"How was she making her money?" asked Vasquez.

"But Analee had a good heart. She was comin' around. Comin' to see that women can control the world—through the power of their souls. Through sisterhood."

"A lot of money went through her account," said Vasquez. He got an angry look from Elena, who thought those five-thousand-dollar deposits should be kept quiet until she found out the source. "Where was she—"

"Mah sister knew how to work the system," said the Reverend. "Ah'll say that for her. Once she matured, she'd have been a fine fund-raiser in mah church. If some evil brother hadn't killed her."

"Which brother did it?" asked Vasquez quickly.

She gave him a contemptuous look. "For 'brother' read 'man'."

"How do you know it was a man?" asked Elena.

"It was a man because the violence of the world grows in the male soul; the love of the world, in the female."

"Do you know anything about her boyfriends?"

"If mah sister had lovers, Ah'd be the last person she'd tell, but Ah'd advise you to look for men's trails—the spore of greed, ambition, an' anger. Not love. Mah sister needed to purge the male in her soul. Someone killed her because of the male in her, the ambition an' hunger for the material." The Reverend rose majestically. "Now Ah have a eulogy to prepare."

"Mumbo jumbo," muttered Vasquez. "You can bet that Bozo had something to do with the murder. He was probably shipping drugs from Houston and she was selling."

"Makes as much sense to figure she was sending drugs to him," said Elena. "They're coming through here from Mexico like quarters through a slot machine. Or hadn't you noticed? I'll check with the Narc Squad to see if there's any information on either of them."

"And I'll nose around here for rumors that she was dealing," he offered, rising.

"You do that," Elena agreed, wishing she had Leo Weizell as her partner, the C.A.P. detective she usually worked with. He wasn't a bigot, he was a lot more fun, and he was a lot better at interrogation. Besides that, he didn't hide behind sunglasses. "How come you're always wearing those stupid glasses?" she snapped at Vasquez.

He halted on his way to the door, face flushed with anger. Then he whipped off the glasses and turned to her, revealing his eyes: one dark brown, almost black, one lighter, closer to hazel. The light one looked strange—bleached. Elena wished she'd kept her mouth shut. Before she could say anything, Vasquez had replaced the glasses and was gone.

12
..

"I'm going over to UTLS to find the boyfriends. You want to come along, Tey?" Elena asked, still embarrassed over her gaffe the day before. She was calling Vasquez from her desk, having just checked to see whether L. Parker Montrose had returned to Los Santos. He hadn't.

"That's off my turf," said Vasquez. "I'd have to get special permission from their police. I'll stay here and see what I can find out about drug dealing."

"OK." Was he about to stop cooperating because she'd pissed him off? "Narcotics doesn't have a thing on Bose since his parole, or on Analee or any other Ribbon. The family's staying in town until the body's released." Elena had talked to Lavender that morning.

"Uh huh."

"Well, I'll see you later today." She could apologize, but that would probably make it worse. How was she to know he had two different color eyes? They weren't that bad, for Pete's sake. She hung up and went to check out a car for the trip to the state university.

Elena loved that campus, which suited the rugged terrain on which it was built: some buildings terraced down into arroyos while others were backed by steep rock bluffs. Little enclaves of desert shrubbery popped up unexpectedly to please the eye. The thick-walled buildings narrowed from base to top with stucco facades and mosaic decorations under red roofs.

She parked in a student lot, hurried across the street, and took a battered elevator with a broken light fixture upstairs, where she found the room number of Ahmed Mohammed. She knocked, and he answered wearing lime green Jockey shorts and struggling into a white terry-cloth bathrobe that looked like a jacket on his seven-foot frame.

"What you doin' at my door, lady?" he asked, sleepy-eyed.

Elena introduced herself and flashed her badge.

"Ain't—whoops—haven't done nothin'." He backed into the room and sat down on the bed, shoving huge feet into rubber thongs. "Jus' got back las' night."

"From where?" she asked, taking a chair by the desk. She could see the evidence of his recent return. He'd unpacked by upending a large zippered gym bag on the floor.

"From Wyoming. Team been on tour."

"That would be—basketball?"

"What else? You don' know Ahmed Mohammed? Ain't—whoops—isn't that a great name? Picked it out my own self. Got a nice ring to it, don' you think?"

"Absolutely," Elena agreed. This young giant had an ingenuous charm that made her want to smile.

"Can't believe you comin' to my room 'thout knowin' who I is—am. Every pro team in the country's scoutin' me. Ain't a shot Ahmed Mohammed can't make—three-pointers, dunks, jumps, free throws—"

"How come you have to jump?" Elena asked, laughing. "Can't you just reach up and drop it in?"

"Near about," he agreed with a smile. "So what you want with Ahmed Mohammed? Want me to talk to some police basketball league? Can't do it 'til the season over. Coach, he—"

"It's about Analee Ribbon."

"What about Analee?" Worry lines leapt up on his high forehead, which looked even higher because he had a shaved-up-the-side haircut with a sailor-hat block of hair perched on top.

Elena sighed. If he'd been out of town, he didn't know that Analee was dead, which meant she'd have to break the news.

"Analee was killed in the H.H.U. library early Tuesday morning. We're trying to talk to everyone who knew her, and I found your number in her address book."

"Analee's dead?" He looked stunned.

"I'm sorry. Was she your girlfriend?"

"Wish she was. Always hoped she would be."

"So you're saying she was just a friend? I understand she came over here to visit several nights a week."

"She come to tutor me an' Rhino Pankins. She's *dead*?"

"Yes. This—Rhino?" What a name! "Would that be—" She glanced at her notes. "—Bulward Pankins?"

"Don' call him Bulward. He don' like that name. I tole him he could change it like I done, but he say Rhino good enough. He jus' kill anyone call him Bulward."

Elena made a mental note: Bulward "Rhino" Pankins dealt in death threats. "Did Analee date him?"

"Din' date neither of us. Her an' Rhino, they been friends since they was kids in Houston. How she die?"

"Someone pushed a statue over on her."

"A *stat*-ue! It hurt her bad?"

"Killed her instantly," Elena assured him.

"I can't believe Analee's dead. I *loved* her."

"So you were out of town early Tuesday morning?"

"Yeah, sure. Laramie. I always thought she might decide to love me back. I'd a married that girl in a minute. Wasn' like I jus' wanted to fuck her—you know? I *loved* her. What'm I gonna do now? She don' marry me, I'll make about twenty million in the pros an' blow it all, end up on some street corner in Paterson, New Jersey, where I come from. 'Thout Analee—"

"Mr. Mohammed, I'm trying to find out who killed her."

"Wasn' me. Ask Coach you don' believe me. I was in Laramie. Pissant lil' town in Wyoming. Why'd anyone wanna kill Analee? Don' make no sense."

"Did you know she had a white boyfriend?"

"Sure. L. Parker."

"Maybe—ah—Rhino was jealous."

"No reason. She wasn' gonna marry no dude named L. Parker. That wouldn't be cool. Anyway, it wouldn'a been

Rhino. He mean an' strange, but she the only one make him smile—or study."

"He's a basketball player too?"

"Naw. Football. Only real good player they got. Football ain't—whoops—isn't—Analee, she always after me 'bout my grammar. Say I gotta talk like a rich man if I gonna be one." He thought a minute and added, "Anyway, football ain' big here." He wiped his eyes surreptitiously on the sleeve of his robe. "Coulda been the white boy, I guess."

Elena left Ahmed sitting on his bed in his green Jockey shorts, shaking his head and saying Analee couldn't be dead. Poor guy. One minute he was on top of the world; the next he was looking at twenty million dollars down the drain and life on a street corner in Paterson, New Jersey. Could he really make twenty million? Probably.

Elena headed for the Athletic Department and had a chat with Ahmed's coach, who confirmed that Ahmed had been out of town. "Look on the sports page," he said. "Kid made thirty-one points in Utah, nineteen in Laramie."

Since Rhino had been described to her as mean and strange, Elena decided to visit the football coach first.

Quickly erasing diagrams from his blackboard when she stuck her head in his door, as if he thought she might be some spy from another Western Athletic Conference team, the coach said, "Rhino Pankins is my fullback. Man could make a first down through a brick wall."

"Really," said Elena. She'd always wanted to meet someone who could do that.

"Yes ma'am, if I had ten more like Rhino, my ground game would be unbeatable. On the other hand, it's a bitch trying to keep him eligible and functioning."

"Not too smart?"

"Hard to say. He's always depressed. *Clinically* depressed. That's what the doc says. We got him on Prozac. Always thought that was for middle-aged women. Like my wife. Wish she'd take some. Have to give him two pills a day, or all of a sudden, he's just sitting there. Not moving. Ever seen anyone like that? We hired this girl from H.H.U. to tutor him and cheer him up. Worked pretty good 'til she got killed.

"Say, is that why you're here? I've recruited some boys

who got in trouble with the law, but Rhino's not one. Kid hasn't spoken since she died. Can't send him to a shrink if he won't talk, know what I mean? It's a thankless job I got here."

"Do you think Rhino could have killed her?"

"No way. Never. He loved that girl. Probably the only person he did love."

"I'd like to talk to him."

"Yeah? Fine with me. No one else has had any luck. He'll be at the football table in the Commons at 11:30. Hasn't stopped eating so far. You know how to get there?"

"Yeah. I'm an alum." Elena headed across campus toward the cafeteria, arriving at 11:45 and locating the jock tables easily because, instead of going through a cafeteria line, the athletes were served family style. And it wasn't hard to spot Rhino Pankins. He was built like a tank and eating as if he might never see food again: otherwise, he was morose and silent. Despite the crowding elsewhere, there were empty chairs on either side of him.

Great. If his own teammates were afraid to sit next to him, *she* didn't relish the prospect. Elena patted her purse for the reassuring bulk of her gun, not that shooting her alma mater's best football player would be a popular move. "I'm Detective Elena Jarvis," she said and took one of the two empty seats.

Rhino Pankins didn't look up. He snagged a bowl of beans and shoveled a pile onto his plate.

"I'm investigating the death of your friend, Analee Ribbon." No sense in beating around the bush. He didn't seem to be listening anyway. Half a tamale made its way from his plate to his mouth. "I could use your help," she said. There was a long silence. How to get him to talk?

She was just about to ask him point blank if he'd killed Analee when he mumbled, head down, still staring at his plate, "You find out who done it. I kill 'im. Then I git the pieces a that fuckin' statue an' stomp 'em to gravel." He looked up with dark, tortured eyes. "Then I set fire to that whole fuckin' university."

"I'd be satisfied with the answers to a few questions," said Elena mildly.

"Because they done killed Analee." He was looking down again, mumbling.

"Who?"

"Don' know."

"Where were you that night?"

"Sleepin'."

"Can you think of anyone who—"

"Go away." Rhino stuffed a second tamale into his mouth and left the table.

Elena didn't have the muscle to stop him, so she stayed to have lunch with the other players, who thought it was a good sign that Rhino was talking again. They said if Rhino claimed to be in bed the night Analee Ribbon was killed, that's where he was; no one was about to call Rhino a liar. They said no way would he have killed her. They'd never heard of L. Parker Montrose and didn't think Rhino was the jealous type. It was more a brother-sister sort of thing with Rhino and Analee. No sex. Plenty of chicks were happy to provide Rhino with sex if he wanted it, which he didn't very often.

Brother-sister? Maybe Rhino'd thought L. Parker Montrose was doing Analee wrong, didn't have honorable intentions toward her, or wasn't the right man for her, in which case Rhino might have felt honor bound to kill—L. Parker Montrose, not Analee. Oh, well.

Elena went back to the coach's office and asked for a blood type on Rhino. Saying, "He didn't kill her. I'd bet on that," the coach provided the information. A positive, the type on the killer's end of the clip arm. Elena couldn't imagine slender Analee bashing Rhino Pankins on the head with a computer gadget. She could, however, imagine him pushing over the statue. He could probably push over the Statue of Liberty. Rhino was definitely a suspect, no matter how much he might have adored Analee. DNA testing would tell her whether he'd been there that night, but DNA reports took forever.

In the meantime, she remembered the coach saying that Analee was paid to tutor athletes. No such payments had shown up in her records. It took two hours to run down the checks. They had been deposited directly into a bank in Houston, no signature on the back but Analee's. It took another hour to get the bank in Houston to tell her that the account belonged to Ray Lee Ribbon. And that's all the bank would tell her, so she still didn't know where the five-thousand-dollar payments were going, or where they'd come from.

The tutoring fees weren't that big. Elena could believe the girl was helping her father out. If he didn't have many gigs in Houston and wouldn't leave town, he might need money but be reluctant to ask his wife. Although she'd have to follow it up, it wasn't a great clue.

13
..

When Elena went into the UTLS dorm, heavy cloud cover shored up by a dark, flat underlayer had turned the mountains black, although the clouds themselves had looked like luminous airplane wings spread above a black runway. When she left the cafeteria, full of Mexican food and jock talk, rain sheeted in cold, diagonal curtains across the campus. She turned up her coat collar, pulled her hood on, and sprinted to her car.

The police radio reported a six-car, two-truck pile-up near the Sunland Park exit, with westbound traffic on the interstate tied up for at least an hour. Grumbling about the carelessness of Los Santos drivers on the rare occasions when rain fell, she started her motor and windshield wipers, turned on her lights, and headed for North Mesa. Once she got past the Kern Place area, water sluiced across the road like flooding in a dry gulch, and motorists plowed heedlessly through the runoff areas, sending up roof-high plumes.

Rain! When you didn't have it—like most of last summer—and everything dried up under water rationing, you wished for it. But when it did come—like now, when the cotton farmers in the valley were probably having breakdowns because crops were still in the fields—you wished the rain would just stop, or that you lived in a city with storm sewers and drivers who didn't believe that speeding was the best way to handle inclement weather.

70

As she approached the Mesa Hills light, easing her car through yet another wash of water, a blue Lincoln slid into the back of a silver Toyota. She eased her car to a stop and fastened a flashing light on top. The Lincoln had steam pouring from bent gaps in the hood; the Toyota's rear end was hidden, but it had, no doubt, buckled as well; the two drivers were gesturing wildly, the flapping of their mouths visible even through the downpour. No patrol cars in sight. Sighing, she radioed in the accident and stepped into the rain.

"Why the hell were you sitting through a green?" shouted the trench-coated Lincoln driver, hair plastered in long strands on his forehead leaving the crown of his head bald and wet.

"I was stalled, you jackass," shouted the Toyota driver. He wore a Dallas Cowboys jacket and a Houston Oilers cap whose brim drooped soggily over his glasses. His car had the logo for an awning and shutter company painted on the side.

"What'd you call me?" The Lincoln owner's face had turned an angry red, and his clenched fists rose threateningly from his sides.

"Just try it, asshole," snarled the shutter man, whipping off his glasses. "You was speedin' an' you rear-ended me. You're gonna pay for my car *an*' the estimate appointment I'm missin'. An' you try to hit me, I'll knock you right on your rich ass."

Elena pushed between the two. "And I'll arrest the first one who commits assault," she said calmly. The two men hadn't noticed her approach. "Detective Elena Jarvis, Crimes Against Persons. I've got a patrol car on the way to investigate the accident, but assault is right up my alley. Either one of you want to try it?" She reached into her purse when neither backed off. "I've got a weapon in here with my finger on the trigger." She lifted the sling bag, gun barrel poking plainly through the leather.

"Hey, lady," said the shutter salesman, "let's not get nervous here." He returned his glasses to his nose. "No one's gonna hit no one. Right, buddy?" He looked at the Lincoln driver, who muttered, "My radiator's broken."

"I'm not nervous," said Elena calmly. "Maybe a little peevish because I'm getting wet. Now, both of you back off."

The two men backed away from each other as a patrol car pulled up behind Elena's unmarked Taurus. She gave a statement to the officer, then drove on to H.H.U.

"Where've you been?" Vasquez demanded when she arrived. "Jeez, you're all wet." He turned to the receptionist and asked her to find a towel, then hustled Elena through the lobby of the station. "Clabb wants a progress report."

Vasquez's solicitude for her bedraggled condition gave Elena hope that he'd forgiven her for having seen his eyes. His aviator glasses were firmly in place, still reinforcing that swaggering macho look. Oh, well, he probably attracted a lot of women that way and saved himself embarrassment over his strange eyes. "I've been at UTLS talking to coaches and friends of Analee Ribbon," she said in answer to his question.

"Lovers, don't you mean?"

"Evidently not. She was tutoring both guys and getting paid for it by the Athletic Department."

Gratefully, she accepted a towel from the receptionist and blotted her face and the wet hair at her forehead. "The football player, Pankins, matches the blood type on the clip and probably doesn't have an alibi." She shrugged out of her jacket and shook the water off it. "Ahmed Mohammed was demonstrably out of town. Of course, Montrose matches the clip blood, too."

Vasquez opened the door to Clabb's outer office and held it for Elena.

His mother had taught him nice, old-fashioned manners. "And even though Analee doesn't seem to have been intimate with the two guys from UTLS," she continued, "with people like Melody Spike spreading that rumor around, Montrose could have killed her in a jealous rage, maybe not meaning to."

"I still like the brother Bose or a friend of his as the killer," said Vasquez. "Drug dealing would explain the money in and out of her account."

They were waved into Chief Clabb's office by his secretary, and sat down to explain the leads they had. Elena was still blotting areas where rain had leaked through her jacket. Clabb ordered a cup of coffee for her and listened, nodding from time to time. At the mention of L. Parker Montrose, Chief Clabb groaned and clapped both hands to his temples as if he'd suddenly developed a headache. "One of our own students? Vice President Stanley will hate that."

"There's always the possibility someone from L.S.A.R.I. did it," she said soothingly, and went on to explain that theory.

"That's even worse," Clabb moaned. His eyelid tic spasmed into motion. "They might kill a second person, and a third. How can we ever hope to protect people here on campus?" Tic, tic, tic. "Parents will withdraw their children. Faculty will resign. Our own officers could quit. One of my men who got spray-painted did. Have I told you that?" he asked Vasquez. "Himmelbrot took a job with some security patrol. He said his wife insisted. His last day is tomorrow, and I don't have a replacement."

"It might be a member of the Feminist Coalition," said Elena, hating to say it. The poor man seemed on the edge of nervous collapse.

"More student suspects? Don't tell me about it."

"It's the brother," said Vasquez, advancing his drug-deal-gone-sour theory. "The brother or some associate of his. Blacks are always killing each other."

"Well, I wouldn't say that," temporized Chief Clabb. "You sound racist, my boy."

"I'm not racist," said Vasquez indignantly. "I'm a minority myself. *You* probably don't even know any blacks." Then, evidently realizing that his tone was less than respectful, he added, "Sir."

"African-Americans," Clabb murmured. "And I knew Miss Ribbon. She was a lovely young woman. Still—" He paused. "—if you're right, that would mean it was—well, more or less her own fault. In that case, the university's image wouldn't—"

Elena stared at him scornfully.

"Or maybe it was the black football player at UTLS," said Vasquez.

"Umm, yes. For the family, that would be a happier situation. Not that they can ever be happy about this," he added hastily. "Incidentally, the memorial service is at four. I think we should go."

"Absolutely," Elena agreed. The last memorial service she

attended at H.H.U. had included cocktails and delicious canapes. Technically, she'd be off duty at four, so she could have a margarita and as many gourmet tidbits as she could grab. Then she wouldn't have to fix dinner. She might even run into Michael Futrell.

"Still, my pick would be the brother, Bose," said Vasquez. "I've already launched an investigation of possible drug dealing on campus."

"Didn't I say he was a go-getter?" said Chief Clabb to Elena. "But if there's drug dealing here at H.H.U . . ."

They left him dithering about the possibility of a new scandal and trying to button the jacket of his dress uniform over his substantial stomach.

"Clabb's a hanger-on from when President Sunnydale was a TV evangelist," said Vasquez once they were outside the building. "I haven't figured out whether he was this incompetent back in California and it didn't show because they didn't have any security problems, or he's getting senile now. Either way, you can tell that he's really losing it under all this pressure. I'll be chief before you know it."

"Uh huh," said Elena.

"I just had a great idea. When I'm chief, I'll hire you to fill my job. In fact, we could give you a double title, assistant chief and university detective."

"You expecting a lot more homicides?" Elena muttered under her breath. She saw Vasquez's offer as a ploy to relegate her to a subordinate position when she was really in charge here.

"I don't see why we have to go to the service," Vasquez continued.

"Because people will get up and talk about the deceased."

"A rosary makes more sense."

"Not if the deceased wasn't Catholic. And it may help us to hear who talks and what they say."

"I wonder why the administration would want to give a black girl a scholarship in the first place."

"She was smart. You saw her records."

"Just making trouble for themselves," he grumbled, then perked up and added, "But if the university's looking for trouble, I'm the man to clean up the mess. Hey, there's

Himmelbrot. I need to say good-bye. Catch you at the chapel."

Elena nodded, climbed into her car, and headed for the computer center. She wanted to find out whether Maggie had any more news on the computer scam. Ex-convict brother or not, Elena couldn't believe anyone as smart as Analee would have been dealing drugs. Not that a computer scam was the mark of a good citizen, but it was less sordid than drug dealing, less violent, less socially disastrous. Elena figured that if Los Santos could get rid of the drug dealers and their customers, they'd cut the crime stats in half.

She found Maggie drinking coffee in a back office and staring unhappily at a computer screen. Maggie's news was, first, that although she'd been changing the passwords every day since she arrived, much to the distress and confusion of registrar's clerks and Charlie Venner, she hadn't been able to keep the scammer out of the system until recently. Nor had she found the Trojan Horse that let him in. Second, no fake transcripts had been entered since Analee's death. That could mean anything: that Analee had been the culprit, that her death had frightened off partners, that Maggie's security measures had finally worked, or that the scammers had run out of people who wanted unearned degrees from H.H.U.

Maggie's third piece of news was that Dr. Erlingson, her Viking-in-a-three-piece-suit research director, had just decided that she should do her master's research on computer stress. "I told him computers don't stress me out, but he insists that they do everyone else. Now I'm supposed to interview every computer user at Herbert Hobart. If he weren't so cute, I'd kill him."

"Is there any way to find out if something was erased from that library terminal we think Analee was using the night of her death?" asked Elena.

Maggie frowned. "Maybe." She thought about it. "Neat idea." She thought some more. "But whoever's doing this stuff is awfully good at concealing or disguising where the transcripts come from. Like the V.P.'s office; I found one from Harley Stanley's office. When I told him, he had a fit, said none of his people would do anything like that. And he doesn't want any of his access privileges canceled, even though he didn't have a clue when I said I wanted to make his machines read-only for registrar's stuff."

Elena didn't have a clue either. Read only? "But you'll try?"

"Sure. You want to go to the service? Melody was planning her remarks when I left. I just wish Analee could have been here to listen. She'd have laughed her head off." Maggie sighed. "She really was a good kid, you know? Talking computers with her was a pleasure. She'd have been smart enough for the computer scam; I just don't think she'd have done it."

"Did she know why you're here?"

"Of course not. I'm undercover." Maggie grinned. "I can hardly wait to tell Dr. Erlingson. Maybe when he realizes I'm not a student, he'll ask me out. On the other hand, maybe he'll resign when he discovers that the university palmed a fake graduate student off on him." She cleared her screen and pulled up another file. "If he comes to the chapel, I'll point him out to you. He's mucho, mucho *cuto*."

"*Cuto*?" Elena winced. "You ought to take a Spanish course, Daguerre. You *are* living on the border now."

"I *am* taking one. Got it off The World Wide Web. *Cuto*'s Spanglish."

Elena rolled her eyes. "See you at the chapel." She went out onto the quadrangle, where rain was still battering walls of flowering bushes alien to the desert and mountains, greedy for water where there was usually so little. They must think they'd gone to heaven, or back to Florida where they'd come from.

The red of the tropical blossoms reminded her of a little patch of flowers she had seen in the fall. They had been growing in Dimitra Potemkin's yard across the street, dropped in a bed of domestic flowers like a Gypsy intruder at a barn dance. Dimitra's wild flowers had small red balls, the luscious color of ripe strawberries, topping fragile, weedy stalks. They had looked good enough to eat, but when you bent for a closer view, they were prickly and covered with hair-thin spines. Beautiful but painful, like everything native to the desert. Even the rain brought flash floods.

14
..

"Our sister is dead," said Zora Lee Ribbon, her rich voice filling the chapel. Elena had asked for a seat to the side, facing the audience. The folding chair they provided allowed her to see the faces of the mourners. Now she glanced curiously at the chapel itself. Curved, cushioned palmwood pews and art deco, stained glass windows showing stylized religious figures, some from religions Elena couldn't identify.

"Who's the one bursting into flame?" Maggie had asked when they entered.

"Zoroaster?" Elena guessed.

"Who?"

"Maybe it's Moses, and the burning bush got him."

"Oh."

"Our sister is dead." Zora Lee had said it three times, until the audience seemed mesmerized by the voice and the repetition.

"In her death, all women have lost a sister. The divine Mother has lost a child."

Somehow, Elena didn't think Zora Lee Ribbon was talking about the Virgin Mary.

"Each of us, no matter the color, has suffered a loss in the death of Analee Ribbon." Zora looked from face to face. Elena did the same, interested in who had come to the service.

"It is the energy of the male that kills, the female energy that weeps, that heals, that is the power for good."

77

Maggie had pointed out Dr. Erlingson, a handsome man with white-blonde hair. He was taking notes. Maybe planning a lecture on matriarchal religions.

"The Mother is omniracial," said Zora Lee, who looked omniracial herself. "She sees no color. She embraces us all. She enriches us with the power of the female soul if we are willing to receive it, if we are not blinded by the gods of the patriarchy."

Elena suppressed a grin as puzzled frowns appeared on male faces.

"Women must unite to save the Earth, which is being debaunched, burned, destroyed . . ."

Elena noticed that Maggie, no feminist, was looking as perplexed as any man in the room. Several rows forward, Melody Spike had a "right-on!" spark in her eye. Across the aisle, Vasquez stifled a yawn and crossed his legs, eyes and emotions, if any, hidden behind his dark glasses. Sarah's Dr. Zifkovitz was sketching on his program between glances at the speaker. He might be drawing Zora, but Elena figured the sketch would look like a toppling tower of blocks. Sarah had described his style as geometric, and had one of his hard-edged masterpieces framed and hanging over the sofa in her living room. Sarah herself, in a beautifully cut black wool suit, listened attentively, tears on her lashes.

Elena glanced sideways toward the speaker, the altar, and the coffin. Analee's body had been released by the coroner and lay before the altar in a white coffin with a mosaic pattern of twining leaves and flowers. Where had the administration come up with an art deco coffin on such short notice? Maybe it was one of their objets d' art.

"Each male birth adds to the fire of violence on our planet. Each female's death sucks water from the wells of peace."

The Reverend must have been reading crime statistics.

"Through me, the divine Omniracial Mother tells you to protect your sisters and, through them, the Earth." Zora Lee raised cafe au lait arms high above her head. She wore a white robe with Grecian lines, her black hair springing out from her head in a great, dense halo.

"Sisters, there is *power* in motherhood. There is *power* in chastity. There is *no* power in giving it away." The last was said in a flat, admonitory tone.

It? Was she saying "Save it for marriage?" That was a nice, old-fashioned sentiment. Grandmother Portillo would like it, although she'd be horrified to hear God identified as female.

"Our sister is dead," said Zora Lee. Her voice had fallen. Her arms had fallen. "Dead before she found the true power of her female soul." Her voice broke, the first sign that she had loved Analee, had cherished her as a blood sister.

Elena, when she first entered, had followed the other mourners to the front of the chapel for the viewing. The damage to the back of Analee's head did not show. With her close-cut hair and elegant face intact, she rested on a bed of leaf-green satin in her mosaic coffin. There had been whispers in the vestibule that Zora insisted the university provide a green satin lining as a sign of spring and rebirth. "No green satin, no service," had been Zora's ultimatum. The heavy white silk robe on the body must have been brought from Houston by Zora. Analee's only jewelry was a gold coin on a long chain.

"Let us pray for the soul of our departed sister." Zora bowed her head. "Let us pray to the divine Omniracial Mother that you, sisters, are not deprived of *your* power by the male violence that desecrates Mother Earth. Amen."

The audience mumbled, "Amen."

President Sunnydale rose from his chair and assumed the pulpit behind the coffin. "Thank you, Reverend Ribbon, for that fine—ah—eulogy." Female ROTC cadets in their vampy twenties uniforms rose and marched forward to escort Zora Lee Ribbon to a place by her mother.

Elena glanced at her program. "Audience participation." A strange way to put it. The cadets marched back.

"At this time," said President Sunnydale, "if any of Analee's friends would like to say a few words, they are welcome to come forward."

Sarah Tolland rose immediately. A cadet raced to offer her arm. Sarah frowned and murmured, "Sit down, young lady. I don't need a microphone or an escort." The cadet turned pink. Sarah faced forward again. "Analee was a brilliant computer scientist. She had the world in front of her. I think she would have achieved great things in our field. That she should be cut off so young and in such a terrible way is a great tragedy. My heart goes out to her mother and her family."

Lavender, seated on the front row, turned to look at Sarah, standing partway back in the audience. The women saw one another through tears. Elena felt bereft. She hadn't known Analee personally, but she was experiencing a deepening connection to her as the investigation progressed. No doubt her fellow officers would disapprove.

"If I had had a daughter, I'd have wanted her to be like Analee. I'll miss her." Sarah sat down.

President Sunnydale cleared his throat and dabbed his eyes with a white handkerchief that featured an embroidered lily, outlined in green.

Old hypocrite, thought Elena. He had a special funeral handkerchief.

"The microphone is open to those who wish to speak," he said.

A young man, nattily dressed in loose trousers, an embroidered vest, and a silk shirt, rose and headed for the pulpit. "As you all know, I'm Happy Hobart, nephew of the founder. I just wanted to say that Analee was a great girl, and in my opinion a shoo-in for Christmas Queen. I was her campaign manager, and I want to thank all of you who planned to vote for her, and to say I hope you'll vote for my next candidate. I'll pick someone that Analee would have wanted to win if she couldn't do it herself."

Now that was tacky—making a campaign speech at the memorial service.

With pretty cadets as escorts, Hobart was followed to the microphone by a handsome young man in a suit and tie, blond hair beautifully cut and styled. "My name is L. Parker Montrose," he said.

Elena committed his face to memory. It was so finely modeled as to be almost effeminate, but he was undeniably good-looking, except for a petulant hardness in the lines of his mouth. She'd grab him immediately after the service; in fact, she was tempted to haul him off right now, before he disappeared on another field trip.

"I've just returned from New England with my recommendations for this season's ski touring in Vermont—not much snow so far and a lamentable tendency in the B&Bs to serve high-fiber breakfasts," he began, then seemed to catch himself. "Well, Vermont's beside the point, except that I'd hoped to take Analee skiing during Christmas break."

Lavender frowned.

"I didn't hear about her death till I got back. What can I say? I'm broken up." He looked haggard but handsome. Elena had heard that he'd been voted handsomest male on campus in his sophomore year. "We were—well, you know— very close friends, which just goes to show that, like her sister said, people and even God can be color-blind. Analee was black, but we were very close. I'll really miss her. She was a fun girl and gorgeous, even if she was black. Which I didn't mind at all. In fact, it was a turn-on."

The rest of the Ribbon family, although not as enraged as Lavender, looked far from happy with his remarks.

"You're an idiot, L. Parker," said Melody Spike, striding forward. Elena turned to watch as Melody shoved first L. Parker, and then the microphone, aside and planted her white gloves on the pulpit, shaking her red curls at the audience. "I don't need a microphone to tell you that Analee Ribbon was a feminist we can all be proud of," said Melody, not bothering to introduce herself. Cadets escorted L. Parker to his seat.

"She was running for Christmas Queen as the candidate of the Feminist Coalition, and she was devoted to the cause. If the army issued us bullets, or even blanks, we, her fellow cadets, would have given her the twenty-one-gun salute, but you can imagine how the male bureaucracy responded to *that* idea. I'm just sorry her sister didn't want her laid out in our uniform, although I couldn't agree more with some of the Reverend's sentiments, except about chastity. That's a crock. Women have as much right to sexual satisfaction as men."

Elena caught the look on Harley Stanley's face. Evidently he didn't consider women's sexual rights a proper topic for memorial comments.

"It's an error in perception," said Melody combatively, "to think of sex as *women giving it away*. Women are *getting it*. If they aren't, something's wrong with the man.

"Also, I want to take issue with the idea that Analee hadn't realized the power of her female soul. No one was a more powerful or a braver feminist than Analee. She was right out there in the forefront of the fight for women's reproductive rights. She knew that ready access, with no nutcase anti-abortionists blocking the way, is the key to women taking their rightful place in society."

Melody shot a hard look to the other side of the aisle, seemingly at a nun who towered over the people around her. Elena had seen that face but couldn't place it.

"Analee was a soldier for her country and for women's rights. For all we know, she died defending the rights, reproductive and otherwise, of her sisters in the Feminist Coalition and elsewhere."

Elena cringed at the look of growing outrage on Lavender's face. Then the service got worse. The person who jumped up next was Ora Mae Spotwood. She had been blocked from Elena's sight line by the nun.

"If you're accusing us, you're wrong," said Ora Mae in a penetrating voice. She made no attempt to move to the end of the aisle or take the microphone. "Analee was one of ours. Her first priority was protecting the fetuses of her race. And the chastity of unmarried black women. She told me herself she understood that these abortion clinics are a genocidal plot against minorities. I couldn't agree with her sister more: chastity and motherhood are the foundations of a decent society. Los Santoans Against Rampant Immorality was proud to count Analee Ribbon among our most loyal members."

"Girl should have been Catholic," boomed a deep voice beside Mrs. Spotwood. Sister Gertrudis Gregory! Finally Elena managed to attach a name to the nun, who was on trial in federal court for grabbing the arm of a coed trying to enter the Health and Reproductive Services Center. Sister Gertrudis Gregory had reduced the girl to tears, either with the power of her grip or the explicitness of her lecture.

Elena remembered the whole story now. The girl, interviewed by the *Times,* said, "She showed me a yucky picture, and I wasn't there for an abortion. I was there for bubonic plague and cholera shots because I'm doing a research trip to India to study resort facilities at the Taj Mahal." The nun was quoted as saying, "Any girl who enters that den of murderers is tarred with their brush." Maybe she'd been convicted. Elena wasn't sure.

"*Roman Catholic*?" exclaimed Lavender, turning around to glare at Sister Gertrudis Gregory. "We're Baptists!"

"We intend to establish a scholarship in her name, Mrs. Ribbon," said Ora Mae, "at some university that doesn't provide abortions to its students and encourage fornication by passing out condoms and such."

"Madam," shouted Dr. Greta Marx, rising from a pew at the back of the chapel, "have you any idea how many people will be on this earth by the year 2010? In third world countries, they'll be eating each *other* because people like you want uncontrolled population growth. Your doctrines are the genocidal plot. You're promoting unwed motherhood, child abuse, famine, war, plague, and all the venereal diseases, including AIDS. I'd like to show you a few pictures of AIDS victims or someone with bacterial-resistant gonorrhea. In fact—" She held up a briefcase and shook it over her head.

Harley Stanley was whispering urgently to the president, who nodded and leaped to his feet. "Thank you, Dr. Marx, ladies, and gentlemen. And now, to continue with our program, Miss Ribbon's brother will read an elegiac poem that he has written in her honor. Mr. Langston Lee Ribbon."

Langston came forward and took the same notebook out of his pocket that he had produced while Elena was questioning him. After slowly turning a few pages, he read, in a melancholy voice, a poem so full of imagery that Elena couldn't follow it—hybrid mimosa springing from ancient muck, melodious miasmas, murmuring maenads. About all she got out of the poem was a feeling of claustrophobic humidity and the idea that Langston Lee Ribbon had a thing for words beginning with the letter M. At the end, he bowed his head and murmured, "Good-bye, little sister." His good-bye was almost drowned out because Gus McGlenlevie, H.H.U.'s "erotic poet," began to clap. The students, taking his cue, clapped as well.

As Langston left the podium, President Sunnydale rose and said, "Perhaps our students don't realize that clapping at funerals is—er—unusual; on the other hand, the moving and—ah—enigmatic nature of the poem we just heard may have made their response so spontaneous as to be—ah—" He cleared his throat. "Now the late Miss Ribbon's father and younger brother will play her favorite song." Ray Lee and Bose came forward, cadets trotting along behind because they hadn't made it to the front row in time. They did get their hands on Langston before he could sit down.

"Mah daughter, Analee, always said Ah did the best "St. James Infirmary" she ever heard, an' it was her favorite song," said Ray Lee Ribbon, towering above the coffin. "We're doin' it for her, Thelonius and me—two verses an' instrumental. The first verse is me to mah little girl. The second verse Analee wrote herself when she was a sweet child. We're gonna make her service like she pictured it." He glanced at his son, who put the sax to his mouth. A flood of plaintively liquid notes poured out, and Ray Lee Ribbon, one great black hand on the altar, the other holding his trumpet, sang the words of a man who had visited the St. James Infirmary, which Elena presumed was in New Orleans, where he found the body of a loved one, a beautiful woman, dead. Several people had said Ray Lee was the best blues singer anywhere. Having heard him, Elena believed it. He made the song a kind of weeping for his beautiful, well-loved daughter, a farewell. His voice was so rich, so low a bass-baritone, so slow-paced and sad, that Elena could have wept with him.

After the initial verse, he lifted the trumpet, and the light flashed gold off the bell as he and his son played. First as if they were one, then as two answering each other's grievous complaints, each phrase a new variation that caught in Elena's throat as if she herself were grieving.

Then Ray Lee let his trumpet fall again and sang the verse that was evidently Analee's chosen requiem:

When I die, bury me in high-heeled shoes,
And white silk for my shroud.

Bose's sax intertwined with his father's voice, a mellow harmony.

A gold piece on my neck chain,
So they'll know I died standing proud.

Ray Lee's voice held the last note with a power that echoed through the chapel. Then he let the note fade as Bose took up the melody on the sax.

They'd carried out Analee's wishes—the white silk, the gold coin, and their song made Elena want to weep, to sing with them, to mourn for all the families who had lost loved ones. When the last golden tones died away, both men playing, chasing one another into stillness, there were tears, even among those who had not known Analee. The chapel was filled with a hushed silence. Earlier combatants had no last words to hurl at one another. Even President Sunnydale forgot to announce what the program said: that cocktails and canapes would be served in the Sacred Vestibule to those who were over twenty-one, soft drinks for those younger.

Elena walked out beside Tey Vasquez, who seemed depressed. "She looked beautiful, didn't she?" Elena murmured.

"I didn't look," Tey muttered.

"White silk gown, gold coin. Just like the song."

"Coin?"

"She's wearing one on a chain."

"Jesus." He was pale.

Touched that the case was finally getting to him, Elena laid a consoling hand on his arm. "We'll find the killer," she promised. "In fact, we better look for L. Parker Montrose once we get free of this crowd."

"Yeah." Vasquez turned away when they had passed through the doors into the vestibule, and she let him go, liking him better for his emotion.

15
..

"What's wrong with these people?" demanded Lavender
Lee Ribbon. "Folks not supposed to treat a funeral like a
debate. Shows no respect for the dead or the family." Before
Elena could answer, a waiter walked between them offering
martinis, margaritas, and wines. "An' what are you doin',
boy?" demanded the mother, stabbing a long finger toward
the tray.

The waiter replied, "Serving cocktails, ma'am. That's an
excellent California chardonnay you're pointing at."

Lavender turned to Elena, who had been hunting L. Parker
Montrose when waylaid. Montrose wasn't anywhere in sight,
and Elena, embarrassed over the behavior of people at the
service, didn't feel that she could walk off and leave Analee's
mother. "They always serve liquor in the church?" asked Mrs.
Ribbon.

"It's an agreement between the president and faculty,"
Elena explained. "They even have Wednesday afternoon
prayer and cocktail parties." She took a margarita, remembering the memorial for Gus McGlenlevie, who, as it happened, wasn't dead after all. The post-memorial canapes had
been fabulous. "Try an hors d'oeuvre," she suggested, beckoning another waiter.

Lavender tried one. "Canned crab," she said disdainfully.
"Shouldn't have let Analee come here. Drinkin' in church!
So, are you ready to arrest someone?"

"We have some leads," said Elena cautiously, "but I can't discuss them." Especially when Bose was a suspect.

"Coulda been a thief," said Lavender. "You looked into that?"

"Because her backpack was missing?"

"Because her necklace was missin'."

"What necklace?"

"Her daddy gave her a chain with a twenty-dollar gold piece on it when she went off to college, one of three he won in a poker game back in New Orleans before we were married. Analee just loved the story about that game, so he gave her one of the coins. For good luck, he said." Lavender sighed. "Ah told Ray Lee that was a mistake—giftin' a live girl her burial wish. But Analee, she treasured the necklace because it was like the one in her song an' because her daddy gave it to her. She never took it off."

"But I just saw it on—on the body," stammered Elena.

"Ray Lee had another one made up when we heard it was gone. Whoever killed her musta taken it."

"We didn't know about the necklace." Someone pushed a statue over on Analee to get a gold necklace? It made more sense than killing her for her backpack, but not much.

Spotting Vasquez, Elena thanked Mrs. Ribbon for the information and excused herself. "Did you find Montrose?" she asked her partner.

"He got out ahead of me."

Elena told Vasquez about the missing necklace.

"So maybe we've got a thief here," he said, pouncing on the information.

Elena nodded. "What we've got is capital murder if the perp actually robbed and killed her."

"Capital murder?" Vasquez looked astounded. "As in a death penalty offense?"

"Yeah, it doesn't sound likely to me either," Elena agreed. "Doesn't *feel* like theft."

He nodded. "The drug connection makes more sense."

"Or jealousy," Elena murmured. "Still, the necklace was gone, and Mrs. Ribbon says Analee never took it off. They had to replace it for the service."

"The other one's probably in her jewelry box," said Vasquez.

"I'll check with her roommates."

"Or maybe she hocked it."

"Who was that boy claimin' to be such close friends with mah Analee?" demanded Ray Lee Ribbon, ending Elena's low-voiced discussion with Vasquez.

Vasquez scooted off, following a tray of margaritas. Elena snagged two pieces of baked Brie in puff pastry and offered one to Ray Lee. "He was evidently her boyfriend, Mr. Ribbon, but I can't tell you much else. He just got back to town."

"Guess that means he didn't kill her," muttered Ray Lee.

Not really, thought Elena, but didn't say so.

"Why would she date a white boy?" Ray Lee seemed genuinely puzzled and hurt.

"There ain't no other blacks around here, Daddy," said Thelonius, who had a saxophone case in one hand and a plate of hors d'oeuvres in the other. He seemed at a loss without a third hand to get the food to his mouth. No drink, Elena noticed. He was adhering to the rules of parole.

"There was Rhino over to the other place. Least, he's a homeboy," said Ray Lee. "She coulda dated Rhino."

"I'd like to know more about Rhino, Mr. Ribbon," said Elena.

Ray Lee shook his head sadly. "Best ask Lavender if you want to know about him."

Elena nodded. "I can't tell you how much I enjoyed your singing and playing, both of you. It was—" She searched for words that would express what she'd felt. "—beautiful and moving," she finished. "It makes me sad to think I can't hear music like that around here."

"Buy you one of Daddy's tapes," suggested Thelonius. He had put his saxophone case between his feet and was munching canapes.

"I'd love to," said Elena eagerly, imagining the pleasure of listening to Ray Lee Ribbon after a hard day on the job. "Will I find them in places like—oh, Blockbuster?"

"Nah," said Ray Lee. "Mine are locally produced. Be glad to give you one, Miss."

"I'd be glad to pay for it."

"Wouldn't say no. You found out who killed mah baby girl?"

"Not yet, sir, but I will." Thelonius drifted off, and Elena took the opportunity to ask about the tutoring checks deposited to Ray Lee's account.

He looked embarrassed, even nervous, and mumbled, "It was her way of helpin' the family. Ah'd be beholden if you didn't mention it to mah wife. Lavender don't approve of takin' money from the children, but sometimes you have to." He sighed. "Sometimes there's no other way. Analee, she was a fine daughter." He looked so heartbroken that Elena patted his arm awkwardly before leaving to find Lavender again. She passed Melody Spike and heard her inviting the Reverend Zora to address the Feminist Coalition.

"Sounds like you all a bunch of loose women," said Zora. "Be a good thing if Ah talked to you. Put you in touch with the power of chastity. Like fastin', it ties you to your soul instead of your body."

Elena overheard Bose telling Chief Clabb that he could always spot a drug user or dealer, and would be glad to hire on with the university force if they had any problems that way. "We may," said the chief. "Do you have a business card, Mr. Ribbon?"

"Say what?" Bose responded.

"Chief," Vasquez cut in urgently. "I need to speak to you."

Had Clabb forgotten that Thelonius was on parole for drug dealing? Had she and Tey told him? Well, Vasquez would do it.

She heard Angus McGlenlevie discussing poetry with Langston, particularly what he called "the crap metaphor." Langston said, "I wasn't talkin' about crap. Ah was talkin' about the black soil of Louisiana. The poem was about roots. A man doesn't mention crap in a poem about his dead sister. Not unless he wants to get exiled from his mama's table."

"Mrs. Ribbon," said Elena, when she found Lavender glowering as President Sunnydale told her about the founder of the university and the sacred video games he had developed for Sunnydale's California ministry.

"California, huh?" said Lavender Lee Ribbon. "Sounds like California. You got news for me, Detective?"

"Some questions. Would you excuse us, sir?" Sunnydale had already turned to shake hands with a professor whom he addressed as "Dr. Er—Ah—" Elena considered it a miracle that Sunnydale had remembered Analee's name. Maybe Harley Stanley had written it on a card for him and hidden it among the flowers by the pulpit. "Mrs. Ribbon, I wanted to ask you about a young man at UTLS."

"Rhino?"

"Yes, ma'am. He seems an angry and dangerous person. And very strong. The killer had to have been strong."

"Rhino'd never have killed mah daughter. Boy could have gone to some big, important school—for football, you understand—but he followed Analee here. She was his anchor."

"Maybe he resented his devotion to her after he got here. That's not exactly a winning team he's on." It made sense. Rhino gave up a place on some high-profile team, and then Analee started dating a white man.

Lavender Lee Ribbon was shaking her head. "What you thinkin'? Jealousy? They weren't sweethearts. They were— well, when Rhino was a little fella—eight, nine—that poor boy was as miserable as a child could be; they beat him at home, an' the children at school laughed at him. He wasn't any prettier then an' had nothin' to say.

"Then Analee took up for him. After that nobody messed with one 'thout answerin' to the other. He mighta killed someone *for* her. Nearly did, one time she had some trouble with a boy in high school. Ah hadda go down to the police to bail Rhino out mahself." Lavender laughed sadly. "Analee with me. Time she got through, Rhino was out an' the other boy was in. That's how it went with those two."

"I see. Thank you." Elena drifted off, plucking canapes as she passed, considering another margarita.

"Can I get you a drink? You must be the only one here without one."

She turned to smile at Michael Futrell, glad to see him again. Sarah had evidently gone home, too unhappy for cocktail parties.

Michael took her arm when she declined a drink and guided her toward an unoccupied, two-person, curved-wood chair that turned out to be surprisingly comfortable. "I've been thinking about who might have killed her," he murmured.

"Your choice managed to get out of here before I could corner him."

"Montrose? Well, maybe, but when you consider environmental factors, childhoods in high-crime areas, that sort of thing, I think one of the African-American boyfriends may be a more logical choice."

"Except that they aren't boyfriends. Where did you hear about them?"

"Not boyfriends? But one of my students hinted that Miss Ribbon was—ah—intimate with two athletes from—"

"I don't think so," said Elena. "Who told you that?"

"A coed named Taffy Foster."

Elena wrote the name in her notebook. "Close friend of yours?" she asked and then wished she hadn't. She didn't have any claims on Michael Futrell.

"You're kidding! Foster has the I.Q. of a mango and the character of an asp." He paused. "Have you heard about the federal court decision on Sister Gertrudis Gregory? The one over there tossing down martinis?"

"No. Are they sending her to jail?"

"Six months. And a fine of a hundred thousand dollars. When she pleaded poverty—members of her order don't own anything—the judge decided the Catholic Church would have to pay. The bishop and the head of the order are having fits, and of course the pro bono lawyers filed an immediate appeal, so she's still out on bail. Whoops, there's my chairman beckoning. Want to meet for dinner when this is over?"

"I'm full of canapes," said Elena regretfully.

"So we'll catch a movie and eat afterward."

"OK." She hoped he didn't like those foreign films with subtitles and nothing happening for two hours except artistic cinematography.

"You're not going to believe this," hissed Maggie Daguerre, grabbing Elena's arm and dragging her behind a potted plant as Michael disappeared into the crowd of tipsy mourners. "You know that dumbhead who spoke at the funeral? Happy Hobart? He's appointed himself my campaign manager. For Christmas Queen. He's got this whole schedule of appearances I'm supposed to make at places like the Polo Club and the Eye-Shadow Society."

"Don't do it," Elena suggested.

"I just called my captain. He says I have to go along; I can't afford to blow my cover."

"Is your captain going to know if you don't cooperate with Hobart? Hobart doesn't know you're a cop, so he can't tell on you."

Maggie looked surprised, then elated. "You're right. And I'm bigger than Happy. Do you know what he said? He said I'm the next best candidate because I'm unusual like Analee— not black, but older with—get this—really big knockers." Maggie was fuming.

"Have you found out anything else?"

"Since I saw you this afternoon? I couldn't get away from Mr. Christmas Boob-Promoter. He'll probably want me to run around with sequined reindeer hanging off them."

While waiting for Michael to break free of his chairman, Elena negotiated the purchase of tapes from Ray Lee. Then she and Michael left. Outside, the sky had cleared, and a quarter moon swung flat over the mountains.

"Aren't you glad you live here?" Michael asked. "Look at how clear that sky is."

She breathed in deeply, savoring the cold, rain-washed air and the bright moon glow in a blue-black desert night. She *was* glad she lived here.

16
..

Elena showed up at the UTLS dorm early to check Rhino's alibi. He was gone, but his roommate, a short black man, knobby thin, answered her knock. The roommate was a long distance runner from Nigeria. She couldn't pronounce his name and had a hard time with his English, which was bizarrely accented and constructed. The strongest impression she got from the conversation was fear; he started to tremble as soon as she asked Rhino's whereabouts on Tuesday morning between two and three, but he insisted that everyone was sleeping. He seemed to think she was going to tell his coach on him, causing him to lose his visa and scholarship.

When she assured him that she was thinking more along the lines of charging him as an accessory to murder if she discovered that he was lying, his teeth began to chatter. "Where was Rhino?" she pressed.

He said something.

"I don't understand."

He hesitated, then went through an elaborate pantomime, kneeling, shaking one hand, throwing it out, staring at the floor. "Shooting craps?" she asked uncertainly.

"Yes, yes. Crappers. Now, no jail?"

"With you?" Violent head shaking. "Then who?" Blank look. "Besides Rhino, who else?" She rephrased the question several times until he understood and led her to a photograph of the football team, pointing to various players, butchering

93

the pronunciation of their names. Fortunately, she could tell by their numbers what positions they played and took phonetic notes on the names as the runner placed a knobby finger on each face.

"Thank you," she said, wondering how he got through his classes. Maybe he read better than he communicated. She spent the rest of the morning locating down the team members identified by the Nigerian runner. All of them initially denied taking part in a craps game. Only when assured that she didn't plan to tell the coach did they admit to gambling in the quarterback's room, Rhino among them, while Analee Ribbon was meeting her death beneath a statue. Elena wondered whether the quarterback had dreamed up the alibi to protect their ground-gaining fullback.

At 11:30 she sat down by Rhino at the athletes' table. "You find him?" he asked after she'd got his attention.

"You lied to me about where you were that night."

He shook his head, which was large, bumpy, and shaved bald, with thick folds at the back of the skull leading into a thick neck.

"Yes, you did." She considered how hard it must be to shave your head. Did he do it every day? Did he ever cut himself? She imagined Band-Aids on his scalp.

"Who says?"

"Eight or nine people."

He glowered. "What they say Ah doin'?"

"You tell me."

"Ah was in bed."

"You want me to go tell the coach that there's some question about whether you were in your bed when you were supposed to be?"

"Don' care."

She looked straight into his eyes and saw tears there. "Rhino?" He turned his head away. "Did you kill her?"

"Course not." There was a hitch of suppressed grief in his voice. "But Ah went against her."

"How do you mean?"

"You know."

"I don't."

"She dyin', Ah shootin' craps like she tole me not to."

"Oh." Elena looked down at her hands so she wouldn't have to see his shoulders shaking. "Rhino." He didn't answer. She put her hand on an impossibly thick bicep. "Rhino? Listen to me. I'm going to tell you what to do."

"Ain't nuthin' *to* do. Ah went against her, an' Ah cain't never change it now."

"Yes, you can. You're going to do what would make Analee happy."

"What?"

"Take your medication. Study. The university'll get you a new tutor."

"But it won't be—"

"No, it won't be Analee, but she'd want you to study." He hadn't killed her. "Then when you're through here, you'll go into the pros. Save your money when you get there. Don't blow it all. And take your medication so you don't feel so bad. She'd want you to be happy."

Rhino wiped his eyes on the sleeve of his sweatshirt and passed her a bowl of mashed potatoes. She took that as a good sign.

17

The gold chain and coin were not in Analee's jewelry box. Elena put out a description to be sent to pawnshops. Then she took the elevator down two floors, caught L. Parker Montrose at his door, and walked him from the dormitory to the humanities building. He was wearing a suede jacket so beautiful it cried out to be touched; Elena restrained herself. Under the jacket he wore a red and blue turtleneck sweater. The sweater had flamingos in a band across the chest. He'd probably bought it in the university bookstore—Miami Beach memorabilia, in keeping with the architecture and landscaping of the university. Montrose kept one hand in his trouser-pocket; he gestured with the other as he talked.

"She was a wonderful girl," he said. "It didn't bother me at all that she was black. Just made the relationship more—piquant, more exotic."

"How did your family feel about her?"

He shrugged. "I'm my own man."

"Which means they didn't like it."

He shrugged again.

"Did she have other boyfriends?"

"Of course not." Some of his breezy confidence leaked away, and the gesturing hand dropped to his side.

"Nobody ever suggested that she—"

"Analee was devoted to me."

"Were you devoted to her?"

96

"Absolutely."

"Where were you the night she died?"

"What time did it happen?" He turned to Elena with an innocent look.

"Just account for your time from, say, ten o'clock on, please."

"I was packing from ten to eleven because I had a trip to make the next day. Then I showered and went to bed."

"What time did you go to bed?"

"Around 11:45."

"When did you get up again?"

"Not until five the next morning. I had a 6:30 flight to catch." He brushed wind-blown hair back from his forehead.

So far his story matched those of the kid who had taken him to the airport and the professor who assigned him the New England trip. But he could have killed Analee during the time he claimed to be asleep. And his body language had gone from confident to defensive.

"Can anyone vouch for you—that you were asleep?"

"I don't see how. I was sleeping alone. *That night.*"

He gave her a cocky grin. Hadn't Melody said Analee went out with him only once a week? So who else did he sleep with?

"Here's my building. Got a two o'clock." He took the steps quickly, waving as he scooted through the etched glass doors. Glad to get away, obviously.

Elena cut across campus to find the names of his roommates, called the suite, found one of them in, and said she was on her way. The roommate, Bunky Fossbinder, was five-four and had a pointed rat's face, all the features feeding into the nose. He was wearing a paisley silk robe. Elena had seen robes like it in the window at Victoria's Secret.

"I don't know where he was that night," said Bunky.

"Could he have been in bed?"

"Well, he wasn't when I went to bed at 12:30. I heard him come in at five and get dressed for his trip. You wouldn't think one person could make that much noise. I didn't get back to sleep until he left."

"Which was when?"

"Five-thirty. Do you think he killed Analee?"

"Do you think he did?"

"It seems a rather extreme way to placate your parents."

"What about his parents?"

"They said if he didn't drop her, they'd cut off his funds."

"Did they?"

"How would I know? He hasn't tried to borrow money."

"Umm. Does he have another class today?" She couldn't remember, and hadn't written down Montrose's schedule—just spotted the two o'clock and dashed to catch him before it started.

"Bunky?" a female voice called from one of the bedrooms.

"He'll be at the Union from three on," said Bunky. "And now, if you don't have any more questions, I was taking a nap." He grinned, and as the smile lit up his eyes and face, he looked like a happy kid instead of a rodent.

Elena got directions from a lady at the desk on the main floor and trudged toward the Union, turning up her coat collar against a sudden drop in temperature. The morning paper had said another front would be coming through. She lifted her face into the wind. Winter was something she missed in Los Santos. Oh, it got cold at night. It even snowed occasionally, dusting the mountain peaks with white, but if any snow fell on the city, it melted off in sunshine by noon. Not like the Sangre de Cristos, where she'd grown up.

In the Union snack bar, which was decorated in stark black and white with a few festive touches of gray, Elena walked up and down the rows of tables and booths, sipping coffee she'd bought at the counter, looking for L. Parker Montrose. When she finally spotted him laughing in a booth full of students, she set her cup down on their table, leaned her hands to either side and, looking him in the eye, said, "You want to come outside for this discussion?"

"I don't have anything to hide," he replied, eyes darting away from hers.

"OK. You lied to me about being asleep in the dorm the night Analee Ribbon was killed. How about that?"

Montrose's mouth opened, but nothing came out. He looked more surprised than alarmed. The girl beside him, a honey blond with a full pouting mouth and sharp eyes, said, "Well, aren't you chivalrous, Parker? If you're talking about the night before Parker went to Vermont—" she stared at Elena. "—he was with me. *All-l-l* night." She smiled.

"Doing what?" asked Elena.

"What do you think?" The smile widened.

"Where?"

The girl hesitated. Parker looked up at Elena, hand waving defensively. "Well, I didn't want to admit I was—" He shrugged modestly.

"Screwing around on Analee?" suggested Elena.

"Why shouldn't he?" said the girl. "Analee was screwing around on him."

"Was she? I asked you where this one-night stand took place? Or was it an ongoing thing?"

"It's an ongoing thing," said the girl. "And the answer is 'in my room.'"

"And your name is?"

"Taffy Foster."

"Thanks," said Elena and left abruptly, catching a look of disappointment on Taffy Foster's face—Taffy Foster, who had told Michael that Analee had African-American lovers at UTLS. Elena decided she wouldn't believe any of them without corroboration. Seeking it, she went back to the dormitory to look for Taffy's suitemates. If Ms. Foster had been entertaining Montrose until four or 4:30 in the morning, surely one of them would have noticed.

A young woman named Marina, who was lying on a taupe silk coverlet, chin on fist as she watched TV, said, "Taffy just *wants* to sleep with Parker. If she had, she'd have been bragging about it. She thinks Parker's unbelievably sexy."

"You didn't see or hear him with her on Monday night?"

"Hey, I was up 'til three watching old movies for my Vintage Cinema course. No boys here. If I'd seen one after watching *Gilda* I'd have grabbed him. That's with Glenn Ford and Rita Hayworth, and it is *hot*—believe me. I mean, Rita Hayworth wears this black satin evening gown—hey, did you know she has Alzheimer's? Or maybe she's dead. I forget. Anyway, she's singing in this—"

"Thanks," said Elena before she had to listen to the whole plot of a movie she'd never heard of. She caught Taffy in the hall that led to her suite.

"What're you doing here?" Taffy asked angrily. "Are you spying on me?"

"Were you lying to me?"

"Of course, I—"

"Be careful. In fact, maybe you ought to get a lawyer."

"Why?" Taffy looked alarmed.

"I'm about to read you your rights."

"I didn't do anything."

"Including sleep with Parker on Monday night and Tuesday morning."

"So, big deal," muttered Taffy. "I was just trying to help a friend out."

"Did you tell him that Analee Ribbon was sleeping with some black guys at UTLS?"

"Why do you think I said that?" Taffy's face had turned sulky, her full lower lip out thrust. "Anyway, she was. Everyone knew it."

"What did Parker say?"

"I didn't say I told him."

"But you did. I know other people you told. Why wouldn't you tell Parker? You thinking of lying again? Get a lawyer first, so I can—"

"So I told Parker."

"And he said?"

"He didn't believe me."

"And you said?"

"I said, 'Ask her if you don't believe me.'" Elena waited. "And he got mad."

Nodding, Elena headed for the elevator. Behind her she heard Taffy Foster mutter, "Bitch." Elena ignored it and stepped aboard when the heavy molded brass doors opened. She stabbed the button for L. Parker Montrose's floor. Parker hadn't returned to his room, but his suitemate and a pixyish girl were cuddled on the sofa in front of the fire in the marble fireplace. A dorm where the students had their own fireplaces! Amazing. They probably had flunkies to build the fires and take out the ashes.

Bunky said Parker would be back in half an hour or so to dress for dinner. Elena said she'd wait, and sat down on the sofa. It was nice to toast her toes in front of a fire on a cold day. Elena never built fires in the round adobe fireplaces at her home on Sierra Negra. Chimney sweeps were expensive, and it was a job she didn't care to do herself. "So, what are you majoring in?" she asked the girl.

"You sound just like someone during sorority rush week," the girl replied.

The conversation didn't get any more interesting until L. Parker Montrose returned and did a double take when he saw who was lounging in his sitting room.

"You lied to me. Twice," she said before he could get a word in. "You weren't in your room, and you weren't in Taffy's room. So where were you?"

"Think we'll head down for dinner," said Bunky. He and the girl left, followed by a ferocious look from L. Parker.

At this moment, Elena would have believed him capable of murder. "Right now you're my number one suspect."

"I'm not saying another word," he snapped. "Furthermore, you ought to know that my parents are very rich and very powerful. You're going to be sorry you ever harassed me."

"Your parents. Right. I hear they cut off your allowance because of your association with Analee."

"They did not."

"So maybe, without any money for a while, you decided to break it off."

"I did not."

"And she didn't like it, so you had a big fight, and she hit you—"

"She never hit me."

"And you chased her and pushed the statue over on her."

"She got killed in the library. I never go there. Ask my friends."

"They're turning out to be liars, too. If you didn't try to dump Analee, your parents must have cut you off. So what are you doing for money?"

Parker stormed across the sitting room and through a partially open door, which he slammed. Elena heard the lock click. She looked wistfully at the cozy fire, then headed downstairs to the lobby, where she could see palm trees tossing and the last red flowers blowing off the bushes, tumbling like drops of blood across the quadrangle.

L. Parker Montrose—a good suspect. Motive. Fake alibis. Lies. Blood match. Could she get a warrant to run a DNA match on him?

18
..

Friday, December 2, 5:30 P.M.

Spectacular red banners streamed across the darkening sky to the west, the sun a great incandescent ball sinking behind the mountains. As Elena paused on the dorm steps to appreciate the sunset, she spotted Maggie sprinting across the grass of the quadrangle. "Shame on you," Elena called. "You're supposed to be dressing for dinner."

"Yeah. Can you beat that? I had to go out to a seconds shop and buy an evening dress."

"You're single and a lieutenant," said Elena. "You ought to be able to afford a new dress." She lowered her voice when Maggie frowned and glanced around. Except for the two of them, the area was empty.

"Hey, if the department paid for it, I would have. Since they didn't, why should I spend my money for a dress I'll never wear again? You want to go out for Mexican food? I don't think I can stand another night of continental cuisine. Especially Friday night, when the chef gets really disgusting."

"My car's around back," Elena said. "I'll pick you up on the other side of the *Charleston Dancer*." There was another of the statues on the quadrangle. A big one.

"Right. We shouldn't be seen together." Maggie jogged off while Elena went for her car.

They decided on La Hacienda, housed in a historic building on the border where, hundreds of years ago, Don

103

Juan de Onate had crossed the river and where, Elena liked to think, her father's ancestors might have passed on their way north to settle near Santa Fe. The large adobe restaurant sat at the end of a little road with a parking lot that separated it from a brushy area where the Border Patrol hunted illegal aliens. Hart's Mill, the original incarnation, had been the last flour mill for travelers on their way to California. The tenements down the road, in front of which children now played, had once been army quarters. Someone had told her the Butterfield stage had stopped here to pick up cavalry escorts through Indian country.

"I'm gonna have *enchiladas verde con dos huevos*," said Maggie, choosing a table that looked out on the road and the highway above it. "I figure I can eat the good, high-cholesterol stuff for about twenty years. Then I'll have to turn vegetarian, or maybe kill myself."

"Two great choices," said Elena. Having eaten with the football players at noon, she ordered the one-egg plate.

"By the way, I was talking to Dr. Erlingson about your falling-statue case. He likes Montrose as the murderer because, as he says, the psychology is right: a snobbish prick going through an adolescent rebellion against his family, Analee his means of pissing them off and making him feel big about himself because he's doing her the ultimate favor by dating her. Then he hears she's going out with two black guys and making him look like a schmuck."

"Did Dr. Erlingson put it just that way?" asked Elena, grinning.

"What do you mean?"

"Snobbish prick? Schmuck?"

Maggie laughed. "So you don't think Montrose did it?"

"Actually, he's a good suspect. If I didn't have to follow procedures, I'd just tackle him and see if he's got a cut on the side of his head."

"A cut?" Maggie pulled over a bowl of salsa and began dipping tostados.

"We think she hit him with one of those clip gadgets you attach to the side of a computer."

"Well, that wouldn't do any damage."

"This one was metal, heavy, and had a sharp edge."

"No kidding? It must have been from the dark ages."

"How's your case coming?"

"Well, that's one of the reasons I wanted to have dinner with you, that and getting something decent to eat and staying away from that damn Happy Hobart, who keeps following me around with campaign advice. Now Melody's after me to cooperate."

"The computer fraud," Elena reminded her as the waiter put plates of enchiladas and side orders of beans in front of them.

"Right. I found a partial transcript from that night. It looks like it came from the registrar's office, but it's done in Microsoft Word, which is one of a number of programs offered to students at the library. Now, it wasn't saved—not in the regular way. But Microsoft has an automatic store feature; it saves every five minutes or whatever you set it for. SVD files instead of DOC or BAK. You can pull up those files if you want to, or you can dump them and just keep the DOC and BAK files."

"Maggie, I have to tell you, this isn't—"

"OK, OK, let's just say that I found this piece of a transcript. In fact, I printed it out for you." She stopped eating and dug into her purse, then tossed a piece of folded computer paper across the table. "Then I cross-checked. This student— the one on the transcript—is not registered and never has been. And that's the last fake transcript, complete or partial, that I've found. None since Analee died."

"It's only been three days."

"You're right."

"But you'll keep checking?" If Analee had been committing computer fraud, that explained the five-thousand-dollar deposits. Or maybe she was getting the money elsewhere, caught the transcript salesman at work while she was in the library to study, and got killed to shut her up or because she tried to blackmail him. Maybe she was partners in the scam and died because the partner wanted to keep all the profits for himself. Or herself. Computer fraud would explain the money, but so would drug dealing. Maybe Montrose was her partner. If his parents had stopped providing money, he'd need a new source.

"I wonder if L. Parker Montrose ever took a computer course," said Elena. Even if he hadn't, he'd have the social contacts to find dumb, rich kids to whom they could sell the diplomas; Analee had the computer expertise. On the other hand, there had been sales last year, too, when there were no big deposits into Analee's account. Maybe his computer expert from last year had graduated. Wrong. No one had graduated from H.H.U. yet, unless you counted the fake grads. But last year's partner might have dropped out.

"Could you find out if someone in Computer Science quit school after last year or early this fall?"

"I guess," said Maggie, sounding reluctant.

That would explain why Montrose was dating Analee. She was the best student in Computer Science. But why would he have been selling degrees last year, when he still had an allowance from his parents? Of course, he claimed they hadn't cut him off at all. But Elena already knew him for a liar in other areas—why not this? She needed to look at his bank account. Maybe he was just greedy, and his allowance had *never* been enough.

Elena tried another scenario. Montrose needed Analee, so he started dating her. She fell in love and agreed to help him with the computer scam. Or she needed the money for some unknown reason. Then his parents found out about Analee, but he couldn't give her up. Maybe *he'd* fallen in love by then. Everyone said she was a great kid. Beautiful, funny, smart. Elena sighed. She needed help from Maggie, who was complaining that she had enough work of her own without doing Elena's.

"I'm more and more convinced that our cases are tied," said Elena. "I think Montrose was her partner."

"Yeah?" Maggie laid her fork on an empty plate. "OK. I'll check him out."

"Could you get hold of his bank accounts?"

"Without a warrant?"

"A warrant would be hard to justify at this point."

Maggie grinned and waved the waiter over. "I'll have another beer. Beer? *Cerveza*!" The waiter nodded and departed. Maggie turned back to Elena. "Honey, there isn't anything I can't get that's computerized. You just won't be able to use it in court.

"If we know he's guilty, there'll be other ways to find the evidence to arrest him," said Elena. "Then I can get a warrant for his bank accounts and see them legally."

"Hey, I saw on one of the local bulletin boards that the brother of your victim is reading his poetry tonight at The Attic," Maggie remarked around 7:30. They'd both had three beers and dessert by then. "Maybe it's one of those poetry slams. What does that mean, anyway? Do they have to hire off-duty cops to keep the poets from knocking each other around? Or maybe the audience attacks the poets. I couldn't believe that poem he read at her memorial service. What the hell does a swamp have to do with his sister's death? I'll bet there isn't a swamp within a thousand miles of here."

"You'd lose," Elena assured her. "There's a bird sanctuary in New Mexico that's pretty swampy. The ground squishes underfoot, and about four million mosquitoes bit me when I went there with a boyfriend. I figured I was a cinch for encephalitis."

"Sleeping sickness?"

"The mosquitoes in this area carry it."

"Jesus." Maggie looked alarmed. "Remind me not to do any bird-watching."

"As for the poetry reading, maybe I ought to go," said Elena reluctantly. "You want to come along?"

"God, no. I'd as soon go to an opera with fat ladies shrieking at me and guys running around in short skirts and carrying spears."

Elena laughed. "Opera's not *that* bad." When Elena was fifteen, her mother had arranged for a group of kids from Chimayo to take advantage of a one-dollar ticket special the Santa Fe Opera ran for young people. Actually, the performance of *La Traviata* had been pretty impressive—the open-air theater in the hills outside Santa Fe, great costumes, and the music wasn't bad. A week later, the Chimayo priest had preached a sermon about exposing impressionable young people to tales about fallen women.

"I guess I'll have to go by myself," said Elena.

"Call Futrell and ask him along. He can protect you. That

place is downtown, isn't it? And there'll be all those violent poets and poetry lovers."

"For Pete's sake, Maggie, I'm a cop. I carry a gun. I even threatened a couple of hotheaded motorists with it yesterday." Still, inviting Michael was a thought. He'd invited her to a movie yesterday, and it *was* an art flick. Elena had fallen asleep about an hour into the movie when the heroine, a Japanese woman, was wandering around invoking the souls of her ancestors.

So if Michael could subject Elena to a bunch of glum Japanese, plus accompanying subtitles, surely she could invite him to a poetry reading. Of course, yesterday had been Thursday and his invitation made on impulse. Tonight was Friday. If he'd wanted a Friday date, he'd have asked yesterday. He probably had plans with someone else.

19
##

The Attic was downtown on Texas Street, its parking lot to the right and a crowd spilling out onto the sidewalk. Elena had gone back to headquarters for her truck, which she parked in the lot, then threaded her way through a long, narrow room with a bare wood floor. Filling the space were small tables and people, many of whom were standing in front or leaning against the bar or the walls between side tables. The bar, festooned with beer signs, ran down the left side of the room. A small, raised stage to one side of the entrance featured a folding chair with a brown vinyl seat, a mike, and a short, leather-faced man wearing a Stetson, jeans, jean jacket, and scuffed boots. He declaimed in rhyme, not all of the rhymes very exact, a poem about cattle, roundups, and other mainstays of the Old West.

Elena bought a mug of draft beer and took a chair toward the back at a table near the rest rooms. Prime location, she thought dryly. If she had to go, she was right on the spot. On the other hand, if there really were fights at these things, she was far enough back to see them start and do her law enforcement duty.

Two mixed-race couples had invited her to occupy the extra chair at their table. The African-American man, dressed much like the cowboy at the microphone, asked if she'd come for the Western poetry. She shook her head. "I came to hear Langston Lee Ribbon." The cowboy's date, a dishwater

109

blonde, had her hair fixed in cornrows, but it didn't look like the real thing—no beads or wraps or any of that good stuff. Elena had always wanted to ask how women did that, how long it took, whether you had to have it dry cleaned.

"Ribbon should be on in about fifteen minutes," said the other man, who looked like the blonde's brother and needed a shave. Elena assumed he was cultivating the scruffy look. His date was a young African-American woman wearing a trim gray suit, the jacket of which she'd hung over the back of her chair. She was snappily dressed, considering the casual attire of the rest of the audience.

At the table next to Elena sat a woman of thirty or so wearing bib overalls with what looked like a long underwear shirt underneath. Her work boots were propped up on an empty chair, and she was talking with disdain about the reading. In fact, a lot of people besides the poet were talking.

"You're a cop, aren't you?" asked Scruffy Beard.

Elena glanced at him in surprise, took another sip of her beer. "That's right."

"For Pete's sake. The cops got something against poetry?"

"Not at all," said Elena. "Like I said, I'm here to listen to Langston Lee Ribbon."

"Looking in his poetry for clues to a crime?" asked the African-American cowboy.

Elena laughed. "Couldn't I be coming for the cultural thrill of it? I heard him read this afternoon at his sister's memorial service."

The four looked embarrassed. "Hey, I'm sorry," said the black cowboy.

"It's refreshing to know that cops like poetry," said Scruffy Beard.

"Especially poetry by a brother," added the young black woman in the gray suit.

"Could you introduce us to him?" asked the blonde.

"Sure," Elena agreed. "If I get the chance, I'll do that." By then the cowboy had finished his reading, a poem about a chuck wagon accident that killed the cook. A rush to the bar followed the scattered applause. When some of the crowd cleared out in front, Elena spotted Langston sitting on a sofa along the side wall between the bar and the stage.

"What kind of cop are you?" asked the blonde.

When Elena hesitated, the black woman said, "Look, don't be embarrassed if you're a meter maid or getting stuck with the typing. In any field you name, women's opportunities are limited." They fell into a discussion of women's rights that ended only when Langston climbed onto the stage and sat down on the folding chair.

A man in a UTLS T-shirt and sandals introduced Langston and lowered the mike so he could read sitting down. Then Analee's brother launched into another of his amazingly convoluted poems. Elena really tried to follow, but trying wasn't good enough. The first poem seemed to be about some symbolic bird of prey. His poem reminded her of Gerard Manley Hopkins' "The Windhover," which she'd read in Freshman English. The Windhover had been a symbol for Christ. She wasn't sure what Langston's symbol stood for; maybe she could say something about Hopkins to him, establish a rapport.

Langston Lee Ribbon had a wonderful voice, like his father's. It was a pleasure to listen even if you didn't understand what he was talking about. Sort of like a church service in Latin. You got with the program even if you weren't too clear on the message. Elena liked some poetry. Her mother, a sixties person, had made her pay attention to rock lyrics, which, according to Harmony, were the poetry of the age. Good lord, she'd missed the last two poems while letting her mind drift. When Langston left the microphone to enthusiastic applause, Elena stood up and waved to him. He didn't look particularly happy to see her as he worked his way back to the table.

"Do you mind?" she asked the overalled woman. She glared but removed her work boots from the chair, which Elena offered to Langston. "This is Langston Lee Ribbon," she said to the foursome she'd joined. They introduced themselves and greeted him with praise that, as far as Elena could see, didn't show any clearer understanding of his poetry than she had.

"Can I buy you a beer?" Elena asked.

"Sure," said Langston.

"Draft OK?"

He nodded. She went to the bar for two more beers, put one down in front of him, and took her seat.

"So what you want with me?" he asked.

"I wanted to hear you read again," she said. Then, turning away so the others couldn't hear, she murmured, "And to ask if you'd thought of anything about Analee that might help me."

He took a long drink of his beer and waved away the cigarette smoke wafting across the table. "Smoke's hard to take since I quit," he said, "hard on my throat an' on my willpower."

"I know what you mean," said Elena. "I still want one occasionally." She'd quit while she was at the Police Academy. Figured she might as well get all the trauma over at once.

The black cowboy and his date hastily stubbed out cigarettes and muttered apologies. The woman in the work boots at the next table lit a cigar and blew smoke in their direction.

"Do you think your first poem was influenced by Hopkins' 'The Windhover'?" Elena asked.

Langston stopped looking morose. "Maybe. You know Gerald Manley Hopkins?"

She nodded. "'I caught this morning morning's minion, kingdom of the daylight's dauphin,'" she quoted.

"Learned it in Freshman English, right?"

Elena grinned. "Right. But I liked it. Maybe because I'm Catholic."

"Yeah, well, Ah like 'The Windhover' too, but mah poem's about a black man breakin' free through art. Got nothin' to do with Jesus. You oughta read some more of Hopkins' work. Now those dark sonnets like 'Ah wake and feel the fell of dark, not day'—stuff on depression; Ah've been that route."

"I'm sorry," said Elena. "Serious depression? Like Rhino?"

"Situational, not clinical," said Langston. "But you find a lot of writers falling into the pits from time to time. It's not your most stable profession. 'Specially if your mama's always after you to get a real job."

"Yeah, my mother always said that a real job was being a folksinger or a teacher, either one of which she considered the height of altruistic public service."

Langston Lee laughed with a deep-throated appreciation that gave Elena an entirely new view of him. "Ah guess you're probably the first cop Ah ever met," he said. "Hope Ah'm not giving you away." He glanced at the other four, who had been trying to look as if they weren't eavesdropping.

"I picked her for a cop right off," said Scruffy Beard.

Langston Lee studied him. "Well, you probably know more cops than Ah do."

"Don't let the beard fool you. It's just that shaving's a pain for me, literally. Shit, I'm twenty-seven years old, and I've still got acne."

"Why don't you try some of that—what do you call it?—peels off layers of your face?"

"Retin-A," said Scruffy Beard in a disgruntled tone. "Leaves you looking like someone scalped your chin."

Langston Lee turned away from the others and leaned toward Elena, mouth close to her ear, and whispered, "Ah've been thinkin' about what Ah said to you—about Analee bein' hung up on money. An' she was, lately."

Because of the noise Elena had to concentrate to catch his murmured words.

"But the truth is, she never was before. She'd a liked to have enough money to buy a computer, but she always managed to get other people to let her use theirs, so she wasn't really too broken up about it.

"But lately—God, she even asked *me* if Ah had any extra, an' she wasn't doin' bad on fellowships. You might look into the money angle; that's the only thing Ah can think of. My sister was really a sweetheart, an' Ah don't know why anyone would have killed her. Ah don't even know why she needed money."

"When did she ask you for help?" Elena murmured back.

"Oh, 'bout a month ago. Ah said if she was really in a bind, maybe Ah could borrow from one of my professors. She said, forget it; she'd take care of things herself."

A month ago? That was during the time when the five-thousand-dollar deposits had been coming and going in her account. What the hell had been happening? And how was Elena going to find out? The boyfriend, Montrose, wasn't talking to her. The two guys over at UTLS hadn't said anything about money except that Analee was getting paid to tutor them; those checks went to her father. Could Analee have wanted Langston to take over helping their father? She could say something about that to Langston, but she hated to embarrass Ray Lee, remembering how he'd said he hoped she wouldn't tell Lavender.

Langston interrupted her thoughts by excusing himself. "Ah gotta go talk to some people over there."

Elena followed the direction of his nod and caught sight of Angus McGlenlevie, the last person *she* wanted to see. She never had liked the self-styled "erotic poet."

"You going to read again?" she asked.

"Nope."

"Then I guess I'll be going." She shook his hand. "Nice to meet you all," she said to the couples and rose to push her way through the crowd.

"Black guy dumped you, huh?" said the woman in overalls and work boots once Langston Lee had disappeared.

Elena stopped. There was no question the woman had addressed her.

"You oughta know enough to stick to your own kind. All of you." She glanced contemptuously toward the two couples remaining at the table. "Where Ah come from, we call it miscegenation."

"How about that?" said the black cowboy. "Miscegenation. An' me a bachelor with no kids."

"Makes me think she doesn't know what the word means," the young woman in the gray suit chimed in.

"Sitting together at a table, even dating—that's not miscegenation," said the cowboy's blond date. "Not that there's anything *wrong* with miscegenation."

"The hell there isn't," snapped the woman in the overalls, her face flushed with anger.

Oh boy! thought Elena. "Look, folks—"

"Maybe you ought to define the word for her, Paul," said the man with acne.

"Sure. It means interbreeding, lady. Or at the least, interracial cohabitation. Do you want me to define *cohabit* for you?"

The woman stood up, knocking her chair over. Elena, anticipating trouble, edged around the table toward her.

"Sounds like where you come from, people don't like education either," said the cowboy.

"You sayin' Ah'm ignorant?" The woman stubbed out her cigar.

Elena was trying to wedge herself between two chairs when the woman lunged at the black cowboy and planted a hamlike fist on his chin, staggering him considerably and shocking him even more.

Two burly men shot out from behind the bar and headed for the table.

"I've got it," said Elena quickly. She'd broken free of the furniture gridlock. "Sit down," she said to the cowboy, who was rubbing his chin.

"Hey, I'm not the one who—"

"I know that. I'm arresting you for assault," she said to the female aggressor, scooting behind her while fishing handcuffs from her purse. She grabbed the woman's wrist and snapped a cuff on it, then grabbed the other.

"What are you—Hey!"

"Detective Elena Jarvis. Crimes Against Persons," Elena said before the other women at Overalls-and-Work-Boots' table could protest the arrest of their friend. Elena flashed her I.D. "You want to clear a path to the door?" she asked the two husky men. "If you're willing to press charges, sir, I'll take her downtown and book her," she told the cowboy. Either way, she was getting the woman out of here before the confrontation ended in a free-for-all.

"Well, I—" He looked embarrassed.

"He does," said the young woman in the gray suit.

"Listen, Leticia—"

"She *hit* you. She insulted *all* of us. You are *going* to press charges, Paul."

"I agree," said his date.

"Absolutely, buddy," said the blond guy. "You gonna let a woman get away with coldcocking you?"

"So I'll press charges. What do I do? Follow you?" Paul asked Elena, giving in to the indignation of his friends.

"Right," Elena agreed, and eight people—two Attic employees, Elena, her prisoner, and the two couples from the table—headed for the door, Overalls protesting all the way.

"You gonna be good, or do I have to send for backup?"
Elena asked once they got to the street.

"I cain't believe you're bustin' me," said the prisoner.

"That's what happens when you attack strangers at poetry
readings."

"I liked that place better when it was just beer and *nachos*,"
the woman muttered. "No damn poetry."

"And keep in mind," Elena added, "you do my truck any
damage, and I'll charge you with vandalism, too."

The aggressive woman, considerably chastened, gave Elena no more trouble during the ride. As they turned down the
ramp into the basement of the jail, the woman muttered,
"What's your problem, anyway? I didn't even knock him
out."

"You assaulted him. In fact, you started the whole thing,"
said Elena, but she was thinking about money. Why did a
person Analee's age, who should have been getting by
comfortably, need so much money that she'd ask her poet
brother for it? An expensive computer? A car? Elena could
ask everyone who'd known the victim whether Analee had
expressed a desire for something like that.

Or an abortion? Had Analee needed an abortion? Had she
had one? Would the coroner's report have mentioned it?
They'd certainly have mentioned a pregnancy.

"What have we got here?" asked the sheriff's deputy on
duty as Elena got out of her truck and opened the door for her
prisoner.

"Random assault by bigot," she muttered.

"Nice outfit," he said to the prisoner.

"Up yours," replied the woman.

20

Elena groped for the telephone with the feeling that she'd just gone to bed, although the digital clock read 5:30, giving her a big four and a half hour's sleep. Booking the cigar lady had taken time.

"It's Vasquez," said a disgruntled voice. "Clabb insisted I call you. He thinks our latest problem's connected to the Ribbon killing."

"What happened?" asked Elena groggily.

"Someone attacked Greta Marx in her clinic last night."

"Is she dead?"

"Unconscious."

Elena threw off the covers and sat up. "What's the connection to Analee?"

"The guy who broke in hit the doctor with one of those statues. Of course, he was probably stealing drugs, but—"

"A *Charleston Dancer*? How big?"

"Bigger than desk size, smaller than full size. Clabb wants you over here."

"I'm on my way." She stumbled out of bed, head aching slightly from three beers with Maggie and two more at The Attic. With the automatic efficiency of someone used to dressing while still asleep, she pulled on jeans and a sweat-shirt, stuffed her feet into comfortable low-heeled boots, grabbed her purse from the coffee table, her gun from the locked drawer in the kitchen, and a half carton of orange juice

117

and a flour tortilla from the refrigerator. It was 5:45 when she climbed into her pickup and headed to the Westside.

You had to figure it was L.S.A.R.I., she decided, even if Vasquez was thinking druggies. L.S.A.R.I. had been threatening Greta Marx. They'd evidently turned to covert, violent intimidation now that they couldn't block clinic access without incurring federal charges. Anti-abortion frustration had brought out the real wackos. Doctors and clinic workers were getting killed in other parts of the country. At least Greta Marx was still alive.

On her truck radio, Elena called for an I.D.&R. team, then slipped one of Ray Lee Ribbon's tapes into her cassette player and sang along with "St. Louis Blues." *I could be a blues singer*, she thought, pleased with herself. Fifteen minutes later, she pulled into the clinic parking lot. The ambulance was leaving. She leaned out and called to the driver, "She still alive?"

He nodded and drove away. The I.D.&R. people had arrived ahead of her and were dusting for prints and taking pictures when she entered. Judging from condition of the lobby, the doctor had put up a fight. Furniture was overturned, papers, magazines, and health brochures scattered. Once I.D.&R. finished, Elena talked to Adam Merton, head of the weekend team.

"No prints on the statue," he said. "We couldn't talk to the doctor because she was unconscious, but I looked at her head while the E.M.S. guys were working on her. I think she was hit a couple of times. The medic agreed. Most interesting thing we found is this." He held up a plastic bag.

"Brown hair?" asked Elena.

"She was clutching it. First, I thought it was real. After a closer look, I'd say it's that acrylic stuff cheap wigs are made of."

Someone had attacked Dr. Marx with a statue, and the doctor had torn hair out of his wig?

"If we're through here," said Vasquez, "I'm going home. My mom gets upset when I'm called out in the middle of the night." Wearing the customary dark glasses, jeans, and a fleece-lined jacket open over a UTLS sweatshirt, he looked a lot cuter than he did in his lavender uniform. "By the way, there's definitely drugs being sold on campus."

"By whom?" she asked.

"Not sure yet, but I think a major deal went down yesterday. Since the brother's still in town, maybe he was behind it. Taking over for his late *hermana*, you know? He wasn't in his room last night; I'll tell you that."

"How do you know, Tey?"

"I've got the desk checking. Maybe you ought to put a tail on Brother Bose."

"You want to talk my sergeant into that?"

"The university expects a lot of cooperation from your department."

"You're getting it," Elena replied. "From me."

"So what have you been doing?"

"Following up on L. Parker Montrose. Also, I talked to Langston last night."

"What about the black guys at UTLS?" Vasquez demanded.

"Both alibied."

"Maybe someone's lying for them."

"I have no proof of that. I do have proof that Montrose and his friends have been telling me lies. And he's a match with the clip blood. Course, we'll need DNA tests to sort out the matches."

"So get them."

"It takes time. H.H.U. is rich. Maybe you people should pay for private tests."

"I'll check it out." Vasquez waved his hand and left.

Had he driven here in the dark with those glasses on? Elena called Maggie, who didn't appreciate being awakened.

"The bank accounts," Elena murmured into the receiver. "Can we do that today?"

Maggie grumbled but agreed. "At least the computer center will be empty, so no one can see the skulduggery going on. You want to come over here for eggs Benedict?"

"Yeah." Elena liked eggs Benedict, a dish to which Sarah Tolland had introduced her. "How are you going to explain my being with you for breakfast?"

"Well, I could say I'm a lesbian and I seduced you last

night. Melody'd love that. Or I could say I'm interviewing you about computer stress."

"I choose number two," said Elena dryly. "I'll meet you in the lobby."

As she crossed the campus, Elena looked up at the pink glow flaring into the night sky from behind the Franklin Mountains. The western slopes were still dark and mysterious, their stark splendor as secret as the dark side of the moon. She shoved her hands into her pockets and admired the white puffs her breath made in the cold air.

Then she glanced up at the ornate wrought-iron lampposts. Sarah said they were copies of the ones in Barcelona, Spain. Elena wondered whether she'd ever see Spain—or anything outside Texas and New Mexico. Maybe she'd get to go to a police conference some year. With her luck, they'd hold it in Omaha, Nebraska.

21
..

Saturday, December 3, 9:05 A.M.

"You see what I mean? Happy's always on my back about the damn campaign," said Maggie. They were walking across the quadrangle to the computer center.

"Maybe if you make a few appearances, he'll leave you alone," said Elena. The eggs Benedict had been great. She'd be happy to eat breakfast in the H.H.U. dining room any Saturday they asked her.

"No, he won't. I've got to solve this case and disappear before the coronation. I'll never hear the end of it at headquarters if I get elected Christmas Queen."

"I think it's terrific," said Elena, grinning. "Didn't you always want to be a beauty queen?"

"Hell, no. I wanted to be the best canoer in Wyoming, and the best white-water rafter in Idaho, and the best police computer scientist anywhere, but I *never* wanted to be queen of some stupid college dance. I don't even like to dance. Happy's already informed me that, as my campaign manager, he'll be my date. The little creep is shorter than me. I swear, if I win, I'm going to wear four-inch heels."

"Good idea. When you dance with him, he'll have his nose in your cleavage."

"You're a big help." Maggie unlocked the front door to the center and led Elena to a small office crammed with equipment.

121

"Pretty clever, the way you wangled the name of Montrose's bank out of him," said Elena.

"Makes it easier if I know what bank's records I need to burgle," said Maggie. She sat down at the desk, turned the computer on, and said, "Don't talk to me for a while."

"Can I go outside and use a telephone?"

Maggie waved a hand in permission as she tapped keys and peered at the screen. Elena closed the door softly behind her and called the hospital for a report on Greta Marx. The H.H.U. doctor had been x-rayed and taken to the neurological unit. That didn't sound good to Elena. Severe concussion was the diagnosis. No fracture, because Dr. Marx had an extraordinarily thick skull. Elena grinned; she could have guessed that.

Dr. Marx wouldn't be talking to anyone until tomorrow, but Detective Jarvis was welcome to call for further updates. "Who knows?" said the doctor. "Greta could wake up and demand to see you. Or start giving lectures on birth control to the nurses. You think the local pro-lifers got to her?"

"I hope she'll be able to tell us," said Elena.

"Well, no one could get me to do an abortion these days. Too dangerous. Even with the new law. Doesn't help to convict the killer if the doctor's dead."

His sentiments made Elena uneasy about the future of pro-choice. She peeked in at Maggie, who seemed totally absorbed in her electronic snooping. *I'm soliciting the commission of a crime*, Elena told herself, then salved her conscience with the thought of Analee in her mosaic coffin. If computer hacking solved the killing, good. An hour later, when Elena was bored to death with poking around the center, Maggie called her in. "The checks from his family stopped in early October. About a week later he found a new source of income. Cash."

"Five-thousand-dollar deposits?" asked Elena, excited.

"It varies. Nothing over ten thousand, which is when the bank has to tell the Feds about cash deposits, nothing under—" She studied a printout. "Nothing under two-fifty."

Elena frowned. "What about spring and fall semesters last year? Any source of income besides his parents?"

"No, but I could only go back to January."

"So there has to be a third person who started the scam. Analee was getting a straight five thou, maybe that's per transcript—if she was in on it. Montrose is getting different amounts—maybe for the contacts he makes."

"Here's the printout." Maggie handed her the information. "Don't let anyone see it, or we'll both be in deep shit."

Elena nodded, and stuffed the papers into her purse.

"I had an idea," said Maggie. "I've been running the names of the fake grads through all kinds of databases, trying to find connections—you know? So far what I've got is that they're all from rich families, they're all short in the intelligence department, and half of them come from around D.C. So let's you and me call a couple of the bigger twits on the list and see what we can find out. We'll say—let's see—we'll say we're from the alumni association."

"If we're from the alumni association, we should know how they've got the diplomas. We might even want them back. Why not say that mutual friends told us about their degrees and ask how to go about getting our own?"

"Even better," Maggie agreed. "We'll use Charlie's phones. He'll never notice the charges."

Elena drew Penelope Joan Rheingold, who, according to Maggie, was the least likely to realize that she was being interrogated by a policewoman. When interviewed at a Virginia horses show by a society reporter from The *Washington Post*, Penelope Joan had confided that she got interested in riding because horses were easier to talk to than people; horses never used hard words. Elena called Penelope Joan, said she'd always wanted a degree, and had heard from a mutual friend that Penelope Joan had mail-ordered a neat one.

"And I didn't have to go to college," Penelope Joan agreed excitedly.

"How'd you do it?" Elena asked, marveling that Ms. Rheingold seemed perfectly happy to talk about her fraudulent degree without asking for any information on the person she was talking to.

"Well, I got this really super ad in the mail that said for twenty thousand dollars, I could be a graduate of a pre— pres—some hard word. Anyway, I could have my own college degree, and I thought, gosh, wouldn't Petey be impressed? Petey's my escort and best friend—you probably know him—and *he* doesn't have a college degree.

"Well, he didn't have one then. He got the same letter and bought a degree of his own. Gosh, was I disappointed! I mean, mine got here in the mail first, but he said, 'Listen, Henny Penny, I've got one coming too.'

"Anyway, as soon as I saw the ad, I showed it to Mummy, and she said she thought that would be really sweet, 'cause she'd always wanted me to be a college graduate, so she ordered one and gave it to me after I fell off my horse at the horse show and everyone laughed. But I don't mind at all, hardly, about falling off, because I have a degree from a pres—pres—a big university. So it came in the mail, you know, and I went right over to Petey's house and . . ."

With hardly any prompting, Penelope Joan talked for forty-five minutes. Elena got the impression that Ms. Rheingold didn't find too many people who were willing to listen to her, except maybe Petey and her horse. The big news was that Penelope Joan insisted the letter had come from Herbert Hobart University. Where else would it have come from? she asked, and it must have been from a very important official there, because you couldn't read his signature—Mummy couldn't either—and no, she didn't think his name was typed anywhere on the envelope or letter, because Mummy had to write her answer to "Dear Sir," and the address was a post office box number; Penelope Joan remembered that because it was 316, her birthday, which she thought was a really good omen. "Now have you got that address?" Penelope Joan asked. "You're going to love being a college graduate."

Elena did have the address. In fact, she had a very complete set of notes on the conversation. After hanging up, she thought about the scam. Twenty thousand was pretty cheap for a degree when you figured that it probably cost more than that for one year of actual study at the university. Analee had been getting only a fourth of the take on each diploma, the number of which had doubled since she started depositing money, if it was diploma money. They didn't really know that. And Montrose—well, they also didn't know that Analee had been killed over money.

But still, if the originator of the plan had killed her, Montrose might be next. Elena turned to Maggie, who had just hung up on Peter Barthholdt III, probably Penelope Joan's Petey. They compared notes. Same story, same postal box. Elena called a retired postal clerk from her neighborhood. He called the post office on Alameda to talk to a clerk who worked Saturdays. Then he called Elena back with the name and address of the person renting the box. Maggie ran the name through H.H.U. files of students and employees, then through the Los Santos directory. No matches.

"Fake name," Elena guessed. "Let's check out the address."

Maggie groaned. "I gotta study. Dr. Erlingson gave me five books on statistics and psychology, each one more boring than the last. Report due Monday. I don't know why I ever majored in psychology."

"I didn't know you had. What about computers?"

"I just fell in with a bunch of hackers in college and took these courses for the fun of it."

"I know this great Mexican restaurant in the Lower Valley, probably not too far from the address my neighbor got from the post office. We could have lunch there and—"

"You're on," said Maggie. "So Erlingson's mad at me Monday. What do I care? It's not as if he's going to ask me for a date if I do the reading."

They had quesadillas, *machaca*, and beer. The investigation of the address was less successful. After driving up and down a country road, they decided that if the street number had existed, it would have been on a goat corral.

"Goats?" exclaimed Maggie. "What kind of a city has goat herds?"

"Chimayo has goats," Elena retorted. "You ate goat at the barbecue after the bicycle race last fall."

"Chimayo's a little bitty *village*! And how was I to know it was goat? I had a broken leg and snootful of pain killers." When Elena glared at her, Maggie added, "It's a nice village. Anyway, I've got to get back and study."

"Just one more stop," said Elena and pulled into a convenience store to call the hospital. Still no visiting. Even for police.

22
∴

Saturday, December 3, 3:30 P.M.

After returning Maggie to campus, Elena canvassed every room on Analee's floor, asking questions. No one had heard Analee mention money or lack of it.

"How would I know?" said a female computer science major. "She always had enough for coffee or a Coke. Her clothes weren't anything special, but she looked good. It would have been rude to ask how much money she had."

A coed two floors down said, "She wasn't one for going out on the town with a gang of students. It's pay-your-own-way, you know? Maybe she couldn't afford it. I never thought of that I guess I figured she was too busy."

"But she was invited?"

"Sure. Analee was a lot of fun. I sat in on an all-night bridge game where they were teaching her to play. She had everyone laughing. And it wasn't that she couldn't get the hang of bridge. When she stopped kidding around, she made four game bids in a row. Remembered every card that went down."

"Were you playing for money?"

"Now that you mention it, she wouldn't. Said she wanted to have fun, not worry about winning or losing. So I guess if you worry about losing, you've got money problems. Why're you asking, anyway?"

"Just trying to get a handle on the case," Elena replied, and went to more rooms to ask more questions.

Three male students she found on the second floor all said that if Analee Ribbon had ever agreed to one of the Dutch nights out, they'd have been glad to pay her way, no matter what the custom was. "She wasn't a big socializer," said one, "but she sure was fun if you could get her to stand still long enough. Remember that skit she wrote after the elections?"

"The Shakespearean voodoo thing?"

"Right. 'The Shakespearean Voodoo Queen Makes Eye-of-Newt-Gingrich Stew.'"

The other two suitemates burst out laughing and began to sing snatches of outrageous political songs that Analee had written. Elena wished she had seen the skit. Evidently Analee had not only a sense of humor but also some of her father's musical talent. As Elena left, the suitemates were reminiscing about the reaction of the Young Republicans to Analee's musical.

Elena took the elevator to the lobby, where she found Tey Vasquez in conversation with a young woman beside one of the boa constrictor lamps. Elena waved and headed for the door, but Tey called to her, "Hold up."

"The mother's going to be guest chef tonight at a place on Cincinnati," he told Elena.

"So?" She wanted to get home. Four and a half hour's sleep last night and no days off all week—she was tired.

"I think we should go. Butter up the family. See what we can find out."

"You go. I'm wiped out."

"Hey, I had to get up earlier than you this morning."

"But I didn't get to bed until after one," Elena retorted.

"Big date?"

"Big bust. Woman slugged a guy at The Attic. I arrested her for assault."

"You're kidding." Vasquez grinned. "Come on. I'll buy you a bowl of Lavender Lee's famous Houston gumbo. You have to eat."

The gumbo sounded good. "I'll pay for my own," she said.

"Can't accept dinner from a fellow cop?"

"We're working a case together."

"Does that mean I can ask you out once we've solved the Ribbon murder?"

"Don't ask me hard questions when I'm this tired. I'll meet you at the restaurant."

"Fine. Twenty minutes?"

Elena nodded, buttoned up her jacket, and headed for the pickup. Temperatures had been in the sixties earlier in the afternoon, but once the sun set, the air turned cold; hot gumbo sounded perfect. She hoped that Lavender Lee Ribbon's family recipe included a lot of spicy ingredients. Punching the button on her tape deck, she sang "Georgia on My Mind" with Ray Lee.

Vasquez followed her up North Mesa and parked beside her truck on Cincinnati, four doors away from the restaurant. What was she going to do if Tey actually asked her out? She liked Michael Futrell, but he issued invitations when he saw her standing in front of him. Once she was off this case, she wouldn't be seeing him in nondate situations, so there might not be any more dates. And he'd never asked her out on a weekend. Maybe he had a more serious romantic interest for the weekends.

"Good thing we came early," said Vasquez, opening the restaurant door for her.

It was a small place with fake Spanish moss draped from the rafters. At least, Elena assumed, the moss was fake. If it wasn't, wouldn't it attract bugs? The tables had flowered tablecloths and intricately woven baskets holding rolls. Customers filled every chair. Light was almost nonexistent. "I'm not sure we did get here early enough," said Elena, trying to spot an empty table through the noisy gloom.

The hostess, a young woman wearing a bandana around her head and long skirts, found them a two-person table so small Elena wondered if gumbo bowls would fit there with the bread basket and hurricane lamp. They were sitting behind a post. "Going to be hard to spot any Ribbons," she remarked. Even so, the aroma was intoxicating.

"You want gumbo?" asked the waitress, poking her head around the post. There was no room to squeeze in between tables. Elena and Vasquez had used up the last inch of space by sitting down. The young woman offered them menus. Tey, after glancing at his, had to take off his dark glasses.

He turned to the waitress, who said, "Hey, weird eyes." Tey turned away quickly and ordered gumbo, then slipped his glasses back on, but not before Elena caught her second glimpse of those strange, mismatched eyes, this time in the red glow of the little hurricane lamp. The impression was eerie.

"Shrimp or chicken?" asked the waitress.

"Shrimp," said Elena.

"Chicken," said Vasquez.

"You're engaged, right?" said the waitress. "And you're going to share bowls, right? And you're going to want to split a dessert, right?"

"We're not engaged," said Elena. "And I, for one, don't plan on having dessert."

"Oh, have some. It runs up the bill and makes my tip bigger."

"What tip?" Tey muttered.

"Well, shit." The young woman went off looking sulky.

Not your everyday waitress. "You know, if you're self-conscious about your eyes, you could wear colored contacts," Elena said to Tey on impulse.

"I'm not self-conscious," Tey snapped. "I like dark glasses." Then he grinned. "Girls think they're sexy."

"Oka-ay." Elena looked down at her menu, deciding she should have kept her mouth shut.

Vasquez took a roll from the basket. "I'd pass the bread, like my mother always tells me, but we're practically sitting on top of it."

"Right. We'll have to put our gumbo bowls in our laps. Your mother must be some dragon on manners."

"Courtesy means a lot to her. We went out to dinner one night, and I held the door for this gal who turned around and gave me a lecture on 'the new women.' She said females can open their own doors. Mama said, 'My son was taught to be a gentleman, young lady, while you need a lecture on how a lady should act in public.' The woman turned bright red, walked through the door I was holding, and glared at my mother for the rest of the evening."

"How did your mother take that?" Elena asked.

"After about fifteen minutes she said, loud enough to be heard, 'That poor woman doesn't know it's bad manners to stare.'"

"Good for your mom. What's your father like?"

"Long gone," said Vasquez, his smile disappearing.

"Oh, I'm sorry, Tey."

"No need to be. He beat my mother up regularly for twenty years."

"My God!" exclaimed Elena, horrified.

"Lucky for us Dad was a long-distance trucker, so he was gone a lot. Otherwise, he'd probably have killed her 'cause she never had any kids after me. He used to accuse her of being on the pill."

Elena thought of her own loving family. Ruben Portillo would no more beat Harmony than he'd rob a bank, and Elena's mother could be irritating when she got on one of her kicks—auras was the latest. She'd visited Elena in the fall and insisted that her daughter spend a whole evening in front of a mirror trying to see her own aura. It had been one of the dullest evenings of Elena's life, and very disappointing to Harmony.

"I guess one son wasn't enough for him," said Vasquez. "He wanted a houseful."

"Did she want more, too?" Elena asked. With a husband like that, Elena wouldn't have.

"Sure. She even went to one of those fertility doctors. Which was a bad move. The beatings got worse when the old man found the bill and the doctor's statement that she should be able to have more children, and maybe her husband should come in for tests."

"Did he?"

"No way," said Vasquez bitterly.

"So what happened? Did they divorce?"

"You're kidding! We're Catholic. No, he was killed in an accident just before I started college. Brakes went out on his truck when he was crossing Transmountain on a run to Oklahoma. He didn't make it to a runaway truck ramp." Vasquez smiled grimly. "That was no big loss to us, but the

company he'd worked for cut off the medical insurance to
truckers' widows a couple of years later. *That* was a disaster
because my mother has diabetes."

Elena nodded. "So you had to quit school."

"Right. She's still got his pension, but it's not much."

"She's lucky to have such a good son." What a strange
mixture Vasquez was—a swaggering mama's boy.

"Nice to have at least one parent who's proud of you," said
Vasquez.

The waitress reached around one side of the post and
deposited a steaming bowl of gumbo at Elena's place. Then she
reached around the other side and served Vasquez, who had to
lift the bread basket to make room. "What am I supposed to do
with this?" he asked.

"I'll take it, or I can take the lamp."

Elena didn't want to eat in the dark, possibly ingesting
something from the gumbo that she wouldn't have put in her
mouth had she been able to see it—alligator, snake. Who
knew what exotic ingredients the Gumbo Queen of Houston
might use? Grabbing the lamp handle and a roll, she said,
"Take the basket." The waitress reached over Tey's shoulder,
but the basket was empty by the time she got her fingers on
the handle. He'd snatched a roll, too.

"So now what?" Elena wondered, looking at her roll.

"Roll in one hand, spoon in the other," he suggested.

"This is wonderful," said Elena after her first mouthful.

They never saw Lavender, so Elena suggested that they
insist on being allowed to compliment the chef.

"Ma'am," said Tey, once they'd made their way into a
narrow, chaotic kitchen located just past the rest rooms, "I've
never had gumbo before. I'm an El Paso boy who grew up on
tacos and *chiles rellenos*, but your gumbo is as good as my
mama's *menudo*!"

Lavender Lee, enveloped in a huge white apron, frowned at
him. "You like tripe?" she asked. "No tripe in my gumbo."

"I had chicken," he replied. "Mexicans like chicken, too,
because in Mexico chickens aren't shot full of hormones and
antibiotics, so they tend to die young. You manage to raise
one to eating weight, you got a real treat."

Lavender Lee laughed. "Did you have the same, Detective Jarvis?"

"No, ma'am. I had shrimp. It was wonderful."

Lavender nodded and reached out to check her pots.

"Mrs. Ribbon, I've got a question," said Elena hesitantly. Lavender turned to her. "Did Analee have some special need for money in the last months of her life?"

"Why would she?" Lavender frowned. "Analee wasn't a big spender, and she had a lot of scholarship money and a job with her professor. She had enough. If she didn't, she could have asked me. Ah've always seen that mah children had what they needed."

Lavender didn't know that her daughter had quit the job with Sarah? Something unusual was at work here: Ray Lee wanting to keep Analee's contributions secret, Analee keeping from her mother the fact that she'd quit the research position she loved, all that money going in and out of Analee's account. And the explanations obviously weren't in Lavender's power to give.

"I've got to get on home," said Tey Vasquez. "My mother's expecting me."

"You live with your mama?" Lavender's eyes softened.

"Yes, ma'am, and I try not to worry her."

"Mark of a good son," said Lavender approvingly.

Evidently Tey Vasquez was no longer "Mr. Assistant Chief" in the mind of the victim's mother. Well, Elena was coming to think better of Vasquez, too. He didn't seem as much a bigot as he had before, perhaps because he was treating Mrs. Ribbon with respect, perhaps because he'd pointed out that he was a minority himself and knew where and why crime flourished. It was true: poverty and discrimination bred crime. Elena sighed.

"Now, you all try a sip of this," said Lavender, dipping her spoon into a pot.

"I really do have to get home," said Tey.

"I'll try it," said Elena eagerly. After that terrific gumbo, she'd have tried anything Lavender Lee Ribbon offered. She swallowed. "What is it?" she asked.

"Turtle soup."

"Oh." Elena wished she hadn't been so venturesome. One

of her favorite pets had been a turtle she and her brother Johnny rescued from the road to Taos when they were kids. They'd named it after the local priest because priest and turtle were the slowest-moving creatures in the town of Chimayo. They'd *never* have made soup of their turtle, Father Ignatius.

23
..

Sunday, December 4, 10:15 A.M.

Once the doctors cleared Greta Marx for police visitors, Vasquez insisted on taking part in the interview. He and Elena met at Sierra Medical Center and found the clinic doctor almost as feisty as usual. "I've got a hell of a headache. What did you expect?" Greta replied when Elena asked how she was feeling. "Have you caught the man who attacked me?"

"He was gone when the night guard found you and called 911," said Vasquez.

"Do you remember anything about the attack?" Elena asked.

"Of course. I caught this stocky fellow hunched over the computer in the reception area, so I yelled at him."

Wrong move, thought Elena and said, "When you encounter an intruder, the department recommends that you get out of there and call the police from another telephone."

"Maybe you don't realize, Detective Jarvis," said Greta Marx, "since you're so free with your advice, that patient files are stored in my computer—which, incidentally, is *not* connected to the university system." She started to push herself up in bed, winced, and lay back. "I can't trust Charlie Venner's system to protect patient confidentiality. The man's an irresponsible nincompoop, both professionally and sexually. So I have my own passwords and security system; however, I think the intruder got through. I'll admit I was across the room, but he had something on the screen."

"What happened after you shouted at him?" asked Elena.

"He jumped over the counter. Surprisingly. A man that stocky shouldn't be able to. He was carrying a lot of weight. Two-oh-five would be my guess."

"Probably not accurate," Vasquez murmured to Elena. "Not when she made the estimate while he was coming at her."

"I heard that," snapped Greta Marx.

Elena thought the estimate might be very accurate, so she wrote it down. Greta Marx would weigh a lot of people in the course of a school year. "So you got a good look at him?" she asked. "At his face?"

"Not really," the doctor muttered. "As I said, he took me by surprise, jumping at me like that, and I had my driving glasses on. Up close his face was blurred."

"Maybe you need bifocals," Vasquez suggested snidely.

"Maybe you do," snapped Dr. Marx. "Then he hit me with one of those *Charleston Dancers*. From the reception room coffee table."

If the guy had hit Greta Marx with a wastebasket or a burglary tool, Elena figured she wouldn't have been called. Chief Clabb was assuming a connection because the weapons in both cases had been statues. And maybe the crimes *were* connected. What if Analee had been pregnant and refused to get an abortion? Montrose, already in hot water with his family, might have killed her at the library in a quarrel over her pregnancy, then broken into the clinic computer to search for and destroy any evidence of her condition. However, Wilkerson, the coroner, hadn't said anything about pregnancy, and he would have; it was a motive for murder. She wondered for a second time if Analee had an abortion at Montrose's insistence, then quarreled with him about it.

Elena pictured Montrose. He didn't weigh over two hundred, although he might have been wearing a heavy jacket that made him look stocky. Surely he wouldn't be dumb enough to send someone else to tackle the clinic computer. And wouldn't Dr. Marx know if Analee was pregnant or had had an abortion?

Well, not necessarily. Analee could have bought one of those drugstore kits, found out she was pregnant, and had the abortion elsewhere at Montrose's insistence. For discretion's sake. Maybe they'd been quarreling about who would pay for it. Maybe Montrose hadn't known where Analee was tested and played it safe. Ready to wipe the records from the computer if they were there. Ready to kill the doctor to protect himself from suspicion in Analee's death. Elena decided to ask the coroner about pregnancy, or signs of an abortion, just in case, and Greta Marx about—

Vasquez interrupted Elena's train of thought by saying to Dr. Marx, "Did you lose consciousness once he hit you?"

"I did not," said the doctor stoutly. "I was dazed, but I went straight for his eyes."

"What color were they?"

"I don't know. How many times do I have to tell you that he was blurry? But I pulled his hair off. Then he hit me again. I saw a bald head as I went down. Snatched him bald-headed." The doctor looked pleased at the thought.

"It was a wig," said Elena. "Brown acrylic." But Montrose wasn't bald. Maybe he *had* sent someone after all.

"Do you go to the clinic late at night on any particular schedule, Dr. Marx?" Vasquez asked. "Could he have known that you'd be there?"

A good question. Vasquez was getting better at interrogation.

"You think he was lying in wait for me?" asked the doctor. "Impossible. I rarely go there after hours. Friday night I couldn't sleep, so I went to catch up on paperwork. The man came for the computer. That's where he was when I—"

"But what would he—"

"I want you to get an expert in there, not Charlie Venner, and see if the fellow's wiped out my files. That would be a *disaster*!" She was beginning to sound panicky. "He must have been one of those L.S.A.R.I. crackpots bent on compromising my effectiveness in fighting venereal disease and unplanned pregnancies. If I don't keep after those girls, they backslide. Get careless. I hope you're conducting your sex life in a sensible way, Detective. Did you read those pamphlets I gave you last spring?"

"Yes, ma'am," said Elena.

"Recruit that new graduate student—Daguerre. She seems

sharp about computers. Fixed a problem I was having when she came in for her physical." The doctor groaned, clasped both hands to her head, then reached for an ice pack on the table beside her. "Girl's the idiot-savant type," she muttered. "Knows all about computers and nothing about her own body."

Dr. Marx looked rather jaunty with the ice pack slipping raffishly over one eye.

"Daguerre is twenty-two and has the body of a woman ten years older. That's *not* good. And on the birth control issue, she tried to tell me she'd been on the pill for twelve years, which would make her ten years old when she started."

"Amazing," said Elena, choking back laughter.

Dr. Marx nodded, winced, and resettled her ice pack. "I told her I didn't appreciate being lied to, and made her take pills with her. And I'll be watching to see that she comes back for more. Probably never took a birth control pill in her life." The doctor harrumphed, then winced again.

"I'll go right out and call her," said Elena, who had to escape before she broke into laughter at the thought of Maggie Daguerre being told with great disdain that she had the body of a thirty-two-year-old woman. Vasquez stayed to ask a few more questions. While he was finishing, Elena telephoned Maggie and talked her into checking out the computer at the clinic. Then she called the coroner's office and got the weekend clerk to look up Analee Ribbon's autopsy. No pregnancy. So much for that, unless Analee thought she was pregnant and told Montrose before she'd had a test. Of course, she might have known she wasn't but lied to him. But why?

"Learn anything else?" she asked when Vasquez came out of the hospital room.

His jaw was set. "Where does she get off giving me a lecture on sexual responsibility? My sex life is none of her business."

"In the age of safe sex, no one's private life is sacrosanct," said Elena cheerfully. "Did she remember anything else about her attacker?"

"Nothing."

"Maybe I should get a police artist over here?"

"Be a waste of time. She didn't see anything."

Vasquez insisted on going to the clinic with Elena to let Maggie in. He really did seem to be getting serious about the case. About time, too. Most of his efforts had been directed toward the drug ring he'd decided was operating on campus. When she asked him about that, he said smugly, "I'm getting there," but became secretive about where he was getting. Nowhere, probably, Elena decided. Just hoping to make Chief Clabb look bad with rumors of drug dealing among the students.

It took Maggie fifteen minutes to break Greta Marx's security arrangements and discover that nothing had been added to or deleted from the clinic's hard disk. The nurse had already ascertained that no drugs were missing. So why had the attacker been at the clinic? To hit Dr. Marx? He couldn't have been sure the doctor would show up, if attacking her had been his primary goal. During the hard-disk search, Vasquez hung around, looking sexy in his dark glasses, boots, and Levis; evidently he didn't wear the lavender uniform on Sunday. When he asked the two women out for a beer, Elena refused, Maggie accepted, whispering to Elena as they left that he reminded her of a rodeo rider she'd once dated.

Elena thought about the attacker as she drove home. Maggie had said the fake transcripts seemed to be entered from all over the place. If the attacker thought the clinic computer was part of the university system, he could have gone there to enter a transcript. Maybe he, not Analee, was the partner in or even the originator of the diploma scam, and Analee had discovered him, blackmailed him. Oh, hell, it just got more complicated. Elena needed to go Christmas shopping, so instead of continuing to the interstate, she turned off Sunland Park Drive into the mall, where the stores would be open until six.

If she didn't get home to Chimayo for Christmas, she'd have to mail the gifts for her parents, her brothers and sisters, her nieces and nephews, her grandmother, her Tía—oh, shoot! She should have asked Dr. Marx and the coroner's assistant if Analee Ribbons had had an abortion. That was a financial problem Analee wouldn't have wanted to tell her mother about.

24
..

"Where have you been?" Michael asked. He'd left a message on her answering machine, which she was returning.

Elena dropped onto the bed. "Christmas shopping," she replied, and leaned forward to slide her boots off. Then she swung her legs up onto the spread and relaxed against the pillows. "You wouldn't believe how many people there were at Sunland Park."

"I haven't even thought about Christmas shopping." Michael sounded amazed.

"I may have to mail the stuff."

"Me, too. Except for my brother—" She heard a voice in the background. "Who's telling me to get to the point, which is to ask if you'd like to go out this evening."

"Well, I—" Did he mean his identical twin, Mark, wanted her to go out with both of them? The idea seemed creepy to her—that they were so exactly alike, and that she might go some place with both of them, maybe have trouble telling them apart.

"It's an interesting event. Not something we're likely to have in Los Santos again."

"What is it?" Probably some dreary cultural thing at the university.

"The Ribbons. Ray Lee Ribbon? It seems he's a famous jazz person."

"He is," said Elena, her interest sparked.

"Well, there's a jazz quintet at H.H.U. They talked him and his son into playing with them tonight. A faculty committee's rented that coffeehouse up on Cincinnati," Michael added. "You do want to go, don't you?"

"Yes, sure." Although she couldn't imagine that anyone from H.H.U. played great jazz, she did want to hear Ray Lee and Bose, and she shouldn't pass up a chance to talk to the Ribbons in any less structured situation.

"Good. Do you like jazz?"

"I like Ray Lee's."

"Then I'll pick you up at 7:40."

Elena glanced at the clock. She had an hour and fifteen minutes to eat and dress. "This isn't formal or anything, is it?"

"I wouldn't think so."

What did that mean? Men never bothered to find that stuff out, and it always ticked her off.

The establishment was dark. At a long counter on the right pastries and exotic coffees were for sale. Wrought-iron ice-cream-parlor tables and spindly chairs crowded the area on the left, and there was a cleared circle for the musicians at the back. Modern paintings hung on all the walls. Elena wondered if Sarah's Dr. Zifkovitz had contributed to the collection.

Elena had always thought of the coffeehouse as a hangout for students and professors from UT Los Santos. Now it was crowded with H.H.U. people, and in the front—good Lord!—there was that portly cellist she'd interviewed on the acid bath case, the one who'd said he had to turn up the Wagner in order to drown out the sounds of Angus McGlenlevie's orgies upstairs. The cellist, looking euphoric, stood behind a bass. She couldn't imagine that neatly mustachioed, middle-aged player in string quartets as a jazz musician.

Behind him was an eerily pale, red-headed pianist, wearing a black shirt with dandruff polka-dotting the shoulders. On the left a trumpeter, looking very professorial in buttoned sweater vest, shirt, and bow tie, fussed with sheet music. If asked, Elena wouldn't have guessed that jazz musicians used sheet music. She'd thought they just winged it, at least on the traditional kind of stuff Ray Lee played.

Another member of the band tuned a banjo. Young, wearing a soft-billed cap, he looked like an English sporting person in his tweed jacket with suede elbow patches, except that he wore jeans with the jacket. He had bushy eyebrows, and curly hair straggled out from under his cap. The last player in the university quintet was a tall, bearded trombonist with deep-set dark eyes and thick black hair tied back in a pony tail, handsome but gloomy looking. None of them looked like they belonged in a jazz band, but then what did she know?

"Where are the Ribbons, Michael?" she asked.

"I'm Mark."

She flushed, embarrassed at her mistake. Of course that was Mark. He was wearing a jock's jacket instead of Michael's usual tweed sport coat.

"Hey, I don't mind taking Michael's place."

His grin had a suggestive quality she didn't much like. "Where's Michael?" she snapped, then regretted the tone. If she wanted to date Michael, she'd have to get along with Mark. She'd always heard that identical twins were particularly close.

"Michael's holding a place in the coffee line. The Ribbons should be along any minute, since this deal was organized in order to hear them play." He picked up a wrought iron chair and plunked it down by the table he'd chosen.

Show-off, Elena thought. Mark, a phys ed professor, was obviously demonstrating his physical prowess—as if she'd be impressed! Fat chance! If she ever had to go out with both of them again, she'd take a good look at their clothes so she'd know who was who. She sat down on the tiny round seat of the chair and found it extremely uncomfortable.

"What kind of coffee do you want?" Mark asked, waving to a sexy female seated toward the front. The woman blew him a kiss.

"I don't know," Elena muttered. "Do they have decaf?" She wanted to get some sleep tonight.

Pulling his eyes away from the interesting display of cleavage, Mark nodded. "They have everything. Want Michael to choose for you?"

"Sure."

He left. Elena hadn't been alone a half minute when she spotted Sarah, clad in an expensive suit. Paul Zifkovitz towered behind her—tall and skinny, with wild, dark hair. Behind him were Colin Stuart and Lance Potemkin, arm in arm. And behind them trailed the whole Ribbon clan except for Zora Lee, who was probably out preaching the gospel according to the Earth Mother. Three bizarre-looking people—from the Art Department?—followed the Ribbons. Elena could have sworn that one of the arty types had clay on his cheek. He was escorting a woman wearing ceramic jewelry with patches of copper glaze.

"Love your outfit," said the woman, pausing behind Elena, who had risen to let the Ribbons by.

Elena had worn a full skirt and matching shawl in Indian colors and patterns that her mother had sent her last week. Harmony was always reminding Elena to pay attention to her wardrobe.

"Where did you buy it?"

"My mother made it."

The woman looked dumbfounded. "Where did she get that fabric?"

"She's a weaver from Chimayo."

"Ah. Let's sit by this woman," the arty lady said to her potter escort.

"She's a cop," warned Zifkovitz.

"So what? Am I prejudiced against cops?" Heavy copper loops swung from her earlobes and touched her shoulders. Elena figured the woman would look like a basset hound by age fifty if she continued to suspend items that substantial from her ears. The party kept drawing tables together on Elena's right until they had created a dam across the room. A young male employee with waist-length hair insisted that they leave an aisle open so patrons could get refreshments. The Ribbons had greeted Elena and taken their seats, Lavender sitting beside Elena. Ray Lee bent down to kiss his wife; he said, "Save me a seat, lover" and edged his way forward with Bose.

"Rina Zifkovitz," said the woman with the earrings and shook Elena's hand.

"Zifkovitz? But—"

"I'm Zif's sister," said Rina, laughing. "I teach life drawing and painting. In fact, your victim was going to model for one of my classes."

"Analee?"

The woman nodded, earrings twisting. "Great kid. Great *body*! Analee was to the young female nude what Donatello's *David* is to the male nude."

"You sayin' mah Analee was goin' to take her clothes off in a room full of artists?" came the ominous voice of Lavender Lee Ribbon from behind Elena. Because of the noise level, Rina Zifkovitz had been talking loudly.

"Yes ma'am," said Rina enthusiastically.

"She'd never—" Lavender began.

"She needed the money," said Rina.

"Did she say what for?" Elena asked.

Rina shrugged. "All kids need money. I've got some wonderful sketches of her. Would you like photocopies?" she asked Lavender, who looked stunned. "I'll send them over to the Guest House. A great beauty died when some clod killed your daughter, Mrs. Ribbon." The artist turned away to answer a question from one of her friends.

"Ah don't believe mah Analeē would have posed naked," said Lavender. "Why would she need money so bad?"

That's what Elena wanted to know.

"Ah guess you're here investigatin'." Lavender muttered. Sorrow had etched new lines in her face in just the few days since they'd met.

"Only if you have anything to tell me," Elena replied. "Actually, I came to hear your husband and son. I've been listening to Mr. Ribbon's tapes ever since I bought them after the memorial service."

Lavender nodded. "So you like jazz?"

"I like *his* jazz."

"You're a good girl." Lavender patted her shoulder.

The woman was obviously no feminist, Elena thought, or she wouldn't call someone pushing thirty a girl. "Thank you," Elena replied politely. Michael sat down and put a cup mounded with whipped cream in front of her. Then he poured something into it. "What's that?" she asked.

"Brandy," he replied. His brother took a chair across the

table but turned it to face the stage and his friend with the cleavage.

"This place doesn't have a liquor license," Elena objected.

"But we've rented it for the night, and we're providing our own booze." Leaning in front of Elena, he said to Lavender, "Can I give you a drop of brandy, ma'am?"

"Don't mind if I do." Lavender held out her cup.

"I'm not sure this is legal," Elena muttered.

"Lighten up, Ms. Cop. Excessive prudery isn't sexy," Mark called over his shoulder.

Michael frowned at his brother, then called, "Mr. Ribbon?" to Langston, who accepted the offer of brandy. "The university lawyer checked it out," Michael assured Elena. "And I'm the designated driver."

"Oh, what the hell," Elena muttered, hoping he wasn't pouring much into his own cup. She took a sip and savored the rich coffee, the cream and sugar, the brandy bite. Heavenly. You could almost forget it was decaf. She noticed bottles being passed around among the art-and-engineering contingent beyond Michael. Sarah waved. To Elena's left, the Ribbons were enjoying their spiked coffee.

In the music circle more spotlights came on, and Ray Lee adjusted the microphone upward—a *long* way up. "We're just jammin' tonight," he said in his slow, soft drawl. The audience clapped enthusiastically. "Never played with professors."

"Ah'm a student," said the banjo picker in the English cap. "Mah daddy gave me a record of yours when Ah was seven or eight."

Ray Lee grinned. "Sounds like you got a fine daddy, boy." He eyed the group. "Everybody know 'Joe Avery'?"

The bass player-cum-cellist nodded. The second trumpet obviously didn't, and thumbed nervously through his sheet music. Poor man; he'd never be able to keep up with Ray Lee Ribbon. The banjo player, however, looked enthusiastic about 'Joe Avery,' as did the trombone player. Who was he? Elena wondered. The pianist was scratching his head, creating a new fall of dandruff.

"Well, just come on in when it starts to sound familiar," said Ray Lee, then nodded to his son. Bose leaned forward and put the sax to his mouth, opening low and slow. The banjo and bass immediately picked up a background beat. Three phrases in, Ray Lee lifted his trumpet and injected a staccato version of the tune. The trombone followed him with a mellow wailing, stuttering improvisation that delighted Elena. The second trumpet stopped playing and frowned, but Ray Lee nodded approvingly, raised his own horn, and blasted into a chorus that caught the others up.

When the song had ended, the professorial trumpet player said sternly to the trombonist, "Rafe, your solo was entirely contrary to every jazz theory this group has evolved." The man with the pony tail grinned unrepentantly.

"Say what?" Bose asked.

"Man didn't like the trombone riff," Ray Lee guessed.

"Yeah?" Bose turned to the trombonist. "For a white boy, you sounded cool to me, bro."

"Jus' jammin', man," said Ray Lee to the trumpet professor. "Gotta let it run."

"Oh, boy," Elena murmured into Lavender's ear. "I hope the white guys don't screw it up."

"Got three who're pretty good," said Lavender knowledgeably. "The bass doesn't look like much, but he plays OK. Banjo too, an' that boy on trombone, well, he's almost good enough to pair up with mah men."

Elena studied him. He looked a lot more cheerful as he worked that trombone slide under the lights. They were playing "Bill Bailey Won't You Please Come Home." Elena sighed happily into her coffee and sat back to listen.

25

The Ribbon/H.H.U. Jazz Band had been playing for almost an hour, getting better with every number. Even the second trumpet had loosened up. Thanks to Michael and his brandy, Elena was feeling pretty loose herself. She and Lavender Lee Ribbon had their heads together singing harmony on "Mood Indigo" when the first set ended and Ray Lee returned to the table with Bose.

"There's the problem with passing around alcohol here," said Elena to Michael. "Bose isn't supposed to be in bars."

Bose looked alarmed. "You gonna git the board to revoke mah parole? Mah daddy said this be a *coffee* place."

"No sweat," said Michael. "It's a private party, so that makes it OK. Who'd know better than a criminologist?"

"And you're the only one who'd snitch, Detective," said Mark.

Michael pulled out his brandy flask. "Have another nip, Elena, and take note that I'm not offering any to young Mr. Ribbon."

"Forget the brandy," said Lavender, moving away a seat.

Elena wondered if Analee's mother was angry because Elena had semi-threatened the freedom of her younger son.

"Ray Lee, you sit down right here," said Lavender. "Ah jus' found you a girl singer for your next set."

"Who?" asked Elena, taking a sip of her brandy-enhanced coffee.

146

"You, girl. You got a fine voice. You're gonna sing when they start up again."

"But I don't—"

"Do it," Mark Futrell mouthed from across the table. Michael wasn't paying attention.

Lavender turned to her husband. "Ah want to hear this girl singin' 'St. James Infirmary.' Got mah mind on Analee. You gotta sing 'St. James' for her, Detective."

Put that way, Elena didn't feel that she could refuse. And why not do it? She remembered every word of Analee's verse, and she'd sung with a rock group at college in Albuquerque, sung folk music and everything else in Chimayo, not to mention singing along with Ray Lee since she got those tapes. She'd do Analee's verse in "St. James Infirmary" and a little harmony on anything else. Sounded like fun. She nodded to Lavender, but when Mark gave her a thumbs up sign, she shifted uneasily in her chair.

"We'll do it," said Ray Lee. "You know, Detective, Ah been thinkin' 'bout some a the questions you asked me first time we met."

"Oh?" Elena sat up straight and made an effort to overcome the laid-back good cheer that had enveloped her.

"Ah 'member now that mah baby girl said—las' time we talked—she said the library was spookin' her. Felt like she was bein'—le's see—stalked. You 'member Analee sayin' that, Lavender?"

"Not to me, she didn't."

Stalked? Too bad Analee hadn't been more specific. Maybe she couldn't be. Not if it had been no more than an uneasy feeling.

The conversation became more general. Sarah came over to talk to the parents of her favorite student. Langston spotted Gus McGlenlevie standing at the pastry bar and went to chat with a fellow poet and share some bourbon. Elena stopped thinking about Analee being hunted through the corridors of that dark library and took time to wonder whether any of these people would be fit to drive home. Bose sulked over his coffee. Hard for him to pass up those tasty dollops of brandy, she imagined. She complimented him on a solo he'd played during "Tiger Rag."

Across the table the trombone player was talking to Mark Futrell about a 6K marathon they were going to run in the spring. Elena didn't think the trombonist looked like a marathon runner—too big a frame. And Mark was too muscular. Marathon runners were supposed to be skinny. "How come your brother isn't skinnier?" she asked Michael.

Michael muttered, "Don't tell me you're falling for Mark?"

Before she could deny it, Ray Lee said, "OK, little lady. We gonna start the second set." He took her arm.

"Where are you going?" asked Michael, but too late. Elena had already been tugged between the tightly packed tables to the musicians' circle.

Ray Lee said into the mike, "Got us another singer." He adjusted it down to her height.

"Don't do that," Elena protested, and her voice filled the room. She turned away from the microphone. "You're the lead singer. I'm just going to do backup."

"Not on 'St. James Infirmary,' honey. Anyway, Ah can bend down. What you gonna do? Stan' on one a them teetery lil chairs?"

Elena certainly didn't want to do that. They were hardly safe to sit on. She'd tried to stretch her legs and came close to falling off.

"I Ain't Got Nobody," Ray Lee told the musicians. Elena couldn't remember any lyrics except the title line. Maybe there weren't any more. Ray Lee and Bose lifted their instruments and started immediately. Feeling the brandy and the music, Elena swayed slowly with the song and snapped her fingers. When Ray Lee nodded to her, it seemed natural to belt out the line. He grinned and bent down to the microphone with exaggerated astonishment to question her declaration of loneliness, then turned to his son. Bose shook his head woefully at Elena. Laughing, improvising on the line, the three finished the song together with the trombone soaring behind them and the pianist running his fingers over the keyboard in variations while the banjo and bass provided background and the trumpet professor forgot to look for sheet music and just played—credibly.

Elena and Ray Lee went on to harmonize on "Just a Closer

Walk with Thee," "His Eye Is on the Sparrow," and "Precious Lord." She wished her mother could hear this. Harmony would have loved it. Why hadn't she thought to bring a tape recorder? Elena asked herself. Of course, she hadn't expected to sing, and once asked, she certainly hadn't expected to have so much fun. Ray Lee Ribbon was a big flirt—winking at her, leaning down to sing with his arm around her. If Grandmother Portillo had heard the three Protestant hymns, she'd have been horrified.

"Now one for mah baby girl, Analee," Ray Lee said, cutting into the applause. He nodded to Elena, and she swallowed hard. She didn't want to screw this one up.

And she didn't. When she'd finished singing Analee's verse about the high-heeled shoes, the white silk shroud, and a twenty-dollar gold piece, Lavender was weeping. Maybe that's what the woman had wanted, catharsis. Elena sang harmony when Ray Lee picked up the chorus.

At Bose's suggestion they ended the set with "When the Saints Go Marchin' In."

"Great voice," said the trombonist as Elena tossed her fringed shawl over one shoulder. "I'm Rafer Martin. You be interested in sitting in? We meet and jam every couple of weeks."

"I'm not employed by the university," said Elena regretfully. It sounded like fun. And he was cute, although she shouldn't be admiring some stranger when she was on a date with Michael.

"I know that." Martin put his trombone into a battered black case. "You're the cop who's investigating Analee's death." He picked the case up. "Analee was one great kid. Took physics from me her first year. Really smart."

"Physics?" Did physics professors wear pony tails? The only physicist she'd ever seen was some old guy who came to town to talk about atomic energy. He'd sounded like he wanted to incinerate the world.

"You got a problem with physics? I promise never to mention it if you'll join the group. Doesn't matter that you're not at the university."

"Do it," said Ray Lee. "A voice like yours shouldn't go to waste, honey."

"OK," said Elena. "Call me."

"Ah knew Analee," said the banjo picker. "Took four CS courses with her. She was the best."

Elena turned quickly and drew him into a hall that led to the rest rooms. "You knew her well?" He nodded. "Do you know why she needed money?"

"Ah didn't know she did," said the young man, who had introduced himself only as Rusty. "But she sure was jumpy—like worried. You know what Ah mean? An' that was a change for Analee."

"Since when?"

"Last few months."

"Did she say why?"

"Didn't say exactly, but maybe it was her boyfriend."

"Montrose?"

"Yeah, Park the Prick. Excuse mah French, ma'am."

"I'm not that old," Elena muttered.

"No, ma'am. Anyway, Analee, she told me she was gonna dump ole Park. Said he was into stuff she just couldn't put up with. Wouldn't say what. Ah thought kinky sex, but Ah'm not that sure he was gettin' any, not from Analee."

That's all Rusty could tell her, but Elena had things to think about. She was glad she'd come tonight, and not just because she'd been invited to join the jazz band. Analee had felt that she was being stalked. She had been desperate enough for money to take a job posing nude, but no one knew what she needed the money for. And she was going to dump L. Parker Montrose because he was into stuff she "couldn't put up with." What?

Having made her way through the maze of tables where people were getting ready to leave, she said to Ray Lee, "I'm glad you told me about Analee's feeling that she was being stalked. It may help."

"Jus' you catch the man who killed her," he replied.

Lavender stood up to give Elena a hug. "Ah knew it would do mah heart good to hear you sing that verse, honey," she said.

Elena sighed. She liked these people. If only she could give them the satisfaction of catching their daughter's killer. Maybe she was getting closer. Although none of it tied together yet, she was accumulating more and more information about the last few months of Analee's life.

26
..

Sunday, December 4, 10:15 P.M.

"I thought we agreed you'd catch a ride home with someone else," said Michael as they stood outside the coffeehouse.

"I don't see anyone offering," his twin retorted. "Anyway, the detective won't mind if I tag along, will you, Elena?"

In answer Elena tapped Sarah Tolland on the shoulder. "Are you and Zif going back to the faculty apartment house?" she asked.

Sarah looked surprised.

"Michael's brother needs a ride," Elena explained.

"You can come with me, Mark," Rafer Martin offered. He had just come through the door, trombone case in hand.

"I think I'm getting ditched," said Mark, grinning. He went off with Rafer Martin, waving to Elena, ignoring Michael.

"Does your brother always want to come along on your dates?" asked Elena once they were in Michael's car. "Can't he get his own?"

"Dozens," said Michael, "and no, he doesn't usually come on to my dates."

"I didn't say he was coming *on* to me."

"Well, he was," said Michael. "And how come you told Rafe Martin to call you?"

"Why not?" she asked, surprised.

"For one thing, he's married."

"So what? I wasn't telling him to call me for a date. Don't turn here. Keep going south and turn left at the Kerbey light."

152

She settled back, adjusting her seat belt. "I've been invited to join their jazz group."

"Do you have time for that?" Michael sounded sulky as he turned off his blinker and continued up Stanton Street.

"Seemed like a good idea to me," said Elena. She directed him through Kern Place.

"I'm never going to find my way back," he muttered.

"Don't tell me you came around on the interstate to pick me up? You ought to get to know the town better, learn the shortcuts. How long have you lived here?"

"This is my second year."

"Well." She laughed, feeling too cheerful to quarrel now that Mark was gone. "I guess I can give you another year before you have to pass the Elena-Jarvis-Finding-Your-Way-Around-Town test. Are you saying you think I shouldn't join the jazz group? Cross over a little to the left and head downhill. Is it because you don't like my voice?"

"Of course not," Michael protested. "I thought you were wonderful."

"Thanks." Elena was exhilarated; she thought that she'd sounded pretty good. "Everyone needs a hobby. Up to now, mine has been patching my house, and to tell you the truth, home repair isn't as much fun as singing Dixieland. Although the brandy may have had something to do with how much I enjoyed singing."

Michael grinned. "And here I was afraid you were going to arrest us all for illegal drinking."

They were laughing companionably when the motor died at the corner of Brown and Murchison. Michael looked discomfited. "Try it again," Elena suggested. He turned the key, but the car wouldn't start. "I thought you just had it fixed."

"I did, but it's a machine. They have a vendetta against me."

Elena opened her door and climbed out.

"Where are you going?"

"Flip your hood release," she said in answer.

"You're going to look at the engine?" He sounded amazed but did as she asked.

Once Elena had the hood up, she couldn't see a thing. "Do you have a flashlight?" she called.

"I think so. In the trunk."

"Turn on your emergency blinkers and bring me the flashlight."

"Do you know anything about cars?" he asked as he carried out her directions.

"After a childhood of aging pickups and secondhand appliances, I can fix anything," said Elena exuberantly, "except a computer." She ducked under the hood, shining the flashlight at various pieces of greasy auto innards. Near the radiator she found the problem. Here you go." She reattached a hose.

"What happened?"

"A hose fell off and triggered a sensor when you hit that pothole. Now get back in and try the engine."

Michael obeyed, and the car started. He set the brake and rushed around to open the door for her, which made Elena grin. Mechanics didn't usually get car doors opened for them by their customers.

Twenty-five minutes later, having taken every side street, they arrived at Elena's house.

"It's faster on the interstate," he remarked.

"Yeah, but look at all the neighborhoods you got to see," she replied. "You wouldn't see those from a highway."

"I didn't see anything. I was too worried about hitting one of those four million cars parked at the curbs."

"Come on in for a cup of coffee," she invited. "Well, actually we've had a lot of coffee, haven't we? How about a—" What did she have in the cupboard? "—liqueur?" Sarah had given her a bottle of Cointreau, which had been languishing, almost full, in the pantry since a dinner party cooked by Elena's mother in September.

Michael looked pleased. Elena, although she knew she had to be up early the next morning, was delighted when he accepted. She felt too wired to go to bed, so she'd just chum around with Michael for a while until she started to get sleepy. She handed him his liqueur in a mug decorated with red chiles.

Stalking, she thought as she sat down on the couch beside him. Had Analee had any *evidence* of stalking? Or had she simply been nervous because she was committing a crime via the library computer? Not that Elena knew for sure Analee had been a party to the computer fraud.

Before she could process any of the other information she'd accumulated that evening, Michael put down his liqueur, untasted, on the oak coffee table and wrapped his arm around Elena's shoulders. "We make a pretty good couple, don't you think?"

"Sure," she agreed.

"You're not really interested in Rafer Martin, are you?"

"What?"

"He *is* married. Even if his wife hates Los Santos and gives him hell all the time."

"I'm sorry to hear it." No wonder the guy looked so sad. Except when he was making music. "He plays a great trombone."

"But you and I have crime in common."

Elena laughed. "Now there's a romantic connection."

Michael kissed her. No little lip brushing this time. He seemed to be in earnest. Elena, who was feeling really good, kissed him back with enthusiasm. He groaned and slid his tongue into her mouth, his hand onto her breast. *My goodness,* she thought. *He's not as shy as he comes off.* She felt a stab of sharp pleasure and let things move along faster than she ordinarily would, certainly faster than she would have in the early months after her divorce from Frank, when she felt suspicious of all men.

Ten minutes later they were entwined on the sofa with her skirt riding up. Michael whispered, "I hope we're both headed in the same direction."

"We are if you've got a condom," she murmured breathlessly.

Michael went still.

"Well, for Pete's sake," she said, opening her eyes. "Surely you have one."

"Aren't you on the pill?"

"Why would I be? I haven't made love since my divorce." The disappointment and frustration spawned a decidedly cranky tone as she pointed out, "The pill only protects you against pregnancy."

"That's all it needs to do unless you think I've got some disease."

"I don't know who you've been sleeping with, Michael." Pushing him away, Elena sat up. "I guess this was a bad idea."

"Maybe so," Michael agreed.

Elena stood and shook out her skirt. It was wrinkled, and she'd have to press the damn thing before she could wear it again. "It's pretty late," she said, "and I go on duty at eight tomorrow morning."

"And I have a nine o'clock class, so I guess I'll say goodnight."

"Yeah, right." She strode to the front door and opened it. "Great evening," she muttered, knowing she didn't sound as if she meant it. Although it *had* been a great evening, right up to the time she discovered that he was contemplating something for which he was unprepared. "It's just as much the man's responsibility as it is the woman's, you know," she muttered. "Just because *you* can't get pregnant—"

"Look, I'm not arguing," said Michael. "I just didn't think—well, I wasn't expecting—"

"Right. Me either," said Elena. "And even if I had been, it takes a while to get back on the pill, and I don't know whether I want to."

"Well, that's certainly your option, but some women carry their own condoms."

"Head east and you'll find the interstate," she snapped.

"I'll do that." He disappeared into the darkness.

For just a minute Elena gleefully envisioned his car dying on him somewhere. He wouldn't know how to fix it. Then she slammed and locked the door and went into her bedroom to undress. Too bad Rafer Martin was married. She wouldn't mind taking up with him. But maybe he didn't believe in being prepared either.

So she wouldn't have to shower in the morning, she headed for the bathroom, and as the hot water beat down on her, she sang a lusty rendition of "The Saints." Then she stepped out, dried off, shrugged into a terry-cloth bathrobe, and went straight to the bedroom telephone, hoping that her ex wasn't on shift or undercover tonight.

"Hello," came a fuzzy voice at the other end of the line.

"Frank, this is Elena."

There was a pause. Then he exclaimed defensively, "Whatever happened, I didn't do it! I haven't given you any grief since your mother sicced that *curandera* on me."

"Right, but she also got you out of that fix, which I won't do unless you return my guitar."

"I don't have your guitar."

"Damn it, Frank, you've got it. You took it for spite after the *curandera* gave you that hallucinogen and you kissed the drug dealer down at headquarters."

"Don't remind me," Frank groaned. "I only kissed him because he looked like you."

"Thanks a lot." Elena could hear an aggrieved female voice in the background. "I want that guitar back, Frank. Just drop it by C.A.P. tomorrow morning. If it's not there, you'll think that mess with the *curandera* was a vacation in the Baja compared to what I'm going to do to you. Now get back to your lady friend."

"You jealous?" Frank asked.

"No way," she replied and hung up. And it was true. The man she'd been married to for six years was with another woman, and she couldn't care less.

Elena didn't bother with a nightgown or pajamas. She slipped naked under the covers and turned out the light, reasoning that her indifference meant she was over Frank once and for all. It was a nice thing to know. Even if she never saw Michael again, she still felt good about the evening because there was the jazz band to look forward to. If they called her.

She'd just snuggled down when the telephone rang. She picked it up and said, "Listen, Frank—"

"Who's Frank?"

"My ex. What do you want, Michael?"

"I just wanted to say I'm sorry for being such a jerk. I shouldn't have started anything I wasn't prepared to finish—I mean finish the right way. You know what I mean."

"Yes," said Elena.

"So, do you forgive me?"

"Sure."

"You're not saying that in a forgiving way, and I wanted to invite you to the Christmas Ball at the university."

"The one where they crown the Christmas Queen?" asked Elena, interest sparked.

"Well, yes, but they also have a multicourse dinner, champagne, and a good orchestra."

Elena thought how much she'd enjoy seeing Maggie Daguerre tramping up to be crowned Christmas Queen of Herbert Hobart University. Even if Maggie didn't win, she'd be a maid of honor or something, and just as furious about the whole thing. Michael would have to be guilty of something much worse than condom deficit for her to be willing to miss a social event with so much entertainment potential. "I'd love to go," she said sweetly.

"Great. Well, I'll say goodnight. I know you have to be up early."

"Uh-huh. Goodnight." She put the receiver down, delighted. She'd been irritated because he only asked her out at the last minute. Now he'd invited her to an important social event, and on a weekend. Of course, that meant she'd need a dress. Well, all right. She'd splurge and buy one. She doubted that Maggie would do the same.

27
..

Elena and Tey Vasquez sat in front of the vice president's desk like two chastised children in front of a schoolmaster. "Did you see the paper?" Harley Stanley demanded, holding up the morning edition. The headline read "H.H.U. Abortions Revealed."

"First a murder, then a vicious attack on our doctor, then a newspaper expose. And now this!" The vice president dropped the front page, picked up a flyer—black ink on red paper—and tossed it across the desk in Elena's direction. "It's the last straw. I want these crimes solved. Before the students leave." He passed a flyer to Vasquez. "Before the adverse publicity keeps parents from enrolling their children here."

Elena was reading. The handout listed by name all the H.H.U. coeds who had had abortions at the university clinic.

"Why has the LSPD assigned only one detective to this case? It's not that I don't have confidence in you, Detective Jarvis, but . . ."

Analee Ribbon's name was on the list. Now Elena didn't have to get an answer to *that* question. And she considered L. Parker Montrose an even better suspect than when she'd learned that his blood type matched that on the clip arm.

"Maybe if you had more help . . ."

According to the banjo player, Park the Prick was into things Analee couldn't tolerate, and she had intended to dump him. Perhaps because he'd insisted that she have an abortion.

159

What did the clinic charge for one? Was that why Analee needed money so badly she'd pose naked to get it? Because she was too proud or too angry to let Montrose pay for the abortion?

"And of course, I have confidence in you, too, Assistant Chief Vasquez. Chief Clabb speaks highly of you."

But *when* had Analee had the abortion? Had Montrose killed her after she said she was through with him? Or— Elena had another idea—had someone from L.S.A.R.I. killed Analee because she'd flouted their most sacred prohibition?

"We *have* to stop this terrible publicity. President Sunnydale called me about the newspaper story this morning."

The abortion list must have come from the clinic computer. How else could anyone get the names? And L.S.A.R.I. was the most likely culprit. The question was when the clinic files had been accessed. Briggs had hinted that Analee was to get the information, but she wouldn't have given him a list with her own name on it. However, they could have stolen the files before Analee's death, in which case they might have killed her. Or during the break-in that sent Dr. Marx to the hospital, in which case Analee was already dead when they found out about the abortion, and Montrose was the killer.

"Where did you get this flyer, sir?" asked Vasquez.

"Where?" The vice president sounded close to hysteria. "They're all over campus!"

"I'll put a stop to this," said Vasquez. He rose and left.

Harley Stanley sighed. "Maybe I was overanxious in asking for more personnel from the city police department. What do you think, Detective Jarvis?"

"We've got a lot of leads in this case, Dr. Stanley." Hit him now while he was scared. "One thing Lieutenant Daguerre and I discussed yesterday is the possibility—"

"Who?"

"Lieutenant Daguerre. She's undercover investigating the sale of H.H.U. diplomas."

"Oh, good gracious. I'd forgotten about that particular contretemps."

"Our cases may be connected."

"Do you think so?"

"Well, we won't know until we find out who's selling the

degrees. To that end, the lieutenant and I want to invite the people who bought the fake diplomas to a—say, an H.H.U. reception in their honor."

"Surely they wouldn't come."

"They seem to be extremely—well, stupid. Rich, but stupid. Or perhaps naive."

"Rich?"

"Very."

"I see." He fell into thought, then said, "By all means invite them. I'll call our Printing Department to authorize invitations and the University Catering Service to plan the event. Of course, President Sunnydale and I will want to be there."

"Actually, it might be better to invite them by phone for some early date. The sooner we can question them—"

"Tactfully."

"Right. —the better off we'll be. We want to solve these crimes before anyone else gets hurt or killed."

The vice president paled. "We'll be glad to pay for the calls and any other expenses. Rich, you say?"

"Yes, sir."

As soon as she left the vice president's office, Elena attempted to locate Vasquez. She couldn't, so she tried for Maggie, who was in class. Finally, proceeding on the hypothesis that the names of the girls who had had abortions *had* been obtained by the person who attacked the doctor, Elena began interviewing the men who guarded the entrances to the university. She found the one who had let the flyer distributor in. That guard had been on duty since six.

"I *saw* the flyers," he insisted. "They advertised a company that takes fashion pictures of students. The kid turned up on his bike just when I came on shift. He was one a those—what'd you call 'em? They look kinda lopsided and Chink."

Elena winced. There had been a Down's Syndrome child in Chimayo while she was growing up, the sweetest boy imaginable. "Could you go over to headquarters so the police artist can draw a picture from your description?"

"You're kiddin'? I thought they only did that stuff on TV."

"And in most city police departments."

"I get off at two."

"Can I schedule you for 2:30?"

"Sure."

Elena made the call from his booth and set up the appointment. The guard was so excited about his role in a TV-type situation that he was glad to let her continue using his telephone. As a result, while he was peering suspiciously into cars and vans, she located Maggie at the computer center and explained that the vice president had approved the reception for fake grads.

"That should be a blast," said Maggie. "I'll call them today. What date?"

"No date is too early if they'll accept," Elena replied. "Can I come over to talk to you?"

"Why?" asked Maggie suspiciously.

"I had another idea."

"Does it mean more work?"

"Sort of, but I'll bet refreshments come with it."

"What kind?"

"Give me ten minutes."

In the allotted ten minutes, Elena talked Maggie into becoming L.S.A.R.I.'s newest recruit from Herbert Hobart. "Just emphasize your Catholicism. Tell them how shocked you were by the flyer."

"What flyer?"

Elena showed it to her. "It has to be the guy who broke into the clinic and the clinic computer, then hit the doctor with a statue."

"So what am I supposed to do if I get accepted?"

"I want you to attend their meeting. Look for a stocky guy who can jump over a counter, who's bald or wearing a wig, and who knows something about computers. You computer people always find each other. It ought to be a cinch."

"Listen, I don't want to hang out with a bunch of—"

"Don't forget, I got your reception approved."

"Right. Now *that* should be fun."

Elena stared at her.

"OK." Maggie sighed. "How do I join?"

"Call Ora Mae Spotwood." Elena thumbed through her notebook and provided the telephone number.

28
..

Monday, December 5, 11:35 A.M.

Because Dr. Marx was unavailable, Elena ran down L. Parker Montrose and dragged him away from his *salade niçoise* to ask if the baby Analee aborted had been his.

Uncertainly flashed in his eyes. "Of course," he said, fists clenched. "Who else's?"

"Analee told you she was pregnant?"

He hesitated, then said, "She knew we couldn't get married. She was being considerate by—"

"You couldn't get married because of your parents?"

"Because we were still in school."

"Then why not use birth control?"

"Condoms don't always work," he replied defensively. "That happened to me once. My dad had to—well—"

"Pay off the girl?" Elena stared at him thoughtfully. He was nervous, upset, and lying. She just wasn't sure what about. Was he afraid the baby *hadn't* been his? Or upset because Analee hadn't told him? Or afraid Elena would find out that Analee *had* told him? Elena decided that even if he were telling the truth, she wouldn't know whether to believe him. But Analee's friends at UTLS might know about the abortion and the father. Maybe Analee had been pregnant by someone else, who killed her because of it, not realizing she'd had an abortion—or *because* she'd had an abortion.

Elena drove down the mountain into a haze of pollution, hoping a wind would come up and blow it away, preferably

163

before she got to the state university. Inversion layers were not one of her favorite characteristics of life in Los Santos. Off and on all winter, they locked pollution in a brown haze over the foothills and the Rio Grande Valley, a curse from the automotive gods.

She caught Rhino leaving a kinesiology class.

"Ah don't see why Ah gotta know how mah muscles work," he muttered, "jus' so long as they do."

"Maybe you'll have to teach it someday."

"Ah ain't gonna be no teacher."

"Well, you might be a coach. After you retire from the pros."

"A coach?" He looked at the book clutched in one huge hand. "This book help me be a coach?"

"Probably. You'll have to read it to find out."

"Ah guess."

Elena caught his arm to keep him from walking off. "I wanted to ask if you ever talked to Analee about an abortion."

Rhino stopped. "Who havin' it?"

"Her."

"She never had no abortion. That white boy she datin' git her in trouble an' kill her 'cause—"

"There's a rumor that she had an abortion."

"Ah don't think she even fuckin' him. Her sister big on not doin' no irre—irresponsible fuckin'. Analee wouldn'a been gittin' it on with him. If he say so, he a liar. Maybe he kill her 'cause she wouldn't."

"Maybe. Thanks, Rhino."

"He kill her?"

Elena sighed. "I'm still investigating."

"You find out, you tell me."

Not till the killer's safely in jail, she thought. Rhino didn't need to go on any vendettas. He had his own problems. "How you doing? Hanging in there?"

"Ah 'memberin' what you said. Got a new tutor. Ain't the same, but Ah say, 'Rhino, think what Analee be wantin'. Sure wish Ah hadn't been shootin' craps that night, though."

"There's no use sweating it, Rhino. It wouldn't have saved her if you'd been fast asleep in bed." Elena patted his arm and went off to talk to Ahmed, but he was out of town playing basketball, so she drove to Sierra Medical Center and visited Dr. Marx.

"How's your head?" Elena asked.

"Well, I'm not seeing two of you today," Greta Marx replied. "Have you found the bastard who hit me?"

"No, but I think you were right about it being a pro-lifer."

"They're not pro-lifers. If they were, they wouldn't be injuring and killing people they disagree with."

Elena couldn't argue with that.

"So why have you decided I'm right about L.S.A.R.I?"

Elena handed her the flyer and immediately discovered that Greta Marx had an impressive repertoire of insults. When she finally finished her remarks on the ancestry of the man who had invaded her computer, she exclaimed, "It's a crime!"

Elena agreed. "Breaking and entering, assault with a—I guess you could call that statue a deadly weapon."

"Of course it is. It's already killed one person."

"Theft of computer files. All felonies. Did you notice Analee's name on the list?"

"She didn't have an abortion."

"Then why was her name there?"

"Same as several of the others, girls who had D&Cs. The stupid, vicious, thieving bastard must have run a search for gynecological procedures and thought D&C was a euphemism for abortion," said the doctor in disgust.

Elena thanked Dr. Marx and went to headquarters to see if the H.H.U. gate guard had managed, with the help of the police artist, to produce a sketch. While there, she picked up a list of private facilities for the mentally retarded and teachers who taught special ed in the public schools.

Using the sketch and the guard's estimate that the kid was about five-five or five-six, Elena made telephone calls from her cubicle until she found a principal in a special school who said her description sounded like Hughie Remman. "But Hughie couldn't be in trouble with the police. He's a fine boy, well adjusted." Elena assured the principal that Hughie wasn't in trouble. Since the boy was in school until 4:30, she interviewed him there.

Hughie climbed happily into Elena's car with the principal as chaperone—just in case Elena was a child molester posing

as a policewoman, she supposed. Following the boy's confusing directions, they cruised until he'd identified his own
house, several blocks from H.H.U. Then he pointed out the
playground of the elementary school where he'd been riding
his bike on Sunday when a "nice man" offered him money to
come back early the next morning to distribute flyers on the
H.H.U. campus. Finally they saw the place where his mommy
had sat in her car to be sure nothing bad happened to Hughie
during his first job. Mommy hadn't wanted him to work for
a stranger, but he'd cried when he thought he wasn't going to
get the money. Did Elena want to see it? It was bigger and
prettier than pennies.

Elena did, and Hughie showed her five silver dollars, which
he counted, very slowly, so she'd know that there really were
five. Then he beamed at the principal, who nodded approvingly
from the back seat. What did the man look like? Elena asked.
"Old," said Hughie. "Like Muncie, the clown. Like Muncie's
hair." The principal explained that the school employed a
red-headed clown for birthday parties.

Had to be a guy wearing a wig, Elena decided, if he looked
like he was wearing clown hair. And how old was old to a kid
whose mental age was three or four? No way of telling.
Hughie couldn't read, so he didn't know what the flyers were
about, but they were red, like the nice man's hair, and there
was a special one for the man in the little house. The entrance
guard, Elena presumed.

Although she showed Hughie her badge, which he fingered
admiringly, let him put the siren on the roof of her unmarked
police car and turn it on, and offered him a ten-dollar bill for
his five silver dollars, Hughie refused to trade because *his*
dollars were pretty and he'd earned them from his first job.
He liked showing them to his friends Min and Benny and
Andy and . . . Elena figured that by the time she got a court
order to dust the coins for prints, Hughie would have handled
off all but his own. Anyway, someone other than the man who
attacked Dr. Marx might have arranged to have the stolen
medical information distributed. Picking a retarded kid was a
smart if cynical move.

At 4:30, half an hour after Elena should have gone off shift, she called Maggie Daguerre. "I've got all kinds of news," said Maggie.

"Do I need to come over there?"

"I don't see why. First, I'm going to a L.S.A.R.I. covered-dish dinner at six."

"Great. That was fast."

"Yeah. Ora Mae Spotwood thinks it's 'really exciting' that I want to join. She can hardly believe Analee had an abortion. Says the poor girl probably joined L.S.A.R.I. because she was eaten up with guilt."

"If they're all that forgiving, maybe they didn't kill Analee," Elena mused. "But Ora Mae knew about the flyer?"

"Uh-huh. She says she found it in her mailbox. So did a bunch of other members."

"Oh, shit," said Elena. "They're not admitting they printed and distributed it."

"Nope."

"Anyway, Analee didn't have an abortion," said Elena. "It was a D&C. But you can keep that to yourself."

"Why?"

"Because you wouldn't have any way of knowing it, and because it'll be interesting to see what the other members say about the abortion. The kid who distributed the flyers told me the man who paid him was old and red-headed, but the kid's retarded; he may think old is thirty-two."

"Some days *I* think it is," Maggie replied dryly.

"And the red hair was probably a wig. So what other news do you have for me?"

"Well, I've already got ten acceptances from fake grads for the reception in their honor. What a bunch of flakes! You wouldn't believe these people. Number three, Happy Hobart's been on my case again."

"About your campaign?" Elena grinned.

"That and this great new moneymaking scheme he has. A computer safe-sex dating service. When he found out I worked at the computer center, he decided to let me in on the ground floor. He thinks we'll make millions."

"Safe-sex computer dating?" asked Elena dubiously. "Is that like phone sex? I guess if you get your kicks by computer, you're in no danger of diseases or—"

"No, dummy. The clients are all tested. Then those who are clean get matched up by computer."

"Right."

"Don't you see? He's into computer businesses. Maybe he originated the diploma scam. I'm going to invite him to the fake-grad reception, see if any of them know him. Someone has to be the contact man among the rich and dumb. It wouldn't have been Analee. Or Montrose. He wasn't in on it last year unless he has bank accounts I didn't access."

"Great work, Maggie!" Was Happy the killer?"

"Yeah. I'm really getting into this detecting stuff."

"I can see that. How're the party plans coming?"

"Don't ask me. Some woman in University Catering's all excited about food with unpronounceable names, and the Guest House is getting ready to put up everyone who accepts."

"Good. Any other news?" There wasn't. "Well, have fun at the covered-dish dinner."

"It's bound to be better than the dorm dining room. *They're* having beef Wellington tonight. Do you know what that is? Melody told me. It's a steak plastered with mashed chicken livers and cooked in a pie, for Christ's sake. At least at a covered-dish dinner, you know you're gonna get some regular stuff."

"Call me tonight after the meeting. And Maggie, be careful. Someone in that group is dangerous," Elena warned.

"Good. I feel like punching someone. Spending time with Melody, especially while I'm eating, does that to me."

29

Elena sat on her bed, brushing her dark hair in long, sweeping strokes. In the living room she had one of Ray Lee's tapes playing and had been singing along to "Tiger Rag." Since the lyrics consisted of one three-word sentence, she'd devoted herself to seeing how many variations in harmony she could come up with.

Before "Tiger Rag," she'd spent an hour playing the guitar she'd found propped against the wall of her cubicle at headquarters. Getting tough with Frank last night had worked, but no amount of newfound enthusiasm for Dixieland seemed to transfer to her guitar. She had been thinking of going to bed when the phone rang.

"You still up?" Maggie asked.

"Just barely. How was the L.S.A.R.I. meeting?" Elena carried the portable telephone with her as she went to turn off the music. Ray Lee had moved from "Tiger Rag" to "St. Louis Blues."

"Interesting. I'm calling from the computer center 'cause Melody keeps walking in on me at the dorm. Yesterday I figured I'd break her of it by walking in on *her*, but that was a mistake. She and some guy were right in the middle of satisfying her feminist right to pleasurable sex. She thought it was hilarious when I bolted."

"Charming girl," said Elena. "What about the meeting?"

"Right, the meeting. Well, they bought my story about

169

being a good Catholic girl shocked to see that list of coeds who'd had abortions. Except that damn Sister Gertrudis Gregory asked me when I'd last been to confession, and if I was ready to go to jail for the pope. Hell, I wouldn't go around the corner for the pope."

"Maggie!"

"Then there was dinner. I bought a dozen tamales on my way over, which they thought was real nice because I'm a penniless scholarship student."

Elena sighed. Obviously Maggie didn't intend to get to the point until she was good and ready. In fact, she seemed to be enjoying the delay. Elena curled up on the sofa, its upholstery woven by her mother in a stylized desert-mountain pattern.

"And just like I thought, the food was great. I ate about half a pound of barbecued brisket and a tub of scalloped potatoes and cole slaw. Drank a lot of iced tea. No beer, unfortunately. Ora Mae said to me, 'You poor dear, you must be starving at that university,' and I said, 'They give us plenty to eat, but it's that fancy stuff that makes gas.' Ora Mae looked shocked." Maggie laughed. "Probably no one's ever mentioned gas in her presence."

Elena tucked the phone between her ear and shoulder and began to rebraid her hair.

"You still there?" asked Maggie.

"Sure. I'm waiting to hear what they had for dessert."

"Do I detect a note of impatience?"

"Not at all," Elena responded dryly. She finished the braid, returned to the bedroom, and slipped under the covers.

"What's that buzzing? Is your phone tapped?"

"The antenna just hit the headboard," Elena replied.

"In other words, hurry up so you can get to sleep. OK. The meeting. Father Bratslowski was ecstatic about the flap over the abortion flyers and called for God's blessing on the brave person who did it. Not a word about who that was."

Evidently the priest didn't consider medical records confidential unless he approved of the treatment, Elena thought grimly.

"The vice president, a guy named Chester Briggs, said he hoped the members noticed that Analee Ribbon was on that list, and that he'd heard from his own sources at the university that she'd been working for the Feminist Coalition."

What sources? Elena wondered. If Briggs took Analee for a traitor to his cause, he might have killed her. The anti-abortionists killed doctors, even receptionists at the clinics; they might kill to keep their plans secret.

"Then he said it shouldn't surprise anyone to hear that Analee was promiscuous. Lots of blacks were promiscuous. I mean, that guy's a *bigot*."

Elena had thought so too. He'd probably been suspicious of Analee from the beginning.

"Then Ora Mae Spotwood got all huffy and said if Analee got in trouble, it was because someone took advantage of her, and she—that's Ora Mae—didn't believe Analee had had an abortion. And furthermore, she didn't believe in violence—they were a pro-life group, after all—and she certainly hoped none of their people was responsible for the injury to Dr. Greta Marx. And she thought what they needed to do was attack the problem at the source, fornication. They needed to promote chastity, because chaste women didn't *need* abortions. And if they did it that way, their members wouldn't get arrested."

Good for Ora Mae, thought Elena. Nothing wrong with advocating chastity, unless you went around killing the unchaste.

"Sister Gertrudis Gregory said she was willing to go to jail for the cause; in fact, she *was* going to jail, and planned to use the opportunity to proselytize women in prison."

Sooner or later the nun would exhaust her appeals and have to serve her sentence. Elena could imagine riots among female prisoners who didn't want to be incarcerated with Sister Gertrudis Gregory.

"Then Chester Briggs said women had to be stopped from killing their babies. Period. A couple of people said if he felt so strongly about it, how come he wasn't at the demonstration that got some of them arrested. After that the argument got sort of nasty until Ora Mae said she'd just had an inspiration, which was that they should have a torchlight parade at H.H.U. in support of chastity."

Poor Chief Clabb, thought Elena. That's all he needed.

"So they discussed that for a while. Some lawyer said as long as they stayed away from the clinic, they couldn't get busted for anything worse than trespassing, maybe disturbing the peace, which was no big deal. It got pretty boring, and they didn't agree on anything."

Good, thought Elena. If they couldn't agree, the parade wouldn't get off the ground. "Be sure to tell me if they set a date."

"Will do. Then Father Bratslowski said a prayer about how God loved the unborn and hated abortion, and we all had coffee and cake while a bunch of the men tried to hit on me; and their wives, if the guys were married, glared; and Ora Mae stayed glued to my side, introducing me to everybody and, I think, protecting my virtue; and Father Bratslowski insisted that I come to his church next Sunday, which is way the hell down the Lower Valley. You still listening?"

"Avidly," said Elena, imagining the effect of voluptuous Maggie on all those moral-majority types—testosterone competing with self-righteousness in an epidemic of hypocrisy.

"Good. I think the most important thing was this Chester Briggs. He made a point *not* to get introduced to me. In fact, when Ora Mae dragged me in his direction, he left. With a piece of cake in his hand. And he's bald and burly. After he was gone, I asked around about him. And get this: he owns a computer repair business, and he's a bodybuilder. So number one, I figure since he's bald, he could be the guy with the wig who hit the doctor and hired the retarded kid to distribute the flyers."

"Different colored wigs," mused Elena, "but you could be right."

"Two, a bodybuilder would be strong enough to push the statue over on Analee Ribbon, and he knew she was an infiltrator. Three, he knows computers. He could have gotten through the doctor's security to retrieve those patient files, and he could have printed up the flyers."

"And four, I didn't like him either," said Elena, instincts abuzz with the possibilities offered by Chester Briggs, remembering that he'd brought flyers to Ora Mae.

"You know him?"

"Met him briefly at the Spotwood house. Maggie, you ought to get a medal!"

"Great. Suggest it to my captain. I wonder if Briggs was part of the diploma scam."

"Anything's possible," said Elena. Chester Briggs! she thought with elation. If he was guilty of everything—the diploma scam, the killing of Analee, the attack on the doctor—well, he could be the explanation for Analee's fear and her death. But not for her financial desperation or the money in and out of her bank account. Elena frowned.

"Anyway, I gotta hang up and call California, issue more invitations to fake grads. Lucky you; you get to go to bed."

"I'm in bed." Before she slept, Elena decided that tomorrow she'd get the L.S.A.R.I. membership list and start checking alibis for the night of Analee's death and the night of the clinic break-in. Tey Vasquez could help. The man was just spinning his wheels on the drug-dealing angle. Maybe they could tie it up tomorrow. Nail Chester the Bigot.

30

Tuesday, December 6, 8:30 A.M.

Elena stopped by the Spotwood house. Because of the attack on Dr. Greta Marx and the distribution of abortion flyers, she requested a L.S.A.R.I. membership list so the police could check individual whereabouts the night of the break-in at the clinic.

"Our people wouldn't do anything so violent," Mrs. Spotwood protested, "and I don't see why I should give you the names." Elena had caught her in a housecoat, bouffant hair wrapped in toilet tissue to protect it while she slept. What a sight!

"I can get a court order," said Elena, "but if you're all innocent, you shouldn't mind cooperating."

"Los Santoans Against Rampant Immorality has nothing to hide, but we do have civil rights."

"You do indeed. I'll get the warrant." Elena smiled. "Then I'll call the TV stations so they can film me when I serve it."

Ora Mae glared at her and, muttering under her breath, rummaged in a rolltop desk. "We're all law-abiding citizens," she declared, handing the list to Elena, "people who are asleep in their beds in the middle of the night. Like Mr. Spotwood and me."

"You told me about the night Analee Ribbon died. Were you in bed with Mr. Spotwood the night Dr. Marx was attacked?"

Ora Mae Spotwood nodded, tears filling her eyes. "I still can't believe Analee is dead. Or that she had an abortion."

"She didn't," said Elena, relenting. No point in keeping that information secret now that Maggie had heard the initial reaction. "She had a D&C."

Mrs. Spotwood frowned. "But isn't that—"

"For some female problem. Heavy periods, I think the doctor said."

"What a relief." Mrs. Spotwood smiled through evaporating tears. "I must tell the membership. I can't bear for them to think badly of such a lovely girl. Do you know she actually made her mother's cornbread recipe for one of our buffets? Did it in a toaster oven at her dormitory."

I'll bet, thought Elena. Analee had probably bought her contribution, as Maggie had done. Elena took the list to the university police station, where Vasquez, looking grumpy, awaited her. Lazy, she thought. He didn't want to make all those calls, which he confirmed by sighing heavily, taking the list from her hand, and detaching one-third of the pages. "Might as well get going," he muttered.

Elena wasn't pleased when she saw her portion didn't include Chester Briggs. She told Vasquez to be particularly nosy about Briggs.

"Why him?"

"Because, Tey, I think he's the one who hit the doctor and stole the medical records. He may even have been the one who killed Analee."

"Why do you think that?"

Irritated, Elena explained Maggie's discoveries, that Briggs was a bodybuilder and computer expert, and her reasoning on the basis of those facts.

"Flimsy," said Vasquez and went into his office.

"Better than phantom drug dealers," Elena muttered, wondering if Tey would take off his dark glasses so he could see the names. She appropriated Chief Clabb's desk, since he'd be attending meetings all morning, and went to work.

By noon she'd called everyone on her two-thirds of the list, written down their alibis, and starred those she wanted to check out. By then Vasquez had disappeared, leaving his annotated list with the receptionist. Thoroughly irritated with

him, Elena read over the alibis and found them mundane.
Beside Briggs's name Vasquez had written: "Briggs out on
business call. Lives with sister, V. Robles. V.R. says B.
always home in bed at 11, up at 7." Elena gritted her teeth,
wrote down the suspect's address, and set out to visit "V.R."
and quiz her about "B.'s" whereabouts on the night of the
clinic break-in. She didn't consider "always home in bed at
11" good enough for a suspect with Briggs's potential.

The small, flat-roofed Briggs/Robles adobe in the Upper
Valley had an overabundance of untrimmed shrubbery, an
unpaved driveway, and the street was full of potholes. A
short, wispy creature answered the door, her gray hair frizzed
close to her skull in an amateur permanent. Behind her, a
vacuum cleaner and a television talk show buzzed.

"V. Robles?" Elena asked.

The woman nodded. "I'm Mrs. Verna Robles, and I don't
want to buy anything—not magazines, not—"

Elena flashed her badge, introduced herself, and Mrs.
Robles burst into tears, catching Elena by surprise. The
brother seemed to be absent. No car or truck stood in the
driveway or under the carport.

"Ma'am, are you all right?" Elena asked.

Mrs. Robles' face was bright red under the tears. "You're
here because I lied about Chester when that other officer
called, aren't you?"

"Yes ma'am," Elena agreed, knowing an opportunity when
she was handed one.

The woman's narrow shoulders slumped, and she stepped
back to let Elena in. Then she turned off the vacuum cleaner
but forgot the television which provided a background to their
conversation. Elena and Mrs. Robles sat down on a squashy
sofa with an ill-fitting, faded, autumn-leaf slipcover.

"Chester acted like he was home," said Mrs. Robles and
blew her nose on a tissue taken from a box on a mahogany
end table. It also held several *Reader's Digest* condensed
novels between bookends that were half-busts of the Reverend Jimmy Swaggert. "He went to bed at eleven."

"Which of the nights was this?" asked Elena gently.

"Friday."

The night Dr. Marx was attacked.

"And I went to bed."

"But you heard him go out later?"

"Oh, no. I'm a heavy sleeper." She blew her nose again. "It's not that I want to keep Chester to myself," she explained earnestly. "My late husband's insurance is more than enough for me to live on, but Chester insisted on moving in with me when John died. Chester doesn't think women should live alone. But I wouldn't mind if he found someone. In fact, I've always hoped my little brother would marry. But, poor boy, he started to lose his hair when he was eighteen—"

"About Friday night, Mrs. Robles—"

"—and went completely bald by the time he was twenty-two. It's hard for a man to get dates when he's completely bald. And that young. There's no hope that the hair will stop falling out when there isn't any left."

"I can see that," said Elena, resigning herself to letting Verna Robles tell the story in her own way, although what Chester Briggs's hair loss had to do with the attack on Greta Marx, Elena couldn't imagine—except that he'd been wearing a wig. "He could get a hairpiece," Elena suggested craftily.

"Just what I said."

"So did he?"

"Wouldn't stoop to such foolishness. His very words."

"Ah." Elena settled back against a lumpy, embroidered pillow.

"So I'd have been delighted to know that he was going out with some nice girl."

Had he snuck out to rifle Dr. Marx's computer, found his sister up when he got home, and said he'd had a date?

"But it can't be a nice girl if he won't even mention her, if he has to sneak out in the middle of the night. It has to be some loose woman he's ashamed of." Verna Robles shed a few more tears. "And Chester's such a force in the movement against sexual immorality and abortion. What would they say if they knew he's associating with loose women?"

"How do you know he is, Mrs. Robles?" asked Elena.

"His shirt. I found it when I collected the wash Saturday morning. *Two* shirts from Friday. The one he wore to work and the one with lipstick and perfume."

"How did your brother explain the second shirt?"

"I haven't asked him." More tears spilled over. "I know I should, but I just can't bear to."

"Have you washed the shirt?" asked Elena.

Mrs. Robles shook her head.

"In that case, I'm afraid I'll have to take it with me. Of course, if you insist, I can get a warrant—"

Mrs. Robles turned pale. "What's he done?"

"I'm not at liberty to say at this time, ma'am."

Verna rose, looking apprehensive. "Well, I suppose I have no choice."

She did, of course, but Elena didn't feel obligated to say more. Impulsively she called, "I'll need a picture, too." To show to Greta Marx. It didn't hurt to ask, and Mrs. Robles didn't think to refuse, although she pointed out that she could only provide pictures of Chester when he still had hair. He'd never allowed any taken after he was twenty-one.

"How old is Chester now?" Elena asked.

"Thirty-nine."

Elena accepted a photograph of Chester with hair on the sides of his head but little on top, took the shirt, studied the lipstick marks on the front, sniffed the perfume that clung to the fibers, and carried her trophies away, leaving Mrs. Robles lamenting the wages of sin as they applied to association with loose women and poor Chester, who couldn't be blamed too much. If he hadn't lost every last strand of hair, he'd probably have married a nice girl by now.

Elena mused on exactly what Mrs. Robles thought the police were pursuing her brother for. In most cases, association with loose women wasn't a crime, not unless you paid for their attentions, pursued them too forcefully when they weren't interested, or committed lewd acts with them in public.

Of course, she didn't mention any of that to Mrs. Robles. Elena just wanted to get the shirt and the picture over to Dr. Marx, who was still at Sierra Medical Center. The shirt, a black and white plaid flannel number, ought to ring some bells with the victim if Chester Briggs was the man who'd hit her.

31
##

From the potholes in the Upper Valley to the traffic on North Mesa, Elena fumed her way to Sierra Medical Center, furious with Vasquez for not pressing Briggs's sister. Dr. Greta Marx, wearing a hospital gown, was lying flat on her back and scowling at the ceiling while a nurse took her blood pressure. Elena showed Greta the black and white flannel shirt, and the doctor said, "You found him."

"I found his shirt. It's got lipstick and even a whiff of perfume on it. Can you identify them?"

The doctor sniffed. "White Linen," she said. "That's my perfume, and the smear looks like Autumn Plum, my lipstick. Must have rubbed off during the struggle." She couldn't identify the picture with certainty.

Elena went from the hospital to court, where she spent the rest of the afternoon getting a warrant to search the house and business of Chester Briggs. Then, while she ate at Big Burger Bayou downtown, she thought about doing the search on her own. From a pay phone she called Leo Weizell, her old partner, to see if he'd returned from Cancun. He had, but protested that he wasn't due back to work until Thursday. Elena explained the situation.

"Damned fanatics," Leo muttered and agreed to go with her. "We're looking for what? Wigs? Flyers with the names of girls who've had abortions? Where do you want to start?"

"His office," said Elena. "It's a computer systems and

179

repair business. Maybe he printed the flyers there. In fact, maybe we can find the files he stole." Elena thought about it. "We need Daguerre," she decided. "I'll try to get her, too. Meet you there at"—she glanced at her watch, gave herself forty-five minutes—"seven."

Next Elena called Maggie, whose initial resistance to expending any more time on Elena's case evaporated when Elena suggested that the warrant would provide an opportunity to snoop in Briggs's computers and see if he was connected to the diploma scam. Maggie agreed to meet them at the Westside industrial park where Briggs had an office and warehouse.

Elena's last call was to Tey Vasquez. "I told you to pay particular attention to Briggs," she snarled. "And what did you do? Let his sister tell you he was in bed asleep."

"Well, wasn't he?" Vasquez demanded.

"No, he wasn't. Of all the alibis that needed to be followed up, his was the one. You don't just accept the word of someone's sister that he's innocent. You go out and look her in the eye. Push her. See if she's lying."

"So *you* went to see her," said Vasquez, sounding petulant.

"Damn right I did."

"How come you didn't tell me you were going?"

"Why would I? You keep saying you don't have any jurisdiction except at H.H.U."

"Well, I just meant I couldn't go invading the other university's territory. It wouldn't be—professional."

"Anyway, you snuck off this morning."

"I went to *lunch*. What are you going to do now?"

"I'm going to search his house and business."

"He's agreed?"

"He doesn't have to. I've got a warrant."

"I'll go with you."

"You don't have any jurisdiction."

"Well, I'm not letting you go by yourself."

"I'm taking my old partner, Leo Weizell. He's as trustworthy a backup as any cop could ask for."

"You're saying I'm not?"

"I'm not saying anything about you, Tey, except that you're careless."

"Well, I don't want you thinking I'm not doing my share. Let me come along."

"Fine," she snapped. "Seven at the Dominguez Industrial Park."

"What about his house?"

"We'll cover the office first."

"Hey, it's already 6:35. You're not giving me much time to get there."

"So you'll be late."

When Elena arrived at the park, Leo was talking to the night guard.

"Hey, kiddo, great to see you." Leo gave her a hug. "Couldn't get along without me, right?"

"Right," said Elena. "You're irreplaceable." She really was glad to see him. "How was Mexico?"

"Terrific. Concepcion loved it."

"She stopped throwing up?"

"Sure has. Now she's walking around with this smug glow, as if she's the first woman who's ever been pregnant. Me, I'm gettin' scared. The doctor says we could be havin' more than one. I told him I didn't have more than one sperm, but he said, like I was some idiot, "Detective Weizell, there's hardly a man alive who doesn't have more than one sperm.""

"Who's she?" the guard broke in. He'd been staring from one to the other as they talked.

"Oh, sorry, Carl. This is Detective Jarvis."

"A *woman*?"

"Last time I looked." Grinning, Leo ogled Elena. "Definitely a woman. And a woman with a warrant. Show it to him, babe. This is Carl Metzger."

"Miz Jarvis." The guard tipped his hat and accepted the warrant Elena had pulled from her shoulder bag. "Looks OK to me," he said after studying it. "Shouldn't I call Mr. Briggs to tell him you're goin' through his place?"

"No," said Elena. "If he's got something incriminating at home, he'd have a chance to hide it if he knows we're searching." Of course, his sister might have warned him by now. Elena was hoping that Verna Robles would be afraid to admit to her brother that she'd been indiscreet. "What are your shift hours, Mr. Metzger?" Elena asked.

"Noon to eight. I'm about to go off duty."

"Have you seen Mr. Briggs today?"

"Sure have. Came in same time I did, left fifteen minutes later, grumblin' about rush orders an' how this one might make him late for dinner."

Great. That meant Verna couldn't call him about her cooperation with the police unless Briggs had a car phone.

"Here's Maggie!" said Leo as a yellow VW Rabbit pulled into the lot. Maggie unfolded herself from the front seat and emerged wearing a pea jacket, jeans, and a knit cap.

"No ski mask?" Elena murmured to her. "You look like a cat burglar."

"It's your unfortunate influence on me," Maggie retorted.

After the introductions, Elena asked the guard if Mr. Briggs ever came back to work at night.

"Not since I been here," the guard replied, "an' I've had this job goin' on two years. Course, I don't always work the late shift. Like now, I'm on noon to eight. Hope my replacement shows up timely. Wife holds dinner an' gets mad as hell if I'm late."

"We ready to go in?" asked Leo.

"Vasquez is supposed to meet us here."

"Who?"

"H.H.U. police. Let him in and send him on down to Briggs's place, will you, Mr. Metzger?" she asked the guard.

"If I'm here. What's that name?"

"Eleuterio Vasquez."

The guard wrote it down, then walked along a row of offices and let them into the premises of Briggs Computer Services, Inc.

Maggie immediately went to the first of four desk-top PCs to search for files. "Fairly simple security," she murmured. Elena and Leo searched drawers and boxes, looking for any sign of the flyer listing the coeds who had had abortions. Tey Vasquez turned up about twenty minutes later and wandered around, hands in pockets, looking at one thing, then another.

"Why don't you watch out front," Elena suggested. "If the guard called Briggs, we want to know when he's coming in."

Vasquez laughed. "You think some computer type's going to be carrying a gun?"

"I am," said Maggie, glancing up at him with a smile, "and I'm a computer type."

Vasquez grinned back at her, settled his dark glasses more securely, and drawled, "Honey, you'd look good carrying an Uzi." Then to Elena, he said, "Why don't I search the back room?"

"Suit yourself." Elena lifted a box marked "Brazos Pinfold Computer Paper" from a pile of such boxes and pulled the flaps loose.

"Found a hidden file," said Maggie.

Leo and Elena looked up.

"Hold on." Maggie tapped more keys. "Got it. That your list?"

Elena rose and went to look. "That's it," she said exultantly. "Can you print it out?"

"Can do." Maggie hit the printer button, and a dot matrix printer began to grind out the flyer text.

"This box has red paper," said Leo, "but there's nothing printed on it."

"When you get through with that file, Maggie, see if you can find his financial records. We want to know if he's tied to your computer scam."

Elena was leaning over Maggie's shoulder when a voice from outside shouted, "Call 911. Someone's broken into my place." Then a burly man in a ski jacket and cowboy hat burst through the door, gun in hand. He shot at Leo, then dodged behind a desk. Leo yelped and went down. Maggie dived one way and Elena the other, terrified that Leo had been hit seriously.

"Police!" Elena shouted. "Throw down your gun!" Had Metzger forgotten to tell his replacement that police were searching Briggs's office? She ducked around the side of the desk to take a look, caught a glimpse of a bald head, fluorescent lights reflecting off the shiny pate. A bullet whizzed by her cheek. The bastard was shooting at *her*. Adrenalin surged through her body.

"Police!" she called again. She could hear Leo cursing. At least he was alive, but was he out in the open where the guy could put another bullet in him? Two more shots rang out, one throwing splinters from the desk into her cheek. Reflexively, she clapped a hand to the side of her face, but her eye was safe. The other shot—well, she heard a slug hit flesh. Leo's? God, his kid wasn't even born yet, and she was the one who'd asked him to—

There was a grunt, a scrabbling sound, and the front door slammed. "Got him," said Vasquez. Elena peeked from behind the desk. Leo had dragged himself into the shelter of a cabinet on the far side of the room, a trail of blood behind him. There was a cowboy hat on the floor, but no shooter.

"Come on, Elena," said Vasquez, running toward the door. "He's getting away."

"Leo's down." She dashed toward her partner, snarling at Vasquez as she passed, "That was Briggs, the guy you couldn't be bothered to follow up on."

"So let's follow him."

"Get an ambulance, for God's sake." She knelt beside Leo.

"Daguerre can—" Vasquez stood indecisively in the middle of the room.

"By God, if Leo doesn't make it, Vasquez—"

"Hey, I'm not dead," said Leo, but he was dead white.

She ripped the bloody pants away from his lower leg, saying, "We need backup, too."

"I'll use your car radio," said Maggie. She was trembling. As she started toward the door, she encountered a different night watchman, grizzled hair escaping from under a haphazardly perched cap. He peered hesitantly around the open door, gun out. "You the cops?" he asked.

"Why didn't you tell him the police were here?" asked Maggie. "He seemed to think we were burglarizing the place." She pushed him aside.

"I never got a chance," the old man whined. "I was on the phone, and he was in a big hurry. Both when he come in an' when he left. You folks musta shot him. I seen the blood dripping off him when he got in his car."

"What kind of car?" Leo asked. Elena was binding his leg with a scarf she had taken from her own neck.

"Blue '88 Chevy station wagon."

"Let me chase him," said Vasquez.

"So do it," Elena said impatiently. "Just try not to kill him before we can question him, OK?" To Leo, she muttered,

"Stupid asshole damned near killed me. What the hell did he think he was doing?"

"Saving your butt, Jarvis," said Tey Vasquez and left in a huff.

"He's got a point, Elena," said Leo. "Briggs shot me. He could have got you too—or Maggie."

Vasquez returned almost immediately and said, "He's long gone. If you'd let me—"

"I should have told Maggie to call in a shooting review team for you," Elena muttered.

"What are you talking about? I was saving your life," Vasquez protested. "What was I supposed to do? Let him kill a woman?"

Elena gritted her teeth. Did Vasquez think he was some knight in shining armor, rescuing the fair damsel? She hated that macho crap. Hell, if she hadn't been moving, a shot from Vasquez' gun would have hit her, maybe killed her. She touched her cheek, which was burning with embedded splinters. Her fingers came away bloody. Her blood or Leo's? And Briggs—he might have bled to death by now or wrecked his car trying to escape while wounded. They'd never be able to ask him about Analee's death.

"How you doing?" she asked Leo, squeezing his hand. "Does it hurt bad?"

"My leg's about to fall off, and you want to know if it hurts?" Leo grinned weakly. "Don't ask me to give up any more vacation time, Jarvis. I should have known better."

"And I shouldn't have let an amateur come along," Elena muttered.

"I saved your butts," Vasquez mumbled, sounding aggrieved.

"If you'd watched the door like I told you, none of this would have happened."

"Yeah, right," said Vasquez. "*I'd* have been shot."

"Everyone's on the way," said Maggie, sirens screaming as she walked in. "I put out an APB on the shooter. Should I keep after the computers? I've got three more to check."

"Do it," said Elena grimly. An ambulance crew followed Maggie in and went to work on Leo.

Maggie turned on the second computer, which showered

her with sparks. "Oh hell. It's been shot," she said. "I'm not working on a machine that wants to electrocute me."

"Try another," said Elena.

"And look at this. The one where I found the abortion file got winged. If the hard disk is gone, we could be screwed on that too."

"Vasquez probably shot it," said Elena, glaring at him. He glared back. The medics shifted Leo to a gurney.

"See you later, babe," he said to Elena.

She nodded. "I'll follow you to Thomason as soon as I can." Two detectives, Beto Sanchez and Harry Mosconi, arrived shortly thereafter.

"Beto, you want to talk to Assistant Chief Vasquez here?" said Elena. "He's the shooter. He and Briggs, the guy Maggie put out the APB on."

"Assistant chief?"

"H.H.U. force. I'll make a statement later tonight when you get back to headquarters. Right now I'm going to Briggs's house and execute this warrant."

She and Beto discussed the situation. "Take Harry with you," Beto advised. "In case the sister's got a gun. Or in case Briggs heads home."

"We should be so lucky," Elena muttered. "He's probably across one of the borders by now. Let's hope it's not Mexico."

"If we'd gone after him earlier—" Vasquez began.

"Oh, shut up." Elena touched her cheek. She was going to look like hell once those splinters were pulled out, but at least her eye was safe. The idea of a splinter in the eye made her queasy.

"I better go over to the Briggs house with you," said Vasquez.

"You better stay here to answer the million official questions you got ahead of you," Elena said, and left with Harry Mosconi.

32
··

"I should never have talked to you," cried Verna Robles as soon as she saw Elena at her door. "Chester was furious when I told him about the shirt. He—yelled at me. He said I was an idiot for thinking he'd been with a woman."

Elena had to wonder whether Chester hadn't done more than yell; his sister had an ugly bruise on her cheek. "Did Mr. Briggs leave the house after the argument?"

"No, he left after he got a telephone call. Left right in the middle of his favorite meal. Pot roast." Verna scowled and, when asked, said that she didn't know who had called but thought it must have been the loose woman whose existence Chester denied. Elena wondered whether someone had tipped him off that the police were heading for his office. Not likely. Who would have done it? "Has he been home since?"

"Of course, he hasn't." Verna's mouth tightened into a circle with wrinkle rays shooting outward. "He's probably with *her* right now."

"We have a warrant to search your house, ma'am." Elena and Harry Mosconi were still on the doorstep.

"What for? I gave you the shirt."

"Your brother shot a police officer while we were making a legal search of his business premises."

Verna Robles' mouth dropped open. "Chester has a gun?" Elena could have sworn she saw fear in the woman's eyes.

"You didn't know that?"

187

"I—I don't believe it. Chester values human life. It's his reason for living—the preservation of the unborn and—"

"We're going to have to ask you to step aside, ma'am," said Mosconi.

"Where *is* Chester?" cried Mrs. Robles.

"We have an APB out on him," said Elena. "He'll be found."

In her living room Mrs. Robles sat stunned, mumbling that association with loose women must have brought her brother to this pass. She didn't seem to grasp the seriousness of his situation, even when Elena explained that Briggs was suspected of stealing a list of H.H.U. abortion patients.

"What's wrong with that?" Mrs. Robles interrupted. "Any girl who'd offend God by having an abortion shouldn't mind if everyone knows."

"We think he attacked Dr. Greta Marx," said Mosconi.

"A woman?" The sister went still, and made no further protest when Elena went off with Mosconi to start the search.

"What are we looking for?" he asked.

"Proof that he was involved in the illegal sale of H.H.U. diplomas at twenty grand each. Connections to Analee Ribbon or L. Parker Montrose. More evidence that he broke into the university clinic, stole computer files, and attacked Dr. Marx. You see that bruise on Mrs. Robles' face?"

"Yeah. Someone gave her one hell of a slap. Think it was the brother?"

"Who else?" Elena sighed, sorry she'd brought trouble to Verna Robles. "How are you with computers, Harry?" They had entered Chester's bedroom.

"Pretty good. You want me to check his out?" Mosconi sat down at an owner-assembled desk with glue blobs at the seams and turned the machine on. "Man, this is a great setup," he exclaimed. "Look at his graphics capability!"

Indifferent to graphics, her conscience troubling her, Elena started with the closet and found a brown wig in a box that was supposed to contain bowling shoes. In the bottom drawer of the dresser she noticed a very wide leather belt. "What's this?" she asked, holding it up.

Mosconi glanced over. "Guy must be a weight lifter. They wear those to keep from getting hernias."

"Now that's interesting. The person who pushed the statue

over on Analee Ribbon had to be pretty strong. You're sure that's what this is?"

"There're barbells here beside the desk," said Mosconi, then continued searching the computer files.

Elena, rummaging in another drawer, found a red wig. "Bingo!"

"What?"

"This must be the hair he wore to hire the retarded kid."

"Your cases are always a pain, aren't they?" Mosconi remarked. "You never get the nice, simple ones where some bastard offs his wife and then cries on your shoulder about how much he loved her."

"I get those, too." Wearing gloves, she bagged the two wigs and continued to search. They could show the red one to Hughie and compare the fibers from the brown one with the fibers Dr. Marx had torn from her attacker's wig.

"I'm considering asking my ex to the departmental Christmas party," said Mosconi. "Think that would be a mistake?"

"I'm the wrong person to give advice there, Harry. I wouldn't invite Frank to my funeral." She glanced at Mosconi. He was in his late thirties, black hair going a little gray, olive skin, nice eyes, crooked nose, and he was six feet tall. "Why don't you ask Daguerre? You're tall enough for her, and you both like computers."

"And get myself on the sergeant's shit list?" Mosconi looked horrified.

"Just a thought."

The house didn't yield anything else of interest. They had Briggs on the clinic break-in and on shooting a police officer, although he'd plead ignorance, say he thought they were burglars. But they had no good evidence that he'd killed Analee, unless you counted the use of the *Charleston Dancer* in both cases and the weight-lifting. No screening officer at the D.A.'s office would recommend going to the grand jury with that. Anyway, they didn't have Briggs in custody yet.

Before they left, Elena called Beto Sanchez at Briggs's office, then at Crimes Against Persons, where he came on the line and said, "We found him."

"That's good news." Elena breathed a sigh of relief.

"Not really. He's dead."

"Gunshot?" Tey would have to go before the grand jury for sure. He'd be no-billed, but the experience might break him of playing gunslinger.

"He wasn't killed by a bullet," said Sanchez. "Man drove right off the Sunland Park ramp and ended up pinned in the remains of his car under the freeway. No skid marks or anything. Either he passed out or he got going too fast and lost control—or maybe he committed suicide. We'll know more later."

Oh God, thought Elena. Now she had to tell his sister that Chester was dead.

"An automobile accident?" Mrs. Robles cried when Elena broke the news. "But Chester was a careful driver. A fanatic about seat belts." Before, she'd looked resentful. Now her lips trembled; her eyes filled with bewildered tears. Elena patted her awkwardly on the arm.

Harry had his own car and went back to headquarters. Elena drove to Thomason General, where a red-eyed, sleep-deprived Emergency Room doctor dug the desk splinters out of her cheek, washed the wounds with disinfectant, and taped on a bandage. The nurse made a few phone calls and told Elena that Leo was in recovery after surgery to remove the bullet from his leg, no visitors allowed until the next day. Trying to quell stabs of guilt over Leo's injury, Elena drove back to headquarters. Leo was the detective in Crimes Against Persons she most liked to work with. Steady as a rock. Not like Vasquez, working one day and goofing off the next.

She met Maggie coming out of an interrogation room in C.A.P. "Find anything else in the computers?" Elena asked.

"Nothing," said Maggie. "Of course, he could be keeping the diploma-scam records on disk only and have the disks hidden somewhere. You look awful."

"Thanks," said Elena dryly. "It's just a bandage over some splinter wounds."

"It's a *big* bandage," Maggie pointed out.

Elena touched it, thinking she'd look like a dork at the H.H.U. Christmas Ball.

"Hear about Briggs?" Maggie asked.

"Yeah. We found the wigs at his house, so we know who attacked Dr. Marx, but we're still stuck with Analee's death and the computer scam. Where would you hide computer disks? Mosconi went through everything Briggs had at home."

"I don't know. A safe deposit box along with the diploma money?"

"It's a thought."

"You shouldn't be so hard on Vasquez," Maggie advised. "You and I could both be dead meat if he hadn't come out shooting."

"He screwed up my case," Elena muttered. "Besides that, he's a sloppy investigator and way too quick on the trigger. Briggs thought we were burglars."

"I don't care what Briggs thought. The jerk kept shooting after you yelled, 'Police.' "

"If Vasquez hadn't shot him, he'd be alive and in custody. How come you're defending Tey, anyway?"

"He's not so bad. In fact, he's kinda sexy—always wearing those glasses. And he stuck with me through every computer check. Took an interest in everything I found. Believe me, I was shaky. I'm not used to getting shot at."

"Well, *he* was doing most of the shooting."

"Jarvis, you ready to make a statement?" asked Sergeant Manny Escobedo, coming out of the interrogation room with Vasquez.

"That's what I'm here for."

"Sorry about Briggs," said Vasquez. He stopped beside her, noticing the bandage on her cheek. "And about your face. You find anything at his house to link him to the Ribbon case?"

"No," she replied. "Just the attack on Greta Marx. I found the wigs."

Tey nodded, and Elena went in to talk to Manny. Where was she going with the investigation of Analee Ribbon's death tomorrow? She'd collected all the keys from the Briggs house, and the coroner's office would give her the keys on his person. Maybe Manny would assign someone to run them down, see if Briggs had anything incriminating stashed.

She'd ask for Briggs's blood type from the coroner, see if it matched the blood on the computer clip arm. Then, if she didn't find anything to connect him to Analee Ribbon's death, she was going after L. Parker Montrose.

"So, Jarvis, what's your version of the shooting?" asked Manny. Then he looked down the hall and saw Maggie leaving with Vasquez. "Say, she's not hung up on that university cop, is she?" Manny and Daguerre had dated a few times. "He's not tall enough for her," the sergeant added defensively, although Maggie topped Vasquez by only an inch. She was a good four inches taller than Manny Escobedo.

Poor Manny, thought Elena. Beaten out by three inches and a pair of sexy sunglasses. She wondered whether Daguerre had seen Vasquez without the glasses.

33
..

Wednesday, December 7, 9:00 A.M.

It hadn't been Briggs's blood on the clip arm, which meant he probably hadn't killed Analee. Discouraged, Elena headed for the university to pursue L. Parker Montrose, whose blood did match.

Vasquez was answering questions at the D.A.'s office downtown, and Chief Clabb was in a snit over the idea that one of his officers had shot someone and might have to go before the grand jury to answer for his actions. He wanted Elena along to placate Vice President Harley Stanley about the bad publicity generated by the incident.

"Vasquez won't be true-billed," Elena assured the chief, "and I'm sure Tey will want to do his own explaining." Having edged toward the door, she hurried away before the chief could protest again, then walked to the dormitory in the hope of finding Montrose's roommate, Bunky Fossbinder.

Bunky invited her in when she knocked. Dressed in his paisley robe, he sat down in front of the fireplace. On the coffee table was a silver tray that curved up in a swan's neck at either end. The tray held an ornate Wedgwood coffee set—pot, cream and sugar, cups and saucers—silver tea- spoons, a plate of pastries, as if he'd been expecting com- pany. He held a cup and offered Elena one. She wondered whether the kid ever went to class.

"Is Montrose good with computers?" she asked Bunky, accepting the fragile cup.

"You really think that he killed Analee?" Bunky passed her cream and sugar. "Frankly, I've come to the conclusion that he was crazy about her. And she *was* a delightful girl. If Parker hadn't found her first, I'd have been happy to date her. I'm a little shorter than she was, but I've never felt I could afford to be sensitive about height."

He leaned forward to pour himself more coffee, breathing in its aroma like a wine connoisseur. "And as I said, she was delightful." He selected several tiny Danish pastries and passed them to Elena. "Did you hear about the letter she sent the student newspaper last year? There'd been a fuss on campus about whether wearing furs was immoral. Analee wrote to the paper to say she thought the anti-fur faction should picket Santa Claus." Bunky's eyes were dancing with glee. "So my fraternity did. We commissioned signs that said 'Save the Ermine' and set off for Sunland Park Mall."

The pastries were delicious. Elena finished the first and bit into the second.

"I'm sure you saw the results in the papers—a riot of weeping kiddies and semi-inebriated college students, many of whom, I'm sorry to say, were deposited in jail for disturbing the peace in that most sacred of American shrines, a mall during the Christmas shopping season."

"Computers," Elena reminded him, sipping her coffee.

"Have you no sense of humor, Detective? The girl was unique. Oh, well, Parker—he flunked the compulsory fresh-man computer course. We're all supposed to become com-puter literate, but Parker flunked. It took him two years to convince the administration to let him substitute a video-game course. Parker argued that it was all electronic, so why not honor our founder, the Video-Game King, by studying his lifework? Instead of wasting time on computers, which Parker never intended to use." Bunky poured more coffee when Elena set her cup down. "The vice president acquiesced this fall—probably because Parker's father endowed a chair in genealogy. That was before the big family conflagration about Analee. The Montroses are genealogy enthusiasts because they believe they're descended from Charlemagne."

"So Parker can't use a computer?"

"Unfortunately, no. I originally thought he appropriated the lovely Analee because she was a computer genius and our esteemed vice president hadn't yet agreed to the course substitution, but I was wrong. Parker was in love—as much as Narcissus can be in love with anyone but himself."

That meant L. Parker Montrose hadn't originated the diploma scheme, although he could have been brought in later for his social contacts, or by Analee when he lost his allowance. "You ever hear rumors that Analee was dating black guys at the state university?"

"Indeed. Taffy Foster mentioned it. I believe I heard it from Melody Spike as well."

"And Montrose knew it?"

"He'd heard, certainly, although I doubt that he believed it. One must look at the motivations of the people who spread the rumors. Taffy wants Parker for herself. Melody undoubtedly thought Analee had other boyfriends because Melody thinks all girls want multiple sexual partners. And it would be reasonable to assume the boyfriends might be African-American because Analee was. I'm hypothesizing, you understand." He beamed at her.

"I see that," said Elena. There was a good mind hiding behind that big nose, killer smile, and stuffy vocabulary. "What do you plan to do when you grow up, Bunky?" she asked out of curiosity.

"I'm pre-law," he replied. "I'd be attending a more prestigious university if I hadn't contracted mononucleosis in prep school and performed lamentably on my SATs. But I'll be accepted to Yale Law." He seemed quite confident for a kid who never attended classes.

"You said Montrose wasn't here the night of the murder; he says he was."

"He's lying. Parker says whatever serves his interests. He has the moral sense of a persimmon."

"But you don't think Montrose believed the rumors about Analee and two black guys?"

"Oh, I doubt it. What Parker lacks in brains and ambition, he makes up for in ego. My suitemate would never believe any love of his could be interested in someone else."

Elena didn't think that answer wiped out the jealousy angle.

"On the other hand," said Bunky, "if Parker did believe it, he'd be furious. In that case, he might have pushed the statue over on her. He's probably strong enough, since he lifts weights."

Montrose, a weight lifter? Better and better.

"He prides himself on his muscles, although I've always thought his largest muscle is in his head. But can you believe anyone would do that to her?" he added, his voice filled with incredulity. "What a waste of intelligence and beauty. And humor. When he brought her up here, she and I engaged in joke duels, one of us starting a joke, the other supplying the punch line. I was unquestionably infatuated with young Analee."

"So maybe you killed her," suggested Elena.

Bunky didn't bat an eyelash. He did give her that great smile. "I'm a lover, not a killer," he replied. "What about you, Detective? Are you ever interested in younger, shorter men?"

Elena blinked. Was he coming onto her?

"I find power an aphrodisiac," said Bunky. "Especially in women. Men can be boring about it. Of course, little, gentle girls are delightful, too."

Evidently Bunky Fossbinder liked all women. Which was a nice trait, Elena thought as she walked to the elevator after getting a list of names from him. Daguerre got on before they reached the lobby. "Going to class?" Elena asked, grinning.

"Escaping from my suitemate and Happy Hobart. They were after me again about campaign appearances. I couldn't get out of the room without promising to address the Feminist Coalition tonight. Can you believe that? I know less than nothing about feminism, and I don't want to be Christmas Queen. At least I won't have to talk very much because Zora Lee Ribbon is the main attraction. She's addressing them on the power of the Omniracial Goddess." Maggie giggled. "Now that ought to be fascinating."

"Maybe I'll go to the meeting," Elena murmured. She could drift around, see if there were any feminists who'd had it in for Analee.

"By the way, the fake-grad reception is set for tomorrow, and I've invited Happy. I didn't tell him what it was; I made out like I was asking him for a date, and he jumped at the offer."

"Maybe we should invite L. Parker Montrose, too," said Elena thoughtfully. "That way, if one or both of them is in on the scam—and Analee's death—it might come out."

"Suits me. How're we going to get Montrose there?"

"Ask Dr. Stanley to issue the invitation. He can say they're going to honor the Montrose family for their contribution of—what was it?—the genealogy chair."

"OK," Maggie agreed. "This place is so weird that anybody will believe anything."

"Tell me about it." Elena went off to track down students whose names Bunky had given her—people who might have some idea where L. Parker Montrose had been on the night of the murder. L. Parker still wasn't talking to Elena or any other representative of the law.

"Elena, what happened to you?" asked Michael Futrell, when they met on the sidewalk outside the administration building.

"What do you mean?"

"The bandage."

Having been deep in thought about her case, Elena had forgotten the splinter wounds. Now she touched the bandage self-consciously as she told him the story.

"My God! If the splinters got you, the bullet must have come close."

She nodded, secretly pleased that Michael looked so upset.

"What we need is the prohibition of all guns," he said heatedly.

"The police, too? If Vasquez hadn't shot Briggs, Briggs might have shot me."

"Briggs wouldn't have *had* a gun if there were real gun control."

"I think it's a little late for this country, Michael. We'd never find all the weapons out there already."

"Have dinner with me."

"OK," she replied, surprised at the abrupt change of subject, then remembered that she was going to the meeting of the Feminist Coalition, so she mentioned that to Michael.

"I'll go with you," he offered. "We can have dinner afterward."

"*You* want to go?"

"In case the feminists get violent."

Elena laughed. "I'm the one with the gun, Michael."

"OK. You can protect me."

34
##

Elena and Michael were sitting forward and to the side of the hall, most of whose occupants were women, many wearing the funky twenties shift-with-epaulettes of the H.H.U. ROTC Cadet Corps. On the platform sat the four remaining candidates for Christmas Queen, three of whom were beautifully dressed. The last, Maggie, wore jeans and a sweatshirt that bore the caption "Love in a Canoe" and a cartoon of two people tumbling into the water. Melody Spike, as chairperson of the meeting, had just given a speech about the opposition of true feminists to beauty contests, which were the result of what she called the "meat-market mentality" of the American male.

"So what are the queen candidates doing here?" Michael whispered to Elena.

"Feminists can support only nominees who have something to offer other than their looks," concluded Melody. "Something that speaks to the pride of women." Then she introduced the candidates one by one.

Taking Melody's pronouncements to heart, Mims Battle pointed out that she wasn't just a pretty face; she had a large collection of designer clothes and spent many weekends each year at Ivy League schools, which she thought added luster to H.H.U.'s reputation. Pamela Froschen announced that she was a Daughter of the American Revolution and had been voted Best Dressed Deb of her debutante year, not to mention she looked good in Christmas colors.

199

"I am very active in campus activities," said Barbie Auchins-loss, the third candidate, "and I don't see what's wrong with being beautiful. I think choosing a beautiful queen to represent the school during the Christmas festivities is very important. You wouldn't want an ugly queen." She stared defiantly at Melody.

Each candidate was asked, during her question-and-answer period, if she planned to stay for Zora's lecture on the Omniracial Goddess. The first three excused themselves by explaining that they had a dates, which sat poorly with the audience.

Maggie, under protest, took Barbie's place on the podium and said, "I'm Maggie Daguerre. Any questions?"

"I suppose you've got a date, too," snapped a young woman in designer eyeglasses.

"Nope. I was supposed to see Dr. Erlingson, but I told him I had a meeting."

"Now I know why she agreed to attend," Elena whispered. "She didn't want to admit to Erlingson that she hadn't read the books he assigned her."

"She'll never get her M.A. that way," Michael replied.

Elena didn't tell him that Maggie wasn't a real graduate student, just a stopgap until H.H.U. could lure some other psych major into Dr. Erlingson's research web.

Under the mistaken impression that Maggie had given up a *date* with the handsome professor, the audience cheered.

"Why else should we vote for you?" asked a cadet when the cheering died away.

"Beats me." Maggie paused as if to think about it. "I can't imagine why you'd want to vote for someone wearing off-the-rack clothes." The feminists shifted uneasily. "Wow, think of what I might turn up in at the coronation ceremonies."

The audience winced. Happy Hobart, her campaign manager, groaned audibly. Maggie grinned as they contemplated the possibility that she would appear at the coronation in some dreadful, unfashionable gown and embarrass everyone.

"Oh, sit down, Daguerre," said Melody testily. She took the microphone. "Before you start worrying about what she's going to wear to the ball, you might notice that she's the only one of the four who refused a date in order to attend the lecture."

"That's not fair," protested Mims, still sulking because the audience had booed when she said she had a date.

"And Daguerre had the best offer," Melody added. "I wonder how many of you would have given up a date with Erlingson for the cause."

"It wasn't—" Maggie began.

"Shut up," hissed Melody.

"I don't think she had the best offer," protested Barbie Auchinsloss. "My date's father is president of three banks and an active supporter of NAFTA, which is some border thing. We *are* on the border, you know."

"Even if she won't admit it, Daguerre is a feminist," said Melody, ignoring the NAFTA girl twice removed. "And look at her. She's making this a woman contest, not a beauty contest, or a breast-size contest."

"Her breasts are bigger than mine," said Pamela Froschen angrily.

"Daguerre is a good role model," said Melody. "Although it wouldn't hurt her to dress more attractively. But I'm willing to take on that problem if she's elected."

There was a exhalation of relief from the audience.

Zora Lee Ribbon stood up and said, "It's unfortunate that you can't vote for mah late sister, Analee, who would have been an omniracial role model. However, in Analee's memory, Ah'd advise you to vote for Daguerre. She does have a job, she does study, and she isn't hung up on trivia like bedspreads and gourmet food. Analee mentioned Daguerre to me as a practical, rational woman."

"Did she mention me?" asked Melody.

"She said you were hung up on bedspreads and sex. Ah'll have something to say about the benefits of chastity in mah lecture." Her voice gained power as she tried to override a chant rising from the quadrangle.

Elena listened, puzzled.

Melody frowned at Zora. "Did you bring a cheering section with you?" she asked.

"God provides," said Zora mysteriously.

The chanting became louder:

Abdicate fornication,
Chas-ti-ty can mean salvation.

"Let's vote on which candidate to support," shouted Melody.

"What in the world is that noise?" Michael whispered.

Ab-di-cate fornication,
Chas-ti-ty can mean salvation.

Elena thought she knew, and wondered why Maggie hadn't warned anyone they'd be here tonight. If the situation hadn't held the potential for violence, Elena would have been amused. Ora Mae's ladies sounded like a squad of high school cheerleaders. Elena pictured them shaking pom-poms outside among the palm trees, imagined their cheer sweeping the country, blowing away audiences at high school football games and halftimes of college games on TV. It might even make Monday night football—audiences of proper ladies rising in waves and chanting about chastity between the beer ads and the men's deodorant commercials.

"Daguerre wins," Melody announced. "What the hell is going on out there?"

"I think it's the Anti-Fornication Brigade," said Maggie. "They're against dating, too."

"Smart-ass," snapped Melody. "Sisters, let's run them off. Cadets, forward!"

"Oh, oh," muttered Elena. "Michael, I'd better round up some help before there's trouble."

"But we've got a dinner date."

"You'll have to give me a rain check."

Elena headed for the aisle, leaving a disgruntled Michael behind while Zora Lee Ribbon rose majestically and took the microphone. "Sisters," she boomed, "do not turn on one another. Those women want, in their own way, to protect your rights."

With the torchlight a flickering menace in the windows of the auditorium, Elena hoped that Zora Lee Ribbon managed to control the crowd.

35

Wednesday, December 7, 9:15 P.M.

Elena took a quick glance at the women of the Anti-Fornication Brigade as they paraded around the *Charleston Dancer* with their torches and banners. Then she ran across the grass in the direction of the police station, where she found two officers overcome by nervous indecision.

"Have you alerted Clabb or Vasquez?" she demanded. They hadn't. Elena telephoned Tey and got no answer. Surely he wasn't still tied up with the D.A. She telephoned Chief Clabb, who lived on campus in a faculty apartment. He didn't want to come over; he wanted her to locate Tey.

Five minutes later the reluctant chief entered the station. "What are they doing out there?" he asked plaintively. "Why can't they leave us alone?"

Elena had been monitoring the situation while she waited. The feminists had streamed out of the hall, but they hadn't attacked the Anti-Fornication Brigade. Instead, people climbed up on the base of the statue and made speeches: Zora Lee Ribbon, Ora Mae Spotwood, Sister Gertrudis Gregory, Melody, several other feminists. Elena couldn't hear what was said, but she could see the reactions of the crowd. The Anti-Fornication Brigade shook their torches periodically and shouted; the feminists shook their fists and shouted. Some threw landscaping rocks at the statue, which seemed harmless to Elena once she was sure they weren't trying to stone opposition speakers.

"Maybe we should disperse them with fire hoses," said Chief Clabb. His hands were trembling.

"You've got students out there," Elena warned.

"I know. Those people might hurt the students. After all, one of them attacked Dr. Marx."

"Chester Briggs did that, but he's dead," Elena pointed out. "And the two groups don't seem to be doing each other any violence." A huge roar went up from the crowd in response to something Zora Lee Ribbon had said.

"Tear gas," stammered Chief Clabb. His eyelid had begun to twitch. "We're going to need tear gas."

"I'd wait," Elena counseled, thinking she really shouldn't be interfering here. Where the hell was Vasquez? She tried him again, got no answer. Clabb was falling apart. She peered out the front window of the police station. People were hurling things at the statue again. No, they were lassoing it. "Good lord!" she exclaimed. They were forming gangs and pulling on the ropes.

"What is it?" the chief asked, peering over her shoulder. She could smell the sweat of fear on the poor man.

"I'm going out there," said Elena. If they actually managed to pull that statue over, someone could get hurt. "I don't want you to panic, Chief," she admonished. "Don't do *anything* unless I signal for help." Shivering at the memory of a falling *Charleston Dancer* and Analee Ribbon's crushed skull, Elena sprinted out of the lobby, then ran full speed across the grass.

"Pull, sisters!" shouted Melody. "That statue has to come down. It makes sex objects of us all."

The women and girls hauled on the ropes, but the statue didn't budge. "For God's sake, Melody," gasped Elena. "Do you want someone to get killed?"

"Butt out, Detective," snapped Major Spike. "My cadets are smart enough to get out of the way."

The women strained. The *Charleston Dancer* continued to dance, hands raised, knee bent, breasts gaily uplifted. "Pull," called the Reverend Zora Lee Ribbon, "for the dignity of women everywhere."

"Although that is a shocking statue," said Ora Mae, edging up to Elena, "I want you to know that I don't approve of property damage."

"Stop it!" Elena shouted, but no one heard. Where was Maggie? Elena herself climbed up on the base. "A statue's already fallen on one girl and killed her!" she shouted.

"It's an inducement to fornication!" screamed one of the rope pullers. "Abomination!" The Anti-Fornication Brigade took up its chastity chant. Faces grew flushed, hands acquired rope burns; the statue stood firm.

"Pull harder, sisters!" cried Zora Lee Ribbon. "Pull! Pull! Pu—" She was drowned out by the roar of a four-wheel-drive vehicle, a battered Jeep driven across the quadrangle grass by Sister Gertrudis Gregory, veil flying.

"Fasten these chains to the hitch," called the nun. The rope gang hastened to obey.

Maggie appeared and dragged Elena off the base. "No use your getting hurt. Nobody's going to stop them. They're crazy." She was shouting to make herself heard.

Elena had to agree. It was a nightmare scene—women of all ages scurrying here and there, chanting, exhorting one another in the flickering glow of the torches and the mellow light of the ornate art deco lampposts, the blithe statue being enchained under the direction of a nun. A slender, childlike girl, whom Elena had seen in Bunky Fossbinder's room, said, "I don't understand. This isn't going to get better jobs or child care for women who need them. I think Melody's schizophrenic."

"Amen," muttered Maggie.

Sister Gertrudis Gregory hiked up her skirts and climbed back into the driver's seat. Anticipating disaster, Elena flew back to the station. From the quadrangle, she could hear crowd roar punctuated by manic laughter.

"Hooray for the nun!" the feminists were shouting as Elena told Chief Clabb to call ambulances just in case. His eyelid seemed to have gone into permanent spasm.

As she turned back to the quadrangle, the dancer tipped, teetered, and came crashing down.

"Our statue!" Clabb cried, horrified.

"Make the call!" she ordered. At least two people had gone down with the *Charleston Dancer*. She headed back across the grass. The fallen were being dragged aside. Idiots! Didn't they know enough not to move an injured person? The rest of the crowd was uprooting shrubbery and piling it around the horizontal statue. Then, cheering, the Anti-Fornication Brigade women threw their torches onto the pile.

To Elena's astonishment, all of them, not just the pro-lifers, were trying to burn the statue. Would bronze burn? She didn't think so. By the time she reached them, the two groups were cavorting around the fire, giving each other high fives. Sister Gertrudis Gregory sprang from her Jeep and slapped palms with Melody Spike, Melody laughing, the sister looking like a member of the Inquisition directing an auto-da-fe. Except that the fire went out before the heretic statue got hers. If the shrubbery hadn't been so green, this mob of crazy women might have burned down the whole campus.

Someone staggered into Elena, and she turned to catch a small, reeling figure—Bunky Fossbinder's pixie girl, for whom feminism had less to do with sex and more to do with jobs and child care. "Are you all right?" Elena asked. There was blood trickling from the girl's hairline, and she didn't seem to understand the question.

"Someone hit me," she said, looking surprised.

Elena breathed a sigh of relief when she heard ambulance sirens. Putting her arm around the girl, Elena led her across the grass.

"Hurts," said the girl as the medics took charge.

Elena then helped two more of the walking wounded, one limping, one clutching her shoulder and screaming. Once they were safely stowed, and to be sure Chief Clabb didn't leap into any belated action, Elena hurried back to the police station. He greeted her by crying, "The head gardener is going to be furious. Look what they did to the shrubbery. And the founder's favorite art object."

"Just blackened," said Elena soothingly. "It ought to clean up OK." Not that she knew squat about barbecued statues.

"Were any students hurt?"

"Definitely one. Possibly three," said Elena, who hadn't identified the others she'd helped.

"Vice President Stanley—" Chief Clabb groaned. "At the very least, he'll want to know why I didn't do anything."

"You did do something, Chief Clabb. You exercised good judgment and kept a cool head. See? They're all leaving."

The ambulances were gone, circling the grassed area that held the charred *Charleston Dancer* and the smoldering Miami Beach bushes, driving out past the guardhouse. The women drifted away, laughing and chatting.

"Nothing terrible happened," said Elena, thinking irritably that Maggie should have warned her that this was coming, and Vasquez should have been available to take charge. On the other hand, maybe it was just as well he hadn't answered his telephone.

"President Sunnydale isn't going to think nothing happened when he sees that statue."

"Hmmm." Given how trigger-happy Vasquez was, he might have come over and shot someone. Elena took a deep, calming breath. She'd been pretty nervous herself. Belatedly, she thought of Michael but didn't see him anywhere on the quadrangle. She hoped the feminists hadn't done him harm. She wanted to go to that dance Saturday night.

Then Elena shook her head, amazed. Just an hour ago, during those silly campaign speeches, she'd been thinking that after dinner, if he had come prepared, she might get back in the mood, that on their last date she'd enjoyed feeling aroused after such a long unloved and unloving drought, although she hadn't appreciated the subsequent frustration. Nothing like a riot to take your mind off sex, she reflected glumly. Some evening! No Michael, no dinner. "I think I'll go home," she said to Chief Clabb.

"I need an Alka Seltzer," said the chief. "Thank God I live close and my wife keeps it on hand."

Elena left the police station, reconsidered, and headed for the dormitory. She found Maggie and Melody in the lobby, getting coffee from the espresso machine.

"It was a triumph of sisterhood," said Melody, "and we owe it all to the Reverend Zora Lee."

"Burning a bunch of shrubbery and a statue was a triumph of sisterhood?" asked Elena. "Chief Clabb wanted to break it up with fire hoses and tear gas."

"We could have taken care of him and his wimpy force," said Melody disdainfully.

"That's why I talked him out of it," Elena muttered. "Too bad I couldn't talk you people out of that statue caper."

"Why?" asked Melody. "We had a great time."

"Three people got hurt."

"All in a good cause," said Melody jauntily. "Well, I'm off to talk to the Reverend. I'm getting kind of interested in this chastity idea. If it really gives women power, it bears looking into."

Maggie watched her go and murmured to Elena, "I'll get a lot more sleep if Melody takes up chastity. In the throes of passion, she's the loudest woman on the North American continent."

"You've done a study on that, have you?" asked Elena dryly. "How come you didn't try to stop the riot?"

"Because I'm undercover."

"Well, why didn't you warn anyone that the pro-lifers were coming here tonight?"

"The last meeting I went to, they hadn't set a date," said Maggie. "Hey, if you think you'd do better undercover with Sister Gertrudis and Ora Mae, be my guest."

Elena gave up. "Do you know who got hurt beside the girl with the bloody head?"

"A mother of three and a fashion coordination major. One broken something—upper body. One leg with a hell of a bruise. The university can pick up the tab for the ambulances."

"The university may be more upset about this than you'd think," said Elena.

"Great. Let's hope they ask to have me reassigned. I've put on five pounds since I got here."

36
..

Thursday, December 8, 8:55 A.M.

CAMPUS STATUE FELLS THREE had been the headline in the morning paper. That wasn't news to Elena, except for the information that one of the injured, Pippa Conroy, was in a coma. Must be Bunky Fossbinder's pixie girl, maybe the one person at that demonstration who had sensible ideas. She wasn't playing at feminism like Melody, and she wasn't some fanatic who wanted to force her moral code on others like Sister Gertrudis Gregory.

Wouldn't you know little Pippa'd be the one with the serious head injury; she'd developed a subdural hematoma. And Melody hadn't suffered so much as a scratch. Elena had turned in a long report on the riot. Whether or not arrests resulted would be decided by people higher up the chain of command. In the meantime, Elena was on her way to see an L.S.A.R.I. leader about Chester Briggs.

"You're actually here," said Ora Mae Spotwood, viewing Elena with dismay when she arrived on the Spotwood doorstep. "Father B. called me this morning to say that the university wants to press charges against us—Los Santoans Against Rampant Immorality."

"What charges?" asked Elena. She hadn't heard.

"Damaging their statue, injuring their students, littering, and contributing to the delinquency of minors. But none of that was our fault. We were having a peaceful, tidy torchlight parade when Analee's sister came out and got everyone upset

210

about the statue. Certainly it's indecent, but I'd never have considered pulling it down. I believe I told you that. Poor Abbie Bentram has a broken collar bone, and her with three children to care for."

"I saw that in the paper," Elena replied. The fashion coordination major had a green stick fracture of the fibula. "A broken collar bone seems minor, don't you think, when you consider that there's a student in a coma?"

"Well, of course, that's too bad, but they didn't have to come out and interrupt our demonstration. We were—we were—*incited* by the Reverend Ribbon."

"And the nun," said Elena.

"*She* was incited. It just goes to show," said Ora Mae self-righteously, "that the old ways are best."

"What old ways?"

"Male preachers."

"Oh, I see." The pope would be glad to hear that he was getting Protestant support in that area. "Are you a believer in the celibacy of the clergy as well, Mrs. Spotwood?" Elena asked.

"Certainly not," said Ora Mae Spotwood. "That's one of many points on which Sister Gertrudis and I disagree. A celibate clergy leads to perversions. People should get married and live normal lives."

"Umm." Elena shifted uneasily. In recent years scandal had rocked the Catholic Church in New Mexico, and she was uncomfortable at the mention of perversions. She'd never known any perverted priests, but she did think they tended to become busybodies because they had no familial responsibilities to distract them from the doings of their parishioners. "Do I take it that the university is going to charge you with luring the Feminist Coalition into an act of statue vandalism?" she asked.

"Isn't that what you're here for?"

"No, I'm here about Chester Briggs." If L.S.A.R.I was to be charged with vandalism, why not charge them with the injuries? Negligent assault? And if the pixie girl should die—well, it didn't bear thinking on, but Sister Gertrudis Gregory had a lot to answer for. Even Zora Lee Ribbon and

Melody, although they hadn't actually hauled that statue over, had certainly encouraged its fall.

"Chester wasn't with us last night. His sister—poor woman—told me he was killed by the police, who were robbing his place of business. Isn't that terrible?"

"And untrue," said Elena. "May I come in?"

"Oh, of course. How rude of me! You're not going to arrest me, then?"

"Not today," said Elena. "I'm a Crimes Against Persons detective, and the statue isn't a person. Until someone addresses the issue of how the statue came to topple and hit those three people—"

"It was an accident! No one would deliberately hurt Abbie, not when she had those three sweet children at home."

"Maybe she should stay home and take care of them," Elena muttered. "Anyway, I'm here about Chester Briggs." They sat down in Ora Mae's living room, which was nose-pricklingly redolent of potpourri. Elena sneezed. Ora Mae said, "God bless you." Elena said, "Thank you," and dragged a Kleenex out from under the gun in her handbag. "Chester *did* deliberately hurt someone."

"Well, he probably thought the police were burglars."

"We weren't," said Elena. "We had a warrant to search his place."

"Why would you want to search poor Chester's business?"

"Because we suspected that he was the man who broke into the university clinic, stole patient files, and then hit Dr. Marx with a statue."

"Oh, I'm sure you're wrong!" cried Ora Mae.

"We've got a lot of evidence to prove it. He's even been identified by the retarded kid he hired to distribute the flyers."

"The retarded should be given gainful employment when possible," said Ora Mae defensively.

Elena ignored that. "And Briggs shot a detective when he found us in his office. If Chester Briggs hadn't died in an automobile accident, he'd be charged with attempted murder."

"An automobile accident?" Ora Mae looked confused but bounced back with, "No matter what anyone says, the dissemination of the names of young women who had abortions was a moral strategy, its purpose to achieve a moral end, which is to say, persuading young women not to murder their babies. And you haven't said a thing to convince me that Chester himself hurt the doctor." Mrs. Spotwood nodded decisively and leaned forward to pluck a browned leaf from a flower arrangement. "As for Chester shooting a police officer, as I said, he must have thought you were thieves. And if you *had* been, he would have been doing what any citizen has the right to do—defend his property. In these violent times, citizens need to be able to defend themselves."

"If there weren't so many people with guns, these wouldn't *be* violent times," said Elena sharply. "So many police officers wouldn't get injured and killed. My partner's in the hospital recovering from a bullet wound. I had to have a dozen splinters taken out of my face." She touched the bandage, scowling.

"Well, I *am* sorry about your partner and your cheek, Detective, but it was all a mistake. Chester wouldn't—"

"If he didn't, how did he get that list?"

Ora Mae Spotwood hesitated. "Chester had a source of information at the university. We always knew when Assistant Chief Vasquez would be off duty so that we could demonstrate with impunity. Although you may not realize it, Chief Clabb is very ineffective; Chester told me that. The insider must have been the person who gave Chester the lists. In fact, the insider probably hit Dr. Marx to protect his identity. Chester, on the other hand, died a martyr to our cause."

"Did Chester leave any records or computer disks with you, Mrs. Spotwood?"

"No. Why would he? He was head of the Anti-Abortion Brigade and kept his own records."

Elena went away wondering who the insider could be, whether there really was one. She didn't have an absolute chain of evidence linking Chester to the clinic break-in because the wig that matched the strands in Dr. Marx's hand was a cheap model that anyone could have bought. And Chester's blood didn't match the blood on the clip arm that Analee had used to fend off her attacker in the library. Could the insider have broken into the clinic, attacked Greta Marx,

or even killed Analee? Elena remembered Maggie reporting
that Chester Briggs claimed his sources knew about Analee
and her connection with the Feminist Coalition.

Elena drove from Ora Mae's brick mansion to the Briggs-
Robles adobe in the Upper Valley. Mrs. Robles, still red-eyed
and hostile, said that if her brother had a safety deposit box,
she didn't know about it, and that Chester had never mentioned an "insider" to her.

"Did he have any friends he was secretive about?"

"You mean beside the loose woman?" asked Mrs. Robles.

"I'm not sure there was a loose woman, ma'am," said
Elena. "Did he have any friends?"

"The Los Santoans Against Rampant Immorality were his
friends," she replied.

Elena sighed. She had not found Chester very charming the
one time she met him. "Any other friends? People he went
out with?"

"Chester didn't go out much. Except to meetings and dem-
onstrations. And on business." Her face tightened in an incipient
attack of panic. "What am I supposed to do with that business?"
she wailed. "I don't know anything about computers."

"Sell it," Elena advised. "Did he have any computer-using
friends? Hackers? People like that?"

"Chester didn't approve of hacking," said Mrs. Robles.

Elena wondered if that disapproval extended to hacking in
the name of the anti-abortion movement. "No one ever came
to the house to see him?"

"No."

"Did he have any hobbies that he shared with friends?"

Mrs. Robles thought a minute. "He had a friend he met at
the gym."

"Tell me about that."

"Chester liked to keep himself in shape. He lifted weights."

Elena nodded. Harry Mosconi had noticed weights in
Chester's room. "What gym?"

"Palomino's."

"What was the friend's name?" It seemed a stretch that his
weight-lifting friend would be the H.H.U. "insider." But still,
it would have taken a strong man to push the statue over on
Analee, and Greta had described her attacker as burly.

"I don't remember. Hispanic, I think."

"Try, Mrs. Robles. It might clear Chester's name."

"What does it matter now?" The sister's shoulders slumped. "I don't believe he did any of that."

Elena gave up. "If you think of the name, call me." She handed Mrs. Robles a card. Then she drove home to change her clothes. She'd have to wait until tomorrow to check the gym. In the meantime, she had to attend the reception for some fake graduates.

37
..

Thursday, December 8, 2:00 P.M.

In the anteroom off the turquoise-and-salmon Presidential Reception Hall, Elena made a quick study of Maggie's information on the fake grads. To ensure the presence of Hubert "Happy" Hobart, the founder's nephew, and L. Parker Montrose, both being possible suspects in the diploma scam, the candidates for Christmas Queen had been invited with escorts chosen for them, "Happy" for Maggie, L. Parker for Barbie Auchinsloss.

"Well, let's hope we catch him," said Tey Vasquez, entering from the president's office. He wore the full dress uniform of the university force in all its lavender splendor. He had omitted his usual cowboy boots, but not his state-trooper glasses.

"Where the hell were you last night?" Elena demanded.

"I wasn't on call," said Vasquez. "Did Clabb say I was?"

"I called you on my own," she snapped.

"Well, my mom's all upset about the shooting, thinks they're going to throw me in jail. I took her out to Leo's for chicken enchiladas and then to a movie."

Elena sighed. She knew that Tey and his mother were close, survivors of his father's brutality, so Elena could understand why the woman would be upset. "Sorry I snapped at you."

"I read about the demonstration. Bad business."

"You can say that again. One of the girls is in surgery right this minute. They're trying to relieve pressure on her brain and bring her out of a coma."

"How did the chief take it?"

"Not well."

"Poor old guy. It's getting to be too much for him."

The condescending tone irritated Elena, and she snapped, "Come on. The receiving line is forming."

"We supposed to go through it?"

"No, just observe and listen."

"You look great. Sorry about the splinters." He touched the bandage on her cheek.

"Thanks." Elena was wearing a dress her mother had made for her from handwoven fabric, a simple sheath with a long matching coat and some silver and turquoise jewelry that Grandmother Portillo had given Elena at her *quinceanera*, the celebration of a Hispanic girl's fifteenth birthday.

Vasquez offered his arm, grinning. "Let's knock 'em dead for La Raza."

Elena had to chuckle. "The last time someone mentioned La Raza to me, it was a fence down on Alameda."

"Let me guess. Jesus Bonilla?"

"You know Jesus?" She glanced at him, surprised.

"Went to high school with him. A gang-banger. Believe me, when I said La Raza, I wasn't thinking of Jesus Bonilla's kind of people."

They took canapes and cocktails and drifted toward the reception line where L. Parker Montrose and Barbie Auchinsloss were meeting the fake grads. Elena would have recognized the honorees anywhere. They were decked out in designer clothes and goofy smiles. None of them seemed to recognize L. Parker Montrose. Which one was Penelope Joan Rheingold? Elena wondered, remembering the telephone conversation she'd had with "Henny Penny."

Dr. Sunnydale was doing the presentation of the queen candidates and their escorts, with some prompting from Dr. Stanley; then Dr. Stanley presented the fake grads, probably because he was capable of remembering new names. The president wasn't. Elena would never forget the memorial service for Gus McGlenlevie, when the president kept referring to Gus as "our famous poet" because he couldn't remember Gus's name.

Harley Stanley said, "Now, let me introduce all these fine young people. Miss Luellen Macabee Schwartz and her cousin Alfred Schwartz of Chevy Chase, Maryland."

Elena, listening, couldn't remember an Alfred Schwartz on the list. Had there been another fake degree since Analee's death? Maggie hadn't mentioned one.

"Mr. Peter Case Bartholdt III, of Alexandria, Virginia."

That was Henny Penny's friend Petey. He looked the way Penelope Joan sounded. According to the files, he'd been nudged out of five prep schools. Elena wondered if he'd ever graduated from anywhere other than Herbert Hobart University.

"Miss Mimi and Mr. Martin Pratt-Carnevon of Washington, D.C."

They were twins. Elena wouldn't have thought there could be two people in the world who looked that amiable and idiotic. Martin was the one Maggie had found written up in the papers for DWI on his grandmother's adult tricycle. Mimi had the largest Barbie doll collection on the east coast. She must be ecstatic to meet someone actually named Barbie.

"Miss Penelope Joan Rheingold of Alexandria, Virginia."

Elena grinned. Who could help it? Henny Penny was giggling, and her slip sagged two inches below the left side of her very expensive, hand-embroidered hemline. She had a large, color-coordinated yellow and green bruise on her elbow. Another fall in a horse show?

"Mr. James Ray Pearson of Gaithersburg, Maryland."

That was the one with the Women's Study courses on his transcript. He didn't *look* like a feminist. Had Analee given him that major after some particularly irritating discussion with Melody? Everyone said that Analee had a quirky sense of humor.

"Mr. Abner Barble Mainz, Jr., and his father, Mr. Abner Barble Mainz, Sr., of Georgetown."

Ah, the banking and finance major. Mr. Mainz, Sr., was scowling, probably looking to defend his possessions, such as his son's expensive but fraudulent degree.

"And here is Miss Daguerre," boomed the president.

"Another Christmas Queen candidate, poor but beautiful, reminding us of the first queen of Christmas, who was also poor, but no doubt—"

"Nice to meet you," Maggie interrupted, glaring toward the president.

"And her campaign manager and president of the junior class, Mr. Hubert Hobart, the nephew of our well-loved founder of blessed memory, Herbert . . ."

Turning her attention to Maggie and Happy Hobart, Elena noticed that he looked pale. Of course, it could be the effect of Maggie's cleavage. Elena would have figured that Happy chose the dress if she hadn't known that Maggie bought it at a "thrift boutique" and had to remove a mustard stain left by the original owner. Maggie had called Elena for advice on stain-removal.

One of the fake grads was jumping up and down and tugging on Harley Stanley's sleeve. "Is that Happy?" squealed Luellen Macabee Schwartz. "Happy Hobart?"

Happy muttered something to Maggie and tried to pull away, but she held him firmly in place while Luellen threw her arms around him.

"You went to school with my cousin Alfie. Remember? He paid you to do his homework. Gee, you're cute. Alfie didn't say how cute you were." Luellen gave Happy a noisy kiss.

Maybe the reception was paying off, thought Elena.

"I get the next kiss," cried Mimi Pratt-Carnevon, pushing past Maggie to descend on the obviously reluctant Happy Hobart. "My cousin Barto was your alumni big brother at Hastings."

"Barto?" demanded Maggie. "Is that the jerk who's coach of the polo team here?"

Don't blow it, Maggie, thought Elena. *Let it run.* Maggie had been furious because Happy insisted on a campaign appearance at the Polo Club, where Maggie had been asked her cup size.

"Hey, Happy," said James Ray Pearson, "remember me? You used to date my little sister. Good thing for you my dad isn't here."

"I know Happy, too," said Penelope Joan Rheingold. "Him and me used to fool around out in the stables while Mummy was doing her yoga. My horse almost stepped on Happy's head. Isn't that right, Happy? An' Happy always fixed Petey's tickets for him." Penelope Joan gave her best friend and escort a playful nudge in the ribs that almost knocked him off his pigeon-toed feet. "Petey lost his license since you went off to school, Happy. Didn't you, Petey? Now we have to go out on dates with the chauffeur, an' it's not nearly as much fun, 'cause he keeps watching us. Doesn't he, Petey?"

Having recovered his aplomb, Happy said cheerfully, "It's sure a surprise to see you guys here."

"An' Petey doesn't like to screw out in the stables like Happy and me used to. Petey says it makes him itch when he takes his clothes off 'cause—"

"That's enough of that, Penelope Joan," said Abner Barble Mainz, Sr., in a loud, disapproving voice.

My God, thought Elena, reeling with the implications, *they all know each other.*

"This is Happy Hobart, Pop," said Abner, Jr. "He's the one who helped me graduate from Hastings."

"Helped you how?" asked Maggie, giving the young twit an encouraging smile.

Way to go, Maggie, Elena thought. *Keep 'em talking.*

"Well, Happy's real smart. He did a couple of things on the computer in the headmaster's office, and I had passing grades." Abner, Jr., looked around the room conspiratorially, then whispered, "It only cost five hundred dollars; I got his special introductory rate."

"Shut up, you idiot," said Almer Mainz, Sr.

Maggie was staring hard at her campaign manager.

"But Pop," said Abner, Jr., looking surprised and hurt, "Happy's a genius with computers."

"Really?" Maggie whirled on her escort. "Then why did you need me in the Love Bureau, Happy?"

"All that was years ago, Maggie," said Happy, an anxious smile hovering on his face.

"Right, Maggie said. Your rates have gone up a lot since then. Now for forty times five hundred you're selling a whole college degree instead of a few grade changes."

"I don't know what you're—"

"You're the one who's been putting transcripts into the computer and selling fake diplomas."

"Maggie, sweetie—" said Happy.

"W-w-what's wrong with my diploma?" asked Penelope Joan, looking as if she might cry.

"It's a fraud," said Maggie.

Elena, who had been watching and listening carefully, was suddenly aware that Tey had moved away from her side, unsnapping his holster. Oh lord, the fastest gun on the Westside was—

"Hubert Hobart, I arrest you—" he began.

"Put that gun up, you idiot," snapped Elena, swinging him around, then gasping because the gun went off and her right forearm began to burn. Around them people were diving to the floor. No one else seemed to be injured, however.

"For Pete's sake, Tey," said Elena, looking at her arm. Blood stained the sleeve of her coat. "You've done it again. First my cheek. Now my arm."

"God, I'm sorry, Elena," he said. "He was pulling away from Maggie. I was afraid he'd escape."

"The hell you were," said Maggie, who had Happy Hobart in an armlock. "You were trying to horn in on the only arrest I'm ever likely to make."

"I thought you were one of the queen candidates," said Petey.

"Yeah, right," said Maggie.

"Gee, this is really exciting," said Penelope Joan. "I'm so glad Mummy let me come."

"But what about our diplomas?" asked Abner Mainz, Jr.

Mainz, Sr., turned red and shouted, "I paid for that diploma, and my lawyer will sue the university if—"

"Goodness, don't worry, Mr. Mainz. We at Herbert Hobart will protect your diploma—I mean your son's. Don't give it another thought," babbled Dr. Stanley.

"What's that supposed to mean?" Maggie demanded. "Those diplomas are fraudulent."

"Bought and paid for," insisted Mainz, Sr.

"Mine, too," said Penelope Joan. "Can your lawyer help with mine, too, Uncle Abner?"

"There'll be no need for lawyers," said Dr. Stanley soothingly.

"Is something amiss?" asked Dr. Sunnydale, smiling beatifically around the circle of stunned pseudo alumni.

Harley Stanley turned to the founder's nephew. "I can't believe you betrayed the university in this way, Hubert."

"If people are going to accuse me of things, I want a lawyer," said Happy.

"What would your uncle think?" chided the vice president.

"That's the ticket, Dr. Stanley," said Maggie. "For a minute there, I thought you were going to back off."

"I'm sure the founder's nephew can't have done anything wrong," said Dr. Sunnydale. "Now, don't cry, young lady." He gave Penelope Joan a kindly pat and a handkerchief with a fish embroidered on it.

"No, indeed," said Dr. Stanley. "I'm sure we can work this out amicably." He cast a nervous glance at the fuming Abner Mainz, Sr. "Perhaps a slight change in the *nature* of the degrees in question."

"I can't believe this," cried Maggie. "I've spent more than a month working on this case, and now you want to settle things amicably?"

Elena detached the cummerbund from her dress and insisted that Tey wrap it around her arm to stanch the bleeding. "My mother's going to kill you for putting a hole in this coat," she muttered.

"I said I was sorry," he replied, pulling the cummerbund tight and tying it.

A towering blond man shouldered his way through the crowd and said to President Sunnydale, "Sorry to be late for the reception, sir. One of our chimps set fire to the animal lab."

"Dear me," said President Sunnydale. "No injuries, I hope."

"We got all the monkeys out, and the Humanities faculty pitched in to put out the fire." Then his eyes fell on Maggie in her low-cut gown. "Miss Daguerre," he stammered, "you seem to be very upset. What's the matter?"

"These people are all crazy," muttered Maggie.

"You're just feeling the stress of taking part in undergraduate activities when you have a graduate student's responsibilities. I suggest that you drop out of the queen race."

"I intend to."

"The election's only a few days away," protested Happy.

"Shut up. You're going to be arrested," said Maggie.

"Now, Miss Daguerre," said President Sunnydale, "we can't have the founder's nephew arrested."

"Oh *really*? Well, that's it." Maggie tugged her neckline up. "I'm out of here."

"I hope you have a wrap," said Dr. Erlingson. "The temperature has dropped considerably in the last hour."

"So I'll catch pneumonia."

"We can't have that," said her chairman. "Let me offer you a ride to the dorm."

"OK." Maggie grabbed his arm and stalked off.

Happy breathed a sigh of relief.

Elena said to Happy, "You're under arrest, kid," and to Tey Vasquez, "I'm going over to the hospital to get my arm looked at. You'll have to take him to headquarters. Turn him over to someone in Fraud and Forgery. And try not to shoot him."

"Dear me," said President Sunnydale. "I think what we all need is a cocktail and a prayer."

"I'll have a margarita," said Penelope Joan, giggling. "Mummy said that's what people drink in the Wild West."

"Certainly, my dear," said Vice President Stanley. "As long as you're of legal age. Otherwise, we have very tasty nonalcoholic cocktails for our younger students and—er—graduates."

If Oz had had a university, this would have been it, Elena thought. Only she didn't remember Dorothy getting shot.

38
∙∙

Elena made it across the reception room, wobbly on her high heels. If she'd known she was going to be shot, she'd have worn flats, although flats wouldn't have done justice to the dress. Harmony sold these ensembles for over a thousand dollars in Santa Fe, and now that trigger-happy Vasquez had put a hole in the sleeve. Mourning the demise of her one good outfit, Elena tottered toward the doors that led outside just as Michael Futrell was entering.

"We seem to keep running into each other," he said dryly. "At least for brief periods of time. Are you leaving? Have you found another riot to quell?"

Elena leaned against the wall by the doors. "Sorry about running off last night, but I had to keep Chief Clabb from using fire hoses or tear gas on the demonstrators. Did you get home all right?"

"I'd have thought that was my line, and yes, I did. Did you?"

"Sure. I take it you participated in the great monkey fire and rescue." She had noted the smudges on his face.

"How did you know about the monkeys?" Michael looked nonplussed.

"The LSPD knows all," said Elena, feeling light-headed. Just a stress reaction, she assured herself. She hadn't lost that much blood.

Sarah Tolland, in a gorgeous green silk suit, and Paul

Zifkovitz, the art professor known for his geometric paintings, burst through the doors. He, too, had smudges.

"Another rescuer of monkeys," Elena mumbled.

"You're bleeding," cried Sarah. "Good lord, what happened? People seem to be leaving the reception. We just saw Dr. Erlingson and his—ah—student. That *is* blood on your arm, isn't it?"

"A mere flesh wound," said Elena. "Gunshot."

"You've been wounded?" Michael looked conscience-stricken.

"'S nothing." Elena pushed herself away from the wall. "Think I'll be running along now."

"What? By yourself?" Sarah protested.

"You should go to a hospital," said Michael.

"I was planning to. Just stopped to chat."

"I'll drive you," said Michael. "I can't believe I didn't notice you were injured."

"We'll all drive her," said Sarah. "I hate these cocktail and prayer fests."

"Good hors d'oeuvres," said Elena.

"Once they've got you patched up, we can go out for a bite at Triangles," Zifkovitz suggested. "They're showing my paintings in the bar."

"Your beautiful coat," said Sarah, turning Elena toward the door. "You finally get something decent to wear, and someone shoots a hole in it."

"You got shot at the president's reception?" Michael shook his head as he escorted Elena, unprotesting, through the doors and down the steps of the administration building. "Who shot you?"

"Vasquez," said Elena, wobbling as she clutched his arm.

"Someone should take away that man's gun," said Sarah. "Didn't I hear that he shot someone else?"

"Me," said Elena. "Well, the desk beside me. That's how I got the splinters. And then he shot Chester Briggs."

Michael walked her across the parking lot toward a gray car.

"I might bleed on your upholstery," she warned.

"That's OK. This is Mark's car. Mine's in the shop again."

He helped her into the front seat, then turned to Sarah and Zifkovitz. "You coming to the hospital with us?"

"Absolutely," said Sarah.

"We could meet them at Triangles," said Zifkovitz.

Elena leaned her head wearily against the seat. "Let's go for the drink first and hit the hospital later."

"Elena, are you feeling all right? How much blood did you lose?" Sarah asked.

"A cummerbund full," Elena replied. "Wonder if Mom can replace the cummerbund and the sleeve. What do you think, Sarah?"

"Just close your eyes and be quiet, Elena," said Michael. "I'll have you to the Emergency Room in minutes."

"Have to arrest you for speeding," Elena mumbled, closing her eyes as he started the car. Sarah and Zifkovitz had climbed into the back seat.

Elena called Crimes Against Persons once her arm had been cleaned and bandaged by a resident at the hospital. She was told that Beto Sanchez and a detective from Fraud had taken the suspect downtown for booking at the county jail. "Beto says if you gotta send in non-C.A.P. perps, to book 'em yourself next time," said Harry Mosconi.

"I'm at the hospital," Elena replied. "I got shot."

"Shit, you and Leo are really having a run of bad luck, aren't you? The doc's gonna keep you there?"

"Just a flesh wound, but I'm not coming back in. How's Leo? You heard anything?"

"The sergeant went over. Says Leo's complaining he may never tap dance again."

"Truly?" Elena felt terrible. Leo loved tap dancing. He'd organized Los Santos' first outdoor downtown tap-dancing extravaganza just a couple of months ago. If Leo couldn't tap dance, he probably couldn't continue as a detective. He'd be relegated to a desk job. He couldn't be her partner anymore. He—

"You know Leo. He's just bullshitting. The doctors say he'll be fine. Now you get yourself home to bed, Jarvis. Do you need a ride?"

"I've got one," Elena replied. And she wasn't going home.

She was having a night out with Michael, one she wouldn't have to break off in the middle because feminists and pro-lifers were lassoing and pulling over statues.

They sat in a room with silver pipes crisscrossing a black ceiling, grotesque mobiles hanging from the pipes, courtesy of some other art professor from H.H.U., Zifkovitz's garish geometric paintings spotlighted on black walls, black table-cloths with silver napkins, and Greek food accompanied by wine that tasted like turpentine. This was Triangles. Evidently a popular watering hole for professors.

Elena awkwardly forked up a piece of pastry, filled with spinach and cheese. It had been precut by Michael. He was all solicitude now, having been really pissed off earlier because she'd dumped him at the Feminist Coalition meeting the night before. Theirs was proving to be a rocky relationship, what with her professional responsibilities and his condom deficit.

"I know Happy Hobart," said Michael. "I don't have any trouble believing that he was selling fake diplomas. He's got some computer scheme going now that provides information on disease-free sexual partners, and he's told everyone on campus he plans to take it nationwide."

"The Love Bureau," said Elena, chasing a piece of feta cheese around her salad plate. They all stared at her. "Well, I didn't name it."

Michael trapped the cheese particle and fed it to her. It seemed to be that or starve, because the doctor had told her to keep her arm immobile for twenty-four hours.

"However, he'd never have killed anyone," Michael continued. "He's not the type, and he was Analee Ribbon's campaign manager. He probably had money riding on her."

"Betting?" asked Elena, stabbing a chunk of stuffed cabbage. The rice and meat fell off.

Michael slid his fork under the remains and fed her that. She was beginning to feel like a baby bird, popping her mouth open to get a bite every minute or so.

"I guess if I tell you he runs a book, you'll arrest him for that, too," said Michael.

"Busy guy," Elena muttered. If Happy Hobart were running a brothel, she wouldn't have gone downtown to charge him tonight.

"From what I hear, L. Parker Montrose is your best candidate for Analee's murder," said Michael. "He has . . ."

The restaurant was almost empty when Elena saw a young man come in and speak to the proprietor at the cash register.

"I wouldn't rule out Hobart," said Zifkovitz. "Those business types will do anything for money. He probably killed her because she wanted too big a share of the profits."

"Umm," said Elena. She was chewing a mouthful of baklava, savoring the nuts and honey, and watching light reflect off something in the young man's hand. The owner looked upset.

"Analee couldn't have been mixed up in anything dishonest," said Sarah, "unless someone forced her into it."

"Damn!" said Elena. They all looked at her, astonished.

"You just solve the crime?" asked Michael.

There's one in progress, Elena thought, fishing in her purse for her gun and slipping off her high heels. She was going to have to arrest that fellow left-handed. "Keep talking," she murmured to her companions as she rose. The young man with the gun glanced her way and, satisfied that she wasn't doing anything more threatening than going to powder her nose, turned back to the proprietor. Elena had the purse slung on her left shoulder, her hand inside on the gun as she turned from the ladies room door and approached the robber from behind, trusting the owner not to give her away. A quick glance toward her table revealed her friends deep in conversation. In her stocking feet, hoping she wasn't getting runs in a good pair of hose, she drew the gun from her purse.

"If you don't open that cash register, Pop," said the robber, "I'll blow a hole in you big enough to hold all the moussaka in Greece."

"If you don't drop that gun, you'll be the one with the hole," said Elena, shoving her weapon into his back. The owner dropped behind the counter. "I'm a cop with a short fuse," Elena elaborated. Her right arm hurt, the painkiller having worn off. "Gun on the counter real slow; then raise your hands, you little creep." She pushed the barrel against the kidney, and he dropped his gun.

"Michael," she yelled as the robber's hands went up. "You're going to have to handcuff this guy."

Michael looked up from the conversation, gaped, and rose. "I thought you went to the rest room."

"I have cuffs in my purse. Hold your hands out in front of you, scumbag."

"What?" Michael exclaimed.

"Not you, Michael; you get the cuffs. He's the scumbag."

Michael fished out the handcuffs and stared at them. Obviously university criminologists dealt with theory, not handcuffs.

"Just put them on his wrists."

He looked dubious.

"I'm not Vasquez. I'm not going to shoot you by mistake."

"Lady, have you got your finger on the trigger?" the robber asked nervously.

"Damn straight," she replied.

"Please, Mister, cuff me, will ya? Before she shoots me."

Michael managed to handcuff the prisoner, who breathed a sigh of relief. "People with guns and shaky hands are dangerous. I coulda got killed there."

"Call 911," Elena said to the owner, who was peeking cautiously over the edge of the counter. "Ask for a squad car to take him in."

"I suppose you'll have to go with him," said Michael, disgruntled.

"I suppose so," Elena replied. "He's my collar."

"I don't suppose we're ever going to have another whole date." Michael led the robber over to a table and pushed him into a chair. "Couldn't you have picked some other restaurant?" he asked.

"You think I don't wish I had? I figured the place would be empty this time a night on a Thursday. An' how was I to know she was a cop? I took you guys for professors."

"Three of us are," said Michael. "You want me to hold the gun?" he asked Elena. When she shook her head, he helped her to another seat so that she could rest her arm on the table across from the robber.

She laid her hand and the gun sideways on the black tablecloth, her finger on the trigger, the barrel pointed at the robber's diaphragm. Aside from solving the diploma scam, this had been a rotten day. Tomorrow she'd have to find out what Happy Hobart's blood type was. See if he matched the blood on the computer clip arm. See if he had a gash on the side of his head.

39
..

Elena began her morning at the county jail, amazed to find that Happy Hobart, even in jail clothing, managed to project a preppy look. But he refused to answer questions without his lawyer present.

"OK, just tell me one thing," she responded.

"No."

She could see that not talking was driving him crazy. Maybe if Maggie were here—Happy seemed to have a crush on her—but Elena hadn't been able to get hold of Maggie. Melody Spike said she hadn't been in at all last night. "Bed's not slept in. At least, I don't think so. It's hard to tell with no bedspread."

The major had a bedspread fetish, Elena decided.

"Try Professor Erlingson's apartment," Melody suggested. "It's all over campus that she left the reception with him and hasn't been seen since. Although I've got to tell you the big money's *not* on her having seduced him."

Instead Elena had tried the university computer center, wondering if Maggie was unaware that Happy had finally been arrested. Perhaps she was still tracking him through the computer. She wasn't at the center.

"Can I go now?" Happy asked.

"My question's not exactly about your computer scam."

"You can ask. I probably won't answer."

She studied him. Great hair styling. "Do you have a cut on

231

the side of your head?" She watched his face for shock, guilt, or at least unease. He looked surprised.

"Why would I have a cut?"

"Can I feel your head?" They were in a small interview room on the booking floor.

Happy grinned. "Why Detective Jarvis, I'd love to have you feel my head."

Elena wanted to kick him, and she figured there wouldn't be anything there—unless he was taunting her, so his lawyer could say that she hadn't had a warrant to feel Hobart's head. Maybe she shouldn't. But what the heck; she was getting nowhere fast with the Ribbon case. Elena ran the fingers of her left hand into the soft hair on one side, then the other.

"That feels great," said Happy. "You've got better hands than my stylist."

Boy, did his hair have body. She was tempted to ask what he used on it. When she didn't find anything on the first try, she stood up, walked around the table, and ran a finger flat against his scalp from his ear to the crown of his head all the way around so she could examine the skin under the hair.

"What are you looking for? Lice?" he asked.

Nothing. No one had hit him with a clip arm. Or maybe he was a fast healer. It had been—what?—ten or eleven days since Analee hit her attacker.

"Hey, you don't have to quit. Don't you want to try again?" he asked when she returned to her seat.

Elena could see why he was called Happy. He had an infectious grin and merry eyes. Perfect attributes for a con man. "Sure you don't want to tell me your story?" she asked, thinking Maggie ought to be here; it was her case.

"I'll be out on bail by noon," said Happy. "Charges dropped by five. Wanna bet?"

"Wanna get charged with gambling?"

"You're no fun, Detective, but you're sure pretty. How do you feel about dating younger men?"

"I'm not as much against that as I am against dating criminals," Elena replied. "Last chance."

"Guard!" called Happy. As he left, he was telling the young sheriff's deputy about the Love Bureau. "The computer matches you to someone with just your sexual preferences, and our clients are all guaranteed disease-free."

"That's pandering," said the deputy.

"Believe me, it's not," said Happy earnestly. "I have a legal opinion on that. Now, you just tell me what you like in a woman and . . ."

Shaking her head, Elena left and retrieved her weapon from a locker downstairs. She crossed the street to her truck, drove one-handed to headquarters, and arranged to have the department vehicle picked up from the H.H.U. lot where she'd left it yesterday. Then she called Dr. Marx, who was back at work, and asked for Happy's blood type.

"I hope this stops soon," said the doctor. "Remember, you can't use these in court or even tell anyone where you're getting the information."

"My lips are sealed," said Elena.

"O positive," said Dr. Marx. "No match."

Elena tried Maggie again and found her in the dorm suite. "Where have you been, Mag? Did you know Hobart's in jail?"

"For how long?" asked Maggie cynically. "What do you bet the damned administration refuses to file charges? Here I catch the guy and—"

"I don't think he killed Analee," said Elena. "No blood match to the computer clip arm, no wound on his head."

"Well, he never seemed like the killer type, just the amoral entrepreneur type. Someone ought to tell the kid that the eighties are over. I figure if we don't get him on this scam, he'll end up in jail soon enough for insider trading or something like that."

"So where have you been? Melody says you never came back to the dorm."

"Yeah. Well, I'll tell you if you promise not to tell her."

"OK," Elena replied, intrigued. She eased her arm in its sling and sat back.

"Let me close the door and get comfortable."

Elena heard a door slam, then what she thought was Maggie punching pillows and settling onto her bed. "I'll tell you what," she said, coming back on the line. "I'm going to stay here at H.H.U. and bug them until they file charges

against that little con artist." More flouncing came over the
line. "What happened last night is Dr. Erlingson invited me to
his apartment for dinner. I guess he could see I was upset and
felt sorry for me. Or maybe it was the dress. He kept staring."

"I'm not surprised," said Elena. "You looked spectacular.
How did he take your being a policewoman instead of a
student?"

"He didn't get to the reception in time to hear that. Some
professor's monkeys set fire to the monkey lab, and half the
Humanities and Fine Arts faculty pitched in. A cellist got bit
by one of the chimps, but that's another story. Dr. Erlingson
still thinks I'm a student, and I didn't tell him any different."

"So what happened at his apartment?"

"He seduced me." Maggie chortled. "Boy, it was great. You
haven't been seduced until you've been seduced by a man
who's actually taller than you and wears a three-piece suit and
rimless glasses. Besides that, he drinks beer and eats frozen
dinners. My kind of guy."

"Sounds wonderful," said Elena, wondering if Dr. Erlingson had taken off his three-piece suit and his rimless glasses
for the seduction.

"It all started out with the *fajitas*. He took this chunk of
frozen *fajitas* out of the refrigerator—which, incidentally, is
gray—and asked me if I liked them. And I said, like a ninny,
'I love frozen *fajitas*.' And he said, looking sort of puzzled, 'I
usually heat them up.' And I started to giggle . . ."

Elena was trying to picture this scenario, the gray refrigerator, the *fajita* conversation—so far it didn't sound particularly romantic.

". . . nervous, you know? That and the martini I had at the
reception. Then he said, 'Ah, Miss Daguerre, I wish you
wouldn't do that,' and I was wondering what I'd done wrong
when he said, 'Your laughter is very infectious.' How about
that? No one's ever told me I have infectious laughter. My
boyfriends were more likely to say stuff like, 'You've got
great tits, Daguerre,' or 'You sure know your white-water
rafting, Maggie.' The guy I lost my virginity to—that was in
a sleeping bag—"

"I believe you've mentioned that before," said Elena, grinning.

"Yeah, well, that guy told me I had great shoulders. We were on a canoe trip at the time."

"Maggie," Elena implored.

"Right. So then he hugs me. With the *fajita* package in his hand. Clasped passionately to my neck, which wasn't too comfortable. Otherwise, being hugged by a guy that tall is great. And he has muscles. I always wondered whether he had any muscles under that suit. He told me once that he was a runner, but I couldn't picture him in running clothes. I'd imagine him running along an H.H.U. sidewalk in this gray three-piece suit, carrying a briefcase."

"Hmmm." Elena turned her chair and stared at the tweed fabric on the wall of her cubicle.

"Then he told me my hair was beautiful, and he ran his fingers through it, which was OK. You can't do my hair much damage. I mean, he couldn't mess it up and then decide it wasn't beautiful after all. Now my cousin Marie Hendaye, she met this cowboy at the Frontier Days Rodeo, and he—"

"Maggie!" Boy, was Daguerre wired.

"Right. You don't even know Marie. She's one of those big-hair-and-lots-of-hairspray people. Anyway, then Dr. Erlingson said he liked the rest of me. He said I have a very 'beguiling body.' His exact words. That really beats 'great tits, Daguerre.' I used to go with this divorced guy who always said that. We broke up because his kids kept spilling cherry soda on my keyboard."

Elena cleared her throat; her arm was throbbing and, fascinating as Maggie's story was, she wanted to get to a water fountain and take one of the pills the Emergency Room doctor had given her.

"So then he said he liked my face and I had beautiful eyes, so I said I liked the way he looked, too, and he invited me into the bedroom."

"Some progress at last," said Elena.

"I'll say. He started unzipping my dress. That's when I almost blew it."

"What happened?"

"Well, I kind of backed off, and he thought I'd decided he was too old for me, so I asked him how old he was. For all

I knew, he could turn out to be younger than me. Wouldn't that be a bummer?"

"How old is he?"

"Thirty-five."

"And he thinks you're twenty-two?"

"Right. Course, it wasn't his age I was worried about. It suddenly occurred to me, while he was unzipping my dress, that all I had on under it was white cotton underpants. Melody's always telling me my underwear is really boring, so I figured he was probably used to girls who have lace and silk underwear that matches their clothes."

Elena remembered Melody's underwear scattered on the floor of her green and lavender room. It *had* matched her clothes.

"I figured mine would really turn him off, but I also figured I had to go for it. I mean, he's going to find out pretty quick that I'm a cop, not a graduate student, and he's probably going to be pissed off that we tricked him. You'd think Harley Stanley would be worried about that, too."

"I think Harley Stanley has a sort-term point of view," said Elena. "As long as things looks respectable, he's happy."

"Uh-huh. Anyway, I let him take my dress off, and he said, "Good lord, Miss Daguerre—"

"He was still calling you Miss Daguerre?"

"Yeah, and I'm still calling him Dr. Erlingson. I'm not sure what his first name is."

"Christian," said Elena.

"No kidding? Anyway, he said, 'Good lord, Miss Daguerre, it's hard to believe that a twenty-two-year-old could look the way you do.' Well, I was about to feel insulted. That's just about what that damn Dr. Marx said to me, and I don't figure I'm in such bad shape. But then he said, 'You're the essence of womanliness.' And he actually picked me up and carried me over to his bedspread, which is charcoal gray, just like the upholstery in his office. I mean, this is a man who's into austerity when it comes to interior decoration."

"He picked you up," Elena prompted.

"Right. I was afraid he'd get a hernia. Nobody's picked me up since I was ten and I broke my leg in the woods playing

Tarzan. My brothers had to haul me home, and they bitched all the way. But Dr. Erlingson never said a word."

"You mean about your weight?"

"Well, actually about anything," Maggie admitted. "But actions speak louder than words. Wow! That man is an insatiable lover. It's going to break my heart when he finds out who I am and dumps me. I had more fun with Dr. E. in one night than I had in any given *year* with Freddie Packer. He was the guy in Cheyenne with the two messy kids. I sent him back to his ex-wife."

"So I take it you liked Dr. Erlingson?"

"Hey, I'm in love. You haven't lived till you've spent a hot night with a Viking in a three-piece suit."

"Right. You never said whether he took it off."

"Of course, he did. And he's got a *great* body!"

Before Maggie could expand on that topic, Elena heard a door banging against a wall and a voice saying, "So you finally got home."

"Don't you ever knock?" That was Maggie.

"So did you get it on with Erlingson?"

"None of your business." That was Maggie again. Then she came back on the line and said, "Gotta go. Big conference on my master's research."

Elena wondered if Dr. Erlingson would suggest that Maggie call him by his first name. Whether he'd ever address Maggie as anything other than Miss Daguerre. In the meantime, Elena had to get over to the university—after she took a pill; her bullet wound felt like the H.H.U. chimp had set fire to *her*. She had two messages from Vasquez to which she intended to reply in person. Maybe she'd shoot at *him* for a change.

40
..

Friday, December 9, 9:30 A.M.

"Where have you been?" Tey Vasquez demanded when Elena walked into the campus station. He seemed rattled. "After I got the Hobart kid to headquarters, I tried all the hospitals. You all right?"

"I'm still in the twenty-four-hour, don't-move-it period; otherwise, I'm OK. Driving's hard."

"Am I going to be charged with shooting a cop?" he asked. "I don't know how much more my mother can stand."

"Maybe you ought to put blanks in that gun," she suggested dryly and started toward his office.

"No way!" he replied. "I don't want to be unarmed if I have to face drug dealers, and believe me, there's buying and selling going on here. These kids think it's no big deal, using cocaine. It's just nobody wants to name the sellers. Even so, I've finally got something concrete."

"Great, but I'll carry the loaded gun in the future." She dropped into a chair—deep-rose brocade and comfortable, hardly what you'd expect in the office of a cop.

"You? You didn't even fire at Briggs."

"Once you've spent time with a shooting review team and a grand jury, you aren't so quick on the trigger."

"Tell me about it. Where do you think I've been the last two days?"

"So what's this 'something concrete' you've got on drug dealing?"

"Montrose."

Elena sat up. Montrose was one of her best suspects.

"I went over to see him. Nobody was there, but the door was unlocked, so I went in. His answering machine was blinking, so I—"

"Without a warrant?"

"I don't need one on campus."

"You do in court."

"Anyway, he had all these messages. People wanted to meet him. Needed resupply. Sweet tooth was acting up. Got the nose itch. One even asked for a bindle. That's a quarter-gram, twenty dollars' worth."

"I know that, Tey," said Elena dryly. "I was married to a narc. What about other terms? Did you hear *paper*? *Diamond*? *Dime*?"

"*Diamond* and *paper*."

Elena nodded. "He's dealing. Did you search his suite?" She hated to hear the answer.

"Didn't have time. Had to show up at the D.A.'s office."

Thank God for small favors.

"But we can do it today."

"Not without a warrant."

"I've got something else. The brother, Bose—I went over to the Guest House when I got back from delivering Hobart. Figured I'd get Bose out of bed, question him while he was groggy. I've had the desk clerks keeping an eye on him, so I know he's been going to bed early. They say his mother damn near tucks him in.

"Anyway, I'm walking in, and guess who I see having a real intense conversation over in the corner of the lobby? Bose and Montrose. I couldn't get close enough to eavesdrop because they spotted me, so I pretended like I had business with the clerk. But Montrose left right away, and Bose headed for the elevator. I guess you think it's not much, but this Bose is out on parole, and Montrose—"

"It's a good lead, Tey." She thought about everything he'd told her. "The question is, can I get a warrant to search Montrose's suite?"

"I'm telling you, we can do it without a warrant. That dorm is university property."

"Montrose has rich parents. Even if they're pissed off at him, they're not going to let him go to trial without an expensive lawyer to defend him. The lawyer will say you violated his constitutional rights, conducted an unlawful search, and that talking to his late girlfriend's brother doesn't make him a dealer."

"That's another thing. The unexplained deposits in her account. She and Montrose must have been in it together. Maybe she and Hobart and Montrose were dealing. And running the computer scam. Look at the timing. She's dead. Hobart's in jail. Montrose needs to reestablish his supply line. Bose is it. Maybe he was in before, and it worked through his sister. Did you know a dealer can buy a kilo of coke for eighteen thousand, cut it, and sell it for a hundred thousand on the street?"

Elena nodded. "Let me check them out at headquarters with Narcotics. Maybe we can get the narcs to put a tail on Montrose."

"Why don't we do it ourselves?"

"Because Montrose and Ribbon know us."

His mouth turned down in disappointment. "I should have been a real cop."

"It would take you longer to make chief," she said dryly.

"But it's good information, right?"

"Aside from the way you got it."

"Nobody knows about that except you and me. I could say I sat down and accidently put my elbow on the answering machine. Triggered the message button without meaning to. Their door was open. And I do have a right to go anywhere on campus I want."

"You have to wonder why a drug dealer would leave his door unlocked. Makes you think he doesn't keep the product there. Where else would he stash it?"

"Some of the callers wanted to meet him at the gym. Maybe in a locker?"

"His roommate told me he was a weight lifter."

"You're kidding. He doesn't look it."

"Good tailoring can disguise that muscle-bound look."

Vasquez glared at her, seemed about to say something, then shut his mouth.

"The weight lifting makes him a possible for pushing the statue over an Analee, that and his blood type."

"He's our man. I can feel it in my bones."

Elena grinned. "Nothing wrong with instinct as long as you back it up by being right a lot of the time. I'm heading back to headquarters. I want to talk to someone in Narcotics."

"Be back here at two. Vice President Stanley wants us in his office then."

"What for?"

"He didn't say, but I imagine he's worried about the founder's nephew being arrested. Didn't I tell you the system favors the rich? You don't have to be around here long to see money in action."

Elena couldn't disagree with him there. She shouldered her bag and walked out to the reception area, where the woman behind the desk said, "Detective Jarvis? I have a message for you." Then the officer shuffled through messages written down on little slips of paper embossed with the H.H.U. seal. "Here we are," she cried triumphantly and handed Elena a slip.

Elena couldn't decipher the message. "What does it say?" She passed it back.

"Oh, silly me, I took it down in shorthand."

Here was one officer who looked and acted like someone at home in the lavender uniform, Elena thought.

"Let's see. Someone—I can't quite make out this name—but someone at the Guest House wants you to come over and see him. He says it's urgent. Well, that's not exactly what he said. He used the F-word. Naturally, I had to think of something else. I mean, you can't put *that* down in a message, can you?"

Bose! Elena thanked her and left. She considered going back to get Vasquez but decided she didn't want him to shoot Bose. Or her.

"Detective Jarvis to see Mr. Thelonius Lee Ribbon," Elena said to the clerk at the reception desk.

"You mean Bose? He's in the game room shooting pool." The clerk pointed to an arch at the end of the lobby. The arch was covered with a beaded curtain like some twenties speakeasy. Through the curtain Elena could hear the steady clink of balls. She walked the length of the empty room, skirting sofas and chairs, tinkled her way through the beads, and watched Bose run the last four balls in the rack. He ended up facing her and planted his cue on the floor. "If pool halls wasn't full a felons, Ah could make mah livin' shootin' pool. But Mama won't let me go into none. Ain't asked my parole officer. He probably say no, too."

"You the one who called and shocked the officer at the station with your language?"

Bose looked astonished. "What Ah say?"

"It's not a word I use except in moments of great stress," said Elena dryly.

"Ah say *mothahfuckah*? Ah don' 'member sayin' that. Look, you the real cop around here, right?"

"I'm a city cop, if that's what you mean."

"Yeah, well, Ah don' trust mah problems to none a them cops wearin' them purple suits, an' Ah got me a real problem."

"Which is?"

"Guess Ah can trust you. Mah mama an' daddy think you cool." He glanced around nervously. "This white dude, he come over las' night tryin' to make a coke connection. Ah don' mean he lookin' fo' a hit. He lookin' fo' a supplier. So what am Ah gonna say? He know Ah in the business befo'. An' he real insistent like." Bose laid the cue on the mahogany table. "So Ah say call me today. Give mahself some time. Ah want that dude arrested. OK? Ah'm clean. Ah don' wan' no trouble with mah mama. Or mah parole officer. He hear some dude hittin' me up fo' coke, Ah back at Huntsville if mah mama don' kill me first."

"He give you a name?"

"Calls hisself L.P. You know. Like the old-timey records."

L. Parker. "Describe him."

Bose did.

"Did he mention he was your sister's boyfriend?" Bose should have remembered Montrose from the memorial service.

"Ah hear him talkin' in the church, but Analee, she never said nuthin'."

"Montrose could be her killer. Maybe she was in the business with him."

"Dope, you mean? Analee too smart to be dealin'. Ah the dumb one. Got caught when the Houston D.A. runnin' fo' office, sayin' send the dealers to jail fo'*ever*. Course fo'ever be five years with good time, but shit, there's first-timers now gettin' probation. So why would L.P. kill her?" Bose's lips drew back in a snarl. "He kill Analee?"

"Maybe." She frowned, thinking hard. "I'll tell you what I want you to do, Bose. When he calls, arrange a meeting. You're going to wear a wire."

"You wan' me to turn snitch?"

"You already have," said Elena, wondering if he'd been deprived of oxygen at birth. The other Ribbon offspring were so smart. Still, he played a mean saxophone.

"You askin' me to do somethin' *dangerous*."

"This is Los Santos, and he's small time if he has to corner a retired dealer. Word won't get back to Houston."

"Retired?" Bose grinned. "Ah like that."

"No one in Houston's going to know." She said it a second time to reassure him. "Except your parole officer. We'd want to tell him what a good citizen you are."

"You think maybe Ah could git mah parole time shortened?"

"Maybe."

"Sure would like to start playin' clubs with mah daddy. Shoulda done it in the first place."

Elena nodded. "You and your father make some team."

"You ain't so bad yo'self, lady."

"I got some practice singing along with his tapes."

"Ah ain't on any a them."

"You were great at the memorial service and the coffeehouse."

"Yeah?" Bose looked as pleased as a child who'd received his first gold star in school.

"So are you in?"

"Wear a wire? Like in the movies?"

"Uh-huh."

"You think he kill Analee?"

"Maybe. We might find that out for sure tonight."

"That mothahfuckah! Ah'll do it."

"Does Lavender let you use language like that?" Elena asked curiously.

Bose's eyes widened with alarm. "You ain't gonna tell her, are you?"

"Not if you do well tonight."

41
##

The plans were set. Two narcs would come over to the Guest House to put the wire on Bose and monitor it. They'd provide backup if the meeting between Bose and Montrose produced enough to arrest Montrose. The only question remaining was whether to tell Vasquez. This would be going down on his territory, because Bose had arranged to meet Montrose in the Guest House game room at ten.

Elena sighed and took the elevator up to the vice president's office. She'd tell Vasquez after the meeting. In the meantime, she hadn't had time to visit Palomino's Gym or even to see how the girl in the coma was doing. Tey was waiting for her. When the secretary waved them in, they discovered Happy Hobart, obviously having made bail as predicted, Vice President Stanley, and a man who was so blatantly a lawyer that he might as well have had it tattooed on his forehead.

"Assistant Chief Vasquez, Detective Jarvis." The vice president waved them to chairs. "I know you'll be happy to hear that we've reached an amicable agreement over this unfortunate matter."

"Why isn't Lieutenant Daguerre here?" Elena asked. "This is her case."

The vice president stroked his chin. "I assumed, since Lieutenant Daguerre solved the mystery, she'd no longer—"

245

"I hope this solution involves your pressing charges," said Elena.

"We've reached a more satisfactory accommodation than that, a solution that not only saves the university adverse publicity but provides considerable financial benefit."

"Then I know Lieutenant Daguerre should be here."

"She's supposed to be out campaigning," said Happy. "The election's tomorrow. If this other thing hadn't come up, I'd be right out there with her."

"May I use your phone?" Elena asked.

"If you insist," said the vice president reluctantly.

Elena located Maggie in her dorm suite and extended the invitation. "I'm afraid you're not going to be too happy with whatever it is they have in mind, but I thought you should be here."

"I'm busy," said Maggie.

"Doing what? The case is over. Your case, anyway."

"I'm studying for finals," said Maggie. "Hell, they start next Thursday. I might as well take the damn things and get the credit."

And make Dr. Erlingson happy for a few more days, Elena thought. "It shouldn't take too long. And you're going to have to report to your captain."

"Oh, right! He's going to be really happy if those schmucks let the little weasel off. That's what they're going to do, isn't it?"

"I guess. You might as well hear it for yourself."

Maggie said to give her five minutes. She showed up with disheveled hair, wearing jeans and her H.H.U. sweat-shirt.

"Christ, Maggie!" Happy Hobart exclaimed. "You haven't been campaigning in that outfit, have you?"

"Oh, shut up, Happy. I'm through campaigning. I'm a cop. Why the hell should I compete in some beauty contest?"

"At least, don't drop out of the race," Happy urged.

"I intend to ignore the whole thing and study for my finals," said Maggie coldly.

"I'm so happy to hear that, Lieutenant," exclaimed Dr. Stanley. "I consider it a great favor on your part. Now, I won't have to disappoint Dr. Erlingson."

"I'm not doing it for you," said Maggie.

"But you're still going to be my date for the Christmas Ball," said Happy.

"You're a felon. I'm not going anywhere with you."

Dr. Stanley cleared his throat. "Actually, Hubert isn't a felon. That's why I've called this meeting. Hubert and his lawyer, Mr. Pendlebaum, and I have worked out a very satisfactory settlement to this problem."

"The only satisfactory settlement would be Hubert here in jail," said Maggie. "Hubert? That's your real name? Jesus, no wonder you're a crook."

Happy grinned. "I'm a benefactor of the university."

"Indeed," said Dr. Stanley. "Hubert has not only recruited these fine young people for the university, but he has generously donated half his earnings to the Hobart Foundation."

"In return for which you don't press charges?" asked Elena.

"What did I tell you?" Vasquez murmured under his breath to Elena. "Money talks."

"What was that, Assistant Chief Vasquez?" asked Dr. Stanley.

"I think he ought to give the university the whole thing," said Tey. "After all, those kids got H.H.U. diplomas."

"We've reached an agreement with the students—well, not students, actually—and their parents, that the diplomas will be changed to honorary alumni certificates. We can't really give them diplomas, can we? However, they'll receive their certificates in May at our first graduation." Dr. Stanley beamed. "Everyone seems quite happy with that compromise. In fact, many of the parents have already donated generously to the Hobart Foundation."

"Does Happy get a cut of their donations?" asked Elena.

"This is not a subject for sarcasm, Detective," said Mr. Pendlebaum. "Serious negotiating brought about this accommodation."

"The result of which is that he doesn't go to jail," said Maggie flatly.

"Exactly," said the vice president. "We can't have the founder's nephew arrested. Good heavens, he's president of the junior class. How would it look? This way we have no adverse publicity and a substantial increase in university funding. What could be more satisfactory?"

"My case isn't settled," said Elena ominously. "I want to know where Analee Ribbon fits into this. She was your partner in the computer scam, wasn't she?"

Happy hesitated and looked toward his lawyer, who nodded. "She was," Happy admitted.

"Who originated it?"

"I did. Last year."

"What about Briggs?" asked Elena.

"Who's that?"

"OK, we'll get back to Briggs later. Was L. Parker Montrose a partner?"

"You're kidding! I wouldn't let him in on anything. In fact, I told Analee he was bad news."

"I see." Elena didn't know whether to believe him or not. "Go on about you and Analee."

"Well, it's not like I didn't need the money," said Happy defensively. "I don't get an allowance, you know. All my uncle left me was tuition, room, and board. My parents gave me a car. That's it. And it was a great business. Worked like a charm until this fall, when I discovered that someone was stalking me in the system."

"Analee?" asked Elena.

"The private investigator and then the detective from Fraud," Maggie guessed.

"I don't know, but I kept getting locked out. And that was before someone began changing the damn passwords."

"That was me," said Maggie.

Happy shook his head. "I never figured you for a cop, Maggie."

"You were telling me about Analee," Elena prompted impatiently.

"So I approached her. Subtly. You know? I didn't want her reporting me if she wasn't interested, but it turned out she needed money, too."

"What for?"

"She didn't say, and I didn't ask. I was just glad to get some help. I'm good, but I don't know a lot about computer security. Just the ordinary stuff."

"So Analee put in the Trojan Horse?" asked Maggie.

"I guess. Yeah. She read all kinds of books on computer security and then got to work."

"How'd she make it look like the transcripts were being entered from other terminals? She was using the library, wasn't she?"

"I don't know how she did that. After she came in with me, she did the transcripts and I located the clients. But then things got dicier, and I wanted to quit. I'd thought up the Love Bureau by then. Not that I said anything about that to her. She was hard enough to deal with in the diploma business; she wanted to do twice as many."

Maggie nodded. "I found them."

"So when she wouldn't let you out of the diploma scam, and you were afraid of getting caught, you solved the problem by killing her," said Vasquez. He turned to Elena. "I think we've got our killer."

"I didn't kill Analee," Happy protested. "In fact, I've got an alibi for that night."

"I'll bet." Vasquez rose, hand on holster. Elena leaped up and used her good left hand to thumb a nerve in his elbow that immobilized his arm. Even if Happy Hobart jumped out the window, plummeted two stories, landed on his feet, and escaped, she wasn't letting Tey draw on anyone else.

"I was in bed with a lady friend," said Happy.

"And you're too much of a gentleman to tell us her name," said Vasquez sarcastically.

"Melody Spike," said Happy without hesitation.

"You're kidding!" Elena exclaimed. "Maggie's suitemate?"

"Ask her." He turned to Daguerre. "You ought to remember, Maggie. You pounded on the door and bitched about the noise a couple of times."

Maggie groaned and turned to Elena. "He's right. I thought she was yelling that she was happy about the sex, although she doesn't usually yell, 'Happy, Happy, Happy.' Just indulges in a lot of shrieks."

"So he was there between two and three?" asked Elena suspiciously.

"Damn right I was," said Happy. "Maggie said, 'Do you two know it's 2:30? Shut up in there.'"

"And they didn't," said Maggie. "That damn Melody makes more noise having sex than any three—"

Dr. Stanley cleared his throat. "Well, it seems that Hubert is cleared in the murder of Miss Ribbon. Of course, you may want to check with Miss Spike, Detective, but I hope this case can be closed discreetly."

"Closed?" Elena stared at him. "We still don't know who killed Analee. Or don't you care? If it was Happy, and it turns out that Melody Spike was faking his visit to give him an alibi, are you going to want us to ignore murder?"

"Really, Detective, I see no reason for you to speak to me like that. I've always been cooperative and—"

Vasquez grabbed Elena's arm and interrupted the vice president. "Detective Jarvis is upset, sir. She's been working on this case ten days now, and the leads keep drying up. You can understand that she's disappointed."

"Of course, of course." Dr. Stanley smiled understandingly at Elena, who was fuming. "And the university appreciates your dedication, Detective. Why don't you go over and confirm Hubert's alibi? That should make you feel better."

"Good idea, sir. We'll do that right away," Vasquez answered for her and dragged Elena toward the door. Happy Hobart was saying to Maggie, "You really ought to come in on the Love Bureau, Maggie. We're going to make a mint."

"In your dreams," said Maggie angrily.

"Love Bureau?" asked Dr. Stanley, sounding worried. "I'm not sure I like the sound of that, Hubert."

"It's a computer dating service," said Happy.

"Perfectly legal," Mr. Pendlebaum assured the vice president.

"Oh, well," said Dr. Stanley. "We like to know that our students will be doing well after they graduate and making substantial donations to our alumni fund, which Hubert here has done earlier than we expected."

"Money," said Vasquez as he closed the door. "That's what talks around here."

Elena took a deep breath. She owed Tey one. He'd got her out of there before she insulted the vice president, which would undoubtedly have got back to Lieutenant Beltran, who would have given her hell.

42

Friday, December 9, 10:26 P.M.

Elena and the narcs, Moro Balderamma and Jack Whaley,
were sitting in the office of the Guest House manager. The
narcs had refused to have Vasquez along on any bust of theirs,
especially given Elena's condition as a result of partnering
him. Thelonius Lee Ribbon was in the game room, running a
rack on the pool table. They could hear his voice calling the
shots, the click of the balls, even the squeak of his shoes as he
moved around the table. The wire was working beautifully,
the tape recorder set to run when Montrose showed up.

"Nice of you to find us a pusher, Jarvis," said Whaley. "Too
bad Frank couldn't be in on this."

"If Frank had been there when I brought the tip in, I'd have
turned around and wired Ribbon myself," said Elena.

"It wasn't a friendly divorce, is that what you're sayin'?"
asked Balderamma, grinning.

"Was yours, Moro?" Elena retorted. She knew more divorced
cops than married cops.

"Can I fix up a wire or what?" said Whaley. "If the kid
farts, we're gonna hear it."

Elena gave him a look. "You're such a charmer, Jack."

"So, Ribbon, you in?" The voice came over the wire.

"That's Montrose," said Elena and switched on the recorder.

"Hey, man, gimme five," said Bose.

The cops heard the sound of hands slapping.

251

"How much you need?" Bose asked.

"A kilo. I'll pay eighteen thousand. A third up front to show good faith on our first deal, the rest when I've sold it."

"Coke?" Bose asked.

"Right. I don't like to handle grass. Too bulky."

"So why you comin' to me, man? This town oughta be coke heaven. You got Mexico right across the river."

"My supplier got busted."

"Gotcha. But that don't say why me."

"Analee said you'd been arrested for dealing. I figured you were probably still connected."

"So you knew mah sister?"

"We were acquainted," said Montrose, sounding cautious.

"You a liar," shouted Bose. "You killed her."

Sounds of a scuffle came over the wire.

"Hey, quit that," from Montrose.

More scuffling sounds.

"Better get in there," said Whaley, straightening from the edge of the desk on which he'd been sitting.

"You pushed that statue over on her, din' you, you honky bastard."

"I didn't. For God's sake, man—"

Balderamma had risen.

"Give it a minute," said Elena. "I've got a case here, too."

"Din' you?" Bose yelled.

They heard the sound of a fist hitting flesh.

"I swear it. I didn't. I was arranging a buy that night. At the Quick Coyote. It's a bar downtown."

"Gimme a name," snarled Bose.

"No one gives up his supplier," Montrose whined.

The two narcs halted at the door to listen.

"Name!" From the sounds—a smack, a groan, a body hitting the floor—Bose had hit him again.

"Chino Allende," Montrose gasped.

"Shit," said Balderamma. "We busted him three days ago."

Montrose confirmed that. "But I told you, he's in jail."

"You tellin' me yo only alibi be in jail where Ah cain't go ask. That right?" Bose hit him again.

The two narcs looked toward Elena, who shrugged. She

thought they'd got all they were going to get, so they went out to arrest Montrose who, when he saw Elena, cried, "This man attacked me. I want him arrested."

"How'd Ah do?" asked Bose.

"Real good, Thelonius," said Elena, patting him on the shoulder.

"You're under arrest, kid," said Whaley.

Montrose turned pale when Whaley grabbed him. Balderamma read him his rights.

"You comin' with us, Jarvis?" asked Whaley.

"He's all yours," Elena responded. "For now. I got to go down to the jail and check out his alibi. Maybe I'll see you there."

"You can't put me in jail," said Montrose. "*He* hit *me*."

"You're screwed, kid," said Whaley. "We got you on tape." Then to Elena, "Don't offer Allende no deals." They took L. Parker Montrose out, Parker saying, "I want to call my lawyer," and Whaley repeating patiently, "After you're booked, kid."

"You tell me what you find out 'bout mah sister?" said Bose.

She nodded. "Call you tomorrow morning."

"Ah not gonna git busted for hittin' him, am Ah? Ah be thinkin' 'bout Analee an' got mad. Analee mah favorite sister. Mah *little* sister. Even if she mad at me for being' dumb, she still love me."

"I'll take care of it, Thelonius," said Elena. "You go on to bed before your mother checks on you."

"Hey, she know Ah'm down here. Ah don' take a piss without Ah tell her. She the one say tell you 'bout the white dude tryin' to make a buy off me. She say anyone sing like you be on mah side."

Interesting way to judge character, thought Elena as she drove downtown to visit the Quick Coyote. She knew the bartender there, Meno. The man never forgot the face of a customer. She and Leo had closed a case because Meno had picked their suspect out of a lineup without hesitation, some guy who'd held up the bar and killed a patron who got macho and tried to grab his gun.

She parked about three blocks from the border, slipped her gun into a waist holster for easier access in case of trouble, then pushed into the Quick Coyote. Three steps inside, she stopped to cough. The smoke was heavier here than in the C.A.P. squad room and the body odors ten times worse. The place was packed with customers well on their way to alcohol-induced friendliness, aggression, or oblivion.

Meno was sliding beers down the long, scarred bar when she squeezed between two guys discussing the sad performance of the university football team.

"They ain't got no one but Pankins," said one.

"An' it takes a while to score five yards at a time," agreed the other, "specially with your team's fumblin' alla time and the other team's rackin' up seven every time they git the ball."

"*Hola*, Detective," said Meno, lumbering down the aisle between the bar and the alcohol supplies, which fronted a mirror that looked as if it hadn't been washed in fifty years. "Get you a beer?"

"Just information, Meno."

"This is *my* territory," said a woman who was probably eighteen but looked twenty-five.

Elena, sizing her up, wondered if she wore that miniskirt out on the street, where the temperature was in the low forties and dropping.

"Back off, Yolanda," said Meno.

"Hell, I will. I'll pull every hair out of her head before I'll—"

Elena brushed back her quilted denim jacket to reveal her waist holster. Meno said, "Cop." The working girl backed away. The two guys discussing football moved off their stools and headed for the door. Elena took one of the stools. Three more customers in her vicinity left.

"You're real good for business," said Meno dryly. He had a knife scar that ran down one cheek onto his neck, and every muscle of his thick shoulders and upper arms bulged through his T-shirt. The Quick Coyote didn't need a bouncer when Meno was working.

"I'll be out of here in three minutes," she promised. "I'm checking an alibi. You know Chino Allende?"

"Yeah, he's in jail."

"I know. Well, I got this guy—Anglo, blonde, blue-eyed, probably around twenty-one, preppy clothes, medium height, well built, snotty—he ought to stick out in here like a sore thumb. You ever seen him?"

"I remember him. Who's alibiin' who?"

"This guy says he was here with Chino late on November 28-29; that would be a Monday night-Tuesday morning."

"He was here. The little prick asked for some English beer I never heard of. 'Round one in the morning. I gave him a Dos Equis. Him an' Chino musta drunk a case between 'em." Meno polished a glass with a rag that needed the attention of a washing machine. "He's usin' Allende as an alibi? Must be in deep shit to admit he even knows Chino."

"So the blond kid was here till three in the morning?"

"Maybe later. Probably waitin' for supplies to come across the border. I had to kick the two of 'em out so I could clean up for the morning crowd."

"You get a crowd in the morning? There must be something about this place I can't see."

"It's the clientele," said Meno dryly. "So if that's it, you're scaring 'em off. No offense meant, Detective."

Elena grinned. "None taken."

She then went to the jail and got the same story from Chino, although he said he and Montrose were just socializing, it had nothing to do with dope. Shoot! Another suspect down the tubes. Happy had an alibi. Montrose had an alibi. Rhino and Ahmed had alibis. The main feminist, Melody, had been with Happy while Analee was getting brained by the statue.

Elena got into her truck, still thinking through her case and her disappearing suspect list. She was left with L.S.A.R.I.: Chester Briggs, now dead, who hadn't been in on the diploma scam but might have taken it amiss if he knew Analee had been a mole in his organization. According to Ora Mae Spotwood, Chester had an inside source of information at the university. So the insider was a suspect, too. And Elena still didn't know where the money in Analee's account had gone.

Tomorrow, although it was Saturday, she'd start on those

leads. Her case was getting cold, and Vasquez was no big help—not when he kept shooting her. She wheeled her pickup into the driveway and trudged wearily into her house. Maybe she'd listen to some Ribbon jazz. Sing along, just in case that physicist remembered to call her.

43
∴

Saturday, December 10, 8:29 A.M.

Elena had found a message on her answering machine when she arrived home from her visits to the Quick Coyote and the jail. Lieutenant Beltran, the head of Crimes Against Persons, wanted her to drop by his office at 8:30. She'd groaned as she switched off the machine, knowing she couldn't put off or avoid the meeting. However, she wasn't looking forward to it, expecting, as she did, that she'd be reprimanded for having failed to close the case after ten days working it exclusively. So here she was, taking a deep breath and knocking on his door.

"My God, you're a mess," said Beltran, staring from the splinter wounds on her cheek to the bandage on her arm. "That campus cop with must be a piece of work. He's the one who shot Weizell, isn't he?"

"No, sir, Briggs did," said Elena. "I suppose Vasquez means well, but I can think of people I'd rather partner."

"Harley Stanley called me."

"Are they going to ask for arrests because their students were hurt when that statue went down?" Elena did want to know, but even more important, she wanted to divert Beltran from the Ribbon case.

The lieutenant looked surprised. "Ah—actually, two of the women who were hurt don't want to press charges. Probably because they were involved in the riot. Incidentally, I hear you were the only person who tried to stop it."

257

"Much good it did. The girl who's in a coma—"

"She's awake now. Out of the hospital."

"You're kidding." Here Elena had been worrying that the girl might die. "Is *she* going to press charges?"

"Jesus, I hope not. If she does, we'll have to arrest the nun and revoke her bail. Then there'll be more letters to the editor about how the LSPD is a bunch of nun-bashers. Damn newspapers. They're saying the Ribbon killing was racially motivated. The local black organizations are getting into it. You get any sense of racial implications?"

"Not really," said Elena. *Here it comes. He's about to say that I'm landing the department in hot water with the richest institution in town, and the chief is calling to ask what the hell I'm doing, blah, blah, blah.*

"The racial accusations were in last night's paper."

"Well, it was midnight by the time I got home."

"Oh, yes, your drug bust. I got a call from the narcotics lieutenant thanking me for your tip and your cooperation. Very good, Elena. Doesn't hurt to foster good feeling between units. How's your case coming?"

"Truthfully?" She sighed. "Lousy. Just when I turn up a good suspect, he or she produces a verifiable alibi."

"You think it could have been a woman?"

"Actually, I don't. The statue's too heavy for most women to push over."

He nodded. "So what have you got?"

"Maybe someone from Los Santoans Against Rampant Immorality."

"Lunatic fringe," muttered Beltran. "I don't like abortion myself, but the law's the law. Any particular one of them?"

"Maybe Briggs, who's dead. Maybe a contact of his at the university, whose name I don't know. My only other lead is the money that came into Analee's account from the diploma scam and then went out again. I'll have to run that down."

"All right," said Beltran. "I realize you're in a tough spot, having to work with that fellow from the university force. Hang in there, and I'll try to keep the H.H.U. administration off your back."

"Thank you, sir." She couldn't believe he'd been so pleasant.

Elena decided that what she needed to do was talk the case over with Leo Weizell. She wished Leo, instead of Tey Vasquez, was working this one with her. What was Vasquez doing today? Sleeping in? Pleased with himself because a drug dealer had been caught, or ticked off because he hadn't been allowed to make the arrest? She'd better call and fill him in on last night's operation. Letting him read a few details in the paper wouldn't make for good relations. She went to her cubicle and telephoned him. His mother said he'd gone to work. She called the campus police station and got transferred to Chief Clabb's office.

"Yeah," said Tey when she started to describe the arrest of L. Parker Montrose. "I was just telling Chief Clabb and Dr. Stanley about how we caught Montrose and how he probably killed Analee."

We? Bose had provided the tip, Elena had set up the wire and made the collar, and Tey was taking the credit? She might have known. "He has an alibi for the night Analee was killed," said Elena.

"Probably a lie," said Vasquez. "As I was just saying to the vice president, I think we've solved the crime."

"We *haven't* found the killer," said Elena grimly, and hung up on him. Obviously Tey wanted to quit working the case and take credit for closing it. So fine. Let him. She was on her way to toss ideas back and forth with Leo. She needed some *professional* input. She also needed a few laughs. And Leo was always good for one—or ten. Boy, she missed him.

She drove to the hospital, taking her pickup so she could head for the Brass Shop to claim her rug after she got through today, hoping fervently that they hadn't given up on her and sold it. The last time she'd called, two days ago, they were holding it and her check, but she'd better get in and pick it up.

Because the only parking spot she could find at the hospital was for the handicapped, she put her police identification on the dash and hurried in.

"Well, it's about time you showed up," Leo grumbled.

"I was here a couple of days ago."

"First you get me shot and end my tap-dancing days forever."

"I did not. The doctor says you'll be fine."

"I'll probably need months of physical therapy to get back my former grace and—"

"You weren't that graceful." She started to giggle. If he hadn't been married to Concepcion, Elena would have dragged Leo off to the altar herself, just to ensure a fun life. Of course, they'd make a silly-looking couple. He was so tall.

"Me? Not graceful? The man who led seventy Los Santos tap dancers into San Jacinto Plaza in a dancing extravaganza?"

"And made all the TV programs by arresting that transvestite tapper."

"What was I supposed to do? Pay him fifty bucks and take him home for the night? He wasn't even tastefully dressed."

"As if you could tell the difference. Anyway, I thought that outfit was pretty nifty—black leather and red roses. What more could you ask for?"

"And after you've got me crippled," he continued, "you can't even be bothered to visit me a couple of times a day."

"I'm visiting you now. Right in the middle of my investigation."

"You're on the weekend shift?"

"I'm on seven days a week until I get this miserable case solved. And I'd like to point out that you're not the only one to get shot." She pointed to her arm.

"Who shot you?" Leo asked.

"Vasquez."

"Your partner?" Leo exclaimed. "The man's a menace. I can see that I've got to help you solve this case, if just to keep him from killing you."

"Right. So here's what I've got." And she told him the long, sad story of her investigation.

"Not much," Leo agreed when she'd finished. "If it was me, I'd go talk to the guys at UTLS again. They seem to have been her best friends. She might have told them things she wouldn't tell people at H.H.U. If I were black, I wouldn't trust whites with any secrets. Same goes for you. You're a cop *and* you're white. The two jocks wouldn't necessarily tell you everything. You need to let them know you're still trying to find out who killed their friend, that you haven't just written it off. Like a lot of people, they probably think the police don't work too hard on a case where the victim's not white."

Elena nodded. "Good idea; I'll check back with the jocks. I also need to track down that money. Find out what she was doing with it. Maybe *they'll* have some ideas." She leaned over to kiss him on the cheek. "Thanks, Leo. I knew it would help to talk to you."

"Any time, Babe."

"Except that you're a sexist pig."

"I forgot. You don't like to be called Babe. How about—" He paused for inspiration. "—Sweet Buns."

"No," said Elena thoughtfully, "I think that's what sexist women call men. I'll call you Sweet Buns, and you can call me Detective Jarvis."

"Good thinking. I want to see Lieutenant Beltran's face when he hears you call me Sweet Buns."

"Hey, he was really nice to me this morning. Downright supportive."

"Yeah? Maybe you're finally off his shit list. You know, I'd try that gym too—Palomino's—the place Briggs's sister told you about."

Elena nodded. "It's on my list."

"You're going to love it. Talk about buns. That's where all the butts of iron hang out. It smells like an old sweat sock."

"I can hardly wait." She rose from the visitor's chair and picked up her sling bag.

"Hey, come back and tell me what you find out. I have to admit it, Jarvis, your visit has cheered me up."

"Me too," said Elena. "Vasquez isn't exactly a barrel of laughs, over and above the fact that he keeps shooting people. But seriously, Leo, are you really worried about how your leg's gonna be when you get out of here?"

"Nah. I'm just bored. And kinda worried. You remember I told you Concepcion might be having two babies? Well, now the doctor's saying maybe three. How am I going to support three babies? And someday they'll want to go to college. What am I gonna do then?"

"They'll get scholarships. There's money out there for smart Hispanic kids."

"Their name is going to be Weizell," he pointed out.

"Doesn't matter. Their mom's Hispanic. That's all it takes.

After I married Frank and changed to Jarvis, it still counted that my dad was Hispanic."

"Well, that's good news. Anyway, the doctor could be wrong about three."

"Yeah, it might be four."

"Bite your tongue." Leo grinned ruefully and added, "Now go get 'em, Tiger. And come back; I want to hear how this turns out. When you catch the guy, you can credit me with an assist. 'Detective Leo Weizell, suffering in his hospital bed, gave me invaluable advice on my case.'"

"I'll be sure to put that in." Elena headed for the door laughing. "In fact, maybe I can borrow a laptop computer from Maggie and you can write the report yourself." Before he could protest, she added, "By the way, the big election for Christmas Queen at H.H.U. is today, and Maggie's a front-runner."

"Daguerre? She's in a beauty contest?"

As Elena left, Leo was howling with laughter.

44
..

As Elena headed toward a public telephone, she remembered that she needed a dress. Michael had invited her to the
Christmas Ball tonight, which was to feature the crowning of
the queen and usher in Dead Days, when students had no
classes so that they could study for finals. She had promised
herself a fancy gown for the occasion. The only time Michael
had seen her wearing anything stylish or expensive, it sported
a bullet hole and bloodstains. With any luck, Tey wouldn't
bring his gun tonight. Rushing into the hospital waiting room,
she snatched up the front section of the morning paper, saying
to the man who was reading the second section, "Can I glance
through this?"

"Help yourself," he replied, eyes red and puffy. Probably
had someone seriously ill in his family. She felt like a heel for
grabbing his paper, which she paged through hurriedly.
There! The Popular was having a sale on holiday dresses,
forty per cent off. And they had branches at Bassett Center
and Sunland Park. She'd just snap up some gorgeous,
forty-per-cent-off outfit before or after questioning Rhino and
Ahmed. "Thanks," she said to the red-eyed man. "I hope your
friend or relative gets better."

"What?"

"Aren't you visiting someone?"

"I'm waiting for my goddamn wife to stop flirting with her
boss, who just had a hernia operation."

263

"Oh. I thought—because of your eyes—"

"Ever heard of pollution, lady?" he snarled. "What'd you think? I been crying? Men don't cry." He shook his paper angrily and stuck his nose into it.

Grump! Serves you right if your wife's down the hall making out with the hernia guy. She headed for the public telephones and called UTLS, hoping Rhino or Ahmed could shed some light on where that money went when it left Analee's account. Now that Elena knew where it had come from—the diploma scam—she wanted to know why Analee had needed that much money, why a girl so evidently likable, so successful in the law-abiding world, had risked a promising future to join Happy Hobart in fraud.

Rhino's Nigerian roommate told her that Rhino had fallen into one of his wordless periods. As she hung up, she decided that if she had to, she'd try to nag him out of it, but she might as well question the talkative Ahmed Mohammed first.

"You woke me up, an' I got a home game tonight," he complained once she'd identified herself. "A tournament game. Don't you read the sports page? We're doin' good. Won two already. You wanna mess up our chances by sending the best player—that's me—onto the court all tired out?"

"I need to talk to you about Analee," Elena replied.

"I been lookin' every day to see who killed her. You don't know yet?"

"I don't know," Elena admitted.

"Well, come on over. Ahmed Mohammed will cooperate. I sure do miss that girl. Ain't—isn't the same, gittin' tutored by some white dude when you's used to black, beautiful, an' female. My life won't never be the same again, that's for sure."

"I'm on my way," said Elena.

"Hey. I ain't had my breakfast. Most important meal of the day. Along with lunch an' dinner." He laughed. "So I gotta get clothes on an'—"

"OK," said Elena. "I'll go shopping and see you in—" she glanced at her watch "—an hour."

"There you go," said Ahmed, beginning to sound cheerful.

Elena hung up and rushed over to Bassett Center, trying to remember how things stood with her credit card. She couldn't recall paying the bill on the first of the month. Which meant they were already charging her interest. She could write a check, but she didn't get paid till next Friday. You couldn't ask a department store to hold your check for a week, and the Brass Shop had her carpet check. They'd cash it as soon as she picked up the carpet.

So it had to be the credit card. She got herself a handicapped spot practically at the Popular's door, put up her police card, and dashed in, then wandered around in circles trying to find the holiday dress department. Once there, she whipped through the sale rack, chose two dresses, beat a slow-moving, middle-aged, size-16 woman into the only unoccupied dressing room, and tried on the dresses, both black. Black was good. It matched her hair and her only pair of dressy heels.

She eliminated the first dress, which was tight in the chest and long in the waist, and bought the second, in which she thought she looked great. It fit like spray paint from shoulders to hips, had patterns of sparkly colored stuff, showed some cleavage but not enough to make her uncomfortable, and flounced out in ruffles to her knees. She splurged on a good pair of sheer black hose to show off her legs, insisted that the saleswoman put the dress in a plastic bag on a hanger so she wouldn't have to iron the thing, and rushed back to her truck.

She hung the dress on the passenger side door and peeled rubber. The dress had cost sixty dollars, marked down from one hundred. Not bad. She wondered if Sarah would think it was tasteful, if Michael would be bowled over. Sarah would probably show up wearing an evening suit. On that thought, Elena pulled into a lot opposite the university dorm, crossed the street, and took the elevator to Ahmed's room. He answered his door in his shortie bathrobe. "I thought you were going to breakfast," she said. Didn't the kid ever get dressed?

"I et, an' I just had me a shower. Robe like this, it saves you some towelin' off."

"Right." She asked her second question. "Did you know that Analee was in business with another student at H.H.U. selling fake diplomas?"

Ahmed smoothed his hair. "I might a known that," he replied cautiously.

"Why didn't you tell me?"

"You din' ask. Anyway, I figured if you thought she was no 'count, you wouldn't care who killed her."

"I'd care," said Elena. "What I can't figure out is why she'd do it. Why'd she need the money?" Elena dropped onto Ahmed's desk chair, tired from the stress of shopping. She'd rather question forty witnesses than go to the mall and try on clothes.

"Analee, she really loved her family."

A memory clicked into place. The tutoring checks had been deposited directly into her father's account. The postcard from Bose said, "Send the money to me." But the sums had been small. The diploma profits amounted to a lot. "She sent it to her father?"

Ahmed nodded. She could tell he was wondering how much trouble he'd be causing the surviving Ribbons if he explained the situation.

"The university isn't charging anyone or pursuing it any further," she said. "They know about Analee and her partner."

"Partner got most the money."

"And he's not going to be prosecuted."

"How come? 'Cause he's white?"

"Because the people he sold the diplomas to have given the university big donations."

Ahmed laughed. "So if I tell you the story, won't get nobody in trouble?"

"That's right. Unless it leads me to the person who killed her."

"Her family not goin' to kill her. Even if they didn't love her—an' they all did—they not gonna kill the girl that's savin' their ass."

"How was she doing that?"

"With the money."

Elena waited.

"Well, Bose—you know about him."

She nodded. "Arrested for drug dealing. Out on parole."

"Well, he did his time, but when he went down, the cops took two keys of coke off him—thirty thousand dollars worth. He like on a credit system, you know? So when he gets out, his connection still wants the money."

Elena nodded. "How does Ray Lee fit into this?"

"Well, he ain't gonna let them dudes kill Bose, so he gets the money from loan sharks."

Elena groaned.

"Well, ain't no bank gonna loan money to pay off a drug debt. But then he got the loan sharks on his ass, so Analee, she couldn't see no way out 'cept she pay 'em off herself, only she don't—doesn't know how. Then along comes this white dude says he needs a good computer chick. He kinda eases into it, you know. Feelin' her out. An' back home, a loan shark's muscle goes after her daddy. Breaks one of his fingers, so Analee she's scared to death for her daddy. They break any more fingers, he won't be playin' his horn no more, an' that man, he can *play*."

"I've heard him. Couldn't he have gone to the police?"

"What, an' say he borrow from sharks to pay off the dealers? Bose end up at Huntsville for parole violation, jus' associatin' with them dudes. Or else the cops, they make him snitch, an' he end up dead."

"So she went in on the computer scam," Elena concluded.

"She had 'em paid off with the last degree. Or would have when the money come in. Suppose that white boy got it all after she died. Now Ray Lee an' Bose, they still short five big ones." Ahmed shook his head. "No wonder they stayin' here long as they can."

"What about Lavender? Couldn't she help?"

"No one told the mama. They all scared a her."

"Analee's boyfriend at H.H.U. was dealing. Tell me the truth, Ahmed. Was she in on that?"

"No way."

"I can't find out who killed her if I don't know everything."

"Analee 'bout to dump that L. Parker Mon-trose. She knew his people cut off his bread, an' he wouldn't say where he was gettin' more. Analee made her bro swear, I mean heavy swear, he don't do no more dealin' or sniffin' or have nothin' to do with drugs if she got him an' Ray Lee clear. She dead down hated that stuff. She was dumpin' L. Parker, an' she was dumpin' the computer dude soon as she got the last five thou.

Goin' back to her job with the lady professor. She *loved* that
job. 'Bout broke her heart when she quit."

It had broken Sarah's heart, too, Elena thought sadly. Poor
Analee. Let your brother get killed, your father crippled—or
risk your own future to save them. Some choice.

"So I'm pretty much back to square one," said Elena
glumly. "Everyone has an alibi. I don't even know how the
killer got into the library. I don't suppose she ever said
anything about someone stalking her in the library, did she?"
Elena asked, remembering what Ray Lee had told her at the
coffeehouse. "After hours when she was putting the fake
transcripts into the computer? Did she ever mention seeing
anyone there?"

"She was tight with the night guard. Hell, Analee was
friendly with everyone who didn't do drugs. I don't think he
a pushed no statue over on her."

"Me neither," said Elena. "He seemed to like her."

"Well, there was one guy, but I don't s'pose it was him. She
saw him prowlin' 'round late at night. Made her real nervous,
dodgin' him so she could get those last records in."

"Who?" asked Elena.

"Hey, wouldn't be a campus cop."

"What campus cop?"

"Can't 'member the name."

"Think, Ahmed."

"Wasn't the chief. He some old guy. Was his assistant.
Some Mexican dude."

"Vasquez?" she asked, amazed.

"Sounds right."

Tey Vasquez?

45
..

Saturday, December 10, 1:30 P.M.

Elena stopped at Taco Bell for a burrito and some uninterrupted thought. Vasquez? But he was her *partner*.

What did she know about him? Well, he was a good son to a sick mother. And he was ambitious. He wanted to be chief. Maybe he also wanted to hurry Clabb's retirement. He always spoke condescendingly about his boss. Was Vasquez setting Clabb up to look even more inept than he was, while Vasquez himself did everything he could to look more competent than *he* was?

Ora Mae had said Briggs had an insider at H.H.U. Verna Robles said her brother had a Hispanic friend he met at the gym. If Vasquez was Briggs's insider, he could certainly make Clabb look bad. He would have given Briggs the guard schedule so Briggs could break into the clinic without being caught. He could have told Briggs which nights Clabb would be on call, so that L.S.A.R.I. could be sure of encountering little resistance when they visited the campus. So that Clabb would look bad. So that Clabb would start to hate his job.

Poor Clabb had been a nervous wreck when she first came to investigate the case and in even worse shape the night of the chastity parade, when Vasquez was conveniently unavailable. Taking his mom to the movies, he'd said so self-righteously. Maybe she ought to check with Vasquez's mother. If Clabb had actually used fire hoses or tear gas on the demonstrators, he might have ended his career as H.H.U.

chief then and there, with Vasquez as his successor—Vasquez, who was so sure of being the heir apparent that he'd offered Elena a job when the time came. H.H.U. detective. Some job! But it could be: Vasquez, wanting Clabb's job, could have used the right-to-lifers to make his superior look incompetent.

And if he was the insider, he'd have warned Briggs about the warrant to search his office and house. Told Briggs that the cops would hit the business first. So Briggs, rushing to his office to destroy evidence, panicked when he found the police there, came in shooting, acting like he thought burglars were in his place. And Vasquez killed him! Or at least caused his death.

To keep Briggs quiet about the connection between them? He wouldn't want Briggs arrested and questioned. Now that she thought about it, Tey had insisted on accompanying Elena and Leo that night, although previously he had backed away from any operation taking place off his own turf.

And he'd come close to shooting Elena that night! Splinter close. Had he meant to get her as well as Briggs? Screw up the case by killing the detective? Maybe that was a little far-fetched.

Elena went over his conduct at the fake grads reception. He'd tried to usurp Maggie's collar. And you don't rush around a crowded room with your gun out. Maybe he wanted to shoot Happy rather than arrest him. With Happy dead, Analee's death could be blamed on him because they were partners in the computer scam. A falling out among thieves. Except that Vasquez couldn't have known until the reception that Happy was the scammer—otherwise, he would have arrested him earlier.

More important, he couldn't have known for sure that Analee was in on it—unless he'd caught her at the library. Ahmed said Vasquez had been there several times, prowling around, making her jittery. Was he looking for her? Had he known that Maggie's investigation had shown the library to be the place where most, if not all, of the transcripts were entered?

She'd have to ask Maggie. So say he knows about the library, is looking for the scammer, and catches her; she hits him and gets away. Chasing her down the stairs, afraid he's going to lose her and the prestige of having caught the seller of fake diplomas, he pushes the statue over on her. Vasquez was into weight lifting—if he was the insider. He probably had the strength to shove the *Charleston Dancer* off its pedestal.

In both cases—at the library and the fake grad reception—he'd have been acting on impulse fueled by an overwhelming desire to make himself look good, and later to protect himself from his first mistake, killing Analee. Elena shook her head, still finding it hard to believe that the man who'd been her partner was the killer.

But maybe he wasn't. She'd need to do a lot of checking before she made any accusations.

She thought of how careless he'd been about looking for evidence in Analee's room. Maybe he didn't care what they found, as long as it didn't implicate him. And who *was* he really shooting at when he'd hit—or come close to hitting—her? Shuddering, Elena left Taco Bell. From the pay phone outside, she called Maggie's room at the university dorm. No one answered. She called the university clinic. No one answered. She called Dr. Greta Marx's university apartment and got the doctor. "I need to know the blood type of Tey Vasquez."

"Who?"

Elena could hear a soprano shrieking in the background. "Eleuterio Vasquez, the assistant chief of the university police force. Don't you have his blood type on file? Didn't he take an employment physical at your clinic?"

"I'm listening to the Met broadcast," said Dr. Marx irritably. "Surely you don't think a campus policeman killed her."

Elena sighed. "When the opera's done, could you go over to the clinic and find out for me? I'll call you back."

"I'll access my computer by phone at transmission," said the doctor grudgingly, "but I'm going to miss part of the opera quiz."

"How soon can I call you back?"

"An hour."

"OK." *The miracles of modern science*, thought Elena, and headed for Palomino's Gym on Doniphan.

"You remember Chester Briggs?" she asked the manager, flipping her badge in his direction and introducing herself once she got there. It did indeed smell like an old sweat sock, and there were at least thirty men whose muscles made them look more mutant than human. They were grunting as they lifted weights and sweated through machine workouts. They were punching leather bags and gasping on benches. A really charming place!

"Chester Briggs?" The manager pulled over a Rolodex and looked up the name. "Member. Bench presses three-fifty."

"Pressed," said Elena. "He's dead."

"You're kiddin'? I remember him. Bald guy. Very faithful to his weight program. Especially considerin' he worked in computers. You don't expect one of those high-tech types to have any real commitment to his body. Since you're a homicide dick, I guess someone murdered him."

"Well, he got shot and died," said Elena evasively. "What I want to know is did he meet someone here, another weight lifter, Hispanic?"

The manager studied another card. "Briggs sometimes had a guest. Don't have his name. Briggs paid the guest fee."

"Do you remember the guy? They may have spent more time talking than weight lifting."

"That would be the guy with eyes that didn't match."

Vasquez! If he was all sweaty, he'd have had to take off his dark glasses.

"I have to tell you—not that I have the figures—but that guy could bench-press more than Briggs. Really pissed Briggs off. I was always surprised Briggs kept inviting the guy back. I mean, like I said, Briggs paid the tab."

"How often?"

"Did the guest with the eyes show up? Every week or so."

"Anything else you can tell me?" Elena was so unsettled by the information that she couldn't think of a specific question.

"Like what?" asked the manager. "Hey!" He was looking through his window into the gym area. "Hey, you. Don't you know how to use that machine? You're gonna fuck it up."

"Can I use your phone?" Elena asked.

"If the call's local, sure." The manager rushed out to chastise the inept member.

Elena called the doctor, who said, "He's A positive. Now can I get back to my opera?"

A positive. The blood type on the killer's end of the clip arm. She tried again and got Maggie, who sounded seriously disgruntled.

"What's wrong?" Elena asked.

"I won the damn election."

"Congratulations. Dr. Erlingson will be proud of you."

"Happy's proud. Dr. Erlingson thinks it's a crock—same as I do."

"Do you have a dress for the festivities?"

"Is that what you called for? To ask if I have a dress?"

"No, I called to ask if Tey Vasquez knew you'd discovered that those transcripts were actually entered from library terminals."

"Sure. He was usually in Clabb's office when I reported my meager findings."

"Thanks. See you at the ball."

"Only if I can't get out of it," Maggie grumbled.

Tey had tried to preempt Maggie's case at the fake grad reception, make the arrest himself, so it made sense that he'd prowl the library after hours trying to catch the computer scammer. And he'd caught her and—well, no use jumping to conclusions. Elena called the H.H.U. police station and talked to a patrolman who remembered her from a previous investigation. He gave her the home telephone number of the guard who'd been on duty when Analee was killed.

"You still usin' my phone?" the manager asked, returning to the battered chair behind his scuffed desk.

"One more call," she said.

"Long distance?"

"Local," she assured him, and called the guard's home number. His wife said he was hunting on his cousin's ranch near the Davis Mountains. Elena wrote down that number, but it *was* long distance. "Thanks for the information and the use of your phone."

"Sure," the manager said. "I guess you're trying to find out who shot Briggs, huh?"

"More like why," she replied. She'd have to go to her office at Five Points to make the long-distance call. Damn!

She hoped Hiram Tully was sitting in his cousin's living room, toasting his toes in front of the fire and readily available to answer her questions. She needed to get home in time to dress for the ball. Michael was picking her up at 7:30.

46
..

Even breaking a few speed limits, Elena had less than three hours left to date time when she arrived at Five Points. She sprinted into Crimes Against Persons, past aisles of empty desks to her cubicle, where she dropped into her chair and snatched from her purse the dress receipt, on which she'd written the telephone number of Hiram Tully's cousin's ranch. She got the cousin's wife.

"Why, they're out in the brush, honey," said the woman. "Who did you say this was?"

"I'm Detective Elena Jarvis of the Los Santos Police Department. I wanted to ask Mr. Tully some questions about a case I'm working."

"'Bout that colored girl got killed by a statue? Isn't that somethin'? Hiram told us about it. He was real fond a that girl. You find out who pushed that statue? Maybe it was someone don't approve of nekkid statues."

"When do you expect Mr. Tully back?" Elena asked.

"Hard to say. Reckon they'll be back for supper. Could be any minute. Could be an hour. Could be two, but my husband don't hunt in the dark, like some. With lanterns, you know? He don't think that's sportin'. An' it's gettin' cold. I reckon they'll be in pretty soon."

"Could you have Mr. Tully call me?" Elena gave her the office number. "He can call collect. I'll alert the weekend operator to accept the charge."

"Sure, honey. I'll tell him."

"Could you ask him to call the minute he gets in? I'm going to wait here for him."

"Why honey, it's Saturday night. Ain't you got a date? Hiram told us you was young an' pretty."

"That's very nice of him," Elena replied. "And I do have a date."

"Then I'll have him call soon as he gets his boots off. Cain't have you missin' an evenin' with your young man."

"Thank you. I appreciate that." Elena hoped Tully did return quickly. She wanted to get home in time to dress. Booting up her computer, she began to write reports on the Ribbon case. Might as well use the time.

At 5:30 Tully hadn't called. Elena telephoned Michael—just in case. Someone picked up but said nothing. "Michael?" Silence. "Michael, it's Elena." She heard the dial tone. Must have called the wrong number, she thought, let ten rings pass. No answer. Not even an answering machine. At six, getting nervous, she tried Michael again. Still no answer. Was his phone out of order? Was he out renting a tuxedo?

Too restless to continue working, she glanced through the reports that had come in since she was last in the office. Autopsy on Briggs—nonfatal gunshot wound to the shoulder. Skull fracture and severe internal injuries from the crash; those had killed him. She looked at the report on cause of crash and frowned. Briggs had gone off the Sunland Park ramp because his brake line was punctured; in the police mechanic's opinion, the puncture must have caused a slow leak.

Had someone—had *Vasquez*?—tampered with the brakes, then called Briggs and told him something that sent him to his car? And to his death? Vasquez must have been surprised when Briggs showed up in the office. Maybe he panicked and shot Briggs, having hoped his confederate would die in a wreck before he got to the office.

Elena thought back to a conversation with Vasquez over bowls of Lavender's gumbo. His father, the abuser, had died when the brakes failed on his truck. To protect his mother and himself, had Vasquez killed before? The father's "accident" was too many years ago to be accessed on the police computer, but maybe—she called the newspaper and asked for Paul Resendez.

"Don't you ever date?" he asked.

"Don't you?" she retorted.

"I'm eaten up by ambition."

So was Vasquez, Elena thought.

"A Pulitzer and a slot on the *New York Times* by the turn of the century—that's my goal. What can I do for you?"

He located the report of the father's accident in the newspaper morgue, but there was no hint of foul play. Elena got the name of the trucking company.

By that time it was 6:30, and she called the Tully ranch a second time.

"They must a got 'em a big buck," said the cousin's wife. "Otherwise, they'd a been home. But don't you worry; I'll have Hiram call soon as he gets in. What time's your date, honey?"

"Seven-thirty."

"Hadn't you oughta be gettin' on home? Hiram could call you tomorrow."

Elena was tempted to agree, but she didn't. "It's important that I talk to him. Tell him I'm here waiting."

"Suit yourself, honey. But good men are hard to find."

Elena thought wistfully of Michael and of her new dress, hanging in the truck. She said goodbye and called Michael again. No answer. Where *was* he?

She tried the trucking company and got a dispatcher who remembered the accident.

"Sure, I was here then. Used to be a driver before I rolled one of them big rigs on ice the other side of Farmington an' busted up my hip."

"What can you tell me about the accident that killed Lalo Vasquez?" Elena asked.

"Brakes went out on him comin' down the east side of Transmountain. He musta been highballin' 'cause he couldn't make the turn onto one of them runaway truck ramps. Ended up in an arroyo surrounded by them Mexican poppies. Real pretty place."

"Any talk about why the brakes failed?" Elena asked.

"You investigatin' Lalo's death?"

"Should I be?"

"Plenty of people din' like ole Lalo. He was a real mean sumbitch. An' there *was* talk. One a the company mechanics, he said—he was drinkin' when he said it—he said the brakes had been screwed up."

"By someone, you mean? Or just worn out?"

"Well, it was an ole rig, an' I guess the company was glad to get the insurance money, but the mechanic, he thought someone had did ole Lalo in. An' I 'member we had a break-in the night before, padlock busted on the gate, but nuthin' was missin' or vandalized."

"Was there an investigation?"

"Nah. They just took the insurance money, paid off the widow, an' that was it. No one was cryin' over Lalo Vasquez. Like I said, he was a mean sumbitch. Ain't gonna do you no good to follow it up now, lady. The truck's long gone. Sold for junk."

"I suppose," Elena murmured and thanked him for the information. She couldn't do anything about Lalo Vasquez's death, but she now had more reason to suspect his son of engineering Briggs's death.

She tried Michael again at seven. And at 7:30, writing more reports in between. Was he standing her up? Or was he at her door, figuring she'd stood *him* up? Surely he'd realize that her work had interfered. No wonder cops were dateless or divorced.

And where the hell was Tully? What if he'd been shot by another hunter? Her father had investigated cases like that in the Sangre de Cristos. If she had to stay here much past 7:30, would Michael wait for her? Maybe he'd be furious and go off to the coronation by himself. Elena sighed. She'd miss the banquet for sure. Probably wouldn't get to see Maggie crowned.

At 9:05 Elena had finished her reports and was wondering if she should dash out to the parking lot, grab her dress, put it on in her cubicle—no, that was no use. She couldn't wear a sexy black dress and boots to the dance, even if Tully did call before the whole affair was over. Hiram Tully called at 9:15.

"What took you so long?" she asked irritably.

"What do you mean? Me an' my cousin just brung home a fourteen-point buck. 'Bout busted our butts gettin' it in the back of the truck, an' that's after we dragged it a mile or two through the brush. I didn't have to call you atall. I'm on vacation."

"Well, I'm sorry to bother you, Mr. Tully," said Elena, backtracking hastily, "but you did offer—"

"We're gonna enter him in the Trans-Pecos Big Buck Contest."

"That's great, but I need—"

"Win us a .270 with a scope sight. That's a huntin' rifle."

"I see. Well, good luck in the contest."

"Put him in the Boone and Crockett Records, too. I mean this buck has it all. Huge beams, champion spread an' height. Best buck me an' my cousin ever got."

"That's terrific."

"I shot him."

"Congratulations." Elena was beginning to wish she could shoot Mr. Tully. "I had a couple more questions to ask you about the night Analee Ribbon died."

"After all this time?"

"Did you see anyone—anyone at all—in the library that night after hours besides Analee?"

"There's never anyone there after hours," he replied impatiently.

In the background Elena heard a man's voice telling Tully to hurry it up if he didn't want supper to get cold. "Not even anyone from the campus police force?"

"Oh, well. Yeah, sometimes."

"That night?"

"Let's see. Yeah, Assistant Chief Vasquez."

Elena felt the hair rise on the back of her neck. "What time was he there?"

"Seen him when I made my one o'clock rounds."

"Where?"

"I covered the whole buildin'."

"I mean where was he?"

"Think he was on Three. That month he come by four, five

times late at night. Checkin' up on me." Tully sounded resentful.

"Did you see him leave?"

"Why would I? I had my rounds to make. He didn't need to be checkin' up on me. I made 'em."

"So you don't know when he left?"

"Nope."

"Did you see him after two?"

"From two on, I jus' check the screens up on Four. I tole you that. You sayin' I'm not doin' my job?"

"Mr. Tully, how you do your job is none of my business. Anything you tell me, I'm not going to repeat it to your superiors. I just want to know about Tey Vasquez. Did you see him on any of the monitoring screens after two?"

"No," he said, sounding sullen.

"Were you watching the screens?" It seemed to her that if Tey Vasquez was wandering around looking for someone entering fake transcripts on library computers, Tully would have seen him.

"You thinkin' Vasquez killed her?" asked Tully cautiously.

"Maybe. But not if he was gone. And if he wasn't, you'd have seen him, wouldn't you?"

There was a silence. "He coulda been the one? Vasquez?" Another silence. "I was sleepin' on the couch in the ladies' rest room on Four," Tully admitted. "Vasquez coulda been in the buildin'. I wouldn't a seen him unless he was still around at six. I checked at two. Then I was tired, so I took a nap."

"Would you say you're a heavy sleeper, Mr. Tully?"

"Pretty heavy. It's not like anythin' ever happens there. I didn't see any harm—I mean, I couldn't know—"

"So if you were asleep on Four, you wouldn't have heard the statue fall on her or seen the person who pushed it."

"I told you, the screens don't look at the atrium. Even if I'd a been watchin', I wouldn't a seen it."

"But you might have seen her hit him when she was on Two, or you might have seen her running from him and him chasing her."

Tully sighed. "Might have. I guess if I hadn't been asleep—"

"I don't think you could have gotten down in time to save

her," said Elena consolingly. "But we might have found out who killed her."

"Vasquez," said Hiram Tully wonderingly. "Why would he do that?"

"I guess he had his reasons," said Elena. *Now all I've got to do is prove it.*

47

Elena gave her quilted denim jacket to the coat checker, who looked at it with disdain. No doubt every Herbert Hobart coed had an evening wrap, Elena thought. She owned a winter coat, but when she'd finished dressing and pulled it out, she'd discovered a splotch on the front. How did those things happen? A stealth leak in the closet ceiling? The untimely death of an insect?

At least, now that she was out of her jacket, she felt that she looked good in the new black dress and hose, the black pumps to which she'd attached gold clasps, a black velvet purse hanging from her shoulder on a long gold chain. Because it held her gun, the evening bag was a bit lumpy, but you couldn't wear a holster with a formal dress. And her hair did look sophisticated; she'd forgone the usual French braid and pinned it into a complicated twist, then added dangling gold filigree earrings.

Not bad for a homicide cop, she decided as she studied herself in the powder room mirror. Maybe, if he was at the ball, Michael would think she looked good enough to forgive for standing him up. He was, after all, a criminologist. He should understand.

Head high, she walked into the Presidential Reception Hall, which tonight was overlaid with Christmas decorations. Men in tuxes and women in elaborate gowns that gave her a moment's doubt about her own were writhing on the dance floor to grunge rock, snatching champagne glasses off trays, wolfing down miniature dessert pastries. Very festive. On the far right a shallow room, open to the dance floor, three steps above ballroom level, held a bountifully laden refreshment table. Perfect. Starving, she headed toward nourishment.

As she picked her way around the edge of the crowd, Elena spotted Sarah, in a navy velvet evening suit, dancing with Zifkovitz, whose tux looked a size too big on his tall, skinny body. Members of the Ribbon family clustered near the bandstand. Melody Spike, wearing a dress that plunged in front to her belly button and in back to her butt, was dancing with a young man in a Christmas green tuxedo. Bunky Fossbinder was pushing a wheelchair in which his pixie girl sat, wearing a gauze turban decorated with a jeweled Christmas wreath flashing emeralds and rubies. And there was Maggie, shoving irritably at her crown until it perched askew, a beautiful giant in high heels and a sweeping red ball gown.

"Lucky you," she called as she and her Viking lover stopped writhing and climbed the steps to join Elena. "You got to miss the banquet and the coronation."

Elena grinned. "Did your fairy godmother come up with that dress? You look terrific."

"So do you, Jarvis. This dress was forced on me by my rotten suitemate, Cadet Major Spike. She was determined not to let me disgrace the Feminist Coalition. I pointed out that I wasn't a member, but when she dumped root beer on my dress, I didn't have much choice. It was this or jeans."

"You must learn to accept compliments and generosity with grace, Miss Daguerre," said Dr. Erlingson. He swept her away again once she had snatched a strawberry-kiwi tart from one of the ornate silver trays on the table.

Good grief, thought Elena, they were still on a Dr. and Miss basis. Then she saw Michael, looking handsome but really pissed off. He was frowning at her. *The best defense is a good offense*, she told herself and tip-tapped toward him on her very high heels—high enough to lift her almost to his height. From that advantageous prospect, she looked him straight in the eye and demanded, "Where have you been?" That seemed to take him by surprise, so she added, "I've been trying to call you since 4:30 this afternoon. Don't you have an answering machine?"

Michael now looked astonished and somewhat confused. He'd obviously expected an apology, not an attack.

"I thought something terrible had happened when I couldn't get hold of you," she continued.

"Well, I—" He paused, frowning. "I do have an answering machine."

"Then you should turn it on."

"And my brother was there part of the time."

"He was?" Now Elena frowned, remembering the first call, when someone picked up but failed to speak.

"And I was at your house at 7:30. I waited a half an hour. Where were you, Elena?"

"Stuck at headquarters trying to call you, Michael. Here I bought this dress especially for tonight—"

He seemed to see her for the first time. "It looks great."

"—and I thought I was going to have to stay home by myself."

"*You* look great!"

"So I decided I'd just come over on my own. I can tell you, Michael, a girl doesn't feel much like Cinderella when she has to drive herself to the ball in a Ford pickup."

"I'm sorry."

"Me, too." She leaned forward and kissed his cheek forgivingly.

"But I was really offended when I thought you'd stood me up." He was beginning to look irritated again.

"Well, surely you realized—"

Their conversation was interrupted when Lavender Lee Ribbon marched up to Elena and demanded to know whether or not Elena had found out who killed Analee.

"Well, I—"

"You haven't. Ah knew it. You probably haven't even been lookin'."

"Believe me, Mrs. Ribbon, I—"

"Mama!" Langston, champagne flute in hand, whispered, "Don't make a scene, Mama."

"Ah don' know why Ah shouldn't. Mah youngest child's been killed, an' they're not even—"

"Mama, I've just been offered a postdoctoral fellowship in poetry here at Herbert Hobart."

"You already got one a them. Why would you want to come here where your poor sister was killed?"

"The famous poet Angus McGlenlevie wants to work with me on an anthology."

"Never heard of him."

"His best-selling book, *Erotica in Reeboks*—"

"What are you sayin', Langston Lee? E-rotica in Reeboks? You wanna work for some dirty-minded poet who writes about sex in tennis shoes? You're doin' jus' fine at University of Houston, where your mama an' daddy can keep an eye on you an' see that you eat. Look at you. Ah been tryin' to fatten you up for years, an' you still look like a scarecrow in a corn field."

"Excuse me, Mrs. Ribbon," said Angus McGlenlevie, pushing between them, "but your son is a great talent—"

"He can be a great talent in Houston," she retorted.

"Langston needs an introduction into the world of profitable poetry, and I'm the man who can—"

"What's that you're wearin'?" demanded Lavender disdainfully. "You look like you're dressed up for a gay-pride parade."

Angus glanced down at his kilts and sporran. Then equally indignant, he snapped, "This is the dress kilt of the Clan McGlenlevie."

"Huh! What you're sayin' is you're wearin' a skirt an' no underpants? Wouldn't expect anything else on a man who writes dirty poetry."

"Erotic poetry, madam," said Gus stiffly, "not dirty poetry."

"Well, Mr. Sex-in-Sneakers, mah boy Langston Lee has got his own Ph.D. Have you got one? Langston Lee was the protégé of Donald Barthelme. Everybody's heard of Donald Barthelme."

"Mama," groaned Langston.

"Donald Barthelme got published in the *New Yorker*. You get published in the *New Yorker*, Mr. Erotic-Foot-Fetish?"

"I'm too avant-garde for the *New Yorker*," said Gus. "And I don't have a foot fetish."

"No one was more avant-garde than Donald Barthelme," said Langston, frowning at Gus.

"Your mentor was the famous postmodernist?" asked English Department Chairman Raul Mendez, who had stopped by to pick up a glass of champagne. He introduced himself to the Ribbons.

"This is my son, Dr. Langston Lee Ribbon," said Lavender, "an' he's not gonna be a post doc to any dirty-minded poet wearin' a pleated skirt and no underpants."

"Your son is old enough to make his own decisions, madam," said Gus angrily. "I've made him a very generous offer. I'm sure he'll want to accept it."

Behind them the band had broken into a samba, and dancers were stalking one another, with dramatic flourishes, across the pink marble floor. Lavender leaned down until she was nose to nose with Gus McGlenlevie, her eyes burning with the protective fire of a mother leopard defending her cub. "Lil white man, Ah'm a Louisiana woman. Ah got mean white blood an' magic colored blood. Ah can put a voodoo curse on you so's you'll never write another word."

Gus went pale.

"Ah can put a curse on you make you soft when you want hard, cold when you want hot, 'fraid when you—"

"This woman is threatening me," Gus cried. "I want her arrested. Detective Jarvis, I demand that—"

Elena, enjoying the show, remembering when Angus McGlenlevie demanded that she arrest Sarah Tolland for trying to kill him with an exploding snail, said, "Voodoo curses work only on those who believe in them, Gus. Are you trying to tell me that you believe in voodoo?"

"Why don't you run along, Angus?" said Dr. Mendez.

"Run along!" exclaimed McGlenlevie. "I'm offering this young man the opportunity of a lifetime, and I'm told to run along?"

"Do you write short stories yourself, Dr. Ribbon?" asked the English chairman.

"Ah used to. Before mah mentor died."

"Have you been published?" Dr. Mendez asked.

"He's been published in *Story*," said Lavender proudly. "In *Southern Review*, in the *Atlantic*—why, Ah've got a dozen magazines and two anthologies on display at Lavender's Gumbo that have stories by mah Langston Lee."

"Excellent. Excellent." Having drained his glass and deposited it on the table, Dr. Mendez was rubbing his hands together. "As it happens, we need someone to teach the short-story course in our creative writing program."

"I suppose he could teach a class while he's a postdoc for me," said Gus.

"Back off, you," said Lavender.

"I was thinking along the lines of an assistant professorship," said Dr. Mendez.

"Now that's a real job," said Lavender.

"Indeed it is, Mrs. Ribbon. And I promise you we'll take good care of him," Mendez assured her.

"You mean you won't let anyone push any statutes over on him?"

"Absolutely not."

"Well, Langston Lee, it's about time you stopped writin' all that depressin' poetry an' got yourself a job with a salary. If they find out who killed your sister, Ah'll consider lettin' you accept the chairman's offer. Ah take it as a good sign that they got a minority chairman."

Even as she was following the development of the Ribbon family drama, Elena was scanning the samba-dancing crowd for Tey Vasquez, but she didn't have to go looking for him. He came to her, drawn by the escalating debate.

"Maybe you don't need to look any further than your own son, Mrs. Ribbon," said Vasquez. "We've reason to think that Bose or one of his drug-dealing buddies may have killed your daughter. She was probably dealing herself."

Lavender's gasp could be heard because the whole group in front of the table had fallen silent. Ray Lee, seeing the expression on his wife's face, hastened toward her, Bose trailing behind.

48
· ·

How did he *dare*? Elena thought, staring at Vasquez. The man was guilty as sin. She was sure of it, yet he looked so smug and confident behind those dark glasses. Unable to resist the temptation, she edged up beside him. "You're saying you've found evidence against Bose?" she asked. When Vasquez turned to her, she slid her fingers lightly through the hair on the left side of his head, smiling as if it were a gesture of affection. Michael scowled at her.

Tey looked startled, recovered, and, giving her a sexy smile, said confidently, "I'll find the evidence."

Only if you manufacture it, Elena thought, for she had found a telltale ridge of scar tissue on the side of his head, slanted from front to back, just as she would expect if a woman shorter than he had swung and cut him.

"You sayin' mah boy, Thelonius Lee, had somethin' to do with his sister's death?" Lavender demanded angrily.

"That's what I'm saying," said Vasquez.

"Ah didn't!" cried Bose. "You tell 'em, Detective Jarvis. Wasn't me."

Tey's accusation, the lying hypocrisy of it, made Elena so angry that she turned on him, hardly noticing that the dancers were now doing the Charleston with as much verve as the lethal statue. "I don't know what evidence *you've* got, Tey," she said, "but the best evidence *I've* got says you were the one who killed Analee."

"Me?" He turned pale. "That's crazy. I'm the assistant chief. I—"

"You were the only other person in the library that night beside Analee and the guard, and he was asleep."

"I wasn't—"

"He says you were, and he never saw you leave. And your fingerprints were on the statue." The minute she opened her mouth to accuse him, she'd regretted it, but she couldn't seem to stop. She wanted to *nail* him. Right now!

"*Everyone's* fingerprints were on the statue."

"And you knew from Maggie that the transcripts entered since October had been created from a library terminal."

"Of course I knew it. I was investigating the case myself."

"Exactly. That's why you were in the library, trying to beat Maggie to an arrest. It was your blood type on the clip arm where Analee hit her attacker. She told friends *you'd* been nosing around there at night. She was nervous about you. With good reason, it would seem."

"Of course, she was nervous. She was breaking the law. But I didn't—"

"I just touched the scar from the computer clip, Tey." The confusion, the dawning realization on his face gave her great satisfaction. "From the cut she gave you. Remember? And a man like you, who can bench-press over—what?—three hundred and fifty pounds?—you'd be strong enough to push that statue over on her. Was she getting away from you?"

"You're talking nonsense. How could a girl get away from me if I didn't want her to?"

"How could she not? Analee was a track star. She ran regularly for the pleasure of it. She could outrun you any day of the week."

"This is some crazy figment of your imagination, Elena. You haven't offered a bit of proof. Why would I—"

"Because you want to look good. Make all the arrests. Make Chief Clabb look bad so you can get his job."

"What's this?" President Sunnydale and Chief Clabb had drifted into the circle beside the refreshment table. "Replace my old friend Chief Clabb?"

"Goodness, Detective," said Chief Clabb, as he selected a brownie decorated with green holly icing, "I think you must be wrong about Assistant Chief Vasquez wanting my job. Why, he's my protégé. And he's too young to be chief."

"Why am I too young?" Vasquez demanded angrily. "I *should* be chief! I caught the man who attacked Dr. Marx."

"*I* caught him," said Elena quietly. "You just put a bullet in him."

"I saved your life."

"Maybe. But why is it you never mentioned that you knew Briggs?"

Vasquez turned red and stammered, "I didn't know him."

"You worked out with him at Palomino's Gym. That's what the manager says. He remembers your eyes." Vasquez blanched, his hand moving protectively to his dark glasses. "You were the insider who fed information to L.S.A.R.I. Told them when to invade the university and make the chief look bad."

Brownie crumbs on his chin, Clabb turned to Vasquez. "You did *that*?"

"My guess is you killed Briggs to keep him from talking when I got the warrant to search his office and house," said Elena.

"I saved your butt that night."

"You sabotaged his brakes—just like you did your father's."

Tey's body stiffened. "You're crazy."

Elena wished that she could see his eyes behind that dark glass. He seemed to have a hunted look, but she couldn't be sure. "You warned Briggs that we were on our way to his office. The guard said Briggs never worked nights. Why was he there unless he'd been warned? And who would have warned him if it wasn't you?"

"I stopped the fake transcripts," said Vasquez desperately.

"By killing the transcript maker," said Elena. "In fact, I think you may have been planning to kill her partner."

"Me?" Happy Hobart, who was reaching for a bottle of champagne on the refreshment table, overheard Elena and looked aghast.

"Unfortunately, Vasquez got me instead," said Elena dryly.

Maggie, who had ended the Charleston with a gasp and a dash for the champagne, shoved the bottle into her campaign manager's hand and told him to get lost. Looking peeved, the founder's nephew hurled himself back into the riot of dancers, who were doing the twist and seemed quite unaware of the drama unfolding in the bower of poinsettias, beverages, and rich desserts.

Elena used the distraction to fumble with the catch on her black velvet bag. "Whatever you did afterward," she said grimly, "you certainly killed Analee, Tey, and I'm arresting you for manslaughter." With the purse open, she reached for her gun.

But she was too late. Vasquez panicked and grabbed Michael with one arm while he drew a pistol with the other. "Back away from me," he said. "I'm not getting framed for something that was an accident."

The damned gun had caught in the lining of her evening bag, so Elena said as calmly as she could, "Let go of Dr. Futrell, Tey."

"I'll shoot him!" he threatened.

Elena took a step forward. The other spectators backed away, gaping. "You'll have to shoot me, too. Killing a police officer is a capital crime."

"Stay back," he warned.

"I'd appreciate that, too, Elena," said Michael.

"Give me the gun, Tey," said Elena, holding out her hand. "At this point all we can charge you with is manslaughter, and a good lawyer can probably get you off. As you say, Analee's death was unplanned. You should have reported it instead of trying to cover it up, but we all make mistakes."

"It *was* an accident. In the line of duty."

"Your lawyer will point that out, but if you kill a police officer, you'll end up with a lethal injection needle in your arm." She motioned with the fingers of her outstretched hand. "So the smart thing is to give me the gun." She carefully failed to mention again the death of Briggs. And the theft of Analee's necklace, which might make her death a capital crime. No use reminding Tey that he would be facing other charges as well. "Tey, you're too smart to dig yourself into a capital murder rap."

The pistol wavered away from Michael's head. Elena, close now, ducked down and slammed his arm upward with her uninjured left hand and arm. Behind Vasquez, Maggie had grabbed the *Charleston Dancer* statue from its bed of poinsettias on the refreshment table. As Vasquez, trying to hang onto his gun, fired into the crystal chandelier, Maggie slammed the statue onto his head with a dull thud that could hardly be heard over the sounds of country music. The students, oblivious, were forming into a line dance. Vasquez slumped, taking Michael with him. Crystal prisms rained down on the pastries.

"Good going, Maggie," said Elena as she scooped up Vasquez's pistol. "See, you're safe and sound, Michael," she added cheerfully. "So I hope you're not mad at me anymore."

"Damn right, I'm mad," said Michael, scrambling to his feet. "I could have got killed."

"Hey, chill out," said Maggie. "Even if Elena hadn't shoved his arm up, I was ready to brain him. So it ought to be my collar, too. Right, Elena?"

"Absolutely, Lieutenant," Elena agreed.

Maggie gave Vasquez's inert figure an indignant look. "Bastard," she muttered. "If he weren't unconscious and if it wouldn't be considered police brutality, I'd hit him again."

"You're a police officer?" asked Dr. Erlingson, looking stunned.

"Yeah, but I'm going to take my finals." Maggie gave him a winning smile.

The students were prancing around the dance floor with their thumbs tucked into nonexistent pockets in imaginary Levis. Michael seemed to have taken Maggie's advice and "chilled out," which Elena was relieved to see. She and Michael smiled at one another. "Dating a policewoman can be an exciting experience, Christian," Michael said to Erlingson, "although they tend to break dates."

"My own assistant chief," said Chief Clabb mournfully. "It's hard to believe. And you say he wanted my job?"

"Looked that way to me," Elena replied.

"And he killed poor Miss Ribbon?"

"He pretty much admitted that, didn't he?" said Elena, relieved. She wasn't sure how the evidence she'd had would have stood up in court, but when Tey claimed it was an accident, he effectively sank his own ship.

Chief Clabb waved two campus policemen over and instructed them to handcuff Vasquez.

"But Chief, we don't have handcuffs," said one.

"We're not even wearing guns," said the other. "Handcuffs and guns aren't part of the dress uniform."

"Someone should have told Vasquez," Maggie muttered. "*He* had a gun."

"Well, tie him up with something," said the chief.

"What?" they asked.

"Drapery cords," said Vice President Harley Stanley crisply. He evidently didn't line dance and had heard the shot. "Our drapery cords are made of the best silk. They're very strong." He waved toward the tall windows behind the table. Their heavy lavender velvet draperies were embellished by silver silk fringe and cords.

"I hope you won't be running off to book him," said Michael to Elena.

"My men can take him to the jail," Chief Clabb offered. "I wouldn't dream of ruining your evening, Detective Jarvis. Not after you and Lieutenant Daguerre have solved all our crimes and saved the life of our hostage professor, Dr. Futrell." Michael scowled. Chief Clabb beamed paternally at Elena and waved to his subordinates. "Carry him out to the anteroom and tie him up, men. Then take him downtown."

"Yes sir," said one of them dubiously, and they carried the unconscious assistant chief away with difficulty, because the dancers were now writhing to a Rolling Stones' song and loath to make way for what they took to be two cops hauling off a third, who had evidently disgraced himself by getting drunk and passing out.

"Ladies and gentlemen," boomed the president, microphone in hand, "I think this calls for a moment of prayer."

The band faltered. The students groaned, but stopped dancing. The president of the Faculty Senate, glowering, signaled the waiters to pass out champagne in accordance with the faculty-presidential agreement: no public prayers without accompanying cocktails.

When everyone had a glass, President Sunnydale bowed his head and intoned in his resonant voice, "Heavenly Father, let us first ask thy blessing on our dear departed Analee

Ribbon. We understand that before her untimely demise she was responsible, along with her friend and the nephew of our founder, Hubert Hobart, for a veritable flood of donations to the Hobart Foundation, which makes it possible for us to continue our academic endeavors in the style to which our students are accustomed."

Elena almost choked on her champagne. But then why was she surprised? President Sunnydale could always be counted on for an unusual prayer.

"Second, Heavenly Father, we ask they forgiveness on behalf of our fallen brother, Assistant Chief—" The president looked helplessly toward Dr. Harley Stanley, who was frowning at him and didn't come up with the needed name.

"Why's he prayin' for that lyin', murderin' honkey?" Bose demanded.

"Come along, son," said Ray Lee, and led Bose toward the bandstand.

"God help me, *Ah'm* not ready to forgive the man who killed mah Analee," muttered Lavender.

"—for the assistant chief," President Sunnydale finished lamely, then perked up. "And third, Heavenly Father, we ask thy blessings on those two fine young Los Santos police-women, Queen Maggie Daguerre, who is also our first graduate student—"

"I can't believe she's a policewoman," mumbled Christian Erlingson and took a big gulp of his champagne.

"—and Detective Elena Jarvis, who solved this most perplexing death on our campus."

"*I* solved the fake diploma scam," said Maggie.

The president raised his head and asked, "What was that?"

"Nothing for you to worry about, sir," said Harley Stanley.

Michael passed Elena the dessert tray, and she helped herself to a tiny lemon tart, then hung onto the tray, setting her champagne glass in the middle. Champagne was OK, but Elena was hungry. She hadn't had any dinner, and it must be getting toward eleven. It seemed more like twelve.

"Lastly, Heavenly Father, we ask that you shower your soothing grace down upon the bereaved family of the late Miss Ribbon, who, I'm told, would have been a shoo-in for

Christmas Queen had she not fallen beneath the library statue. Amen."

The band launched into a Tejano number and the students, puzzled but game, returned to dancing.

"It seems to me that those statues are dangerous," Elena said when the president came over to shake her hand. She had to let Michael have the pastry tray, but she took it right back. "Six people have been hit by them now, one dead. You ought to get rid of them."

"Oh, we couldn't dispose of the statues," said the president, horrified. "The original was the founder's favorite. And as the National Rifle Association says, 'It's not the statue that's lethal; it's the person wielding it.' "

Elena doubted that the N.R.A. ever gave much thought to statues, but she got the point. The president wasn't going to get rid of the *Charleston Dancers*.

"Herbert Hobart said that statue was the essence of carefree and joyous youth," President Sunnydale explained.

"Mah Analee's not carefree an' joyous," said Lavender bitterly. "She's dead."

Elena sighed. There had been a hundred stories about how witty and intelligent Analee Ribbon had been. But not carefree. She'd had her family to protect. She'd even committed a crime for them, although she'd never have been prosecuted for it, not when Happy Hobart was being viewed as a benefactor of the university for roping in the "honorary alumni."

Well, Happy was going to turn another five thousand of his profits over to the Ribbon family; Elena would see to that. But it wouldn't bring Analee back. She was dead because Vasquez had been ambitious.

"Ah, but you're wrong, my dear Mrs. Ribbon," the president was saying. "I am sure that, as we speak, your daughter is in heaven, carefree and joyous, working away on God's computer."

"God's computer?" echoed Lavender Lee Ribbon. "Nobody talks about God's computer in mah church. You people are bi-zarre."

Elena grinned. Lavender Lee Ribbon evidently didn't realize

that she'd stepped into the Land of Oz when she came from Houston to claim her daughter's body.

Then suddenly the band stopped playing. The crowd fell silent. The dancers stopped dancing, because on the stage Ray Lee Ribbon and his son, Thelonius, having borrowed instruments, had stepped forward in front of the musicians. The plaintive notes of "St. James Infirmary" floated over the heads of faculty and students, between the pink marble columns, through the Christmas holly, shivering the champagne glasses and the hearts of all those who had loved Analee Ribbon.

Elena put down a miniature chocolate eclair to listen, wishing she'd known Analee. Michael laid his hand on her shoulder. Maybe she'd consider inviting him in tonight. Of course, they'd arrived in separate vehicles. But the prince had followed Cinderella home. Eventually.